Nobody's Angel

Also by Karen Robards

THIS SIDE OF HEAVEN

KAREN
ROBARDS

Delacorte
Press

To my nephew, Bradley Nicholas Johnson,
born January 5, 1991.
And, as always, with much love to Doug, Peter,
and Christopher.

Published by
Delacorte Press
Bantam Doubleday Dell Publishing Group, Inc.
666 Fifth Avenue
New York, New York 10103

———————— **1** ————————

"Susannah, you cannot be serious! You cannot really mean to *buy* a man!" Sarah Jane Redmon's dark brown eyes grew wide with alarm as she took in her older sister's grim expression. There was no reasoning with Susannah when she looked like that, as her family knew from long and bitter experience.

"Pa'll have a fit." That gleeful prediction was made by Emily, at fifteen the youngest of the quartet of Redmon sisters, as she stared over the smaller Susannah's shoulder at Craddock, the family hired man. Craddock was sprawled in a drunken stupor across the newly purchased provisions that filled half of the back of the wagon. Snores so loud as to be embarrassing on this unaccustomedly busy street in the center of Beaufort issued from his open mouth. He lay on his back, muddy boots protruding over the edge of the wagon, a nearly empty bottle tilted precariously in his hand. A silvery string of drool stretched from his slack lips down toward the sack of flour on which his head rested.

"Pa never has a fit at anything Susannah decides. He always says she likely knows best, and so she does." Amanda, seventeen, was the family beauty, and she knew it. She was charming, gay, and much spoiled, though Susannah had tried her best to leaven with firm discipline the worst effects of too much indulgence of her whims on the part of nearly every male Mandy had ever met. But Susannah would be the first to admit that her efforts had resulted in only a tentative success. Men responded to Mandy's radiance as naturally as flowers turned their faces to the sun, and Mandy thrived on their attention. Even as she smiled affectionately at Susannah, her attention was distracted by a trio of fashionably dressed gentlemen passing by on the street. Mandy tossed her auburn curls for their delectation. One gentleman, responding to Mandy's flirtatious glance by slowing and tipping his hat, was seconds later frozen to the marrow of his bones by Miss Susannah Redmon's icy glare. He had no way of knowing that her daunting frown came from much practice and meant nothing personal at all. Thinking the dagger look dredged up for himself alone, the gentleman, much chastened, hurried to rejoin his friends. He would have been affronted had he realized Susannah was barely aware of him as an individual. Her reaction had been no more than a reflex, engendered by endless years of warding off her younger sisters' beaux. Acting as mother-dragon to them had become as natural to her as breathing in the dozen years since their mother's death.

"At least the cursed man sold the sow and her piglets before he succumbed!" Susannah scowled once more at Craddock, then gave up the exercise as useless. He was as insensible to her displeasure as the wood on which he lay. Curbing the impulse to kick the iron wheel nearest her, she dropped her parcels on the floor of the wagon and crawled up beside them. Leaning forward, she thrust her hand into the bulging pocket of Craddock's coat, averting her nose from the smell of sour whiskey that hung around him like a noxious cloud. With a feeling of relief, she found what she sought, an oily doeskin bag well filled with silver coins. Closing her hand around the bag, she offered up a silent prayer of thanks that Craddock had not drunk away her money. She pulled the bag free and stuffed it into the reticule that dangled from her wrist.

"Would you get down? If anyone should see what you're about, they'll likely think you lost to all shame! To actually put your hands on his—his person is beyond what is permissible—and your backside is up in the air!" Sarah Jane's eyes darted nervously over the people making their way along the street. She dreaded encountering someone who knew them, but only strangers were at hand, drawn to usually sleepy Beaufort by the spectacle that was at that moment taking place down by the waterfront. Convicts brought over from England were being sold for indentured servants at public auction, and the event had attracted scores of spectators. A festive atmosphere imbued the town.

" 'Tis our money, goose, from the sale of the hogs we raised! Would you have me leave it where it was, to be spilled out when Craddock rolls over or stolen by some thieving passerby?" There was affectionate exasperation in the look Susannah sent her next sister as she clambered off the buckboard. Susannah loved the twenty-year-old dearly, but ever since Sarah Jane had betrothed herself to a young minister she had become such a pattern card of rectitude that she occasionally verged on being downright annoying.

"Oh, stop being such a prig, Sarah Jane!" Emily was not as fond of Sarah Jane as Susannah was. "I think Susannah is right to want to buy a man! There's too much work for all of us as it is, and with you getting married there will soon be even more!"

"I hadn't thought of that." Mandy sounded taken aback. One result of so much pampering was that the third Redmon sister was just a tad lazy. Mandy worked when there was no help for it, but any time she could avoid a chore she found unpleasant, she did so.

"But to actually purchase another human being! It goes against everything Pa has ever taught us!" Sarah Jane said. " 'Tis promoting slavery, and you know how Pa feels about that!"

"If Pa dislikes it, then he'll just have to dislike it. It's all very well to spend all one's time ministering to the less fortunate as he does, but someone must do the chores. I grant that Pa showed fine Christian principles in employing the town drunk as a hired man, but it just has not worked out as he had hoped. Though he does not see it, of course." Susannah fought a disrespectful tendency to roll her eyes heavenward. She had long since decided that the unquenchable optimism of their father, the Reverend John Augustus Redmon, minister of the fledgling First Baptist Church on the outskirts of town, was a cross she had to bear. Hard-headed pragmatism about the mundane realities of life such as food and shelter was beyond him. The Lord would provide, the Reverend Redmon always maintained, even when faced with the direst circumstances. Then he would smile his sweet, vague smile and refuse to trouble his head with the difficulty a moment longer. The aggravating thing about it was, he was usually right. The Lord—with a little help from His handmaiden Susannah down below on earth—usually did.

"Can't we go home and discuss this there? We're attracting attention." Sarah Jane cast another embarrassed look over her shoulder at the teeming street.

Following her gaze, Susannah saw that Sarah Jane was right. Passersby, particularly the male ones, were ogling the sisters with interest. Nosy things, Susannah thought with a narrowing of her eyes, not realizing that the four of them, each so very different, made quite a picture as they stood arguing in the street. Closest to the sidewalk was Emily, with her carroty red hair cascading down her back from a simple ribbon at the crown of her head. She was clad in a daffodil yellow frock that flattered the youthful plumpness that she had not yet outgrown. A splattering of freckles covered her nose because, scold as Susannah might, Em could never be bothered to wear a sunbonnet. She was a pretty girl, though quite eclipsed by Mandy, who stood beside her. Mandy was reasonably tall—she and Emily were much of a height—but willowy where Emily was plump. Her apple green dress had been chosen to set off her lissome figure, just as her lace-trimmed sunbonnet had been carefully selected to provide maximum flattery for her porcelain complexion and auburn curls. If she was not quite a world-class beauty—her nose was just a trifle too long and her chin too pointed—she was the closest thing to it that Beaufort possessed, and she was, in this, the year of our Lord 1769, the belle of the county.

Sarah Jane, who stood opposite Emily, was plainer, with a quiet kind of attractiveness that would stand her in good stead as a minister's wife. Her eyes were large and grave, her soft brown hair was never in disorder, and, though she was shorter than her younger sisters, her figure was trim. She wore a white dress sprigged with pink and a pink sunbonnet on her head. As always, she looked as fresh and good as a loaf of new-baked bread.

Sandwiched between Sarah Jane and Emily, Susannah drew about as much notice as a squat brown titmouse might when flanked by a bright-colored pair of tropical birds. She was small of stature, smaller even than Sarah Jane, but sturdily built where the other girl's bones were fragile. Her dress was loose-fitting, designed for comfort and modesty rather than to show off a figure that she felt called instead for concealment. Fashioned with chores rather than high style in mind, the garment was made of tan calico chosen for its resistance to showing dirt. A peach-colored sunbonnet was perched on her head more to keep the bright May sunlight out of her eyes than to protect her fair skin, about which she rarely troubled herself. Its too-large brim, coupled with the rather limp bow with which it tied under her chin, had the unfortunate effect of seeming to overpower her small face, making it appear both plain and square. Her hair was a nondescript color midway between blond and brown. By dint of much effort, it was slicked severely back from her face and bundled into a cumbersome knot that stuck out awkwardly behind the sunbonnet. It was coarse as a horse's tail, so thick that she could barely drag a brush through it, and wildly curly to boot. The bane of her life when she was a girl, her hair was just one more thing she had learned to live with. Each morning she attacked it with water and a brush, tamed it into a style that was relatively tidy if nothing else, and forgot about it until it worked free of its pins or in some other way demanded her attention. She had a pair of large, well-shaped, thickly lashed eyes that were unfortunately of no more remarkable a color than hazel, a small pert nose, a wide, full-lipped mouth, and a jawline that was nearly as broad as her cheekbones. No beauty, she, and she knew it. She looked like what she was, a twenty-six-year-old woman who had been left on the shelf and had no interest in or hope of attracting men. Nearly all of the speculative glances directed toward the quartet of ladies passed right over Susannah's head to fasten on her sisters.

"There is nothing more to discuss, though you're right, we are attracting attention. Pile your packages in the buckboard, my dears, and let us be on our way." Susannah looked around, acknowledged the justice of Sarah Jane's observation, and reached for her sister's parcels. Sarah Jane clutched them closer and took a step backward.

"Susannah, you cannot be serious! How can you even think to do such a thing, when you know our father must strongly disapprove?"

"Sitting up half the night at old Mrs. Cooper's bedside, then rising this morning to discover Ben gone with all his chores undone and none but us to do them, as well as the prospect of nursing Craddock through his latest binge and doing his chores, too, until he recovers, has doubtless addled my brain," was Susannah's tart reply, but she forbore to wrestle her sister for her packages. The "Ben" to whom she referred was another of the Reverend Redmon's charitable impulses. Left fatherless by a fever that had swept the community some years back, Ben was a gangly youth who found trouble as naturally as a compass needle finds north. He had been hired to save the girls such chores as chopping wood and building fires, and he had performed faithfully for nearly a year. Then, two months ago, he had fallen in love. As a result, he was now as unreliable as Craddock.

"Having a dependable hired man would certainly make life simpler, but the fact remains that a bound servant is not the same thing as a hired man, and . . ."

"Sarah Jane, you know Pa won't agree to pay a hired man properly, and that's why we can never keep one. I say that Susannah's had a splendid idea!" Mandy's sherry-brown eyes sparkled with excitement.

"I cannot like . . ."

"You cannot like anything, Sarah Jane, since you became betrothed to that goody-goody Peter Bridgewater!" Emily placed both fists on her hips, standing arms akimbo as she glared at her sister.

"Don't you dare malign Peter!" Sarah Jane said, flushing. "He is a most estimable man, and . . ."

"We know he is, Sarah Jane, and Emily was wrong to speak of him so. I've told you before that you must learn to guard your tongue, Em. Peter is Sarah Jane's choice, and in time I am sure we will all grow to love him as a brother." Susannah strove to keep the doubt she felt from being reflected in her voice. In her opinion, her sister's fiance was a prim fool, but Sarah Jane was so in love that no words of caution could sway her. So she held her tongue and had warned her two youngest sisters to do the same if they wished to maintain warm contact with Sarah Jane once she was wed.

It was obvious that Emily had, for the moment, forgotten Susannah's warning. She snorted. Sarah Jane bridled and opened her mouth to reply.

"What has any of that to say to the purpose?" Mandy broke in, dismissing the incipient quarrel with a wave of her hand. She addressed Sarah Jane. "The point is, do you want to do Craddock's work? There are the provisions to be carried in, the horse to be rubbed down and fed, the hogs to be slopped, the cow milked, and all that as soon as we get home. And Ben's work, as well. And our own."

"Pa . . ." Sarah Jane's voice trailed off as the force of this objection sank in. Her younger sisters, sensing her wavering, swooped upon her. Lacking Susannah's reluctance to assault their sister physically in the middle of a public thoroughfare, Emily and Amanda wrested Sarah Jane's purchases from her feebly resistant fingers and dropped them atop Susannah's packages, then added their own shopping to the pile.

Most of the paper-wrapped parcels contained laces and ribbons and cloth that would be used in the fashioning of Sarah Jane's bridal clothes. But each girl had had pocket money of her own to spend as well and so had bought a few personal fripperies. These unaccustomed luxuries were placed in the buckboard with more care by their respective owners. Only the prospect of Sarah Jane's upcoming wedding had convinced their father to countenance such a large dispersal of funds in the name of female vanity, and the largess was not likely to be repeated any time soon, as they all knew. The Reverend Redmon's custom was to donate every coin not actually needed for his family's survival to better the lives of his congregation. But on this occasion Susannah had said, in her decided way, that Sarah Jane must have a trousseau, and when Susannah made up her mind about something their father invariably acquiesced. Amanda and Emily had begged to be included in the shopping expedition, and Susannah had agreed.

That morning, after completing all their own chores and Ben's, too, they had set out for town. Craddock had accompanied them, along with a prime sow and her piglets, culled from the herd that Susannah painstakingly raised. The money from their sale she meant to use to purchase passage aboard a ship for Sarah Jane and her husband-to-be, so that when September came, bringing with it Sarah Jane's wedding, the newlyweds might travel in some comfort and style to Richmond, Virginia, where Peter Bridgewater had already gone to take up the ministry of a church. But September was some four months off, and the need for a hired man was immediate. The securing of a ship's berths could wait.

Ever since she had first seen notices advertising the auction, Susannah had silently debated the advisability of acquiring a bound man. The physical labor required to work the farm was beyond her and her sisters' strength, and Craddock was prone to periods of alcohol-induced "illness" that made his help a chancy thing at best. There had been some thought lurking around the edges of her mind that she might acquire the indentured servant when she had set this particular day as the one for their shopping expedition. During the course of the morning, her baser instincts had warred with what she knew to be her father's lofty code of morals. The Reverend Redmon's scruples had nearly won, despite the fact that trying to run the house and farm, fill the part of minister's lady to the congregation, raise three lively younger sisters, and at the same time keep her father from giving away every scrap of food in the larder were leeching away Susannah's reserves of patience, to say nothing of her strength. Craddock's latest fall from grace had been the last straw. Sometimes practicality had to outweigh principles, and the simple truth was that the Redmons sorely needed a man to do the heavy work that farming required.

Her father might be appalled, but he would in the end accept her decision, Susannah knew, just as he always did. Over the last twelve years, he had occupied himself more and more with spiritual concerns, leaving more problematic earthly matters to her discretion.

"You cannot—you haven't enough money!" There was triumph in Sarah Jane's voice as she thought of the most telling objection of all.

Susannah patted the reticule that swung from her wrist. The silver clinked comfortingly. "Oh, yes, I do."

"But that's the money for my wedding trip!" Sarah Jane said, then immediately looked guilty. "I—I didn't mean to sound so selfish, of course you must use the money as you see fit, but . . ."

"You will get your trip, dear, don't worry. I'll sell one of the hogs I was saving to slaughter in the autumn. Pa would doubtless just give the meat to someone anyway, so it will be no real loss."

"How greedy I must be, to wish you to do that! I cannot. . . ." Sarah Jane looked and sounded stricken with guilt.

"Oh, hush up, Sarah Jane, do! You're making me sick!" Mandy, who had as little patience as Emily for Sarah Jane's recently acquired piety, cast her sister a disgusted look.

"Now that's enough, all of you. If you wish to come with me, you may. If you do not, then you may stay here. But I am going to the auction." Having had quite enough of the discussion, Susannah picked up her skirt, turned, and moved briskly toward the sidewalk.

"But, Pa . . ."

"I am bound and determined in this, Sarah Jane. So you may as well stop fussing, because it will not do the least bit of good." Susannah spoke over her shoulder as she stepped up onto the plank walkway fronting the shops.

Sarah Jane looked as if she meant to say something more. Concluding that further remonstrances would prove useless, she refrained. As they all knew, when Susannah was bound and determined to do something, the earth might move beneath her feet, the sky might rain bolts of lightning down on her head, and the voice of God might call her to account, but still Susannah would go ahead with what she intended to do. Mule obstinate, their father called her on the infrequent occasions he had disagreed with his oldest daughter's judgment, usually without much success. And, Sarah Jane reflected unhappily as she followed the bustling form of her diminutive sister, mule obstinate was just what Susannah was.

2

"Beaten biscuits! Who'll have my fresh beaten biscuits?" The cry came from a plump farm woman with a cloth-covered basket over her arm as she made her way among the newly arrived spectators.

"Crabs! Live crabs!" A grizzled fisherman had made a booth out of a wooden crate, which presumably held the crabs in question. He had set it up at the edge of the green on which the auction was being held.

"Rice! Get yer rice!" Next to the fisherman was an old woman bent over a steaming pot that she stirred intermittently as she exhorted passersby.

These voices and others rose over the buzz of the gathered crowd, lending a carnival atmosphere to the proceedings. Susannah slowed her pace as she drew nearer to allow her sisters to catch up with her. Emily's eyes were wide, and Mandy's cheeks were flushed with excitement. Sarah Jane merely looked worried, but even had she wished to she would not have been able to renew her protests because of the sheer volume of the activity around them. Enterprising hawkers peddled everything from pecans to hair ribbons at the top of their lungs. People everywhere moved, some leaving, more coming. Women in bright cotton dresses and with deep-brimmed sunbonnets on their heads clutched unruly children by the hand as they all strained to get a good view. Gentlemen in long-tailed coats and top hats rubbed shoulders with trappers in buckskins and roughly dressed farmers. Horses were tied to any conceivable hitching post. Wagons and carts with everything from farm implements to crated chickens in the back headed in both directions, clogging the street that ended at the green. A special stockade had been constructed to hold the convicts prior to the sale, and the auction block had been built just to the south of it. Only the week before, a ferry had crossed the Coosawhatchie River to discharge the human merchandise. The convicts had landed originally at Charles Town, the rumor went. From there they had been brought to Beaufort, considered the most prosperous small town in South Carolina, a distinction of which its residents were justly proud. It was hoped that the relative wealth of Beaufort's citizens would make the effort worthwhile.

As the sisters approached the green, they were passed by two men, one after the other, each with what was obviously a newly purchased servant in tow. The first convict they saw had his wrists bound and was hobbled about the ankles with a short length of rope. He was forced to adopt an ungainly gait somewhere between a trot and a hop to keep up with his new master, to whom he was tethered by a rope that passed around his neck. The second convict had been left unbound, except for the tether-rope around his neck, and followed his new master with his head down and his feet dragging. Both men were unkempt and filthy, and for a moment, a flicker of doubt arose in Susannah's mind.

"Susannah, they look misused!" Sarah Jane exclaimed almost in her ear.

"What am I bid for this fine specimen here, a good worker, like all Scots, and strong as an ox?" The auctioneer boomed from the block, extolling the virtues of a stocky man with a shock of red hair who stood regarding the crowd with a cocky grin despite his predicament.

"Now there's a likely-looking fellow," Susannah said, distracted from Sarah Jane's protest by the activity on the block. A little distance away, a trio of matrons spied the sisters. They waved and called greetings, the sense if not the actual words of which were apparent.

"Good afternoon, Eliza, Jane, Virgie!" Susannah called back. Mistresses Eliza Forrester, Jane Parker, and Virgie Tandy were members of the Reverend Redmon's flock, and the sisters knew them well. Smiling, returning waves and greetings, Susannah missed her chance to bid on the man.

"Going once, going twice, gone to Tom Hardy for two hundred pounds! You can pick your man up over here at the side, Mr. Hardy—and pay your money, too, of course."

The auctioneer was Hank Shay. Susannah had known him, or rather known of him, in a vague sort of way from birth. He was an itinerant who traveled the Carolina coast, fetching slaves and bound servants impartially from the large port towns and peddling them across the countryside. His sales were notorious, and the Reverend Redmon had been known to denounce him as a hawker of human pain and suffering. He was a large-bellied, bald, and florid-faced man in his fifties, with a voice that boomed like thunder. It was booming now, as he called for bids on yet another unfortunate.

"Are you going to bid or aren't you?" Mandy prodded Susannah's arm, while Emily, clasping her hands in front of her plump bosom, regarded the goings-on around her with transparent delight. Sarah Jane, on Susannah's other side, looked distressed.

"Please reconsider, Susannah. These men—they're criminals, remember, or they wouldn't be here. You might buy a thief, or even a murderer!"

"A murderer!" Mandy's eyes brightened with obvious fascination at this prospect. Susannah felt another quiver of misgiving—until she thought of all the work that waited at home. She would not allow herself to be swayed from her chosen course by Sarah Jane's negativity.

"Stuff!" she said stoutly. "If the men were dangerous, they wouldn't be offered at public auction, now would they? Over here!"

She raised her hand and called out as the auctioneer took the bidding up to eighty pounds. Shay saw and acknowledged her bid, while Sarah Jane muttered what sounded like a plea to the Almighty to restore her sister's good sense.

It occurred to Susannah, as the auctioneer called for more bids, that in her haste not to be dissuaded by Sarah Jane she hadn't spared more than a glance for the fellow she'd bid on. Accordingly, she stood on tiptoe and craned her neck and thus was able to get her first good look at the man on the block.

He was tall, she thought, comparing his height to that of the auctioneer and the two burly guards who, armed with coiled whips and rifles, stood on either side of the platform. If the breadth of his shoulders was anything to judge by, he was also large-framed, but something, his current dire circumstances or perhaps a recent illness, had rendered him so thin that his clothes hung on him as though they'd been made for a far bigger man. His hair straggled about his shoulders and seemed to be very dark, but it was so matted and filthy that its precise color was impossible to determine. There was a gray cast to his skin, and a scruffy dark beard obscured the lower part of his face. His eyes—like his hair, their color was impossible to determine— appeared sunk into their sockets. As he stared out over the crowd, they seemed to glitter, and his lip curled into what looked like a snarl. His arms hung limply in front of him. The irons that linked his wrists appeared to be weighing them down. His fists were clenched, which Susannah took as another sign of belligerence. This is a bad one, Susannah thought with an inward shiver, and vowed to bid no more on him. Sarah Jane's warning no longer seemed quite so farfetched.

"Who'll give me a hundred? Come on, now, a hundred! You, Miss Redmon? No? You over there?"

Someone must have raised a hand, because Shay picked up the beat. "I have a hundred. I have a hundred! Will you let this big, strong fellow get away from you for so paltry a sum as that? I . . ."

"Why's he still got the irons on, Hank Shay?" a male voice called out.

"Gave you trouble, did he?" A guffaw accompanied this sally from a farmer at the edge of the crowd. From somewhere an object was let fly. It sailed past the convict's head, just missing him, to splatter against the far edge of the platform. An overripe tomato, judging from the mess it made when it landed, Susannah saw. The man didn't even duck, let alone flinch, but his eyes seemed to burn just that much brighter. The curl of his lip grew more pronounced. He emanated waves of hostility so intense they were almost palpable as his head turned in the direction from which the missile had come, and his gaze raked the crowd.

"Enough of that now, you boys, or I'll be having you hauled up before the magistrate! I don't take kindly to having my sales disrupted, as you'd do well to remember!" Having dealt with the tomato-thrower and his friends, Shay's angry bawl moderated, and he addressed himself to the farmer and his confederate. "The irons are a precaution, no more. You can see for yourself that this one's big, and he's strong, too, I can vouch for that! He'll be a fine worker for the lucky bidder what gets him! Do I hear a hundred and ten?"

The bidding continued, but Susannah paid little attention as she had no intention of joining in. The convict looked sullen at worst, ferocious at best, and was definitely not the man she sought. Still, she couldn't help but feel pity for him, just as she would feel sorry for any poor creature who had so obviously been ill-treated. Like a bear that had been baited, he bristled with hatred. But who was to blame for that: the bear, or the one who had done the baiting? she asked herself. She could not condemn him for his fierceness, though it bode ill for his future. Only a fool would buy a bound man who looked as if he would positively relish murdering one in one's bed.

"He can read and write, the King's own English, too! That should up his price considerable! Some canny buyer will be gettin' a real bargain for a hundred and sixty pounds! Do I hear a hundred and sixty?"

Shay got it, but the bidder sounded reluctant. This man was not going to sell for as much as Shay wished, it was clear. Indeed, from the ferocious way the convict was scowling at the crowd, Susannah was surprised at anyone having the nerve to bid on him at all. But Shay had said he was an educated man. Was that true, Susannah wondered, or merely one of the auctioneer's devices to drive up the bidding? The convict certainly did not appear educated, though if one looked closely it was possible to discern that his clothes had once been fine. He was dressed in black breeches, now badly torn and stained, an equally deficient shirt that must once have been white, a ragged waistcoat fashioned from what might have been gold brocade, and a pair of flat brogues that were sadly at odds with the rest of his costume. He wore no stockings, and his hairy bare legs were plainly visible below the kneeband of his breeches.

The red-haired man had been far more prepossessing, and certainly more suited to Susannah's purpose. But something about this one roused her compassion.

When Shay pushed the bidding up, Susannah stood silent. Mandy and Emily watched the proceedings wide-eyed. From their expressions, it was clear they were pleasantly titillated by the convict's aura of ferocity, but they had no wish to take him on as a family servant. Sarah Jane looked uneasy, as if she really feared that Susannah might be so lost to all judgment as to buy such an obviously unsuitable man.

"Afternoon, Miss Amanda, Miss Susannah, Miss Sarah Jane, Miss Emily. Ladies, what are you doing here? I could hardly believe my ears when that villain Shay addressed Miss Susannah by name and I saw you were bidding. Don't tell me that the good reverend countenanced any such thing, for I'll not believe it!"

This greeting, boomed without warning from just behind Susannah's left shoulder, was more than audible. She turned her head sharply, to behold, as she had known she would, Hiram Greer. He was a prosperous indigo planter who had long had an eye on Mandy. As he was nearly as old as their father, and homely and brusque-mannered to boot, none of them had ever given his suit serious consideration, though he was quite wealthy. Mandy, for all her flirtatious ways, had never purposefully encouraged him. But still he fancied himself her future husband and therefore adopted a proprietary manner toward the rest of the family that set their collective teeth on edge. Barrel-chested and stocky, of average height, with thinning, grizzled hair and coarse features, Hiram Greer was a bull of a man in both appearance and manner. Susannah couldn't abide him, although, as he was a leading member of her father's small flock, she had perforce to be polite.

"Good afternoon, Mr. Greer." Though she gave his question no direct reply, he was not the man to recognize and accept a rebuff.

"Good God, ma'am, when I saw you here with your sisters I thought my eyes were playing tricks on me! Did you know you actually bid on that scum? For you cannot have done it on purpose, surely! But you should realize that if you raise your hand Shay up there takes it for a bid. Fortunate for you that others have topped you, or you might have found yourself saddled with a hooligan you never wanted and your father to answer to for it! Let me escort you ladies away from here!"

He took Susannah's arm without waiting for her reply and would have pulled her with him willy-nilly had she not jerked her elbow free.

"You quite mistake the matter, I assure you, Mr. Greer," she said firmly. "I have no wish to move an inch from this spot. Indeed, I am here for the express purpose of securing a bound man."

So saying, she lifted her chin and fixed her eyes firmly on the platform again. Shay called for more bids. The convict bared his teeth as if daring someone to buy him. Shay, looking ugly, sent the man a sideways glance that bode ill for his future if he remained in the auctioneer's care. For a long moment no one bid, and then a man near the middle of the crowd raised his hand.

"One seventy! I have one seventy! A ridiculous price for an educated

NOBODY'S ANGEL   13

gentleman strong enough to work like a field hand while he keeps your books! Come on, folks, are you going to let Mr. Renard there get away with rob- bery?"

"Renard can have the taming of him! He's got the stomach for it. The rest of us are a mite more squeamish about how we use the whip!"

The catcall produced a tidal wave of guffaws. Georges Renard was a cotton planter from the up-country, and his cruelty was legendary. Slaves on his plantation were routinely whipped to the brink of death for such sins as what Renard perceived as laziness. Rumor had it that nearly as many who survived died, but the veracity of that was generally discounted; after all, Renard was a businessman, and slaves were valuable pieces of property. Su- sannah shuddered to think what he might do to a man so obviously bent on defiance as the convict.

"You'll not buy that one," Greer said, his voice commanding. "Do you hear me, Miss Susannah? I'd not sleep easy, worrying about you and yours, with the likes of that around. If you must buy a servant, I'll choose him for you. There's a man to be put up a little later that I've had my eye on for myself. He's an older fellow, but stout looking, and in for no more dangerous a crime than forgery. I asked. When he's put up, I'll buy him for you. Consider it a gift."

The munificence of that offer drew a gasp from Emily and a blush from Mandy. It annoyed Susannah so much that she had to draw in a quick, steady- ing breath to keep from losing the temper that was one of her gravest faults.

"I thank you for the offer, but I've quite decided on this one," she said, realizing even as the words left her mouth that she had, indeed, made up her mind. She raised her hand.

"One eighty! I have one eighty!" Shay acknowledged her gesture almost instantly, while Greer's face reddened, and the girls made a collective sound that might have constituted shock, or, in Sarah Jane's case at least, a realized fear. "Will anyone go one ninety? No? What about one eighty-five? No? This is your last chance, good people, for the bargain of the year! Are you going to let Miss Redmon steal him out from under your nose for a measly one hun- dred and eighty pounds? Any bids? Any bids? No? Then going, going, gone, to Miss Redmon for one eighty! You've made yourself a mighty fine purchase, ma'am!"

"Oh, Susannah!" Sarah Jane moaned. Susannah wasn't sure that she didn't feel like moaning, too. Already she was having second thoughts. But with Hiram Greer bristling beside her and so many other eyes turning to seek her out, this was not the moment to indulge in them. She stiffened her spine and thrust up her head and marched through the crowd toward the auction block where the convict was being led down. Behind her trailed Hiram Greer, for once shocked into silence, and her sisters. With the sinking feeling that she had let pity and annoyance lead her into making a grave error, Susannah counted out the required amount of sterling to a man who sat behind a table just beside the platform guarding a cash box. The man recounted the cash, then handed her a piece of paper—the Articles of Indenture, she later discovered—and the frayed end of a rope. The other end of the rope was attached to the neck of the man she had just bought.

Her eyes were wide as she followed that rope to its end.

3

The crowd eddied around the auction block, appearing to Ian Connelly as a single colorful, noisy mass. Individual faces blurred before his eyes as he stood like a stone behind the table where Shay's assistant, Walter Johnson, greedily counted the cash that would purchase—purchase!—him, just as he himself had once purchased a horse or a cow. Equally indistinct were the strangely accented voices that rose and fell against his eardrums. Their cadence served as a stomach-churning reminder of the rhythm of the waves that had slapped ceaselessly against the hull of the ship that had carried him from England. His head was pounding, though whether from the stifling humidity, which was like nothing he had ever experienced, or from the effects of the starvation they had finally used to tame him, it was impossible to say. The sun—surely this was not the same sun that gently warmed the Irish countryside or chased away the sober English mists—beat down without mercy on his uncovered head. His legs felt odd, boneless almost, his knees shaky. It had taken every iota of his willpower, first to stand without wavering on the platform and then to make his way down the makeshift wooden steps to the trampled grass. Hatred was what kept him going—black, burning hatred of his enemies, who at the moment constituted most of mankind.

"Move, you!" One of the men employed by Shay to guard the cash box shoved Ian from behind without warning. He stumbled, caught himself. He snapped his head around, fists clenching as he snarled at this newest tormentor. The offender took a hasty step back. Then the man remembered who he was and where he was and stepped forward again, ostentatiously shaking out the whip in his hand as if using it would be a pleasure.

"Not here, fool. Shay'd mislike it," one of the other guards muttered, stepping between them. The first guard looked around, nodding sullenly.

"Aye, you're right," he said, and coiled the whip again. Ian felt some of the tension leave his shoulders. He would not have surrendered to another beating without a fight.

But the guard had not quite finished with him. He shouldered his whip and picked up a length of rope, fashioning what looked like a hangman's noose at one end. He stepped forward and with a smirk flung the loop around Ian's neck.

"Goes against me grain, but I guess we'll just have to let your new owner deal with you. How does it feel to be a slave, me fine lordling?" This taunt was uttered under the man's breath so it would not be overheard.

Ian's fists clenched. Bloodlust boiled in his veins, but he kept the urge to do murder under careful control. To snap the slimy little worm's neck would afford him only the most momentary satisfaction, for which he would then pay with his life.

The bastard wasn't worth it.

The frayed hemp chafed Ian's skin as the guard, jeering, deliberately tightened the noose about his neck, then jerked him forward another dozen or so paces. But after all the suffering he had endured over the past six months, he barely noticed the small discomfort. The real prick was to his pride; in some strange fashion the rope around his neck galled him more than the irons linking his wrists. The guard—Ian had had no dealings with him before and thus did not know his name—was no better and no worse than he had come to expect his captors to be. They were jackals, all of them, quick to rend the flesh of the weak. They had best pray God help them all when he was restored to himself again.

But he had not been whipped, whereas, only two days before, no more than an insolent look had earned him a beating that had brought him to his knees. Why not? His brain, dulled by the heat or the smell or his own damnable physical weakness, took a moment to come up with the answer: he was no longer their property to abuse as they pleased.

He had been sold. He was free of the sadistic crew.

Now he had only his new owner to contend with.

Ian's gaze, drawn more by instinct than by any conscious act of will, followed the path of the rope to the small, capable-looking hand that clasped its other end. A woman's. He'd been bought by a woman. As his eyes rose to the face that went with that hand, he felt a burning sensation build deep inside his belly. He knew what it was: shame. He thought he had grown immune to that long since.

But being sold like an animal to a woman was as degrading as anything he had so far experienced. Once, in what seemed another lifetime, he wouldn't have spared a second glance for a dowdy dab of a female such as the one who now stood regarding him with what appeared to be both resolution and dismay. She was tiny, the top of her head reaching no higher than his shoulder even when she stretched herself to her full height, as she was clearly doing at that moment, and he was not standing particularly tall himself. And she was plain. Dumpy was the word that came to mind as his gaze slid over her. Her face was square, and her body looked square, too. Her bosom seemed ample enough, and her hips, but only the smallest indentation between hinted at any proper kind of female waist. Her fashion sense was clearly nonexistent. The gown she wore, of a faded tan color that appeared to be sprigged, most improbably, with orange flowers, was unbecoming, and her orange bonnet was worse. Even his toothsome Serena, with her tall, lissome figure and raven hair, would have looked less than beautiful in a rig like that.

During the passage over, he had spent weeks chained in a dark, rancid-smelling hold, lying spoon-fashion on one of a tier of wooden pallets, with men crammed before and behind him. He had held on to his sanity by imagining what his future might hold. As soon as the ship docked, he would be sold at auction, he knew. He would become the property of a farmer, or a merchant, or one of the planters who, he had heard, ruled this part of the New World, Carolina it was called, like the nobles ruled England. But he didn't mean to be anybody's bound servant for long. At the first opportunity that presented itself, he would do whatever he had to do to regain his freedom. If violence against his new owner was necessary, well, he was no stranger to that. But a woman had never entered into his plans. Even such an obviously unfeminine one as this. Violence against women was where he drew the line.

Or at least, it was where he had drawn the line. Before. But circumstances had changed, and so had he.

To be free again, he would do whatever he had to do. The stone walls of Newgate and the stinking bowels of a ship had held him; this little dab of a woman would not.

"Thank you," she said to Johnson as he handed her the Articles of Indenture. It was the first time he had heard her speak. Her voice was low and deep, her words slurred in a melodious fashion that was far more feminine than her appearance. Against his will, Ian felt himself drawn to that voice. It was lovely, soothing as a lullaby in this nightmare which had so unbelievably caught him in its toils. "Now you may strike his irons."

"Ma'am?" Johnson gaped at her. Ian blinked. Surely she was not going to make it as easy for him as all that.

Her eyebrows lifted. They were thick, straight, a shade or so darker than her hair, and very expressive. "I said I want his irons removed. At once, if you please." That she was accustomed to being obeyed was unmistakable despite the velvety drawl. Johnson looked at her uneasily, wetting his lips. Ian watched her too, beneath lowered lids that he hoped masked the sudden gleam in his eyes.

"Now, ma'am, I daren't do any such thing. Yon's a bad lot. Violent, as we've learned to our cost. 'Tis attempted murder that brought him here, and . . ."

"I have no use for chains. I would not treat a dog so, so please remove them."

Johnson, cut off in mid-protest, shrugged and signaled to one of the guards to do as the lady wished. An anvil was dragged over, and Ian squatted to place his wrists on the iron. A mallet slammed home with the clang of metal against metal. One pin and then the other shot from its casing. The mallet grazed his wrist with the final blow. Ian ignored the small hurt, as he had learned to ignore most unpleasantness. He was alive, and that was what mattered. And he meant to stay that way.

Perversely, now that his arms were free, Ian found himself questioning the lady's good sense. He rose slowly, so as not to make the pounding in his head worse, rubbing his numbed wrists and then spreading his arms wide. The muscles of his shoulders and back protested the unaccustomed movement, but it was a good kind of pain, and he welcomed it. He had not known such freedom of movement for almost half a year. The guard jumped hastily back at his sudden movement; Johnson's hand strayed to the pistol at his waist. But the lady watched him unmoved, her head cocked a little to one side, her hand still clasping the end of the rope that encircled his neck. Had he been more himself, Ian would have found the situation utterly ridiculous. She could not have been more than an inch over five feet tall, if that, while he stood six feet two in his bare feet. Though she was sturdy for her size and he was emaciated, he could have picked her up and held her immobile with one hand and wrung her neck with the other. Yet she had ordered his irons removed. What would she do if he turned ugly, pray?

"Susannah, be careful, please!"

This plea and the sound of shocked giggles from just beyond the woman drew his eyes. Glancing over the top of that hideous bonnet with no trouble at all, Ian beheld a trio of girls clustered at the lady's back. One was lovely, the other two merely passable. All three were looking at him as if he had sprouted horns through the top of his head. The quiet-looking one in the pink bonnet held her hand pressed to her mouth as she stared at him in open fear. Ian had to repress an urge to bare his teeth at her, just to give her a taste of what she so obviously expected.

"See here, Miss Susannah, I'll take the miscreant off your hands for you, give you back the money you paid for him to the pound. 'Tis no shame to admit you've made a mistake." The speaker stepped up to stand beside the woman, looking down at her. He was a choleric-looking fellow who might have passed for her father but for his manner of addressing her.

"I do not want the miscreant taken off my hands, thank you very much, Mr. Greer. I am convinced that he will suit my purpose admirably." For all her frumpishness, the lady could summon the cool hauteur of a duchess. She even managed to give the impression of looking down her nose at a man who was half a head taller than she.

"When the animal tries to murder you all in your beds you'll sing a different tune, my dear, but 'twill be too late then. If you will not think of yourself, at least think of your poor innocent sisters." Greer wore a bottle-green frock coat that would have been the better for being thoroughly brushed and a pair of black breeches that seemed to have been made for a much trimmer man. He looked every inch the bumbling provincial and would have been laughed out of London or Dublin had he blustered about so there. Here, it seemed, he was an important man, and one who was used to being obeyed. The lady's intransigence caused his face to turn even redder than nature and the hellish New World sun had rendered it.

"He is not an animal but a human being, and he will certainly not try to murder us in our beds. How absurd you are to even suggest such a thing!"

That decided speech, delivered with a lift of her too-square chin, made Greer look apoplectic. His lips clenched, and his eyes promised trouble as they darted from her to Ian and back.

"Absurd, am I? When even the likes of Hank Shay and his men were afraid to strike his irons? I am not the absurd one here, I fear!"

"Nonsense."

"Nonsense!"

"Nonsense."

Her cool stare seemed to drive Greer over the edge. Before Ian realized what the man was about, Greer snatched the rope out of the lady's hand and yanked it hard. Ian's head was jerked forward, the hemp bit deeply into the skin of his neck, and he had to bite back a pained oath.

"Mr. Greer!"

Ian's hand shot up to close over the man's fist even before the protest was out of the lady's mouth. His eyes blazed, his fingers tightened, and he knew the momentary urge to bring the bleating fool to his knees with the sheer pressure of his grip. But to humiliate the man publicly would be to create a dangerous enemy, and Ian already had enough of those. For a moment, just a moment, his eyes locked with Greer's. He slowly eased his grip before releasing the man entirely and stepped back.

"You'll pay for that!" Greer danced with rage. He shook his fist at Ian, who watched him without expression. The man talked a good game, but he was careful to stay out of reach. Ian had known many like him, all loud bluster until put to the test, and then the first ones to hightail it to safety. His eyes narrowed with contempt.

"I'll have you whipped till you bleed, you insolent bastard! Hell, I'll do it myself, with pleasure! You'll learn to lay hands on your betters at your peril! You won't be so high and mighty when the cat's slicing your back to ribbons!"

The past eight weeks had rendered Ian sensitive to that particular threat. Rage rose in his throat, bitter as bile. By the skin of his teeth he managed to bite it back, but his eyes glittered ferociously at Greer, causing the man's words to falter.

"That's quite enough, Mr. Greer! You are making a spectacle of yourself, and us as well, to no good purpose. I will thank you to leave the management of my people to me." The gentle slurring of the lady's words in no way mitigated their bite. She took the rope from Greer's hand, then stepped around him, showing him her back in no uncertain manner. Then the lady looked up, all the way up, to meet Ian's gaze. Her eyes matched her voice, Ian saw: soft and unexpectedly lovely.

"You need have no fear," she said. "You will be kindly treated, and you will not be whipped. You may put that concern from your mind."

"Susannah, I think you should at least give Mr. Greer's caution some thought. This is no three-legged dog or one-eyed cat, but a man." The chit in the pink sunbonnet spoke urgently to his new owner's back. Though the comparison made no sense to Ian, Susannah—like her voice, her name was surprisingly feminine—appeared to understand it without the least trouble. She inclined her head.

"I'm well aware of that, Sarah Jane. But I am certain that Mr.—" she looked down at the papers in her hand, then back up at his face—"Mr. Connelly will do us no harm. Will you, Connelly?"

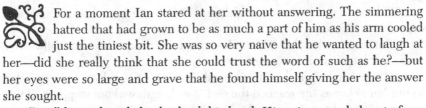 For a moment Ian stared at her without answering. The simmering hatred that had grown to be as much a part of him as his arm cooled just the tiniest bit. She was so very naive that he wanted to laugh at her—did she really think that she could trust the word of such as he?—but her eyes were so large and grave that he found himself giving her the answer she sought.

"No," he said, and slowly shook his head. His voice sounded rusty from long disuse. The timbre of it surprised him.

She smiled at him then, and he was interested to discover that her face was quite transformed. "There, you see." Her eyes left his to swing around triumphantly to the group behind her.

" 'Twould be useless to tell you that I think you've done a very bad day's work for yourself, 'tis clear. You are one of God's angels here on earth, Miss Susannah, as we all know. You would not recognize evil if it stood grinning at your right hand. I honor you for that even as I fear your very goodness will cause you to come to grief. But whether you wish it or not, I feel I must do what I can to keep you and yours safe."

Greer transferred his gaze from the lady's face to Ian's. Ian regarded him with no expression whatsoever. Greer's fists clenched, and his voice grew harsh. "Despite what you may think, Miss Susannah here and her sisters are not unprotected. Do you in any way cause them to come to harm, or offer the least insult to her or hers, and I'll peel the hide from you inch by inch with my whip whether Miss Susannah says me yea or nay. Then, if the offense merits it, I'll have you dragged before the magistrate and with God's grace see you hanged as you doubtless should have been to begin with. Do you hear, fellow?"

Ian stiffened, but did no more than that. The man was a bully and a fool and not worth the price that he would have to pay did he crush him like an ant. But his hatred, slightly cooled, boiled anew.

In some strange way, Ian realized that he welcomed the emotion's resurgence. It strengthened him, fortifying him against pain and fear—and the ridiculous softening he had felt in himself as he had stared into Miss Susannah Redmon's smiling eyes. It had been so long since he had known true goodness that he had almost forgotten what it was like.

"I'll thank you to save your bullying for members of your own household, Mr. Greer." If Susannah's eyes had been smiling when they met Ian's, they were smiling no longer as she turned them on Greer. Instead they flashed angrily, and her chin came up as she fixed Greer with a look that was as daunting as if the lady had been twice her present size, and a man to boot. "Now I must ask you to excuse us, please. Come along, Connelly. Come along, girls."

Without so much as another glance at Greer, she turned on her heel and started to walk away.

"But, Susannah . . ." The pink-bonneted girl protested in a faint voice as she fell back out of her sister's way.

"Hush, Sarah Jane," said Susannah, and she tugged on the rope that bound Ian to her as she reached the end of its length without stopping. It was an absentminded tug, Ian thought, but still it was too much. The hemp stung as it dug into the raw welt left by Greer's harsh jerking of the rope, but the pain was nothing compared to the sting to his pride. He was having none of being hauled through the crowd at the end of a tether. He did not move but put both hands up to loosen the knot and slip the loop over his head.

At his refusal to budge, the rope went taut and stopped Susannah in her tracks. She looked back over her shoulder at him to find the noose no longer about his neck but rather held in both his hands. Her expressive eyebrows lifted in silent inquiry. By way of a reply, he dropped the noose to the ground. His eyes challenged her to protest.

Instead she nodded once, in a decided way. "You are quite right, of course. I should not care to be dragged about at the end of a rope, either. Now please follow me."

Somewhat to his own surprise, Ian obeyed. With neither chains nor rope to hold him, freedom beckoned ever more brightly. But he could not very well just turn and walk away, however much he was tempted. Someone would surely give chase. He would be recaptured, probably harshly punished, and certainly guarded far more carefully in future. It was clear that his new owner had more heart than sense. He could tarry awhile in her household, regaining his strength and formulating a plan for the future, without fearing either physical abuse or humiliation. For the first time in a long time, his prospects looked bright.

At the thought, Ian felt a lifting of his spirits. Unfortunately, his body did not respond quite as swiftly to the renewal of hope as did his mind. As he set one foot in front of the other, Ian was disconcerted to realize just how weak he was. He had to force himself to concentrate even on so simple an act as walking, had to will his feet to obey the commands of his sluggish brain. Something—the heat, the sun, the damned sickening smell of rotting vegetation that permeated the place—was making him dizzy.

So dizzy was he that he was barely aware of the curious eyes that fixed on him from every direction as he followed his new mistress through the throng. He was only peripherally conscious of Susannah being greeted by what seemed to be half the matrons present, to which obviously expectant salutations she responded with no more than a smile and a wave. Trailing not too far behind him came the three girls he assumed were her sisters. He knew they were there because he could hear them whispering. One of them giggled.

That pricked the vertigo that half-blinded and deafened him. The chit snickered at him, of course. The burning shame reared its head again. How had he, Ian Connelly, fallen to such depths of ignominy? But he knew very well, of course, and knew who was responsible, too. He could consider himself fortunate that he'd not been murdered outright. But what had been done to him was almost as bad.

His sentence was seven years. Seven years was not that long a time for a man of thirty-one to wait to get his revenge. Not that he had any intention of serving out the period of his indenture, of course. He could walk away from his dowdy new mistress any time it suited him and catch the next ship back home.

And then there would be bloody hell for his enemies to pay.

A few people with skin in various shades of coffee hovered on the edge of the crowd. They were conventionally clad, the women in long dresses that were certainly finer than the one Susannah wore and the men in shirts and breeches such as any man would wear. But the darkness of their skin made them stand out. Ian blinked at them curiously as he passed. With a sense of shock he realized that he was seeing African slaves. He had heard tell of such, of course, but had never laid eyes on one before. As they left the green, he stared at a tall, ebony-skinned woman with a turban wrapping her head who was approaching along the street. She wore a starched white apron over a full-skirted dress of pale blue calico and walked a pace or so behind a fashionably dressed lady who was presumably her mistress. To his shock, Ian found that the African woman was eyeing him with every bit as much curiosity as he felt toward her. It hit him then that he, as a convict who had been indentured, was as much an oddity to her as she, an enslaved African, was to him. It occurred to him that they had a great deal in common.

"Convict! Convict!" A rock flew out of nowhere to hit Ian's shoulder and bounce off. He flinched, looking sharply around as his arm came up to ward off other missiles. A tow-headed urchin of perhaps nine years was already running back to join a snickering group of his friends, who peeped around the corner of a dry goods shop.

"Jeremy Likens, you stop that at once! Or I'll have a word with your mama! And the rest of you had best behave yourselves as well or there will be a painful reckoning for you all in the very near future!" Susannah clapped her hands sharply to emphasize her words, and the boy looked alarmed as he scuttled out of sight. His friends had withdrawn around the corner already, and not so much as a hand or foot remained to be seen of them.

"Sorry, Miss Redmon. Please don't tell Ma!"

"Sorry, Miss Redmon!"

"Sorry!"

The culprits peeped out at them and were dismissed by Susannah with a stern look and a monitory gesture. Ian was impressed anew with the respect she seemed able to command at will. More than one able-bodied man of his acquaintance would not have been able to deal half so effectively with such a gang of restive boys.

"You are not hurt, are you, Connelly?" She did not stop walking but slanted him a glance over her shoulder. Those kind eyes were accented by lashes as long as his thumbnail, Ian noticed, and her nose was small and surprisingly pert. Had she possessed a better figure and a keener sense of style, she would not have been so very unattractive after all. But she was waiting for an answer. His head was throbbing and the sidewalk was beginning to undulate beneath his feet, but the spot on his shoulder where the rock had struck troubled him not at all.

"No," he said after a moment spent summoning the word to his tongue. Then, as an afterthought, he added, "Ma'am."

That bow to courtesy earned him a glimmering smile. She half-turned, slowing as though to allow him to catch up. It was her sisters she waited for, of course. He was not quite so lightheaded that he did not realize that. But the smile was for him, and once again Ian was struck by what a smile did for her face.

"I did not think so, or I would have been more severe. Jeremy is not a bad boy, you see, but he is much interested in impressing his friends. His mother is a good woman, but his father is a notorious scoundrel, and that makes Jeremy susceptible to such behavior as you bore the brunt of."

"You would find excuses for the Devil himself, if he came in the guise of a child," the lovely one said, as, cautiously giving him a wide berth, the three girls scooted around him to gain their sister's side.

"I make no apologies for liking children." Susannah's answer was brisk as she turned her back and quickened her step again.

"By rights you should have some of your own, Susannah," Miss Pink-bonnet put in.

"She must needs be married first, dolt, and no one's come asking her that I have seen." That leveler came from the plump one in the yellow dress.

"Hush, Em!" said Miss Pink-bonnet, with a conscious look over her shoulder at Ian.

"It's all right, Sarah Jane. Emily is telling no more than the truth and must not be scolded for that." Susannah sounded untroubled, and Ian deduced that her apparently unwed and unsought state was not something that bothered her unduly. To his surprise he found that he rather admired her for that. Almost all the females with whom he'd been acquainted up till now had viewed marriage as their ultimate goal in life.

They turned onto a wide avenue lined on both sides with shops, the four girls in a fluid cluster with Ian a few paces behind. The few people who were not attending the auction sauntered along, in pairs or singly. The ladies they passed were surprisingly well-dressed, Ian considered, taking into account Susannah's appalling gown and the provincial nature of the area. Some carried baskets over their arms to hold their purchases, while others clung to the arm of a male escort. Nearly all called or nodded greetings to Susannah and her sisters, their faces reflecting their curiosity as they discovered Ian, filthy and tattered, lurching in the ladies' wake. Had he been feeling more himself, he would have snarled at the most avid, just to hear the women squeal and to see their eyes widen with fear. But he was growing more and more woolly-headed, and it required all his concentration to keep on his feet.

"Here we are." Susannah halted before a dusty, iron-wheeled wagon. Her sisters stopped too, as did Ian. A man sat on the high plank seat, his head in his hands, the picture of misery.

"Miss Susannah," he said thickly, glancing up. The movement must have pained him mightily, because he groaned and dropped his head back into the cradle of his hands.

"I have a very great deal to say to you, Craddock, but I will reserve it for a later time. You will oblige me by getting into the back, if you please."

"I didn't mean . . ." the man began miserably, but Susannah cut him off.

"At once, Craddock." Her voice was cool and perfectly polite, but Craddock said no more. Moving as if he were eighty years old and crippled to boot, he got down and crawled into the wagon-bed, where he sat with his back propped against an ironbound barrel and his feet dangling toward the street.

"You may get into the back as well, Connelly." Susannah turned her eyes on him. There was nothing of feminine coyness in the look, nothing that said that she was conscious of herself as a woman at all, but only the kind of directness that he might have expected from another man. A redoubtable woman was Miss Susannah Redmon, Ian found himself thinking even as he took a step forward to obey. But that step proved to be a mistake. His head whirled, and all of a sudden the ground seemed to tilt.

"Connelly, are you all right?"

Ian swayed. Susannah moved toward him, frowning into his face, and placed a steadying hand on his arm. Ian heard her voice, felt the surprising coolness of her fingers against the bare skin of his forearm where his shirt had been ripped away, and smelled the fresh scent of soap and—was it lemon?— that hung about her person. Then, so suddenly that he was at a loss to do anything about it, the sidewalk seemed to heave beneath his feet. His knees buckled. He felt himself collapsing and clutched at the nearest solid object in a vain attempt to save himself.

That that object was Miss Susannah Redmon and that his arms were around her pulling her down with him was the last conscious thought he had before he spun away into oblivion.

5

Susannah pulled the horse to a stop before the two-story white clapboard house that the Redmons had called home since before her birth. Brownie, the family dog, rose from her preferred spot on the front porch directly in front of the main door to yap a welcome. She was a fat brown creature whose sole claim to distinction was that she had only three legs; her left hind leg had been amputated by a carriage accident some years before. Susannah had been in town that day and witnessed the accident and had brought the maimed stray home to save it from being "mercifully" shot. She had nursed the dog back to health and now Brownie's missing limb slowed her not at all. Only her age-acquired girth hampered her movement. But she was still capable of a mighty bark. Chickens that had been scratching in the yard clucked and fluttered, alarmed by the dog. From the pasture near the barn, Old Cobb the mule brayed a welcome to his stable-mate Darcy, who drew the buckboard. Darcy nickered back. Clara the cat, roused from her nap, stretched lazily on the porch railing, adding her voice to the general hubbub. Susannah, accustomed to being welcomed in such a fashion, paid no attention beyond telling Brownie, in a distracted tone that did no good at all, to hush. Her shoulder ached from where she had hit the ground when the bound man had collapsed on her, but she ignored the pain that shot down her arm as she moved.

"Craddock, you take his shoulders. Girls, you may help me with his legs."

"You can't mean that you expect *us* to move him?" Mandy pouted prettily. Unfortunately, the effect was entirely wasted on her sister. Susannah finished wrapping the reins around the knob at the front of the buckboard that had been put there for just such a purpose and gave Mandy an exasperated glance. The four of them were crowded onto the plank seat, and until that moment both Mandy and Em had been crossly remarking on how very cramped they were and how glad they would be to reach home. Now neither of them, nor Sarah Jane either, made the least effort to get down. Only Crad-dock, grimacing as if every muscle pained him, clambered to the ground.

"Yes, I expect you to help move him. How else are we to get him inside, pray? In his present sorry state, Craddock could not lift much more than an egg without help."

"Surely you don't mean to take that convict into our house!" Sarah Jane's eyes widened as she turned them on Susannah.

"Where would you have him taken? The barn? Craddock's quarters? Mayhap the chicken coop? Or shall we let him sleep in the loft with Ben? He's ill, and he'll need nursing. Of course I mean to take him into the house, for now at least. It ill becomes you, as the daughter and prospective wife of men of God, to speak of convicts in that tone." Susannah jumped to the ground. Her jarring landing sent pain shooting along her shoulder again, but she dismissed it. As always, she had too much occupying her mind to pay heed to any trifling physical discomfort.

"You are right, of course, and I don't mean to sound uncharitable, but— but he's filthy! And 'tis anyone's guess what he may try to do to us when he recovers! The only thing we know about him is that he has been convicted of attempted murder. You could be endangering all of our lives! I declare that I will be terrified to sleep in my own bed with that con—er, that man in the house!" There was real distress in Sarah Jane's voice.

"You're as poor-spirited as a declawed crab lately, Sarah Jane, do you know that? *I* have no objection to helping to carry him in, or to having him in the house, either," Emily said, sounding virtuous. She was seated next to Mandy who still occupied the far right end of the bench, and she did not let Mandy's presence keep her from jumping to the ground. She simply pushed her sister out of her way. Mandy, thrust from her perch without ceremony, fortunately hit the grass feet first, stumbling forward as she landed before finally gaining her balance.

"Em, you great cow, be careful what you're about!" Mandy, clutching folds of her elegant skirt in both hands, whirled on Emily, who was grinning widely as she watched her sister's less than graceful descent. Even as she appeared ready to box her sister's ears, Mandy recollected her status as a young lady rather than a squabbling child. Her eyes left Emily to shoot self-consciously toward Craddock. A large component of Mandy's reach for self-control stemmed from the knowledge that a man—even so ineligible a one as Craddock—was witness to her behavior, Susannah knew. She stifled an in-ward sigh. Really, Mandy in the throes of man-fever was getting to be almost more than she felt equipped to handle. But of course she would handle it, because who else would if she did not?

Emily was sensitive about her weight, as Mandy of course knew very well, and was still young enough that she felt no compulsion to preserve her dignity. She flushed with anger in turn, "Don't you dare call me a cow, Amanda Sue Redmon! You're nothing but a—a preening peahen yourself! All you care about is your mirror! You're lazy, and vain and—and . . ."

"Emily! That's quite enough! You're far too old for such tricks as pushing your sister from the wagon, and for name-calling as well. And that last goes for you, too, Mandy. Words can be far more hurtful than deeds, remember." Susannah never raised her voice, but the authority that sprang from years of acting the mother to her sisters silenced both girls. They glowered at each other, but neither said anything more. With an inward prayer to the good Lord above to grant her patience, Susannah walked around to the back of the buckboard, beckoning her sisters to follow her. They did, although Mandy and Em both looked sulky and Sarah Jane was openly dubious. All four of them clustered around the end of the wagon, silent for a moment as they stared at the sprawled figure of the indentured man.

His legs, bare from just below the knee down, stuck out over the edge of the buckboard. They were hairy and dirty, and decidedly unprepossessing. The brogues he wore looked too small for him, and the bottom of one foot could be seen through a large hole worn in the sole. His breeches were tattered, permitting indecent glimpses of male flesh to anyone who cared to look, which Susannah emphatically did not. His shirt was little more than a gray rag, and only the gold waistcoat, which amazingly still retained a button that held it closed at his waist, kept his chest from being bare. Aware of her young and innocent sisters' eyes fixed on what was visible of the convict's very masculine, hair-covered chest, Susannah felt another stab of misgiving. Here was a complication to her compassion that she had not considered: what effect would the addition to the household of a virile and very likely completely amoral male have on the girls?

Sarah Jane was probably right, Susannah admitted to herself with a sinking feeling. She should never have allowed her annoyance at Hiram Greer and a certain sympathy for the convict's plight to move her to purchase him. Problems of all sorts were very likely to ensue, and more problems were something she certainly didn't need. But the deed was done and could not be undone. She must take care to keep Mandy and Em, whose youth rendered them most vulnerable, from close contact with the man.

And if he proved to be the kind of rogue who preyed on young girls? Susannah felt queasy at the very idea. Then, as she bethought herself of the stout iron fry-pan that hung from a hook in the kitchen, she felt marginally better. Should the need arise, she would clout the varmint soundly on the head, then sell him to Hiram Greer for his pains! Though perhaps, if she were lucky, it would not come to that.

"Craddock, you get up there behind his head and lift his shoulders. Mandy, you and Em take his left leg. Sarah Jane, help me with his right."

"Yes'm." Craddock crawled up in the wagon to do her bidding. Her sisters also moved to obey, though a tad reluctantly.

"Susannah, he stinks," Em said, wrinkling her nose as she made a discovery that had become known to Susannah an hour or so previously, when she had struggled to get out from under the man who had collapsed on her. Susannah was well-accustomed to nursing the infirm; it was one of the duties she had willingly assumed when she took over her mother's place as the female head of the minister's household. But even she had known an instant's hesitation before sliding her hands around the convict's hair-roughened and filthy leg. Her sisters, whom she had never allowed to be exposed to the very intimate tasks involved in nursing a man, could not be blamed for their obvious reluctance to touch him.

"Yes, he does," Mandy chimed in. Grimacing, she let go her grip on the man's ankle and stepped back.

"So would you if you had not bathed for months," Susannah said. Before she could expand on this theme, Mandy, an expression of relief easing her frown as she looked beyond Susannah's shoulder, interrupted.

"Here's Ben, thank goodness!" she said.

Susannah's hands dropped from the convict's leg as she turned to watch the approach of their second hired man.

"I'm real sorry about this mornin', Miss Susannah," Ben said, hanging his head guiltily as he hurried toward them. Tall and bone thin, with a shock of auburn hair and a spattering of freckles to go with them, Ben was not an unattractive boy. Susannah liked him, and as a rule he was as biddable a youth as one could wish to encounter. But his recent devotion to Maria O'Brien, youngest daughter of a dirt farmer who, with his large family, barely managed to eke out a living some four miles distant, had rendered him all but useless. She gritted her teeth to hold back the scolding she knew would be better rendered in private and indicated the bound man.

"We'll talk about this morning later. Right now, you can help Craddock carry this man inside."

Sarah Jane, Mandy, and Emily stepped back from the wagon with varying degrees of relief. Ben's eyes widened as they found the unconscious figure thus displayed.

"Who's he?" Ben asked.

"Our new bound man," Emily said. She and Ben were much of an age, and Susannah suspected that Em found Ben rather attractive. But Ben seemed totally unaware of Emily as anything other than a daughter of the family, so Susannah hoped she had not much to worry about from that direction. Certainly she was not about to borrow trouble by planting a warning to stay away from the other in either Em's or Ben's ear and thus sow seed on what might prove all too fertile ground.

"Bound man?" Ben let out a whistle of surprise, his eyes shooting to Susannah. The look on her face must have been daunting, because he clamped his lips together and positioned himself between the convict's ankles without another word.

"Lift, then, when I say." Craddock took charge as he saw that his helper was to be the boy whom Susannah well knew he bullied when he thought he could get away with it. Craddock gave the word, and between them he and Ben managed to lift the man from the wagon.

"Dad-blum, he's heavy!" Having been sternly weaned from profanity in the year he had been with them, Ben had substituted a variety of colorful expressions for the swear words he had grown up with but was no longer permitted to utter.

"He don't look like hardly more than a skeleton, neither," Craddock marveled as he, backing, struggled to negotiate the two smooth gray rocks that served as porch steps without dropping his burden. The convict's head rested against Craddock's thin chest. His bristly black beard and the unkempt, overlong tangle of his hair were largely responsible for the ferocious look of him, Susannah judged with a slight feeling of reassurance as she followed them onto the porch. A slanting ray of light from the late afternoon sun touched a lock of filthy hair as it straggled down over the bound man's forehead. Susannah saw that it was not just dark but jet black beneath the grime that caked it. She had no chance to notice anything more about him as she hurried around the trio to open the door.

"Where do you want 'im, Miss Susannah?"

"In the parlor." She led the way, untying her bonnet as she went. A row of pegs had been set into the wall at the base of the stairs. As she passed them, she hung the hat there, then ran both hands over her head in a gesture as automatic to her as breathing.

There was a company bed in the parlor, pushed against the wall opposite the fireplace over which hung Grandma and Grandpa Durham's pictures. The portraits were huge and dark and would have been grim had not Susannah remembered her grandparents so warmly. They had died not long before Susannah's mother, their daughter, who had hung their pictures in the place of honor in the little used room reserved for important visitors. Two rocking chairs on either side of the fireplace, a wooden settee, and a pair of fine walnut bookcases filled to overflowing with books completed the room's furnishings. Susannah hurried to the iron bedstead and whisked back the intricately patterned quilt that she had spent many a winter night piecing some two years before. The linen, having been put on fresh after the bed was last used by a visiting minister six months previously, was clean. At her direction, Craddock and Ben lowered the convict to the bed.

He looked filthier than ever against the snowy sheets.

"He'll need to be bathed and put into some clean clothes," she decided. "Ben, you can help me. Craddock, you can carry in the shopping, and you girls can put it up and start supper. Pa should be home before long."

"He was leaving with John Naisbitt when I got here," Ben said. "He tole me to tell you that Miz Cooper done died."

"Oh dear." Susannah, having spent a large part of the previous night at Mrs. Cooper's bedside, had suspected that the old woman would not long survive, but she had not expected her to pass from this life quite so soon as this. She would have to hurry over there and help the woman's daughters lay her out, then stay to comfort the grieving family. There was the funeral to think about—she played the church clavichord that had been shipped from England at great expense—and her father's best suit, which he would need to officiate at the service, to sponge and press.

But first the bound man's needs must be seen to.

"Start undressing him, Ben," she said, shooing her wide-eyed sisters out before her as she left the room. "Sarah Jane, you might get together some bread and molasses for me to take with me when I go over to the Coopers' tonight. The family will doubtless be too upset to want to think about cooking. Mandy, you and Em get supper started. There's a chicken plucked and ready to go in the pot, and you can fix dumplings and greens to go with it. I'll take some of that with me, too. Oh, and be sure and save the water the chicken's cooked in to make broth. We'll need it for him."

Her head jerked in the direction of the parlor and left her sisters in no doubt of whom she referred to.

"I thought the whole idea of getting a bound man was so that we'd have to do less work, not more," Mandy muttered as the girls disappeared into the kitchen. Craddock, his arms full of the day's purchases, shouldered his way through the front door. Susannah, prudently ignoring Mandy, who had a point, went up the narrow staircase that led from the sitting room—a large, less formal parlor where the family spent most of their time—to the second floor. There were four bedchambers abovestairs. The Reverend Redmon had the largest one, directly over the front parlor, while Amanda and Emily shared the next largest, located over the sitting room. Susannah and Sarah Jane each had a small room at the back of the house to herself. Susannah's room was above the rear porch and overlooked the family cemetery where her mother and grandparents lay, along with her four baby brothers who had not survived infancy. Susannah said her nightly prayers on her knees before the single long, narrow window that opened onto her room, instead of beside her bed as she had been taught. Sometimes her mother's and grandparents' faces got mixed up with her conception of God's and she quite forgot who she was talking to, but it was comforting, nonetheless.

Her father's room was, as usual, untidy. Papers and books were strewn about, along with the clothing he had discarded when he had changed to go to the Coopers'. If she hadn't done the straightening up herself, she would never have believed that the chamber had been spotless just that morning. Her fingers itched to restore at least a modicum of order to the room as she crossed to the tall bureau that stood against one wall, but she resisted. There were too many chores awaiting her that were more urgent.

Remembering Mandy's words, Susannah stifled a sigh. The bound man's collapse had made him just one more task to be dealt with, another problem rather than the solution she had bought him for. Last night she had not seen her bed until the wee hours of the morning. Tonight she would be lucky to lay her head down at all.

She was tired, bone tired, but there was nothing to be done about that. If she just kept plugging away, putting one foot in front of the other and doing each task as it arose, eventually she would get everything that was needful done. She always did.

The Lord never sent anyone more of a burden than he could bear. That bit of Scripture was the talisman that had kept her going for years. She repeated it aloud to ward off the exhaustion that, as she glanced toward the bed, momentarily threatened to overwhelm her.

It worked. Almost at once she felt better. Extracting a linen nightshirt from the bureau, Susannah turned and hurried back down the stairs. The appetizing aroma of supper cooking wafted into her nostrils. From the kitchen, she could hear her sisters bickering good-naturedly about everything from the amount of greens to boil with the chicken to the eye color of the man Mandy had flirted with in town. Susannah rolled her own eyes heavenward as she made a quick foray through the battle zone to collect a pitcher of warm water, a bowl, a sliver of soap, and a towel. There was a trick to not allowing herself to be drawn into any of the sundry discussions that flew about the room, and that trick was selective deafness. Firmly rejecting Mandy's offer to help—she knew full well her sister considered caring for the bound man both more interesting and easier than her kitchen duties—Susannah finally made it to the parlor with her booty.

Ben looked up as she entered. "Lookit this, Miss Susannah."

The bound man—Connelly, she must remember to think of him as Connelly now that he was to be a member of the household—lay on his stomach. He was naked, or at least she presumed he was naked, though Ben had drawn the quilt up to his waist, so she could not be absolutely sure. Susannah's first thought was that his back was far darker that the rest of his coloring would have indicated. Then, as she came closer, she saw that the darkness was a combination of severe bruising and dried blood, and she drew in a sharp breath.

"Looks like he's been beat bad."

Without answering, Susannah set her provisions down on the small table that stood beside the iron bedstead. With hands that were carefully steady, she lit a pair of candles so that the parlor's perpetual gloom would not distort her judgment. Finally, as the candles' warm yellow glow spread to illuminate the area in question, she turned to look again at Connelly's back.

As Ben had observed, the man had been badly beaten.

There were dozens of wounds crisscrossed on top of one another, some half healed, some oozing pus, some raw and obviously fairly fresh. The abused flesh was swollen and painful-looking. The smell from it reminded Susannah of meat gone bad. She had nursed many people and animals through a huge variety of injuries and illnesses, but nothing had ever angered her so much as did the condition of her new bound man's back.

"Fetch my medicine case," she said tightly.

"Yes'm." Ben, with no more than a single look at her expression, was out the door with as much alacrity as if she had taken a lash to his legs. Susannah smiled sourly as she reflected that it was the fastest she had ever seen the boy move.

Turning to the bedside table, she washed her hands and wet the towel. Taking the soap in her hands, she sat down on the edge of the bed to do what needed to be done.

The first order of business was to give the bound man a quick, much needed bath.

6

The last bed bath she had given had been to Mrs. Cooper just the previous night. Washing Connelly was a whole different experience.

Not that Susannah had never given a man a bath before. She had, on several occasions, in the course of her nursing duties. But it occurred to her, as she carefully soaped Connelly's left hand, rinsed it, and patted it dry, that every single man she had cared for so intimately in the past had been ancient and, if not on his deathbed, near it. Never had she had occasion to bathe a man who could be no more than a decade or so older than herself. The experience was almost unsettling.

But to allow herself to be disturbed by such a mundane task was ridiculous. He needed care, and it was up to her to provide it. Perhaps lack of sleep was making her unaccustomedly skittish.

He had beautiful hands, Susannah noticed as she soaped the long, strong fingers. The nails were ragged and caked with dirt, but the fingers themselves were straight, the fingertips elegantly rounded. His palms were broad, and the faintest sprinkling of black hair covered the backs of his hands. His wrists were bony but thick, as befitted a man of the size she judged that, under normal conditions, he was.

With his hands clean, she saturated the towel and lathered soap into it. Somehow she could not feel quite comfortable about running her bare hands over his flesh, no matter how pure were her motives. Some small part of her, which she steadfastly determined to ignore, was very much aware that the sprawled body beneath her fingers belonged to a man. The tiny flicker of feminine awareness was like nothing she had ever experienced before, and she wondered at herself. She was long past such foolishness, not that she had ever indulged in it anyway.

His arms were long and hard with muscle, despite their lack of excess flesh, and his forearms were dark with hair. Thick black tufts grew in his armpits. His shoulders were smooth-skinned and broad enough to cover half the bed. She noticed these attributes as she washed him simply because she could not help it. That she should find his person so very intriguing vexed her, but there was nothing she could do to keep her eyes from seeing and her brain from registering various masculine details. Almost against her will, as she washed down both sides of his rib cage, her eyes absorbed the powerful symmetry of his upper torso, from his wide shoulders to the intriguing hollow of his spine, where the quilt fortunately cut off her view. For all his leanness, his build was superb. Restored to health, she guessed, he would be a very strong man.

Which was why she had bought him, of course. For his strength. There were plowing and planting and harvesting to be done, and fences to build and mend, and the roof of the barn to be repaired, and a new pond to be dug, and —and dozens of things about the place that needed doing that she could not at the moment call to mind. Connelly must perform all these tasks, and more. If the question of his strength interested her, then that was why. Certainly there was no other reason.

"Here's your case, Miss Susannah."

Susannah had quite forgotten Ben's errand. Startled by his return, she glanced around to find him right behind her, proffering her case. To her annoyance, she felt heat rise in her cheeks as she met his gaze. Which was ridiculous, she told herself sternly. She had done nothing, thought nothing, that should make her feel in the least guilty.

Nevertheless, guilty was precisely how she felt.

"Put it on the floor here beside me."

If her words were short, it was simply because she was tired. Ben complied, then straightened. She smiled at him to lessen the impact of her tone. He looked relieved, and she felt guiltier than ever.

What was the matter with her today?

"Can I do anything else for you, Miss Susannah?" Ben's diffidence did not help matters. He sounded as if he were actually afraid of her. Was she really such an ogress? Perhaps she was. Most everybody seemed to be scared of her at one time or another. But someone had to keep them all in line, and by default the job had fallen to her. Not that she regretted the circumstances of her life, but still it would be nice to be as young and full of anticipation of life's possibilities as her sisters. Sometimes it seemed to Susannah that she had never been young.

"I am going to need a big bucket of warm water, a couple more towels, another cake of soap, and a paring knife. Would you fetch those for me, please?" She smiled at him again, and this time he smiled back. Susannah felt a little better. Maybe she was not so terrifying, after all. Maybe her view of the world was unaccustomedly black at the moment because she badly needed a decent night's sleep.

"Yes'm." Ben took himself off, and Susannah applied herself once more to the task at hand. Before she medicated and bandaged Connelly's back, she wanted him to be as clean as she could render him under such constrained circumstances. Cleanliness was all important to the recovery of health, as she had seen demonstrated over and over again.

His arms, the uninjured portions of his back, his shoulders and neck were clean. Susannah moved down to stand at the foot of the bed. Folding back the quilt so that his legs were bared to the knees, she proceeded to wash his feet. Like his hands, they were long and strong-looking and beautifully made. There was a large, horn-thick callus at the base of his big toe. Susannah remembered the hole in his shoe. He would not be wearing those brogues again. She made a mental note to have Ben carry them to the cobbler in town. The cobbler could use the shoes for a size gauge as he fashioned Connelly some sturdy work boots, two sizes bigger.

"Do you need help, Susannah?" Mandy popped up in the doorway, her eyes bright with curiosity as she took in the sight of her oldest sister running a soapy cloth along the bound man's calves. Connelly was covered only from the small of his back to just above his knees, and Mandy's eyes widened at so much masculine nudity on view. Susannah frowned at her and moved instinctively so that her body was between her sister and the bed, blocking much of Mandy's view. But before she could send the girl away, Ben returned, lugging a steaming bucket in one hand and carrying the other items she had sent him for in the other. Mandy had perforce to step into the room so that Ben could pass. With Susannah distracted by Ben's arrival, Mandy approached the bed. Susannah did not become aware of what her sister was about until Mandy stood beside her, gaping down at the nearly naked man lying prone on the white sheet.

"Ben can render all the assistance I need in here, thank you very much. As you have so much excess energy, you may go upstairs and tidy Pa's room."

"But, Susannah . . ."

"Go do it, Mandy. And when you have done, go back to the kitchen and help Sarah Jane and Em. Your presence is not required here."

"But what happened to his back?"

"That is not your concern, is it?" Instinctively Susannah sensed that Connelly would not relish having the world at large know of the punishment he had endured. She had already seen that he was a fiercely proud man and not one to easily accept public humiliation. Just why she felt compelled to spare him from further embarrassment she could not say. But she would, and did, reflexively shelter as best she could any living creature battered by life's blows. She supposed the urge to protect Connelly sprang from the same source.

"It looks dreadful!"

"Amanda, go on now. Shoo!" The firmness in Susannah's voice brought a momentary pout to Mandy's face. Mandy glanced swiftly from her sister to Ben, who was in the act of setting the bucket down on the floor and placing the other items on the bedside table.

"Oh, very well," Mandy said. Turning, she left the room. Susannah felt some of the tension leave her shoulders. Mandy could still act like a spoiled little girl, and she was perfectly capable of throwing a tantrum if she failed to get her own way. Susannah guessed she owed her sister's restraint to Ben's presence. Perhaps Mandy's dedication to attracting male approval had some vestige of a silver lining, after all. On that comforting thought, she picked up the paring knife and proceeded to trim and clean Connelly's nails.

"Ben, I want you to help me scoot him so that his head hangs over the side of the bed. I can't stand the idea of leaving his hair so dirty," she said when she was done.

"Yes'm."

Between the two of them they managed to get Connelly positioned. He stirred during this procedure, grunting, but then lapsed back into what Susannah believed was nothing more serious than a profound sleep. His skin was hot to the touch, indicating the presence of fever, but not so hot as to cause her a great deal of anxiety. It was obvious to her that, whatever ailed her bound man, he would recover if provided abundant food, water, rest, and nursing care. Then he could begin to help about the farm, and perhaps she would cease fearing that she had made a dreadful mistake in purchasing him.

"I'll hold his head, and you pour half the water in the bucket over it. We'll need the other half for rinsing." Susannah pulled up a nearby chair and sat, taking Connelly's head in her hands. He lay face down, and his head was surprisingly heavy. She tried not to feel distaste at the griminess of his hair as it curled around her fingers or at the filthy state of his skin.

"Yes'm." Ben did as he was told. The warm water gushed over Susannah's hands and wrists as she held the dead weight of Connelly's head over the slop jar, one of which was kept beneath every bed in the house in case of need.

"What the bloody hell?" Something, presumably the water rushing over his head, roused Connelly with a vengeance. Susannah gasped and sat back as, without warning, he braced his hands against the mattress and jerked his head from her hold. Though she quickly regained control of herself, Susannah was aware of the still-quickened pace of her heart at her bound man's unexpected resurrection. She watched warily as he levered himself into a sitting position. Streams of water ran down his face and neck and onto his chest. Blinded by the soaked curtain of overlong hair that plastered his face, Connelly shook his head, spraying droplets like a wet dog, and uttered an oath so foul that Ben, bucket suspended in his hands, swallowed and glanced wide-eyed at Susannah. Then Connelly brushed the offending strands back with both hands. Susannah unexpectedly found herself pinned by a pair of fierce gray eyes.

"It's all right. We're merely washing your hair," she said. Though her heart continued to pound, she tried to make her tone soothing. The color of his eyes, which she had not noticed before, came as a surprise. With his black hair and swarthy skin, she would have expected them to be brown. But they were the gray of the sea during a storm, cloudy and turbulent and changeable. Just now they were glaring at her as if he meant to leap on her at any moment and tear her limb from limb.

"The hell you are." The words were a throaty growl. It occurred to Susannah that perhaps he had forgotten who she was and the altered circumstances of his life. Certainly he could have no idea how he had come to be in this room and this bed. The realization reassured her. All she needed to do was make him aware of what had transpired and that dangerous look would vanish from his face. The key to handling him was to be gentle, so as not to frighten him. She would treat him just as she would any injured, snarling animal.

"You do remember me, and the auction this afternoon? I am Miss Susannah Redmon, and I . . ."

"No bloody woman is washing my hair!" His voice was hoarse, scratchy, furious, and its intonation was unmistakably British. He glowered at her as angry dark blood rose high in his cheeks. His shoulders were dauntingly broad and tensed as if ready for battle. His fists were clenched, and his torso was rigidly erect, though she guessed that it must be costing him considerable effort to keep it so. Thankfully, the quilt was puddled around his vital parts, but he was bare as a babe both above and below it.

Though she tried not to let her gaze rest there, Susannah could not help but observe his naked chest. It was wide and furred with a wedge of thick, curling black hair that narrowed to a thin line as it trailed past his navel to disappear beneath the quilt. The sheer masculinity of that hairy chest caused the tiny flicker of feminine awareness she had struggled with before to flame anew. Conscious of her pinkening cheeks, praying that he would not notice, Susannah dragged her eyes back up to his face.

Then she almost wished she had not.

With his soaked black hair pushed sleekly back from his forehead while the ends cascaded in a wild tangle to his shoulders and his bushy black beard obscuring the lower half of his face, he looked like the savage she had been busily assuring herself he wasn't.

Had she permitted herself to, Susannah would have felt just the tiniest tremor of alarm. After all, what did she know about this man? As Sarah Jane had pointed out, only that he had been convicted of attempted murder. And that he'd been beaten mercilessly for some unknown reason. Neither fact was reassuring. But she'd made her bed, as the saying went, and now she had no choice but to lie in it.

"Wash your hair yourself, then," she said and, scooping up the cake of soap, held it out to him. Her tone was admirably cool despite her inner unease. When dealing with potentially dangerous creatures, she had learned that it was important not to let them get the faintest whiff of fear. And something told her that her new bound man was a very dangerous creature indeed.

7

Connelly looked warily from the soap to her face. Then, to Susannah's surprise he took it, rubbing it between his hands until it lathered, then rubbing the lather into his hair. He repeated the process until frothy white bubbles nearly covered the seal-black strands, then spread the lather over his face as well. His eyes remained fixed on Susannah for the most part, though they flickered occasionally to Ben. They were hard and narrowed and dark with suspicion. She was reminded once more of an animal at bay.

"Is there water in that bucket?" The raspy question was addressed to Ben, who blinked.

"Y-yes, sir."

"Bring it here, then."

With a quick glance at Susannah to secure her permission—she nodded almost imperceptibly—Ben carried the bucket to Connelly's bedside.

"Put it on the floor."

Ben complied, then stepped back. Connelly shot him a warning glare, then sent Susannah another one. Before she realized quite what he intended to do, he grasped the edge of the mattress with both hands and his upper body jackknifed over the side of the bed. He thrust his whole head into the bucket and stayed submerged for perhaps a minute. When he withdrew his head, tossing it, he again slung water everywhere as his eyes darted to Susannah and then Ben. Having apparently satisfied himself that they intended no threatening moves, he bent and wrung out his dripping locks over the bucket.

"Would you care for a towel?" Susannah held out one. Her extreme politeness under the circumstances sounded almost ludicrous to her own ears, but the effect she strove for was one of unthreatening calm. Those gray eyes gave her a distrustful look, but he took the towel and rubbed it vigorously over his head and face.

"Ben, fetch me a dry quilt. And a bowl of broth and a cup of water from the kitchen." Susannah's voice was quiet.

"Yes'm."

"And Ben—there's no need to tell my sisters that he has awakened. If they ask, you may tell them that the broth is for yourself."

"Yes'm."

Ben hurried to do her bidding. Left alone with the bound man, Susannah was conscious of feeling more than just a little bit nervous. But she camouflaged the sensation, masterfully, she thought, by bending to her medicine case and extracting from it a squat jar, a vial, and a roll of bandages.

"What's that?" He was regarding her with acute suspicion, even as he dropped the used towel to the floor. She noticed that he was careful not to rest his back against the iron headboard and guessed that it must be painful to the touch.

"Salve for your back, for one thing."

"What the hell do you know about my back?"

Susannah sighed. Dealing with him carefully and kindly was one thing, but allowing him to show her the rough side of his tongue was something else. It was time to establish, very gently, just who was in charge.

"'Tis obvious to anyone who has seen your back that you have been severely beaten. The wounds are festering, and you may count yourself fortunate not to have contracted blood poisoning. This salve will take away the infection and the pain and promote healing. If you will lie on your stomach, I will apply it for you. And you will please put a curb on your tongue. We do not swear in this house."

"Is that so?"

"Yes, it is. Will you lie down? I do have other things to do this evening besides attending to you."

He looked from her to the medical necessities in her hand, seemed to weigh the matter, then did as she asked. As he sprawled on his stomach, Susannah noticed that he was careful to keep the now-damp quilt wrapped around his waist. At least he was not the sort who got a thrill out of displaying their private parts to women.

She rose and moved to the bedside table, where she put down the vial and the bandages. The other jar she opened, scooping out the white paste inside with one hand. Then she set the jar down and, leaning over the bed, proceeded to apply the salve liberally to Connelly's abused back.

"What the devil is in that stuff? It burns like hellfire!" He went rigid beneath her hands as the medicine started to do its work.

Susannah slapped an extra measure of salve on one particularly raw spot for good measure.

"Perhaps it will teach you that I mean what I say: in this house, such language as you just used is forbidden."

"What are you, some kind of nun?" From the sounds of them, the words were forced through his teeth.

Susannah was silent for a moment as she screwed the lid back on the jar and returned it to her medicine case. She picked up the roll of bandages.

"Would you sit up, please?"

He scowled warily at her over his shoulder, still grimacing from the sting of the medicine, but did as she asked.

"Can you lift your arms?"

Silently he complied. Susannah began to wind the bandage around his back and chest. With his eyes on her, the task was difficult. She was all too conscious of his gender and her own. He had nipples, hard male nipples that were flat and brown and as unlike her own as it was possible for two of the same species to be. The hair on his chest was thick and black and crisp, and it felt soft against her fingers. As she registered this she almost dropped the roll of bandages, rescuing it only with a clumsy save that made her feel like a fool. Glancing at him because she could not help herself, knowing her cheeks were brick red and afraid he might be able to guess the cause, she was unsettled to find that he was watching her almost mockingly.

"No, I see you're not a nun," he said.

The gibe made her blood heat with shame; hard on the heels of shame came anger. Susannah gritted her teeth.

"It is time we got something clear between us, I believe. I am the mistress here, and you are my servant. You will be well and kindly treated, but you will speak to me and my family with respect and abide by the rules of this house. I hope I am making myself understood?"

She finished her task as she spoke and tied the loose ends of the gauze in a knot at his side. He slewed his head around to look at her.

"And just what will you do should I choose not to be respectful or abide by your rules?" It was both taunt and challenge.

"As much as it would pain me to abandon a task I have undertaken, I would be forced to sell you to someone else. Mr. Greer, for one, would be glad to take you off my hands, I'm sure."

"Are you threatening me?" If there was renewed rage in his voice, and Susannah thought there was, he had no time to give it fuller rein, and she no time to reply. Ben entered just at that moment, carefully carrying a tray on which a steaming bowl and a tin cup were balanced. Over his shoulder was flung a quilt from the linen press upstairs.

"Where do you want I should put this, Miss Susannah?"

Susannah beckoned, and Ben brought the tray over to where she stood by the bedside table. With her back turned to screen her actions from view, she quickly unscrewed the lid of the vial from her medicine case and dribbled a little of the brownish liquid contained therein into the broth. She recapped the vial and set it down again.

"If 'tis food, give it to me," Connelly said.

Ben glanced at Susannah. Taking the spoon that rested beside the bowl, she quickly stirred the broth, then nodded. Ben set the tray down on Connelly's lap.

Good manners, if Connelly had ever possessed them, lost the battle to hunger. Taking the spoon from the steaming bowl, he dropped it on the tray, then picked up the bowl itself and carried it to his mouth. Both Susannah and Ben watched wide-eyed as he tilted the dish, pouring the contents down his throat so greedily that the bowl was emptied in a matter of minutes.

"Is there more?" he asked hoarsely, lowering the bowl and running his tongue over his lips to catch any stray drops.

"As much broth as you want," Susannah answered, feeling her compassion stir anew as she realized that the man was, literally, starving. "Though solids must wait at least until the morrow. You don't want to eat too much at first."

For a moment she thought he would argue, but he did not.

"Then bring me more broth," he said. Susannah nodded at Ben, though she really didn't think that Connelly would be awake for long enough to enjoy it. To recover fully, he needed rest as much as food. And, since she had to leave her sisters alone in the house with him and basically unprotected (young Ben didn't count), she had decided to take no chances in case he should feel inclined to mayhem. To ensure all of them a peaceful night, she had added a few drops of laudanum to his broth. It should take effect soon.

He swallowed some water and set the cup back down on the tray still half full.

"You were not deprived of water as well as food, I see." Susannah's observation was carefully neutral.

For a moment he just looked at her, as if uncertain how, or whether, to respond. Then he gave the merest suggestion of a shrug.

"Water is essential to life. Food, unless withheld for a very long time, is not."

As she had expected, within minutes his eyelids began to droop. He swayed, and one hand went out to steady himself against the mattress. Susannah reached over to lift the tray from his lap and set it out of harm's way.

"Were I you, I would lie down now and rest until Ben returns," she suggested soothingly, turning back to plump his pillow with practiced hands.

Connelly managed to focus his eyes on her face for an instant, but Susannah could see that it was an effort. Then his lids closed, and he sighed.

"Feel—strange," he muttered, even as he permitted her to ease him over onto his stomach and down onto his pillow.

"No doubt you will feel better in the morning," she answered, but she doubted if he heard her.

"I've brought more broth, Miss Susannah," Ben said from the doorway.

Susannah straightened to look at him. "He'll not be wanting it after all, Ben. He's asleep."

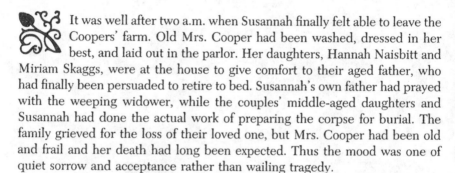 It was well after two a.m. when Susannah finally felt able to leave the Coopers' farm. Old Mrs. Cooper had been washed, dressed in her best, and laid out in the parlor. Her daughters, Hannah Naisbitt and Miriam Skaggs, were at the house to give comfort to their aged father, who had finally been persuaded to retire to bed. Susannah's own father had prayed with the weeping widower, while the couples' middle-aged daughters and Susannah had done the actual work of preparing the corpse for burial. The family grieved for the loss of their loved one, but Mrs. Cooper had been old and frail and her death had long been expected. Thus the mood was one of quiet sorrow and acceptance rather than wailing tragedy.

Climbing up into the buggy with her father, glad that for once she did not have to drive home alone, Susannah stretched her tired back, wincing a little at the soreness of her shoulder. The bruise was already deep purple, and it made itself felt whenever she moved. It also reminded her of a problem she had managed, for a few hours, to push to the back of her mind—Connelly. She had yet to tell her father what she had done.

Glancing along the seat to where he sat, fragile in his black suit, white-haired, his back erect despite a weariness that must surely be as great as her own, she knew that the moment of truth was at hand. But he forestalled her.

"Walter Cooper asked that you play Milton's *Hymn to the Creator* at the service tomorrow."

Susannah nodded. "Mrs. Cooper loved that song. She asked me to sing it to her just last night."

"She was a fine woman. Heaven is the richer for our loss."

"Yes."

Conversation died. The muffled thud of Darcy's hooves against the dirt road was echoed by the plodding hoofbeats of her father's horse, Micah, who was tied behind. Except for the rustling of the wind in the trees and the shrill call of a nightbird from some distance away, there was no other sound. The silence would have been comfortable had Susannah not been on tenterhooks about the confession she had to make. There was no good reason not to speak. The revelation would get no easier for being delayed.

Susannah took a deep breath. If it had to be done, then it was best done quickly, as her mother had often said. But still she hesitated, reluctant to spoil these few moments that she had alone with her father. For a moment, just a moment more, she would hold her tongue and savor the peace of the night. It was cooler now, the temperature having dropped some twenty degrees from what it had been that afternoon, and the smell of growing things and farm animals and salt water combined to add just the suggestion of a spicy tang to the air. Above, twinkling far out of the reach of a forest of tall pines, dozens of stars studded the deep blue satin of the sky. A half moon, frosty white, lit the dirt road, making it simple for Darcy to find his way home.

Which was fortunate, because her father's hands were slack on the reins, and his eyes, like hers, were on the sky above. But while she was indulging in a very worldly reluctance to broach an unpleasant subject, he was undoubtedly engaged in godly thoughts of the world to come. With his full white beard and rippling mane of hair turned to glowing silver by the eerie light, he looked like a Biblical prophet come to life. Susannah's heart swelled with a fierce love for him. He turned his head as if sensing her regard, and smiled his gentle smile at her before resuming his study of the heavens. Susannah, the knowledge of her transgression heavy as an anvil inside her, felt like the lowest worm alive.

"Pa, I bought us an indentured servant today. A man." Her words were abrupt.

For a moment she was not sure he heard or understood, but then his eyes dropped from their contemplation of God's wonders to fasten on her face.

"You did what, daughter?"

"I bought us a bound man."

"*A bound man?*" The Reverend Redmon sounded as if he had never heard of such.

Susannah persevered, though she felt her stomach clench at the thought of how she must displease him. "Yes, a bound man. Craddock is a drunk, and Ben is no more than a boy. Sarah Jane will be married in September, and there is too much work for the rest of us to do. Anyway, much that needs doing is heavy work, man's work. So I bought us a bound man to do it."

There was a moment of profound silence. Then the Reverend Redmon shook his head sadly.

"Have all my teachings on the evils of slavery fallen on deaf ears? Moses was a slave, and . . ."

"I know all about Moses, Pa, and I feel just as you do about slavery. But this man is not a slave. He is an indentured servant, bound to work for us for seven years to atone for his sins. He was duly sentenced by a court of law." Susannah's hands were cold, and she twisted them in the material of her skirt to warm them. She hated to set herself up in opposition to her father, not because of any scoldings or punishment she might suffer—he was not the man to dispense either—but because he was so sorrowful when one of his children distressed him. She felt guilty for having done something she had known from the onset he would dislike, and angry at herself for feeling guilty when, after careful deliberation, she had concluded that a bound man was truly necessary to the running of the farm. Someone had to be concerned with clothing and feeding them and keeping a roof over their heads, and by default the job had fallen to her. Her father was as blind as a mole to the wretched practicalities of life. But all the justifications in the world still didn't make her feel any better. His reproachful gaze made her want to cringe.

"Doesn't the Scripture say that the punishment of the wicked is righteous work?" In the face of his silence, Susannah fumbled for an argument that might persuade him that her deed had not been so truly dreadful after all. The quote popped into her head, and she used it thankfully. The Reverend Redmon latched on to it as if it were a lifeline, nodding his head and frowning as he considered. He hated to be at odds with her or her sisters, Susannah knew. It distressed him, disturbed the comfortable tenor of his life. Long ago she had realized that, if she really wanted something, she had only to stand her ground against him. Hers was the stronger will, the more determined personality. It shamed her sometimes to realize how easily she could bend him to her way of thinking. Yet, for all her headstrong ways, he, who was surely the saintliest of men, continued to think her the best of daughters. Only she knew how very far she fell short of his image of her.

The Reverend Redmon's brow cleared. "Well, yes," he said. "I suppose you're right."

"He's been whipped and mistreated. We can restore him to health as well as godliness."

"Indeed we can." He smiled at her then, clearly happy to have the sticky issue so neatly resolved, and just as they reached home, too. "You've done the best thing, I've no doubt. 'Tis quite likely that your rescue of the unfortunate creature was divinely inspired."

Divinely inspired. Of course he would think so. Susannah smiled a little sourly as she went to relieve Ben, whom she had left sitting with Connelly. The parlor was dark except for a single candle near the bed that was guttering in its own tallow. Connelly lay sprawled on his stomach on the bed, her father's nightshirt, which she had instructed Ben to wrestle him into, straining across the breadth of his shoulders. Had he not been so emaciated, and had the nightshirt not been loosely cut for comfort, the garment would not have come near to fitting him. As it was, though the nightshirt was far too short and too snug, it at least rendered Connelly minimally decent.

"Is't mornin' already, Miss Susannah?" Ben yawned, rousing from a near doze. He had been slumped in a rocker drawn up near the bed.

"No. It's the middle of the night. Has he wakened?"

Ben shook his head. "He ain't so much as sneezed since I been sittin' here. Didn't even move when I put that nightshirt on him, and that was a chore, let me tell you."

"I can imagine. You've done a good job, Ben. Go along to the barn now, and help Pa with Micah. Then you can go to bed."

"Yes'm." Ben rose, stretching. He looked down at the still figure in the bed. "What about him?"

"I'll sit with him for a while. Go on, now. And, Ben . . ."

"Yes'm?"

"Be sure you get your chores done in the morning before you go see Maria, you hear?"

Ben had the grace to look shamefaced.

"Yes'm. I'm right sorry about this mornin'."

"We'll forget about it, shall we? As long as it doesn't happen again."

"It won't, Miss Susannah. I promise."

Though the words were fervent, Susannah knew from experience that it wasn't likely to be longer than two days before the promise was forgotten. But she didn't say so, and Ben took himself off. Susannah bent over the bed, her hand reaching automatically to settle on her patient's forehead.

It was only slightly overwarm. Thankfully she reckoned that if he were going to contract a raging fever, he would likely have done so by now. Though the man must have the constitution of an ox not to have succumbed to one, given the poisons that had festered in the raw meat someone had made of his back.

"Is this the man?" Her father entered, his voice hushed as he frowned down at Connelly.

"Yes."

"Poor, wretched fellow. As you said, we will heal him in body as well as in spirit. The good Lord was with him, to guide him safely to our door."

"Yes." If there was a bright side to anything, her father could be trusted to find it. Susannah smiled at him affectionately. "You should go up to bed now. There's much that needs doing tomorrow."

"You're right, of course." He patted her arm. "And I am fatigued, I must admit. You'll be coming to bed soon yourself?"

"There are a few things I must do. But I'll be along presently."

"What would we all do without you, Susannah?" he asked, sighing. He left the room. Susannah, listening, heard his footsteps as he ascended the stairs. His tread was light, lighter even than Mandy's, although she weighed hardly more than a piece of thistledown, and the realization clutched at her heart. Over the last year or so her father had been losing flesh. Soon she feared that he would be scarcely more than a collection of skin-covered bones. She must see to it that he ate more and rested more. That was all he needed, she assured herself. Certainly there was nothing more wrong with him than that. To imagine anything else was to borrow trouble, and she had enough real problems to worry about without doing that.

With her father gone, the quiet was broken only by the harshness of Connelly's breathing. Automatically Susannah touched his cheek above his bristly beard, and it felt no warmer than had his forehead. Very likely, with the laudanum to aid him, he would pass what remained of the night in sound sleep. The temptation to do the same herself was great. She was so tired she could scarcely keep her eyes open, and the coming day already beckoned, filled to bursting with chores to be done. Did she lock the door between the parlor and the rest of the house, he could not wander even if he did awaken. His life was not in danger; there was no earthly reason to sit up all night with him. She craved just a few hours' sleep.

Conscience warred with fatigue, and fatigue won. She would be up soon after dawn, in any case, so he would not be left alone for long. Touching his forehead one last time to assure herself that a raging fever had not sprung up in the last minute or so—it had not—she surrendered, aided by a yawn so wide that it hurt her jaws. Did she not get some sleep, she would be of no use to anyone on the morrow.

First blowing out the bedside candle, then closing and locking the parlor door, Susannah went up to her room, where she changed into her nightdress and washed her face and teeth. She loosed her hair, brushing it until it crackled and stood out like a tawny cape around her shoulders. A faint sound from belowstairs made her pause, brush in hand, and cock her head to one side. What was that? It came again, a muffled scratching noise as if someone, locked in, were trying to get out.

Out of where? The only locked door in the house was the one to the parlor. Had Connelly awakened? Surely not—but what was that sound?

She put the brush down on her washstand. Gathering up her rose-colored quilt, she wrapped it around her shoulders, then started downstairs, a candle held high in her hand and her hair, which she customarily plaited before sleeping, floating behind her.

Belowstairs, the house was dark and still as a grave beyond her small pool of light. The parlor door was closed and locked, just as she had left it. The key still stood undisturbed in the keyhole. Had she imagined the sound? Surely not.

But even as she thought it the sound came again, so unexpectedly that

Susannah jumped, causing the candle to flicker. Her eyes fastened on the door in time to see it move. The key jiggled in the lock—and then a faint meow from the other side of the panel solved the mystery.

"Clara!" Susannah scolded even as she unlocked the door and the cat sashayed out. "How did you get in there? You should be outside."

Clara purred loudly, weaving about Susannah's ankles. Susannah set her candle down on the stand at the base of the stairs and scooped the cat up, holding her under one arm and rubbing behind her ears as she headed toward the door. Clara was a Calico, with orange and black spots competing for space on a ground of thick white fur. She was a big cat, nearly twenty pounds, and would have been beautiful had she not lost an eye and part of an ear in an unfortunate accident that had brought her, bleeding and near death, to the Redmons' barn. Susannah had found her and nursed her back to health and had been rewarded for her pains with Clara's undying devotion. The ear was still raggedy, but the eye had quite healed over and was not at all unsightly as the resulting sealed slit was located in a semi-circle of black fur that gave rather the appearance of a pirate's patch.

"Go catch a mouse," Susannah murmured as she pulled the door open and set Clara on the porch. As if she understood, Clara meowed softly, then with a wave of her tail headed across the porch and down the steps to vanish in the darkness. Closing the door, Susannah retraced her steps to the parlor. For a moment she did no more than peer inside, wondering if Clara had disturbed her patient. She heard nothing, not the smallest rustle of bed-clothes. Despite the candleglow that lit the hall, the nether end of the parlor where the bed stood was in deep shadow. She would just nip in and check on Connelly before she went abovestairs again.

The incandescence behind her provided just enough light to permit her to see that he had shifted position since she had left him last. His breathing was softer, and he seemed not so deeply asleep. Perhaps Clara had disturbed him. Frowning, Susannah bent over the bed. Her hand found his forehead, rested there—and then, so quickly that she was paralyzed with the shock of it —her wrist was imprisoned in a grip of iron. The quilt slid from her shoulders as one hard jerk brought her off balance. Her knees collided with the mattress, and with a shocked gasp she tumbled down onto the bed.

9

Susannah no sooner felt the softness of the mattress beneath her back than he was on top of her. The fall jarred her bruised shoulder, and she would have cried out had she had the chance. But the weight of his body crushed the air from her own. She tried to catch her breath, tried to speak, but the sheer size of him suffocated her. He was muttering something, his whisper hoarse and fierce in her ear, but she could not understand the words. Nor could she see his face. Her nose and mouth were pressed into the warm, hair-roughened skin left bare by the throat opening in the nightshirt he wore. The scent of the soap she herself had made and used on him just hours earlier filled her nose; the taste of it was in her mouth.

He shifted just a bit so that he was not completely on top of her, and she managed to turn her face to the side and suck in air, blessed air that expanded her lungs and restored her brain to full functioning again. The shock of being so brutally grabbed was subsiding. A burgeoning fear took its place. Did he mean to kill her—or what?

His mouth nuzzling her neck confirmed her second worst fear. She stiffened, afraid to move as the prickliness that was his beard rasped over the tender skin of her jaw and throat. His lips were warm and moist, and his mouth was open. She knew because she could feel his teeth nibbling on the tender cord that, with her head twisted to the side, stood out beneath her ear.

His tongue touched, then followed the swirls of her ear, dipped inside the shell-like hollow. Susannah lay frozen, afraid to move for fear of goading him into doing something even more dastardly.

His teeth found and nibbled on the delicate lobe. To her horror, Susannah realized that the sensation would have been quite tolerable had the circumstances been different. But she feared what he would do next. Though she had never personally experienced the kind of carnal love that men expected of their wives, she knew the basics of how it was done. It was clear that carnal love was what Connelly had on his mind. He was heading toward it faster than a pig on a greased slide.

She had to stop him. But how? With her right hand trapped beneath the weight of his body and her left hand imprisoned by his grip on her wrist, she was helpless. She could not even kick. His thigh lay over her legs, pinning them down. The sheer size of the man completely overwhelmed her.

His tongue traced the line of her jaw, rousing goosebumps in its wake. Then his mouth nuzzled the soft skin just beneath her chin. Susannah felt her body stir in response to the rasping heat of his mouth. The novel sensation startled her. She twisted her head away, struggling desperately to be free. Unheeding of her efforts, he trailed tiny, stinging kisses over the soft skin of her throat.

"Stop this!" She hissed the command into the hollow of his shoulder, where her face had come to rest. "Do you hear me? Stop right now and we'll forget all about this! You'll not be punished, I give you my word."

If he even heard her, the combined threat and promise moved him not at all. He kissed her averted cheek, the corner of her eye, her temple. His body was poised over hers, still pushing her down into the mattress but with his weight shifted slightly to the side so that she could breathe. His imprisoning thigh, bare where her father's too small nightshirt had ridden up, rubbed up and down over her own. Susannah realized to her horror that she could feel the heat and texture of it so well because her own thighs were bare, too. Either the motion of his leg or the fall and her subsequent wriggling or some combination of the two had caused her nightdress to be pushed up almost to her waist.

The thought of screaming, which had been anathema to her only moments before—how shaming to be found in such a position by her family!—occurred to her again, but she was loath to do so. Besides the embarrassment of it, there was the very real danger to her sisters and her father when Connelly was confronted. With a sinking feeling, Susannah realized that all five Redmons together were no match for the man that she herself had brought down upon them. Unless her father thought to snatch up the fowling piece from where it was kept beside the kitchen door before he responded to her cries—which of course he would not do. Her father would never have such a practical thought as that.

If she did not find some way of stopping Connelly quickly, she would soon know more about carnal love than she had ever thought to learn. She would be raped and ruined, through no one's fault but her own. The thought galvanized her.

"Connelly, you must let me go! If you don't, they'll hang you for this!"

Her threat seemed to move him not at all. He kissed the corner of her mouth in a most loverlike fashion by way of reply. It occurred to Susannah then that, thanks to the effects of the laudanum that she herself had given him, perhaps he was not really awake at all, only roused to some semi-somnolent state by her presence in his bed. Perhaps he was in the midst of an erotic dream and was acting it out on her person!

"Connelly! Wake up!"

The only answer was his mouth sliding along her cheek to nibble the tip of her chin. Despairing, she bucked against him, trying to throw him off—she had about as much chance of that as a lamb trying to rid itself of a wolf who had it by the neck, she thought—and in response he shifted slightly. Susannah thought her resistance might finally be getting through to him—until she felt his knee slide between her thighs.

For an instant, no more, she registered the hard strength of the thigh that parted her legs, the roughness of the hairs on it abrading her delicate flesh, the heat of his skin, with a stab of excitement as shocking as anything he was doing to her. Fright and outrage and the strong moral sense that had been drummed into her from childhood banished the heated flicker almost at once. But there was no ridding herself of his encroaching knee. It was wedged between hers, and the whole length of his thigh descended behind it, working at opening her legs further. Her strength was no proof against his, and inexorably he got what he wanted. For a moment, as her legs were pried apart only to close desperately around the thigh that denied them as they sought to close again, she felt the solid strength of his limb pressing hard against the most secret place at the juncture of her thighs. The sensation was as startling and physical as the jar of being thrown from a horse.

His thigh pressed harder against her, and her mouth went dry.

Whether she was shamed at being discovered in such a fix or not, whether she endangered her family or not, this had to end. Susannah opened her mouth to scream. Before so much as a squeak could emerge, Connelly covered her lips with his own. Susannah gagged, nearly choking as he thrust his tongue deep into her mouth. His weight was on her again, his arms around her, his head bent to hers as he ruthlessly plundered her mouth. He tasted of chicken broth, and his mouth was hot and wet and greedy as he sucked at her lips and tongue, then nipped at what he captured with his teeth. His thigh moved up and down between hers, pressing against the place that, no matter how hard she fought to keep it from happening, was rapidly becoming the center of her consciousness. She squirmed to escape the shameful friction, but that only made matters worse. Gasping, she abruptly ceased her struggles as an undulating wave of white heat radiated down her legs and up her spine.

Was this how men enticed women into carnal love? She'd wondered, of course, about how it might feel, she who had never had so much as a beau. Though Sarah Jane would never think to discuss something so improper with the older sister that she very nearly regarded as a mother, Susannah had once overheard her hesitantly confiding in Mandy a fear of what might await her in her marital bed. If this was what carnal love was like, then there was nothing to fear at all but much to look forward to when it was done within the sacred bonds of matrimony.

But this was not her marital bed, and Connelly was not her husband. The pleasures that were snaking over her body were sinful, and she would not permit herself to feel them. She would not!

His mouth freed hers and slid along the side of her cheek to her neck. Her hands were suddenly free too, as he shifted again, lifting his hips even as he moved his hands down her body, learning the shape of her. His fingers found and closed over her breasts, cupping the soft globes, teasing the nipples through her thin cotton nightdress. Susannah gritted her teeth against the sudden terrible urge just to surrender that weakened her. Ever since Sarah Jane's betrothal, she'd been coming to terms with the idea that she would likely go to her grave a maid. The knowledge should not have bothered her—but it did. The future that her sisters took for granted—marriage, children, a husband to teach them about carnal love—was not for her. Her duty was to her father and sisters. By the time they no longer needed her, she would be too old to make a full life of her own. Plain or not, practical or not, she wanted to learn the lessons of loving just as other women did. Here was her chance; she had only to lie very still and let him. . . .

Then his other knee wedged in beside the first. Before Susannah knew what was happening, her legs were spread wide.

"No!" Sheer, instinctive panic triumphed over every other consideration, and she lashed out, hitting him as hard as she could in the temple with her balled fist.

"What the hell!" To her combined surprise and relief, he fell back with a yelp. Susannah suddenly found herself free. She scrambled for the edge of the bed, only to be brought up just short of her goal by his hand catching and twisting the flying ends of her hair.

"Let me go! Let me go, do you hear?"

"Damn it, woman, what did you hit me for?" He actually sounded aggrieved. She glared at the dark shape of him, which was all she could see through the gloom, and was surprised to find that she was shaking. She, who never trembled at anything.

"What did I hit you for!"

Maybe he truly had no idea. If her theory was right, perhaps he was only now coming properly awake, with no notion of the shameful nature of what had transpired between them. She prayed God that it was so. How humiliating, if he should recall how he had mauled her. He had touched her in places she had never even touched herself and bared her to the waist and—and . . . If he remembered, she would never be able to look him in the face again. He was silent, giving her no clue as to his thoughts, but through the darkness she could feel his eyes on her. All at once his hold on her hair tightened. Susannah was suddenly, sickly afraid. Perhaps he meant to drag her beneath him again and finish what he had started. Perhaps he'd been awake the whole time and was bent on rape. Fear and fury combined to make her shake so much her teeth would have rattled had she not clamped them together.

She sensed as much as saw him sit up and felt a tug on her scalp as he leaned away from her. He tugged harder, and she was forced to lie on her side as he reached for something on the opposite side of the bed without releasing her. She heard the fumble of metal against metal, smelled the sudden acrid scent of a spark being struck, and then the bedside candle was lit. She realized he must earlier have seen the candle and where she kept the flint and steel. As the flame struggled into fitful life, his grip on her hair eased, and Susannah was able to sit up again. She scooted as far away from him as his grip on her hair would permit. Unable to get away or do anything else, she turned with an awful sense of fatalism to look at him.

Connelly's eyes were moving over her, taking in everything from the riotous tumble of tawny curls that spilled over his fist to pool on the mattress beside where she sat to the twisted-to-the-point-of-indecency nightdress. They rested momentarily on the swell of her breasts pressing against the thin cotton and widened even as her arms clamped over her chest to hide her bosom from his view. Undeterred, his gaze slid along the rest of her. Her legs were bare to the tops of her thighs, and he missed not an inch of their slender length all the way down to her small toes. Quickly Susannah pulled her legs beneath her and adjusted her nightdress to cover them. She was blushing so furiously that her skin felt as if it were on fire, and she knew he must see.

When she dared glance up, Connelly was scowling at her as fiercely as if she had somehow wronged him. There was a red mark on his temple where she had clouted him. Her father's nightshirt strained across the daunting width of his shoulders and was twisted over his broad chest, and Susannah dared not look lower for fear of what she might see. His black hair was wildly tousled. His lips were clamped together, and his expression, coupled with his barbaric beard, made him look like a savage.

Just thinking of how her body had responded to the brute's touch made her want to cringe. She had to glance away. Was she really so desperate that any man would do?

"What the devil are you doing in bed with me?" It was an accusation if she had ever heard one. Her eyes snapped back to his face.

"What am I doing . . . ?" Her voice failed her. How was she to answer that? If he truly did not recall what he had done, then she had no wish to remind him of the embarrassing particulars. The shameful memory would be hers alone and thus not nearly so degrading. Though even if he had been wide awake, which was still quite possible, he could have no way of knowing how her body had quickened to his touch—could he? Of course he could not! The man was not telepathic, after all! Only she could know how fiercely her body had responded, and she would take her guilty secret to her grave.

"If you bought me thinking to use me as a stud, lady, you miscalculated. I bed whom I please, when I please. I don't perform on command."

"What?" Susannah's jaw dropped. As the shocking nature of the insult sank in, her fists clenched. The jumble of emotions that moments earlier had set her atremble now coalesced into one blinding burst of heat, and her temper soared to flashpoint so quickly that she felt as if the top of her head might explode.

"Why, you ungrateful, ignorant savage!" she hissed. "To think that I saved you from Hiram Greer! To think that I saved you from Georges Renard! To think that I was actually kind to you! You deserve to be whipped! You deserve to be hanged! You deserve to be cut up for hog slop with a dull knife! How dare you say such things to me! You—you churlish lout!"

As she paused for breath, his eyes ran over her again, and this time there was a flicker she could not quite decipher in the gray depths.

"I don't bed women out of gratitude."

Susannah's eyes flashed, and words so bad that she couldn't believe she knew them bubbled to her tongue. She bit them back, grabbing at the section of hair he held and yanking at it to free herself. Her efforts were futile. She only succeeded in hurting her scalp.

"Let me go! At once, do you hear?"

"Or . . . ?" He mocked her, his fingers twisting deeper into her hair.

"Or I'll sell you to Hiram Greer before sunset tomorrow! When I tell him what you—how you insulted me, he'll have you whipped to within an inch of your life!"

"And when I tell him—and everyone else who'll listen—just how you climbed into bed with me, and how hot you were to be ridden, you won't have a shred of reputation left. And don't think I won't shout the details to the world, because I will." His lips twisted into an evil smile as Susannah stared at him, aghast.

She had not climbed into his bed, of course. That was patently false, whether he believed it or not. But there was just enough truth in the rest of his accusation to make her quake inwardly. He could not know the longings his hands on her body had awakened—could he?

"I don't respond well to threats," he added as if by way of an explanation.

"Neither do I," she said through her teeth and yanked at her hair again. This time, whether because his grip had loosened or because of the savageness of her jerk, she managed to tear her hair from his grasp. She leapt from the bed, putting several paces between it and her person for safety's sake. Her quilt was on the floor near the bed. She snatched it up, wrapped it around her shoulders, and felt marginally safer as she turned to face him.

Several long strands of her hair still clung to his hand, and as she watched he wrapped them around his fingers.

"A keepsake," he said, as if she had asked for an explanation, and leered at her.

Susannah's head threatened to explode again, but this time she managed to keep the lid on her temper.

"Just in case you seriously don't know how this—farce—began, let me set you straight. I was roused from my bed by a noise, and I came in here to check on you. When I touched you to ascertain whether or not you had a fever, you grabbed me and pulled me into bed with you. Then you—you . . . I had to fight to get free and finally had to resort to striking you to bring you to your senses."

There was the briefest of pauses. His eyes narrowed, as if he were mulling over her words.

"That's not how I remember it, sweetheart," he said softly and smiled the wickedest smile Susannah had ever seen.

"You are a spawn of the Devil!" She was so furious that she could barely get the words out. "And I am not your sweetheart. For as long as I manage to restrain myself from selling you, you will address me as *Miss* Susannah."

Without waiting for what he might reply, she turned on her heel, clutched the remnants of her dignity around her like her quilt, and walked with head held high from the room.

10

Susannah felt as if she'd spent the best years of her life doing little but making bread. She mixed, kneaded, and baked twice a day, and never a night passed that dough was not rising in her kitchen. The rooster had crowed his good morning not a quarter of an hour before, and here she stood in the kitchen, making bread for supper. The morning's loaves were already in the small baking oven set into the side of the huge fireplace that took up most of one wall of the kitchen. Soon they would be done. The wonderful warm scent of them wafted through the kitchen.

The rest of the family would be up within the hour, expecting to eat. That was the way their day always began, and that was the way it always would begin, world without end, as long as Susannah was there to take care of them. Except that Susannah, for some reason she couldn't quite fathom, was suddenly dissatisfied with the routine. Her life was busy, and she knew it was good, but—but—but what? She should be thankful, not repining. She was blessed. What was the matter with her, that she should secretly long for something other than the plenty she had?

Gruel bubbled over the fire. With molasses dribbled over it, and plenty of fresh bread and butter, it would make a hearty morning repast. With the girls to help, it would not take long to clean the kitchen, and then perhaps she could get out to work in the garden for a little while. Weeding was something she truly enjoyed.

"Is there anything else you need me to do, Miss Susannah?" Ben came in through the back door, his arms full of sticks so that she could feed the fire. He'd not forgotten, and she had already praised him lavishly.

"You can feed the chickens."

"Yes'm."

He dropped the sticks into the basket by the hearth and went out. Craddock should be up, too, milking the cow, but Susannah had no expectation of seeing him until she sent Ben to rouse him. He liked his sleep almost as much as he liked strong drink, which was another reason he had never been able to keep a job before.

Craddock was next to useless, and Ben was a flighty boy. They added to, rather than alleviated, the burden that rested on her shoulders. That burden had grown increasingly heavy over the past few months, until she had feared she might crumple under its weight. So what had she done? She'd bought a bound man to make her life easier. That was selfishness, pure and simple, and, as her father had always said, selfishness carried a high price tag. Now she was having to pay that price.

Connelly. She could not think of him without wanting to cringe. It was almost impossible to believe that she, who had never so much as exchanged a flirtatious glance with a man in her life, had found herself half-naked in bed with her bound man just the night before. When she remembered his hands on her breasts and his knee between her legs—to say nothing of the rapacious way he had kissed her!—she felt physically ill.

When she remembered how her body had responded, she felt sick to her soul.

What had passed between her and Connelly made her feel so guilty, angry, and ashamed that she could scarcely face herself in the mirror. How could she, her father's daughter, supposed paragon of righteousness whose virtue was admired and praised by all, harbor such dark yearnings? Her father, did he know what she had done (please God that he never learned of it!), would blame the Devil for tempting her. Susannah knew better; she blamed herself.

Almost worse than the memory was the prospect of dealing with Connelly when he should awaken. Whenever she thought of facing him again, she wavered between blushing with shame and sizzling with fury.

One thing she couldn't do was sell him. At the thought of his blabbing his version of what had happened between them to so much as another living soul, her blood ran cold.

How had she gotten into such a fix? By being mule-obstinate, that's how. Everyone from Sarah Jane to Hiram Greer had tried to tell her that she was making a mistake in buying the man, but she had been too stubborn to listen.

Were it anyone save herself, Susannah would have said that such a comeuppance was richly deserved. As she made the admission, Susannah kneaded and slapped the pasty mass that had swelled almost to her elbows as if it were her new bound man's leering face.

A sound from the parlor stiffened her spine into ramrod erectness. Or, rather, not so much a sound as the cessation of sound. She had not realized how attuned she had been to the harsh rasp of Connelly's breathing. Was he awake so early? Her stomach tightened at the thought.

Folding the dough over one last time, Susannah covered it with a cloth and left it to rise. She walked with measured steps across the wide plank floor of the kitchen through the front hall. In the open doorway that led into the parlor she stopped, wiping her hands on her apron, and then, because there was no help for it, looked toward the bed.

Connelly was raised up on one elbow, looking right back at her. The one long window was situated to catch the morning sun. Bright rays illuminated every corner of the room. Caught in a wash of shimmering daylight, Connelly looked more brutish than ever. He would have been right at home on the deck of a pirate ship or bellowing over-warm ditties in a smoky taproom while deep in his cups.

Had she lost her mind, to quicken to the touch of a man like that?

"Water," he said, the word scarcely more than a croak.

With a curt nod, Susannah forced back the jumbled images of the night before that haunted her and retraced her steps to the kitchen to fetch water from the bucket by the back door. Carrying the dipper carefully, she returned to the parlor. For no more than the merest second she hesitated in the doorway, wary about approaching him. She squared her shoulders and forced herself onward.

If she were ever to put the previous night behind her, she would have to face him down. If her stomach clenched at the very idea of going near him, she must be the only one to know it.

In her experience, the only time a dog bit was when it sensed its victim was afraid of it. She would approach Connelly with the same cautious authority that she would show a vicious dog.

To get close enough so that she might hand him the dipper, she had to put herself within grabbing range. So be it, she thought, lifting her chin, and walked right up to the side of the bed. If he was to live in their household—and thanks to her own folly, he was—she could not avoid him forever. Let him think that she was calm and in control.

"Thank you." He took the dipper from her, closing his eyes as he drank. Unable to help herself, she took a single step back away from the bed.

When he had finished, he opened his eyes to survey her from the top of her severely styled hair to as far down her apron-covered gown as he could see.

"You're prettier with your hair down," he said.

Susannah nearly choked. "My appearance is no concern of yours!"

"True." He held out the dipper. Susannah took it back, careful not to let her fingers brush his. His eyes met hers. She misliked the gleam in the gray depths. It was almost—avid. She braced herself for what he might do—or say.

"Is there anything to eat?"

It took a moment for that to sink in.

"You're a bold rogue, I'll say that for you," Susannah said through her teeth. "To behave as you have, and then calmly ask me for something to eat! What will you do should I choose not to feed you, pray?"

The shoulder that was uppermost shrugged. His eyes never left hers, though the gleam faded slightly. "I've starved before."

What could she say to that? It was not in her to let even so undeserving a creature as he was starve. Without another word she left the room. When she returned, she was carrying a tray that held a bowlful of steaming gruel sweetened with molasses, two large chunks of hot, buttered bread, and a mug of sweet tea.

"Here," she said ungraciously, plopping it down on the mattress beside him. Some of the tea sloshed out onto the tray.

"You won't join me?" He looked up at her then, and for the first time she thought she saw a glint of genuine humor in his eyes. Was he teasing her? If so, then it was a mistake, because she didn't find even the smallest detail of what had passed between them the night before to be a matter for joking.

"No."

With that blunt reply, Susannah turned and went back into the kitchen, where she busied herself with the thousand and one chores that awaited her. A full day's housework had to be crammed into the morning so that she might spend the afternoon at the church helping to prepare for Mrs. Cooper's funeral, which was scheduled for four that afternoon when the worst of the heat would have subsided.

"Susannah!"

Susannah stiffened. Surely Connelly would not be so bold as to call her by her given name.

"Susannah!"

He would. She took a deep breath and a firm hold on her temper and walked into the parlor.

"I would have more."

"You are to address me as *Miss* Susannah, and you know it," she said frigidly.

"After the kisses we shared?" His teeth gleamed at her. He was teasing her, the dastard! Susannah saw red. A long-handled spoon was in her hand. She hurled it at his head as if the spoon were an axe and his head a chunk of wood and she would split the wood in two. He ducked, falling backward, then yelped as he landed on his back. The spoon thudded harmlessly into the wall a scant six inches above where his head had been, and then fell with a clatter to the floor. The tray, upset by Connelly's dive for safety, slid off the bed to land with a crash beside the spoon.

"Let us get one thing perfectly clear," Susannah said, unmoved by both the upended tray and Connelly's obvious discomfort as he rolled gingerly to one side. "If you push me too far, I will sell you, no matter what black lies you're prepared to tell."

So saying, she turned and stalked from the room. Her hand trembled as she added more water to the kettle over the fire. The gruel was bubbling ready, the bread taken from the oven, sliced for Connelly, and what was left waited cooling on the table. She must rouse her family—but first she had to get herself under control. It would not do to let her father or her sisters see that she was upset. They would inevitably question the cause.

Turning, she nearly jumped out of her skin. Connelly stood in the kitchen doorway, the tray with bowl and cup and spoon on it in his hands, one shoulder braced against the jamb. He was watching her, his expression inscrutable. His black hair stood out wildly around his head. His beard made him look fearsome. He was tall and lean and, except for one small detail, looked every bit as menacing as he had the previous afternoon on the block. That detail was his attire. Her father's nightshirt did not even reach his knees and fit him so snugly that she could see the outline of the bandages she had wrapped around his chest. What else she might be able to see of him she refused to put to the test. After one comprehensive, shocked glance, she lifted her eyes to his face.

"You cannot walk about the house like that!"

"I brought you the tray." His tone was almost placating.

"You should not be out of bed." Unwillingly, she put down the bucket she'd been using to fill the kettle and moved to take the tray from his hands. The bowl looked almost as if it had been licked clean, she saw as she dumped the tray and its contents into the pan by the back door for later washing. This evidence of his hunger would have touched her had she not been well beyond being touched by him.

He was still standing in the doorway watching her when she turned around.

"Are you still hungry?" The words came out grudgingly. She couldn't believe she'd said them. She didn't care if he was hungry! In fact, she liked the idea—but no, that wasn't quite the truth. The base, worldly part of her might be able to think of his hunger as a measure of revenge for her humiliation, but the part of her that was still her father's daughter must offer him food.

"I could eat."

Without another word Susannah heaped another bowl full of gruel and dribbled molasses on it, then slapped it down on the table.

"Sit and eat, then," she said shortly, pouring tea into a mug and slapping that down, too.

"You're a kind woman, Sus—*Miss* Susannah," he said, and to her fury the faintest suggestion of a grin seemed to lurk beneath the camouflage of his beard.

"No," she said very clearly, stopping what she was doing to face him, her arms folding over her chest, "I am not. For you must know that at this very moment I am battling the most awful urge to clout you over the head with my fry pan."

He paused in the act of shoveling gruel into his mouth to eye her with interest. "Are you, indeed?"

"Yes."

"Ah," he said. "A woman of spirit as well. I like that." And he commenced eating again.

Susannah sizzled. Before she could erupt, Ben entered the kitchen through the back door.

"I fed the chickens," he said, then stopped as he discovered Connelly. "You're up, then," he said to Connelly.

"As you see."

"I helped carry you in."

"Ah," Connelly said, his eyes sliding back to Susannah. "I wondered how you managed that."

"Connelly, this is Ben Travers. He'll be helping you about the farm." Susannah made the introduction in a frigid voice as she turned to lift the pot of gruel from the fire.

"Good morning, all." Her father's voice as he walked into the kitchen from the hallway made her start, and hot gruel slopped over her hand. Wincing, she set the pot down on the trivet with a grimace, then wiped her hand on a towel. It was not a bad burn, the skin was barely red, but it would not have happened had she not jumped. She would not have jumped had she not felt so guilty about the night before and about being found by her father with Connelly now. She only hoped the reddening of her cheeks would be attributed by him to the heat of the fire.

"Morning, Pa," she said gruffly, turning to find him taking his place at the head of the table. He was fully dressed, in black as befitted his calling. As she watched, he smiled his gentle smile at Connelly, quite undeterred by the bristly fierceness of the visage across the table.

"You must be, umm . . ." The Reverend Redmon's voice trailed off as he obviously searched for the name.

"Ian Connelly."

"Welcome, Mr. Connelly. I am the Reverend John Redmon. I hope you will soon feel at home with us."

Connelly's eyes narrowed for a moment, as if he suspected Susannah's father of mockery. But something, perhaps the old man's luminous hazel eyes, must have persuaded him that the Reverend Redmon was quite serious.

"Thank you, sir," he answered with grave courtesy. Susannah would never have believed him capable of such a tone. It was all she could do to keep her mouth from falling open. But her father seemed pleased by the response, and suddenly Susannah realized that the rogue was cleverer than she had thought. He changed his manner to suit his audience.

"Are the girls up?" she asked her father in a tight voice.

"They were moving around when I came down."

"I'll go hurry them along, then," she said and escaped from the kitchen. When she returned, with her sisters' promise of no longer than two minutes more, she was both surprised and relieved to find her father breakfasting alone.

Her swift glance around the room must have asked the question she couldn't quite put into words.

"Ben went to fetch Craddock, and I sent our new bound man back to bed, though he assured me that he was ready to work. I feel it best to give him a few days to recover his strength, and so I told him. He seems like a good man, Susannah. You made the right decision, just as you always do."

"I'm glad you think so," Susannah said, not knowing whether to be pleased or sorry that her father had been so taken in. But then Ben came in with Craddock, and Sarah Jane and Em trooped downstairs—Mandy had not quite finished with her hair, Em said, but would be down momentarily—and suddenly Susannah was so busy with the tasks of everyday life that she had no more time, for the moment, to worry about her bound man.

11

"On your way back from dropping off the basket at the Likens', you might stop by the church and remind Pa that the Eichorns' baby was born yesterday and they are wanting it baptized. It's sickly, so he'd best plan to go over there this afternoon," Susannah said. She was standing in the kitchen over the flour bin, a rectangular, table-like contraption that held flour in one side and corn meal in the other. Emily and Sarah Jane, the latter with a filled basket over her arm, were moving toward the back door. It was late the following morning, and Susannah was not in the best of humors, though she was doing her utmost not to let it show.

"Poor Eleanor! She wanted this baby so much! After losing the other two, it seems that God could let her keep this one."

"It is not your place to question God, Em."

"Would you stop being so sanctimonious, Sarah Jane? I declare, you've become as sober as a judge!"

"That's enough, Emily!" Susannah intervened more sharply than was her wont. Both Emily and Sarah Jane looked at her, surprise at her tone plain on their faces. It was not like Susannah to be cross. "You might also stop by the spring and bring in the buttermilk as you come home," she added in a milder tone.

"And just where is Mandy this morning, while we run all these errands?" Emily asked, aggrieved.

"Mandy has gone for a ride in Todd Haskins's buggy. He and his sister came by less than a quarter hour ago to take her up with them." Susannah was once again making bread. She punched the unwieldy dough beneath her hands with rather more force than the activity called for. The Haskinses were a wealthy planting family, members of the well-established Episcopal Church whose towering spire had long been the tallest point in Beaufort's skyline. The aristocratic Episcopalian congregation tended to look down their collective noses at the upstart Baptists, but Todd Haskins' infatuation with Mandy was strong enough to cut through such minor social barriers. Nevertheless, Susannah saw no future in the acquaintance and did not wish to encourage it. It was not likely that young Mr. Haskins had marriage on his mind. But should the question ever arise, the difference in religion would prove a sticky issue with her father and doubtless with the Haskinses as well.

"Should you have permitted that, do you think?" Sarah Jane asked, frowning. She was well aware of Susannah's concerns on that head.

"And why should Susannah have been against it, if you please? Mr. Haskins is as handsome as a dream, and rich, too. I wish someone like that would show an interest in me, and I'll just wager you do, too," Emily said.

"You forget that I am betrothed, Em."

"No, I don't, but I wish you would! Honestly, Sarah Jane, you are the most . . ."

"If you two do not hurry, it will be nightfall before you so much as set foot outside the back door!" Susannah said with a snap. She felt as though she could not bear another moment of their bickering. Emily promptly shut her mouth, looking hurt, while Sarah Jane shot Susannah a questioning glance. Susannah pummeled the dough as if it were her own ill humor. Out of the corner of her eye, she saw Em and Sarah Jane exchange shrugs, and they quit the house without another word.

Susannah breathed a sigh of relief as she was left alone at last. She loved the girls dearly, but of late they had been, each in her own way, something of a trial. Emily was experiencing the usual adolescent growing pangs, Amanda was attracting beaux by the score, and Sarah Jane was growing more prim with every day that passed. All three required tactful handling, but today diplomacy seemed to be beyond her.

"Good morning." Deep in disgruntled thought, Susannah started, then looked around to see Connelly standing in the kitchen doorway looking at her. She had not seen him since yesterday's breakfast, quite deliberately. She had kept herself and her sisters out of the house as much as possible, first doing chores about the place and later enlisting them all to help her with Mrs. Cooper's funeral. They would ordinarily have attended the service, of course, as the minister's daughters, but Susannah had had them scrub the church from top to bottom and decorate it with flowers and then practice the *Hymn to the Creator* so that the four of them might sing it as a quartet. As a result of all this preparation, Mrs. Cooper had had an unusually fine funeral, and the family had been lavish with their thanks for Susannah's efforts. Only Susannah knew that much of the thanks should rightfully go to her bound man. Had she not been wishful of keeping herself and her sisters out of his way, she would not have done so much.

And so she felt guiltier than ever.

"Did Ben not bring your breakfast?" After that first quick glance, she looked back at her dough. But she did not need to look at Connelly to see him. His piratical image was permanently engraved on her mind's eye, as she had found to her dismay both yesterday and last night. Even while she was in church, his long, hard body and wolfish eyes would flash into her consciousness. As a result, she had spent a third nearly sleepless night.

"Yes, he did, and all my meals save breakfast yesterday. I suppose I should be grateful that I was not left to starve."

"Yes, I suppose you should. What are you doing from bed?"

"Do you really need to know?" He walked across the kitchen and out the back door. Surprised, Susannah left the dough to rise and followed him. What was he up to now? She didn't trust him an inch! Though where he could go barefoot, clad only in her father's nightshirt, was a mystery. He had just stepped off the back porch when she reached the doorway.

"Unless you want to get an eyeful, I suggest you go back inside," he said over his shoulder. "I'm in search of a water closet."

"A water closet?"

"Am I presuming too much to suppose you have one?"

When his meaning hit her over the head with the force of a brick, Susannah turned bright red.

"It—it's up the hill, behind the chicken coop." She popped back inside the house. Once again, he'd embarrassed her to her toes, and she was perfectly sure that he knew of her discomfiture and was enjoying it. Were she of a mind to think of it that way, she might consider that she would, in this particular instance, have the last laugh. In England, they might have such amenities as water closets, but in the Carolinas one made do with a wooden seat over a hole in the ground and considered oneself lucky.

He was back so quickly that Susannah suspected that he had not made the trek up the hill after all.

"Is it always this damned hot here?" He stood just inside the kitchen, wiping the sweat that already beaded his brow.

"We do not use profanity." She scraped the scraps she had saved from breakfast into a pan for the hogs as she spoke.

"Well, is it?"

"It's been hotter than usual the last week or so."

"Thank God for that! Else I'd melt in a month."

"We do not use the Lord's name in vain, either. And I meant that it's hot for May. It does, however, get far hotter in August."

"Christ!"

"Connelly!" Susannah rounded on him. "My father is a man of God! You will not use the Lord's name in vain in this house! Nor will you use profanity! Am I making myself clear?"

He leaned a shoulder against the wall and crossed his arms over his chest, eyeing her. He would have been the picture of arrogant masculinity had it not been for the ridiculousness of a man of his size wearing her delicately built father's nightshirt.

"Perfectly, *Miss* Susannah." If there was a touch of mockery in the title he gave her, Susannah chose to ignore it.

"Good."

"What's that you're making there?" He nodded at the pan that rested on the scrubbed pine table at her elbow.

"Slop for the hogs." She turned back to it.

"Hogs!" He sounded as if he'd never heard of such creatures.

"Yes, hogs." It gave Susannah quite a bit of satisfaction to add, "That's one of the reasons I bought you—to take care of them."

"You want me to take care of hogs?"

"Yes, I do." She turned from the table with the pan of food held in both hands before her. He took one look at the mixture and the scraps of food floating in the remains of last night's milk and quickly averted his gaze.

Susannah stopped where she was, eyeing him. It was clear that he found her pig slop distasteful.

"What did you do, before?" Real curiosity prompted her question. Though she had never been there, she was sure there must be pigs in England. If he had never tended any, he must not have been a farmer. Shay had said he was an educated man, and his manner of speech bore this out. Had he been a clerk, perhaps? Or was that too honest a profession for the likes of him? It occurred to her to wonder, with a renewed sense that buying him had been a dreadful mistake, exactly how much help he would be with the chores. Perhaps he was one of those who was afraid of hard work.

"Oh, this and that. Nothing that would interest you, I assure you," he said, confirming her worst fear.

"Well, around here you will work, and work hard," she promised him grimly and, stepping around him, took herself and her pig slop out the door.

12

Susannah returned from slopping the hogs by way of the front door, having detoured to rescue an inattentive robin from Clara. On edge as she walked through to the back of the house, expecting to encounter Connelly with every step, she was surprised to discover that he was nowhere to be found. The parlor door stood open, and she saw at a glance that he was not there. He was not in the sitting room, either, or the kitchen. Blast the man, he'd caused her more aggravation in less than a day than the most troublesome of the parishioners had in their entire lives.

Where was he?

Perhaps he had stepped out to visit the "water closet" again. Susannah put water over the fire to boil—it would soon be time to begin preparing the noonday meal—and then, when Connelly still had not returned, decided to look abovestairs for him. Surely the man was not bold enough to venture into the family's private sleeping rooms—though she would not put much beyond him. But he was not abovestairs.

Frowning, Susannah gathered up an armload of clothes that waited on the landing to be washed and retraced her steps to the kitchen. Where could he be? Dirty clothes in hand, she went to the back door. She would do the wash this afternoon and in the meanwhile would add her bundle to the pile already waiting on the back porch for her attention.

When she found Connelly, he was so close at hand that she wondered that she had not heard him. He was running a comb through his hair on the rear porch, near the end where the kitchen, which extended from the house like the short end of an L, formed a solid wall. Washtubs and washboards hung from pegs on that wall, and the growing pile of laundry waited beneath them. The broom and various other utensils leaned into the corner. A washstand was kept on the porch for visitors, with soap, a comb, a razor and strop, and a small mirror hung above it. Connelly stood with his back to her before the washstand, lather covering the upper portion of his beard, stooped slightly as he peered into the mirror. He was wearing his filthy breeches—she'd had them on the porch waiting to be washed—and nothing else. Feet, calves, and upper torso were completely bare, except for the bandage that wound around his back and chest. Her father's nightshirt lay discarded in a crumpled ball near his feet.

"Just what do you think you're doing?" she asked, after she recovered somewhat from the shock she had suffered upon setting eyes on him. That he was totally without modesty had already occurred to her when he had cavorted about the house clad only in the too-small nightshirt. Now he was half-naked and seemed totally unconcerned by his state.

Despite the best will in the world not to look, her eyes slid over his body. He was so thin that his ribs showed, but his shoulders were broad and his legs long and powerfully muscled. Susannah felt a blush heat her cheeks as she realized that his buttocks were nicely muscled, too. An uncomfortable memory of how heavy he was, appearances to the contrary, and how hard his body was to the touch arose to plague her. She banished it almost instantly, but not before sudden, acute embarrassment threatened to overcome her. Her instinct was to avert her eyes, but she guessed that he would get too much enjoyment out of seeing her stare at the wall or the yard or anyplace but his person as she spoke to him.

"Shaving. Want to watch?" He glanced at her over his shoulder as he spoke, and it was clear that he had noticed her discomfiture and was laughing at her. Of course—he could see her reflection in the mirror. Doubtless he'd gotten a good view of her blush. Unable to help it, Susannah blushed more hotly and felt like throwing something at his head again. But she'd already made enough of a fool of herself where he was concerned and had no wish to add to her folly. She was the mistress, he the servant, and she meant to cling to her dignity throughout the rest of their dealings if it killed her.

"I'm glad you feel so much better. Perhaps by tomorrow you'll be ready to start taking on a few chores. Light ones, of course." She could do nothing about the color that she was sure still blazed in her cheeks, but her voice was steady.

"Like slopping the hogs?" He twanged the razor along the strop and then brought it to his face.

"And feeding the chickens, and fetching the water, and grooming the horses, and planting seeds and . . ."

"Whoa! I thought you said a *few* chores."

"Those are a few chores. I hope you're not lazy."

"I hope not, either. I guess we'll find out, won't we?" He turned his head to flash a glance that was almost teasing at her. Nearly a quarter of his face was cleared of brush, and he was starting to look different. Not quite so brutish.

"If you don't work around here, you don't eat," Susannah said and turned back into the house. When she returned a few minutes later, she was carrying a pair of gray hose she had just finished knitting and one of her father's shirts. The shirt was sure to be hopelessly too small for him, but it was the best she could do for the moment. Certainly it was better than having him go around bare-chested. What was left of his own shirt was fit for nothing but the ragbag, once it was clean.

"When you've finished, you may put these on. I don't know how things are done in England, but around here we're careful of our modesty. I expect you to keep yourself decently covered in future."

"I've finished." Connelly turned away from the washstand, a towel to his face as he wiped away the soap. "And speaking of modesty, given the fact that you've already seen me in the altogether—it *was* you who bathed me, wasn't it?—I don't see that it matters."

"Caring for an unclothed sick man is a very different matter from being constantly confronted with an unclothed healthy one, especially in a household that consists mostly of young ladies. I've my sisters to think of."

"Ah, the three twittering birds from the auction. I remember." He finished with the towel as he spoke and tossed it in the general direction of the nightshirt. About to inform him that the pile of laundry waiting to be washed was the other way and that he might add towel and nightshirt to it, Susannah never got the words out. Her attention was distracted by his face. For a moment—she prayed it was no longer than that—she stood staring at him, as stunned as if she'd been pole-axed.

He was breathtakingly handsome. Never in her wildest flights of fancy would she have guessed the degree of masculine beauty that could be hidden by a well-grown beard. His cheekbones were high, his jaw chiseled, his chin square with the slightest suggestion of a cleft in its center. His nose was long and straight, his mouth perfectly carved. And he was young. Too young. Almost as young as herself. Susannah's shocked gaze turned to one of near-horror as she realized just what she had done.

This time she'd set the fox loose among the chickens and no mistake. Her sisters, or at least Mandy and Em, were going to go wild when they saw him.

The sound of a buggy pulling up in front of the house made her jump like a scalded cat.

"What ails you?" he asked, frowning.

"Put on that shirt," she hissed. Turning so fast her skirt swirled, she went to see if she could head Mandy off at the door. Though she could not forever keep her sister from getting a look at their bound man, at least she could prevent her from seeing him half-naked. But his face was the real problem. How long did it take a man to grow a beard?

Mandy was waving good-bye to Todd Haskins and his sister as their buggy rolled away. Susannah emerged onto the front porch, and managed a feeble wave herself in response to their shouted greetings. To think that only that morning she had been worried about Todd Haskins turning Mandy's head. A boy of twenty, with fine fair hair and a peach fuzz chin, Todd was handsome in a callow kind of way, but even with his family's wealth and position added in he was no match for the gray-eyed devil that she herself had brought right into their house.

Mandy would be dazzled. The thought almost made Susannah groan.

"Just think, Susannah, Mr. Haskins has told me that his mother means to give a grand party! There'll be music and dancing, and Miss Haskins said that she'll make sure I'm invited!" Mandy was almost at the porch, looking lovelier than ever as her cheeks glowed pink with excitement. Her dress of simple white calico sprigged with rosebuds showed off her figure to perfection. The straw bonnet that Susannah herself had decorated with ribbons to match was vastly becoming. Beaming with anticipated pleasure, Mandy looked as beautiful in that moment as she ever had in her life. Susannah saw her sister's attraction with the fresh eyes of fear and felt her heart sink.

She already had ample personal evidence of the kind of rogue Connelly was. If he could practice his wiles on herself, he would certainly not keep his hands off a beauty such as Mandy out of gentlemanly decency or out of respect for her youth and innocence. As for Mandy, Susannah shuddered to consider what a task it would be, keeping her sister away from Connelly once she set eyes on him.

"Baptists do not dance, dear," she murmured distractedly as Mandy picked up her skirts and stepped up onto the porch beside her.

"But surely just this once . . ." Mandy's voice broke off and her eyes widened as they looked beyond Susannah's shoulder. Susannah did not even need to glance around to know what had brought that arrested expression to her sister's face. The doorway was behind her, and Connelly was standing there. Susannah knew it as well as if she had turned around to see him herself.

"That cannot be the bound man," Mandy breathed.

Susannah did turn then, to see Connelly running his eyes over Mandy with open appreciation. The knave! Did he lay so much as a finger, or speak so much as an overwarm word, to her little sister, any of her little sisters, Susannah would fill his hide full of birdshot! And so she meant to warn him before he was an hour older!

"You must be Miss Susannah's sister." His clipped English was nearly as captivating as his appearance, Susannah realized. The deep, gravelly voice was surprisingly attractive, now that it came from the throat of a heartbreaker rather than a lout. He should have looked ridiculous, standing there in his stockinged feet and disreputable breeches, with their father's full-cut shirt strained to the point of ripping over his shoulders, but he did not. In fact, he looked spectacular, certainly far more spectacular than any male Mandy, or Susannah for that matter, had ever seen. The wrap-around shirt would not close over his chest, though he had thrust the ends of it into the waistband of his breeches as was proper. A deep vee of masculine chest was exposed down the middle, revealing everything from the pulse in the hollow of his throat to much of the thick wedge of black hair that covered his chest to the swathe of white bandages that thankfully covered some part of what otherwise would have been on display.

"I'm Mandy."

"Miss Amanda," Susannah said, her eyes fixed meaningfully on Connelly. His gaze flicked from Mandy to Susannah, and suddenly an amused gleam appeared.

"Run along upstairs and change, dear. I need you to fetch me a few things from the garden." Susannah's voice was as steady as she could make it. Knowing Mandy as she did, she was aware that the least hint of opposition was all that was needed to set the seal on a situation that already promised to be vexatious enough.

"Oh—all right." Mandy glanced back over her shoulder at Susannah as if just then remembering that she was there. She must be dazzled by Connelly, Susannah thought grimly, to agree to picking vegetables without broaching so much as a single argument. Mandy hated anything to do with dirt.

"And I need *you* in the kitchen," Susannah added to Connelly as he stepped aside to allow Mandy to pass by him. He smiled at her sister, just faintly, but the effect was maddeningly sensual. Susannah felt the temperature of her own response to the slow lift of his lips and could have kicked both herself and Connelly.

"Yes, ma'am," he said, his eyes sliding to Susannah now that Mandy was past him. Susannah realized that he was laughing at her, though his face had sobered. Amusement lurked in the glinting gray eyes. Ignoring the teasing look, Amanda walked into the house.

"What was your name?" Mandy stopped at the base of the stairs to glance back at Connelly, who had entered behind Susannah. The look she gave him was flirtatious, but then Mandy would flirt with a doorpost, Susannah reminded herself as she tried not to succumb to utter dismay. "Campbell, Crane, something like that?"

"Connelly," the blackguard said. "Ian Connelly."

"Connelly." Mandy smiled blindingly at him. "How nice to have you join our household. I'm sure you'll be very happy here."

"I'm sure I will, Miss Mandy."

"The vegetables, Amanda," Susannah prodded with an edge to her voice.

"I'm going, Susannah dear."

The sweet-as-molasses reply—Susannah dear, really!—was followed by a

truly inspiring demonstration of how to seductively climb a flight of stairs—
skirt gathered so as to show off the curve of her neat little behind and a
discreet bit of stocking at the ankle, hips swaying, back erect. The minx!
Where had she learned to move like that?

Susannah vowed to have a long and pointed talk with Mandy in the near
future.

"You need me in the kitchen?" Connelly's voice was bland as Mandy
disappeared around the curve in the stairs. Susannah might have been taken
in had not his eyes given him away. They gleamed at her, more amused than
ever.

"If you dare . . ." she began in a fierce undertone, only to be interrupted by the sounds of Em laughing and footsteps crossing the front porch.
Emily and then Sarah Jane walked through the doorway. For the moment it
took their eyes to adjust from the full sun outside to the comparative darkness
of the hall, they were unaware of Susannah's and Connelly's presence.

"Do you suppose Mrs. Likens really hit her eye on a door?" Em sounded
uneasy.

Sarah Jane grimaced. " 'Tis possible, I suppose, but I would deem it
more likely that the door was Jed Likens' fist."

"But surely he . . ." Emily suddenly became aware of the two figures
standing silently at the foot of the steps. She broke off her words, blinking at
them in surprise. As the full glory of Connelly's altered appearance sank in,
she gaped, then blushed with confusion.

"Oh, my goodness!" she said, her hand flying to her mouth.

Sarah Jane, who had far more presence of mind than Emily, confined her
reaction to no more than a single surprised glance at Connelly's face before
her eyes slid to Susannah.

"This is Miss Sarah Jane, and Miss Emily," Susannah said tersely, nodding to each girl in turn. "As you can see, Connelly is much recovered. Did
you remember the buttermilk?"

"I left it on the porch," Sarah Jane replied.

"Connelly, would you fetch it to the kitchen, please? You two had best
change. There's a lot of work to be done."

"There's always work!" Emily groaned.

"There's always food, too, and clothing, and shelter, and so you should be
thankful," Susannah said.

"Yes, indeed, that's true," Sarah Jane told Emily as she shepherded her
younger sister up the stairs before her. "Besides, you know what the Scrip-
tures say about idle hands. . . ."

"Oh, Sarah Jane, just for once would you hush? I am so sick of you
forever prosing on!"

The two disappeared around the bend. Connelly appeared in the doorway, carrying the milk jug. Tight-lipped, Susannah turned and went into the kitchen. He followed her, setting the jug on the table. She moved to the flour bin, dumping the dough from the bowl and shaping it into loaves without even having to think about it. She had performed the task so many times she could have done it in her sleep.

"If I dare what?" he asked then, leaning a hip against the table and folding his arms over his chest as he watched her.

Susannah's hands stilled, her fingers sinking deep into the dough, ruining the shape of the loaf. Her eyes were angry as they lifted to his face.

"If you dare so much as glance sideways at Mandy, or Sarah Jane or Em for that matter, I'll take the fowling piece there and blow you so full of holes you'll look like a sieve!" she hissed.

13

"Saving me for yourself, are you?" the swine asked, apparently unmoved by her threat. Picking up an apple from the bowl in the center of the table, he bit into it with relish.

Susannah stared at him for a moment without speaking. The question was so plainly intended to provoke her to anger that she felt her temper subside a little. Carefully, she reshaped the loaf she had destroyed and put it and its fellow into pans for baking.

"I mean what I say, and so I warn you," she said, picking up the pans and moving across the kitchen to thrust them into the baking oven.

"Miss Mandy . . ."

"Miss Amanda!"

"Miss Amanda, then, is certainly lovely, but a trifle wet behind the ears for my taste. And your other sisters are not quite my style, so you may set your mind at rest. You have no need to be jealous."

"Jealous!" For a moment Susannah could manage no more than that. Then, as she glared at him, ready to annihilate him with any weapon that came to hand, the teasing glint in his eyes gave her pause. He was deliberately baiting her, for no other reason that she could think of than that he enjoyed watching her lose her temper. She would not give him the satisfaction. Instead she stooped, retrieving from the floor near the fireplace a basket of turnips that she had brought up from the root cellar earlier.

"You may peel these," she said, setting the basket down on the table with rather more force than was necessary and laying a knife down beside it. "That should not tax you overmuch."

"What the devil are they?" Thwarted in the teasing game he apparently derived so much amusement from, Connelly took another huge bite out of the apple and frowned down at the contents of the basket.

"You're swearing," Susannah pointed out, tight-lipped, as she crossed to the tall cupboard opposite.

" 'The devil' is swearing?"

"Yes, it is." Opening it, she began to search among the jars for the dried herbs she would need.

"And I thought I was being quite mild. See how I try to accommodate myself to your requirements? I'm even prepared to peel your strange vegetables."

"They're turnips."

"Ah." He finished his apple and set the core down on the table.

"You may put that in this bucket. I save scraps in it for the hogs." Susannah pointed to the bucket in question.

Connelly looked mildly revolted but picked up the core and lobbed it through the air. It landed with a dull thump, right on target. Susannah turned back to the cupboard. The jar she sought was on a shelf right in front of her nose, and she was sure she would have seen it much sooner had she not been distracted by Connelly.

"I need the turnips shortly so that they may have time to cook." This pointed reminder made Connelly sit down at the table and pick up a turnip in one hand and the knife in the other.

"What do you want me to do?" He turned the turnip over in his hand, eyeing it with clear misgiving.

"Peel them, as I said. Then cut them in quarters, and put them in here." She banged an iron pot down on the table beside him.

"Yes, ma'am."

Though she hated to leave Connelly alone, lest Mandy or one of the others should change more quickly than was their habit and appear in the kitchen, she needed ham hocks from the smokehouse to cook with the turnips.

"I'll be right back," she said in a tone of grim warning and hurried off on her errand so fast that she was near winded when she got back. Connelly was alone, she was relieved to see, seated at the table, his head bent over a turnip as he painstakingly wielded the knife on it. He was concentrating so hard that he barely glanced up as she entered.

Pausing just inside the back door to catch her breath, Susannah's eyes widened as she looked at the mound of cut-up turnips in the pot. It was minuscule, yet the basket was more than three-quarters empty.

"What have you done to the turnips?" she asked, mystified.

"Rather you should ask what the turnips have done to me," he said sourly, looking up. "I cut my thumb." He held up the afflicted member as if to provide proof. A small nick on the ball of his thumb was barely beaded with blood. Such a scratch was totally undeserving of sympathy, and he got none.

"Where are the rest of them?" Susannah set the ham hocks down on the corner of the table and came closer to peer inside the pot.

"The rest of what?"

"The turnips!"

"They're all right here. What do you think, they jumped up and ran out the door while you were gone?"

Susannah flashed him a narrow-eyed look for his sarcasm. The heaping basket full of turnips, most of which had been peeled, occupied no more than a quarter of a pot they should have filled to overflowing.

Then she found the reason. Looking from the misshapen white blobs in the pot to the peels on the table, she saw that most of the meat remained on the peels!

"Look what you've done!"

"What?"

"You've peeled away half the turnips!"

Connelly frowned defensively down at the mound of peels. "I did not!"

"There's hardly enough left to provide a spoonful for each of us! Have you never peeled a vegetable before?" Susannah was more aghast than angry. Her hand rested on the back of the chair on which he sat as she shook her head disbelievingly at him. Seated, his head reached clear to her shoulder. She was reminded suddenly of just how large a man he was. He looked up at her, his hair brushing her hand as he tilted his head back so that he could see her expression. The slight contact drew her eyes. Washed and combed, the thick strands were as black and sleek as a starling's wing, with just the faintest hint of curl at the ends. Like his face, his hair was beautiful without being in the least feminine. Disturbed that she should even notice, Susannah quickly removed her hand.

"I must confess that peeling vegetables is not an occupation that has previously come my way," he said.

" 'Tis obvious." Susannah took the knife and deftly peeled the few remaining turnips herself. "See how it's done?" Only the thinnest layer of peel was removed, leaving large, glistening-white turnips, which she dropped into the pot on top of their misshapen brethren. She then salvaged what she could of the vegetables he had mangled and picked up the ham hocks to add them to the pot.

"What are those?" He frowned at the pink meat.

"Ham hocks." She put them in the pot and moved away to add water, first to rinse and then to boil.

"Ham hocks? But they look like—pigs' feet."

"They are," Susannah said, glancing back over her shoulder at him.

"We're eating turnips and pigs' feet?" He sounded so revolted that she almost had to smile.

"Yes, we are. They're delicious, you may take my word for it. Only today we'll have to have eggs as well, since you wasted so many of the turnips."

"Eggs I can handle. I like mine soft-boiled."

"Do you indeed?" Susannah hung the pot containing the turnips and ham hocks on the crane over the fire. "I hope you like collecting them as well as eating them. The henhouse is up the hill. You can see it from the back door."

"You want me to collect eggs?" His voice was curiously doubtful, but Susannah scarcely noticed as she frowned over another problem.

"I suppose you'll have to wear Pa's clogs. They're on the back porch. They'll be too small, of course, but they have no backs and I am sure you can squeeze in your toes."

"I'll wear my own shoes, thank you."

"I've sent Ben to town with your shoes, to get you some boots made. Pa's clogs will have to do till the boots are ready. You may take the basket the turnips were in for the eggs. And hurry, if you please. I have any number of things to do besides cook this afternoon."

He pushed his chair back and stood up. "The eggs are in the henhouse, you say?"

"Up the hill." She nodded, busy measuring out flour for the dumplings that would be needed to fill out the meal.

He hesitated the barest second, then without another word picked up the basket and padded out through the door. Moments later, through the kitchen window, she saw him following the well-worn path up the hill, moving a little awkwardly as he worked to keep her father's too-small clogs on his feet. The basket was tucked under his arms, and Brownie waddled along at his feet.

Mandy came into the kitchen, dressed in a sky-blue frock that was never meant to go gardening. A gay smiled curved her lips until, looking about the kitchen, she perceived that Susannah was alone.

"Where is he?"

Susannah added the dumplings to the boiling water and, wiping her hands on a towel, turned to frown at Mandy.

"If you mean Connelly, he has gone to fetch some eggs."

"Oh." She was obviously disappointed but brightened again almost at once. "That shouldn't take long."

Susannah had hoped not to have to warn Mandy off—in her experience, such an action was usually counterproductive—but the gleam in Mandy's eye presaged trouble. It was always possible that a few timely words might make Mandy stop and think before she plunged rashly ahead.

"Amanda. You will remember that he is our bound man. Moreover, he is a convict. As a beau for you, he is not to be considered. You may flirt with

Todd Haskins or Hiram Greer or just about anyone else you please, but leave Connelly alone. Do you hear me?"

"But he's gorgeous, Susannah! Whoever would have thought it, as dirty and scruffy as he was when we brought him home?"

"You are not listening to me, Amanda Sue Redmon! I rarely forbid you to do anything, but I am forbidding you now—you are to stay away from Connelly! The man is dangerous!"

"Do you really think so?" Mandy sounded as if she found the idea thrilling.

Susannah gritted her teeth. She should have known better than to say such a thing. Had her wits gone begging lately? "I will make a bargain with you, Mandy. Do you truly wish to go to the Haskinses' party?"

Mandy's eyes widened. "Above all things!"

"If you behave yourself with Connelly—and I will be keeping an eye on you, so do not think to fool me that you are when you are not!—you may go to the party."

"And dance?"

"I would not go that far. You may watch the dancing."

"Oh, very well. If only I may go!"

Pa would be greatly distressed when he discovered that she had given Mandy permission to attend a party where there would be dancing. The teachings of their church severely frowned on much congress between unmarried couples. On the other hand, the alternative was far worse. Connelly could be injurious to far more than Mandy's reputation, though Susannah didn't mean to tell her father that. If Susannah had learned nothing else over the past dozen years, she had learned that it was sometimes necessary to compromise the lofty principles her father adhered to in the face of the reality of raising three lively girls.

"All right, then. You may attend the Haskinses' party, on the condition that you behave yourself with Connelly. Do we have a bargain?"

Mandy hesitated, then nodded, her beaming smile breaking out. "Oh, Susannah, may I really go to the party? I had not thought—I am so excited!"

"Yes, I can see you are. Don't chatter of it to all and sundry, now. Some of the parishioners will think it scandalous." But Susannah had to smile, despite her various misgivings, in the face of her sister's incandescent joy.

"You are so good to me, Susannah! Will there be time for you to make me a new dress, do you think? That green silk I bought in town the other day will be perfect!" Amanda twirled around the kitchen, stopping only to hug her sister enthusiastically.

"If you are going, I suppose you must have a new dress." Susannah returned Mandy's hug, only to have her twirl about the room again when she released her. Susannah watched Mandy with wry indulgence. What must it feel like to be that young?

"I must tell Em and Sarah Jane. Might they go, too?"

"Emily is too young, and Sarah Jane will not wish to, I think."

But Mandy had already flown from the room to share news of her good fortune with her siblings. Susannah looked after her for a moment, smiling. Mandy had been more work to raise than the other two put together, and there didn't seem to be any prospect of that changing very soon. But even if she could, Susannah realized that she would not alter so much as a hair on her sister's head. Susannah thought that over for a minute, then amended it, rather ruefully. There were a few things she might consider changing about Mandy, but not many, and Mandy's warm-hearted exuberance more than made up for her faults.

Only then did Susannah realize that Mandy was gone, and the vegetables were still unfetched. She opened her mouth to summon her sister back, then closed it again. It would be easier, and quicker, just to fetch the vegetables herself.

Picking up a basket, she went out the back door and across the porch. She had no more than set foot on the grass when a burst of wild barking from Brownie caused her to glance up the hill from whence it came.

She was just in time to see Connelly burst through the henhouse doorway, his arms raised to cover his head and an enraged red hen flapping and screeching behind him as it clung with its claws to the back of his shirt.

14

 "Bloody damned creature! Get it off me!" Connelly ducked and twisted, trying to dislodge the angry bird as Susannah rushed up the hill to his rescue.

"You're frightening her! Stop flailing about!"

"Frightening *her*! What do you raise here, killer chickens?"

Finally Connelly succeeded in knocking the hen to the ground. She landed, squawking and flapping her wings. Brownie, barking hysterically, darted at her, while some half dozen other screeching hens flew through the open henhouse door, passing not more than a foot above Connelly's head. Connelly ducked, cursing and throwing up a protective arm. The downed hen took wing to join them, chased by Brownie, who had not seen so much excitement in years. The entire flock landed clumsily in a nearby tree, while Brownie made excited, noisy leaps halfway up its trunk. Susannah, who had rushed to the rescue only to arrive seconds after Connelly rid himself of his attacker, burst out laughing.

She laughed so long and so hard her sides ached when she at last straightened up again. Never could she remember having seen anything so funny as Connelly on the run from her favorite hen.

"Hilarious, is it?" He had straightened to his full height now and had both arms crossed over his chest as he regarded her with disfavor.

"Yes." Susannah wiped streaming eyes. "Her name is Elise. She's ten years old, and she's a dear."

"If you are referring to that chicken, she bit the hell out of my hand!"

"You're swearing."

"So I am."

"Well," conceded Susannah with a chuckle that threatened to dissolve into a full-blown laugh at any second, "perhaps this time you have cause. Did she really bite you? No, of course she didn't. Hens don't have any teeth. They can't bite. She merely pecked you."

"Oh, is that all? It hurt like he—like the dickens, let me tell you."

"What did you do to her?"

"I couldn't find any eggs, and the old biddies were all sitting around staring at me and clucking. I thought they might be hiding them, so I tried to shoo them off their nests. That one attacked me."

"Oh, dear," said Susannah unsteadily and started laughing again. She could just picture him, all six-feet-plus of menacing man, being made uneasy by the bright gazes of a roomful of nesting hens. Judging from his expression, he didn't much appreciate her amusement at his expense, so after a moment or so she heroically swallowed her chortles.

"Don't tell me," she said when she had herself under control, "you've never gathered eggs before?"

"No, I never have."

"Have you ever even been on a farm before?"

"Of course I've been on a farm."

"You have?"

"To collect the rent." The admission was somewhat sulky. Susannah lifted her eyebrows at him, and he shrugged. " 'Twas one of my jobs, once."

"You've never peeled vegetables, and you've never gathered eggs. Can you plow? No, of course you can't. What can you do, if you don't mind my asking?"

He narrowed his eyes at her. "I can ride with the best, drive to an inch, wench, dance, drink anyone you care to name under the table and never show it, play cards and win, and shoot the wick out of a candle at fifty yards, among other accomplishments that I cannot at the moment call to mind."

"Oh." Susannah heard this list with doubt written on her face. Then, in a more positive tone, she added, "Shay—the auctioneer—claimed that you can read and write."

"Oh, yes, I can read and write. How remiss of me not to mention that. Don't tell me that you cannot?"

"I can, and my sisters, because our father is a learned man and wanted us to be educated."

"How forward-thinking of him."

"You say you collected rents at one time. How else did you earn your living?"

Connelly hesitated a moment before replying. "I managed," he said curtly.

"Indeed? From your current circumstances, I cannot judge that you managed any too well."

"You know nothing of what brought me to this pass."

"I would be glad to listen, if you should care to tell me."

"I don't need a mother confessor, I assure you." Suddenly, he sounded almost hostile.

Susannah's lips compressed. "Everyone needs someone to tell their troubles to, I've discovered. 'Tis nothing to be ashamed of. Nor is being ignorant of farming, though when I bought you I'd certainly hoped . . . But 'tis too late to repine. Perhaps you can help me with the books, and Pa with his sermons. He cannot see any too well anymore and needs someone to write them out for him. And I will teach you farming."

"Do you have to?" There was a rueful note to his voice. Looking up at him—Susannah realized that the top of her head barely reached his shoulder and that she had to tilt her head back to a considerable degree to meet his eyes—she saw that he was smiling down at her. It was not the sensuous smile he had turned on Mandy, but a real grin. The humor of it reached his eyes, warming the gray depths to devastating effect. Susannah stared, startled as she realized anew just how very handsome he was. In her amusement, she had quite forgotten that he was the physical embodiment of a female's dream.

"Certainly I do," she said severely, flustered to realize that, like Mandy, she was in grave danger of falling under the spell of those reprehensible good looks. "We'll start right now. You may come with me, and I'll show you how to go about gathering eggs."

"I'd really rather not."

"You're not a coward, are you? Come, Elise and the others are still in the tree. There can't be more than a dozen left in the henhouse."

"How reassuring," he muttered, but he did follow her inside, ducking through the low door. Just over the threshold, Susannah stumbled over something and looked down to find one of her father's clogs. Her eyes widened, and she glanced back to discover her bound man in his stockinged feet—only the stockings were well muddied now, and probably wet as well. Her lips twitched, and suddenly she was more at ease with him again.

"Here is one of your shoes," she pointed out. Spying its mate in a pile of straw, she added, "And there is the other."

"Thank you, but I prefer to be without them. Just in case we have to run for it."

"Don't be absurd!" The basket he had carried lay overturned near the second shoe, its bottom crushed. He had apparently stepped on it in his haste to escape the henhouse. It was ruined, of course. But Susannah was smiling as she retrieved the clogs and placed them in her basket. "If you will look in the empty nests, I'm sure you'll find some eggs."

"Yes, but will the guardians the others have left behind attack me?" He was eyeing the ten remaining hens with trepidation. They looked back at him unblinkingly, their little black eyes gleaming. Having collected eggs from the time she could walk—it was a task generally allocated to the younger members of a household—Susannah found his caution as ridiculous as it was endearing. She thrust her hand beneath a feathered breast, felt around, and came up with an egg. The hen—Ruth was her name—clucked, but she did not offer to peck.

"See?" she said, holding the egg up to demonstrate. "And you have the advantage over me. You are tall enough to be able to reach into all the nests, where I have to fetch a stool for the ones on the top row."

She turned up the end of her apron to receive the egg and its fellows, as her basket was filled with his clogs. She rooted beneath another hen, came up empty. His eyes never leaving Matilda and Mavis, the closest of the roosting hens, Connelly took a careful step, and then another, until he stood beside her. He had to stand quite close, because the henhouse, a shed-like structure with a tin roof and neat rows of straw-filled nest boxes, narrowed at its far end. His legs brushed her skirt, and Susannah was suddenly very aware of his nearness. All at once the confines of the henhouse seemed far too restricted.

"You may check the top nests. I cannot reach them." It was all she could do to keep her voice steady.

"That's easily remedied," he said.

Susannah felt his hands grip her waist from behind. Seconds later he was lifting her clear off her feet. In her shock, she forgot to hold on to the edge of the apron and the single egg they'd found dropped to the floor. It broke, but she was barely aware of its fate. Her hands flew to his, and instinctively she clutched his fingers for balance as he held her high.

"Now you may check the nests for yourself," he said, and she knew he was teasing her even though she could not see his face. Her hands tightened over his. The warmth of his fingers beneath hers, the strength of his hands clasping her waist, set her senses atremble.

"Put me down!" she said fiercely, struggling to be free.

"Not till you check the nests." His hands tightened. His fingers dug into her flesh. In the face of his strength she felt suddenly helpless, and the sensation was unnerving.

"I said put me down!" The ferocity in her voice was quite out of proportion to the situation, she knew. But the awful burning sensation that pulsed to life inside her frightened her.

Clenching her teeth, she dug her nails into his fingers. She must have had the good fortune to connect with his cut thumb, or perhaps with the place where Elise had pecked him, because he yelped and released his grip, dropping her onto her feet.

Out of breath and red-faced, Susannah scrambled quickly out of his reach.

"You are never to put your hands on me in such a way again, do you hear?

And you may gather the rest of the eggs yourself. I have things to do in the house."

His eyes narrowed on her, but Susannah did not wait to hear what he might reply. Turning on her heel, she fled.

15

Speculation narrowed Ian's eyes. He watched Susannah retreat in disorder, well aware of what caused her flustered withdrawal—she wanted him. He had known too many women not to recognize the signs.

The dowdy little dab of a female who had bought him at auction was eager for him. Eager and resisting of the notion at once. The situation should have been laughable, but it was not.

Ridiculous as the admission undoubtedly was, he would not be averse to bedding Miss Susannah Redmon. The lady had unexpected depths.

To begin with, she was not nearly as plain as she appeared. The night he had awakened to find her in his bed, she'd been surprisingly alluring. In his dreams he'd been making love to Serena, and to find that the silken thighs he'd parted and soft breasts he'd caressed so enthusiastically belonged to Susannah instead had been quite a shock. What had been an even bigger shock was to discover, unless his mind was playing tricks on him, that Susannah's body was as enticing as her day-to-day appearance was not. Though he had not been quite himself on that never-to-be-forgotten night, his hands still burned with the shape of her. Hard as it was at first for him to believe, the prim minister's daughter seemed to have a figure that a courtesan would kill for. Her breasts were full and beautifully shaped, soft and rounded and womanly, crowned with nipples that had stiffened to instant attention as soon as he had touched them with the balls of his thumbs. Her hips were as lushly female as her breasts. And that was where the deception came in. Her gowns were cut almost straight from breasts to hips. He suspected that she deliberately disguised the asset that would have made her figure breathtaking—an unbelievably tiny waist.

Looking back on those few minutes when he'd had her beneath him in his bed, he'd thought that her waist had felt amazingly small and supple beneath his exploring fingers. Today, when he had lifted her, he'd had his suspicions confirmed—her waist was so small that he could span it with his two hands.

He burned to see her naked.

To think she worried about his seducing her pretty sister. The notion was almost funny. Little Miss Mandy was lovely, but he had known many lovely women. His own Serena was a diamond of the first water. Beside Serena, Mandy's beauty blazed about as brightly as a candle's light when compared with that of the sun. He didn't lust after Mandy.

He lusted after Susannah.

The contrast between what she was and what she appeared to be intrigued him. With her hair scraped so tightly back into that hideous knot that it seemed practically colorless, her square face pale and unsmiling, and her figure hidden by those truly atrocious gowns, she looked plain to the point of being homely. But he had seen her with her hair loose so that it tumbled past her fanny in a wild riot of gold-shot curls. He had seen her face flush with temper and her hazel eyes turn to bright green-gold with it. And he had discovered the luscious woman's body that she concealed beneath her gowns.

He had discovered something else, too—the lady was not quite as resigned to aging spinsterhood as she liked to appear. He didn't remember everything about that night, but he remembered how she had responded to him.

He remembered the smell of lemon that clung to her hair, and the clean taste of her skin, and the incredible softness of her.

And he was curious.

He hadn't felt this way about a woman in years.

There was no hurry about returning home, after all. His enemies would still be waiting, smug in the mistaken belief that they had rid themselves of him at last. He could take a few weeks to satisfy his curiosity about this most unexpected turn of events.

"Miss Redmon! Miss Redmon!"

The cry, with its clear note of distress, jerked him out of his introspection. Ian's head came up, and he strode to the door. A tow-haired boy burst from the woods that lay beyond the henhouse, racing right past Ian as he stood in the doorway to run pell-mell down the hill toward the house. The youth looked vaguely familiar, but before Ian could even attempt to cudgel his memory for a name, Susannah stepped off the back porch into a blaze of bright sunshine, her hands outstretched to catch the boy.

"Jeremy! Whatever is the matter?" Her hands closed over Jeremy Likens' thin shoulders. The child was shaking, his eyes bright with unshed tears, his chest heaving with some combination of emotion and exertion as he struggled to get the words out.

" 'Tis Pa! He's killin' Ma! He's hit her with the shovel, and she's bleedin' bad! You gotta come, Miss Redmon! You gotta come!"

"I'm coming, Jeremy." Susannah stepped back up on the porch and hurried into the kitchen. Seconds later she emerged with her father's old fowling piece in her hands. Jed Likens was no good, a violent, brawling man who frequently beat his wife and seven children. Annabeth Likens, Jeremy's mother, was a meek, colorless little woman who attended church when she could, with bunches of her children in tow. Susannah was often impatient with her quiet acceptance of the abuse that darkened her life, but Annabeth had no notion of how to end it. Susannah had dispensed advice and comfort and practical assistance to her many times over the years, and the whole family—with the exception of Jed—had come to regard her as a friend.

"He hit Cloris with the shovel, too. I think she's dead. You gotta hurry, Miss Redmon! You gotta hurry!" Jeremy was sobbing, dancing from one foot to the other as he waited for her. Cloris was his oldest sister. At thirteen, she was notorious around Beaufort for the way she made up to men, and Susannah guessed that it was just a matter of time until she had an illegitimate baby growing under her skirts. But for all her waywardness in that direction, she was good to her mother and tried to help with her brothers and sisters. There was not a mean bone in Cloris's body.

"Go on, then. I'll follow you."

Jeremy tore back up the hill. With her skirts caught up in one hand and the fowling piece tucked beneath her arm, Susannah followed at a run. She was panting by the time she reached the wood but did not slow her pace even when a stitch hit her side. For Jeremy, to whom familial violence was an everyday occurrence, to run for help, the situation must be desperate.

The Likens place was just on the other side of the hill, across Silver Creek, where Susannah and the girls waded in summer. The path crossed the stream at a narrow section, and Jeremy leaped it easily. Susannah, not quite as limber, splashed through the cold water, wetting her shoes and stockings and the hem of her dress. Even as she struggled up the bank, she could hear shouts and screams from Jeremy's family. Their rundown farm lay in a muddy field at the bottom of the hill.

Following Jeremy, Susannah emerged into cleared ground and bright sunlight. In the moment it took her to absorb the scene, she was nearly upon it. Cloris Likens, in a muddied white dress, her blond hair darkened around the forehead with blood, was screaming as she tried to crawl up the steps of the ramshackle house. Her father had not killed her, Susannah realized with relief. Annabeth Likens lay on the ground a short distance away. She was on her back, with her shouting husband astride her. Both his fists were in her hair, and he was pounding her head into the hard ground. Like Cloris, Annabeth was screaming. Two young children huddled together, crying loudly, while a third boy, Timmy, who was seven, pulled at his father's shirt, trying to get him off their mother. A vicious sweep of Jed Likens' arm sent Timmy flying. The boy's head hit a stump, and for a moment he lay stunned. Then he, too, started to cry and sat up. Jeremy rushed to take his little brother's place in defending their mother. Likens, looking around at his older son with a snarl, sent him reeling back with a vicious shove.

"Jed Likens, that is quite enough!" Susannah barely had the breath to speak, but she leveled the fowling piece at Likens and held it steady. He glanced around, saw Susannah and her weapon, and let loose with a string of curses that would have made St. Peter blush. His hands left his wife's hair. Annabeth's head fell back, and her screams turned into wrenching sobs. Weeping noisily, she implored the good Lord and Miss Redmon to help her.

"This ain't none of yer business, you old busybody! You get yerself back to yer damned church, and let me manage my family!"

"Let Annabeth up. I mean it, Mr. Likens."

"She's a lyin' bitch, and she deserves every lick she gets! Did Jeremy there run blabbin' to you? You gonna pay for that, boy! Jest you wait!"

"If you so much as lay a finger on Jeremy, or any of the rest of them, again, I'll have you arrested, and so I warn you."

"Cain't have me arrested. I'm the bleedin' master around here. You spew out all them fancy words, and you don't know nothin' about nothin'. This here's my family, and I can learn 'em like I see fit. Ain't no concern of yours what happens to 'em, and I mean to see that you remember it in the future." With that, he got off his wife's body and stood glaring at Susannah, fingers flexing, an evil smile playing around his mouth.

"You take one step toward me and I'll blow you clear to the next county, Jed Likens."

"Don't you hurt her, Jed! Don't you go hurtin' Miss Redmon, now!" The wail came from Annabeth as she turned over on her side and sought to lock her hands around her husband's ankle. Likens kicked her in the stomach without even glancing down. Annabeth cried out, and curled into a little ball with her arms cradling her stomach, keening loudly.

"You won't shoot me." Likens took a step forward.

"What makes you think I won't?"

"You ain't got the stomach for it, church woman."

Susannah kept the fowling piece pointed at his middle, while inwardly she fought the urge to take a step back. He was calling her bluff, and both of them knew it. To her horror, she discovered that she could not, in cold blood, shoot the man.

He took another step toward her, then another, his confidence increasing as she didn't pull the trigger.

"I'm gonna whip your ass for you, bitch," he said, gloating.

"Oh, no, you're not," said a gravelly voice from behind Susannah. To Susannah's surprise, the fowling piece was plucked out of her hands. Connelly moved to stand beside her, the weapon cradled familiarly in his arms, its mouth pointed directly at Likens, who stopped in his tracks.

"You'd best get out of my sight in a hurry. If Miss Redmon here can't blow you to hell, I sure can."

"Who the hell are you, and what business is this of yourn?"

"I said get, and I mean get." Connelly moved the fowling piece almost casually, but the gesture's effect on Likens was galvanizing.

"I'm goin', I'm goin'!" He looked around at his frightened family, his expression ugly. He spied his hat on the ground, picked it up, and slapped it against his thigh before clapping it on his head.

"There'll be a reckonin' for this day's work," he said, his eyes fixing on Susannah for a moment before sweeping his family again. As Connelly jerked the fowling piece, he turned and shambled off.

"Ma! Ma, are you bad hurt?" Jeremy and the younger children ran to cluster around their mother. Susannah sagged, momentarily weak with relief. An arm came around her waist, supporting her, and she glanced up to find Connelly frowning down at her.

"Are you all right?"

For a moment, just a moment, she permitted herself to rest against him as she closed her eyes. He took her weight with ease, sheltering her against his side. The sheer impropriety of the situation occurred to her, and she straightened. His hand continued to ride her waist. The warm strength of his fingers was comforting, but of course she couldn't allow him to hold her like that. He was her bound man, not her beau.

"Tell me that in another minute you would have blown a hole through him." There was a roughness to his voice that made her glance up at him again.

"I couldn't just shoot him," she confessed.

His eyes darkened, and a curse seemed to hover on the tip of his tongue. "If you couldn't shoot him, then you had no business getting yourself in the middle of something like this. What do you think would have happened if I hadn't followed you over here? Hell, the bastard nearly killed his own wife."

"Don't swear," she said automatically.

"An occasion like this calls for some swearing. You could have been badly hurt, you little fool."

To be scolded was a new experience for Susannah. She had ruled the roost at home for years, with none to say her nay. Connelly's words put her back up, but they warmed her at the same time. It was a novel sensation, to have someone looking out for her.

"But I wasn't," she said quietly, and stepped away from him. As she went to help Annabeth and Cloris, she was conscious of Connelly's eyes boring into her back.

With the big-eyed children clustering about, Susannah set about putting the mess to rights. Annabeth had a cut on the back of her head and numerous bruises, but she was not seriously injured, despite the copious amount of blood that stained her gown. Cloris, who'd taken a hard blow with the sharp side of a shovel while coming to her mother's defense, was dizzy and had to be carried inside. At Susannah's direction, Connelly lifted the girl as if she weighed no more than a feather and carried her in to lay her in the middle of the one big bed. Annabeth fussed over her daughter, while Susannah sought to comfort the frightened children.

"Jed will be back, you know," Susannah said to Annabeth at last. Despite the bruises that were beginning to discolor her face and the already present black eye, from what Susannah suspected was a previous beating, Annabeth behaved as if nothing had happened, tending to Cloris, whose head was bound up in a towel, and starting supper at the same time.

"He'll be different when he does come back. He's always like that. Jed's not a bad man, Miss Redmon. He just—explodes, and then he's sorry for it."

"For your own sake, and your children's, you should think about leaving, Annabeth. You know we have those old slave cabins out behind the barn. You and the children can move into one until you can get things straightened out."

"I know, and I thank you for the offer. But I'll stay. It'll be all right, you'll see."

In the end, there was nothing to do but leave them there. Susannah only hoped that Annabeth was right about her husband's probable change of mood.

"Do you always take on everybody else's troubles?"

They were on their way home. Connelly had been mostly silent since he had called her a little fool, and Susannah had been content to have him remain so. He was far from properly respectful toward her. Even if one totally disregarded their infamous encounter of two nights before (and how she wished she could disregard it!), he had laid his hands on her person more in the brief time she had known him than had any other man in her entire life. Yet even in so short a time as they had had together, she knew she liked him, especially when she forgot about his staggering good looks. She felt comforted to have him by her side. If he had not been there to stand between her and Jed Likens, the Lord alone knew what might have happened. But he had protected her, in a masterful way that was quite foreign to anything she had ever experienced. How then was she to set him in his place when next he stepped beyond the line, as he was certain to do?

"Susannah."

She had known he would do it.

"*Miss* Susannah," she said. They were nearing the stream. She was in front, Connelly behind. His hand on her arm stopped her. The sleeves of her dove-gray linen dress were turned back to the elbow in deference to the heat. The garment was loose, as were all her dresses. A plain white apron was pinned to her waist and covered most of her bell-shaped skirt. She wore neither bonnet nor gloves, and his hand curled around her bare forearm.

She felt the warm strength of his fingers clear down to her toes. Hadn't she, not an hour before, ordered him never to put his hands on her again? She ought to remind him, she knew, but to do so might only make him aware that she had reasons other than propriety for wanting to avoid his touch. Turning, she glanced up at him, to find that he was looking down at her intently, a frown drawing his brows together over his nose.

"Do you always take on everybody else's troubles?"

"I try to help people when I can." It was shady in the woods, and cool. Tall pin oaks draped with thick gray curtains of Spanish moss blocked the sun. The path beneath her feet was slippery with vines. Behind her the stream tinkled. Birds called overhead.

Susannah felt as though the whole world had suddenly fallen away, leaving the two of them alone.

"Is that why you bought me? To help me?"

"I bought you to work the farm." She had trouble getting the words out. He was close. Far too close.

"You made a mighty poor bargain, then."

"Maybe. Maybe not. That's up to you, isn't it?" Unobtrusively, she tried to pull away. His hand tightened on her arm, slid caressingly down to her waist.

"You have the softest skin. Almost as soft as your heart."

Susannah caught her breath, for a moment unable to believe what she had heard. His fingers circled her wrist, his thumb tracing a slow arc over the translucent skin where her veins showed blue. It was all she could do not to shiver.

"Are you flirting with me, Connelly?" she asked in her sternest voice. Steeling herself, she looked up at him with a frown.

He grinned, a wide grin that showed even white teeth and that danced in his eyes.

"Yes, Miss Susannah, I am," he said, lifting her hand to press it against the warm smoothness of his freshly shaven cheek. "Your bound man is flirting with you. So what are you going to do about it?"

Then, still grinning, he turned his head so that his lips seared her palm.

16

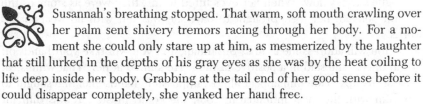 Susannah's breathing stopped. That warm, soft mouth crawling over her palm sent shivery tremors racing through her body. For a moment she could only stare up at him, as mesmerized by the laughter that still lurked in the depths of his gray eyes as she was by the heat coiling to life deep inside her body. Grabbing at the tail end of her good sense before it could disappear completely, she yanked her hand free.

"If you are hoping to charm me for some nefarious purpose of your own, you are wasting your time," she said jerkily. Turning about, she marched along the path that led to the house. Her back was ramrod straight, her gait steady, and only she knew how much effort it cost her to keep them that way. Her muscles were as weak as warm mush, and her knees had a most regrettable tendency to tremble.

"Susannah."

Her shoulders stiffened. There was laughter in his voice. She should turn and berate him for the familiarity. But if she did, if she looked up into his too-handsome face to find him smiling down at her in that teasing way that was probably totally calculated but was almost impossible for her to resist, she would be in danger of falling completely under his spell. That complication to her life she didn't need. What the rogue could hope to gain from charming her she couldn't imagine, but that he had some purpose in mind she was quite sure. She wasn't stupid, after all. Why else would a man who looked like Connelly be expending so much effort on a plain spinster like herself?

"Have you never had a suitor?"

The question flicked her on a raw spot she hadn't known she possessed. It was one thing to acknowledge the truth to herself and quite another to admit to Connelly that no man had ever found her attractive enough to pursue.

Ignoring him, she strode on, head high. Time enough to remind him of his place when she had regained control of both her body and her emotions. To confront him now would be an act of pure folly.

"Damn it, Susannah! Wait a minute." He caught her arm, throwing her offstride. Even as she tried to jerk free of his grasp, he turned her to face him. He held her about the elbow, his grip not hurting her but as unbreakable as a shackle. The fowling piece that he had carried tucked under one arm he very carefully set aside. His newly-freed hand slid around her other elbow, and she was well and truly caught.

Held fast, Susannah disdained to struggle. He was very close, so close that the hem of her skirt overlay his toes. She had forgotten that he wore no shoes but only her father's gray stockings, now wet and muddied almost to the knee. The knowledge that he had come after her in stockinged feet might have softened her had she allowed it to. But she was thoroughly on guard against his rogue's tricks now. When her eyes lifted to his, they were as stony as the ground beneath her feet. Brought to bay, she was left with no weapon but words.

"You will address me as *Miss* Susannah, and you will take your hands off me, at once," she said in a positive fashion. He smiled at her. That whimsical twist of his lips made him appear almost impossibly handsome. She sought to cow him with the most intimidating look she could muster. It was difficult when the object of that look was more than a foot taller than herself.

He laughed. Her lips tightened, and sparks of anger brightened her eyes.

"Does everyone do as you tell them?" he asked, grinning.

"If they're wise." She spoke through her teeth.

His grin widened. He made no move to release her. His eyes sparkled with amusement as they slid over her face.

"I never was very wise," he said, as if making an admission.

"Quite obviously not."

"I like shrewish women. Shutting their mouths can be so entertaining, especially if one goes about it in the right way."

"Connelly . . ." It was a warning.

"Ian," he said. "Say Ian, Susannah."

Had she not been on guard against his blandishments, it would have been all too easy to succumb to his coaxing rogue's tongue. As it was, she stiffened her spine and glared at him.

"I will do no such thing," she said.

"You will." He sounded disconcertingly positive.

"I won't."

"Will."

"You're being childish as well as foolish, and I demand that you let me go at once." She tried to pull free, only to confirm what she already knew—she was trapped until he chose to release her.

"Taming you is going to be a delight."

"Taming me?" She could scarcely believe her ears.

"Gentling you, rather. Breaking you to bridle."

"I," said Susannah with a great effort at self-control, "am not a horse. And you are about to get yourself in a great deal of trouble, sirrah! I can sell you, you know."

"But you won't. Think how someone else might mistreat me. You wouldn't like to see me hurt, would you?"

"At the moment I can think of nothing I would like better." She gritted her teeth. "If you do not let me go . . ."

"Call me Ian, and say please, and I'll consider it."

He was laughing again, the devil. Susannah, dander up, lifted her half-booted foot and slammed her heel down hard on his stockinged toes.

"Ow!"

Taken by surprise, he yelped, jumping back. Suddenly freed, Susannah whirled, snatching up her skirts. Dignity or no, she ran for the house. She had outfoxed the fox, but only for the moment. What payment he might demand for her victory, should he catch her, she trembled to imagine.

He did not catch her. She was fleet of foot, but she suspected he did not seriously give chase. She arrived at the back steps, flushed and winded, to find her sisters in the kitchen and a hideous smell permeating the house.

"Where have you been?" They all three turned to stare at Susannah as she stepped through the door.

"At the Likens'—I'll tell you the whole story in a minute. What is that smell?"

"The turnips burned dry. When they stunk up the whole house was the first we knew that you'd gone off somewhere." Em sounded accusing.

"I went ahead and made a corn pudding, Susannah. 'Twas the best I could think to do." Sarah Jane turned from the fire, wiping the back of her hand over her sweat-beaded forehead.

"That will be fine, with the ham hocks. They didn't burn, too?"

"No."

Connelly stepped onto the back porch just then. Though Susannah couldn't see him, she was as aware of his presence as if he stood directly beside her. There was the slightest pause, and then he appeared in the back door, barefoot, with the fowling piece in hand.

Three pairs of eyes went from Connelly to Susannah.

"Did he go with you?" Mandy sounded put out.

Susannah sighed. "Let's get the meal on the table, and I'll tell you the whole story," she said with a mendacity that her father wouldn't have approved. Because of course she meant the whole story of what had happened at the Likens'. What had occurred later, in the wood, she would keep to herself.

Over the course of the next week, Susannah worked hard to keep herself and her sisters out of Connelly's way. Her efforts were aided by the fact that she no longer considered it necessary to have him sleep in the house. Obviously, the man required only minimal nursing care. On Tuesday next, a fortnight from the time she had applied her special healing salve to his back, she would reapply the medicine and change the bandage. Other than that, all he seemed to need was feeding up.

He ate all the time, in enormous amounts, as though there were not enough food in the world to fill him up. Though she hated to admit that the thought of his being hungry disturbed her, Susannah took to cooking huge quantities of foods she thought he might like. He seemed especially partial to chicken and dumplings and devoured so much of her bread that she started baking an extra two loaves a day. One of her guiltiest secrets was the amount of pleasure it gave her to watch him eat food she had cooked.

"Is it my imagination, daughter, or are you providing us with a great deal more sustenance than we are used to?" the Reverend Redmon asked at the breakfast table one morning. He surveyed the plenty spread out before him with mild perplexity. Susannah had made hot water cornbread and served it with fresh-churned butter and honey and thin slices of ham. In addition, there was the usual gruel and molasses, soft-boiled eggs to suit their bound man's preference, and a large rasher of bacon.

Susannah was just setting the bacon on the table as her father spoke, and she could not help the quick color that stained her cheeks as she sent him a startled glance. As he was usually oblivious of what was put before him, she had not expected him to notice.

"My theory is that Susannah is trying to make us all as fat as Em," Mandy said with a saucy smile at Connelly, who sat across the table from her.

"Mandy!" Susannah and Sarah Jane protested in shocked unison. Em, fortunately, had not yet come down.

"I think, rather, that Miss Susannah is trying to fatten *me* up," Connelly said, with a comically rueful gesture at his high-piled plate. His intervention shifted attention to himself from Mandy, which, Susannah guessed, was his intention. Certainly it saved Mandy from a scolding. Susannah suspected that Mandy's remark had been designed to draw their bound man's attention to her own svelte shape. But with their father present, and Connelly himself as witness, now was hardly the time to say so. Mandy's callousness to her absent sister's sensitivities called for a reprimand. But for the moment Susannah was too preoccupied with Connelly's embarrassingly accurate assessment of her intentions to spare more than a rebuking glance for Mandy.

"Is that so, daughter?" the Reverend Redmon asked with interest. Susannah, who was busy filling everyone's mug with fresh milk, felt more color heat her cheeks. Really, her father's obtuseness was sometimes as much a curse as a blessing!

"Connelly needs a great deal more meat on his bones if he is to do heavy work," she said primly, hoping that none of those around the table would read more into her actions than practical self-interest. She set the milk jug down and took her own seat. Asking her father to please pass the cornbread, she sought to turn the conversation in a new direction, without success.

"She has been feeding me up for years," the Reverend Redmon said to Ian in a confidential tone as he complied with Susannah's request. "For some reason, females seem to be born with a need to stuff their menfolk with food."

"They do, don't they?" Ian agreed, and the two exchanged a purely masculine look of amusement. Susannah, sure that she must be scarlet by now, nearly choked on her cornbread. Whatever else he might be, Connelly was certainly not one of her "menfolk"!

" 'Tis not to be wondered at, if Susannah is forever trying to tempt your appetite," Sarah Jane said to their father, unknowingly earning Susannah's gratitude by drawing all eyes to herself. "You eat no more than a mouse. You must think of the congregation, Pa, and how much they depend on you. To keep up your strength, you need to eat."

"My daughters are forever trying to mother me, as you can see," the Reverend Redmon said to Ian. He smiled his luminous smile. "But they are good girls, nonetheless. I would not be without them."

Before Ian could reply, Em entered with a complaint against Mandy for borrowing her new embroidered handkerchief, which Em assured everyone Mandy had not been given leave to do. By the time that dispute was settled, the conversation had taken a different turn entirely. To Susannah's relief, no further mention was made of the bounty that graced their table. For future meals, she took care to cook less lavishly. She still pandered to Connelly's enormous appetite, but not, she hoped, so that anyone, including the man himself, would notice.

A previous owner of the farm had built half a dozen one-room cabins just beyond the barn. Intended to house slaves, they had been largely empty in the twenty years since the Reverend Redmon had acquired the property. Now Craddock occupied one, and Susannah put Connelly in another. Swept and scrubbed, furnished with a rope bed, a thick corn-husk mattress, a washstand, a table, and chairs, it was more than adequate for his needs. Susannah slept much easier knowing that Connelly was out of the house.

So as not to tax his slowly returning strength, and also because, with his lack of farming knowledge, he was pretty generally useless, she assigned him to tasks that required education rather than brute strength. For years she had had the job of keeping track of contributions to and disbursements from the church, and it had grown to be a considerable burden. Not without some misgivings, she set Connelly to work at it in her stead. He proved to be adept with figures, even discovering a mistake in addition that she herself had made. Since the books were kept at the church, the job also took him away from the house. Relieved to have at least one time-consuming chore lifted from her shoulders, she made up her mind to delegate it to Connelly permanently, though it brought him in close contact with her father. But with Connelly's facility for changing his stripes to suit his audience, Susannah was confident that this posed no problem. Indeed, the Reverend Redmon seemed to enjoy their bound man's company and spent several mealtimes firing questions at him concerning the fine points of theology as practiced by the Church of England, of which Connelly had apparently been a member.

Watching her father's eyes sparkle as Connelly capped a particularly spirited argument with a Latin quotation that, as the girls had not been schooled in that language, only the two men could understand, Susannah had to smile. The Reverend Redmon obviously relished such discussions even when Connelly got the better of him. It occurred to Susannah then that their bound servant might have been just what the Reverend Redmon had needed: another man, an educated man, who could serve as a counterpoint to their previously feminine household. Certainly her father seemed much less ethereal these days than he had before Connelly had joined them.

Sunday morning came again, with its usual rush to get ready for church. The entire family attended, including Craddock and Ben and, for the first time as he had been deemed too weak the previous Sabbath, Connelly. Susannah thought Connelly might protest when informed of what was expected of him in the way of religious observance, but he did not.

What he did was present himself, promptly at seven in the morning, to drive the ladies of the family to church.

The Reverend Redmon had already gone ahead on Micah. Craddock and Ben would, as usual, follow in the buckboard. Susannah, Sarah Jane, Mandy, and Em always went by buggy, with Susannah driving. They liked to arrive early, so as to practice their music and because, as the minister's daughters, it was fitting that they should.

When Susannah stepped out onto the front porch, expecting that Craddock would bring the buggy around as he always did on Sunday morning, she was surprised to find Connelly leaning against the porch rail, waiting for them. She was clad in her best black poplin, with a crisp white lawn fichu covering her shoulders and pinned by a silver brooch at her breast. The dress was cut loosely through the bodice, with a full bell of a skirt, and Susannah considered it most appropriate for a spinster of her age to wear to church. A head-fitting white lawn cap with a small upstanding frill framing her face was tied beneath her chin. Her short sleeves were turned back to reveal the white frills of her chemise. Her one frivolity, transparent black lace mittens, covered her arms from her elbows to the middle of her palms. Her fingers were bare. This was the costume she usually wore to church, and always before she had been quite content with it. Now, with Connelly's eyes running over her from head to toe, she wished, for the first time that she could remember, that her dress was just a little more becoming. Maybe a softer color . . .

Connelly straightened away from the railing. All thoughts of her own attire vanished, quite eclipsed by her wonder at the splendor of his. Darcy, hitched to the buggy that waited before the porch, nickered a greeting when he set eyes on Susannah. Susannah's attention, however, was riveted on Connelly.

He was dressed in black breeches—not his old, disreputable ones but an altogether better-looking pair. He wore his own waistcoat of gold brocade that she had washed and mended, a white linen shirt, and a frock coat of dark blue linsey-woolsey. A neckcloth, slightly limp but perfectly serviceable, was tied in an elegant knot beneath his chin. Gray wool stockings covered his calves, and flat-soled, black leather shoes with small silver buckles were on his feet. His hair had been brushed straight back from his forehead and caught up with a black ribbon at his nape. In one hand he held a three-cornered black felt hat.

Except for the shoes, which had been made for Sunday best by the town cobbler and sent out along with a stout pair of work boots, his clothes were not new, Susannah knew, nor even his own. But as he put his hat on his head and came toward her, he looked so much the fine gentleman that she was momentarily shocked speechless.

"My goodness," she said when she could speak. "Where did you get all that?"

"Your father very obligingly made me free of your church's poor-box. A few things were a reasonable fit."

"My goodness," she said again, blinking. As her sisters spilled out onto the porch behind her, she firmly marshaled her wits, which, for a dreadful moment, seemed to have gone abegging.

"Why, Connelly, you look quite swooningly handsome!" This was said by Mandy, of course, as she brushed by Susannah to greet their bound man with a bewitching smile. Mandy had kept to the letter if not the spirit of their bargain, though she flirted with Connelly every time she laid eyes on him. But then, flirting to Mandy was as natural as breathing, and Susannah had seen to it that she had had no opportunity to be alone with the silver-tongued rogue. Now, with her auburn curls artfully framed by the upstanding poke of her straw bonnet and her gown of lavender and pink striped silk cut to show her slender figure to best advantage, Mandy was a vision. For a dreadful, shocking moment, as she watched Mandy smiling up at their bound man, Susannah suffered the first pang of jealousy she had ever felt in her life. So unprecedented was the emotion that it took her a moment to discern exactly what it was that made her stomach churn. Then it hit her—she was jealous, fiercely, greenly jealous, of her own dearly beloved little sister and their bound man!

"Why, thank you, Miss Mandy. And you look as beautiful as always. Tell me, do you ever get tired of men telling you that?" He was quite as bad about flirting as Mandy, as Susannah had discovered to her cost.

"Oh, no, never!" Mandy breathed, not one whit abashed by the scoundrel's blatant flattery. Susannah, fixing Connelly with a warning glare, caught Mandy's arm and turned her in the direction of the carriage.

"We must hurry, or we won't have time to practice that new song. Sarah Jane, Em, get in." Susannah mentally congratulated herself, so composed did she sound.

But Connelly, moving with lazy grace, somehow managed to reach the buggy before any of them.

"Miss Mandy?" With the merest lift of a smile that did strange things to Susannah's heart, Connelly held out his hand to her sister. It took Susannah only an instant to realize that he meant merely to hand Mandy into the buggy. But it was a very long instant, an instant in which, to her own dismay, her fingers instinctively clenched into fists.

"Why, thank you." Mandy dimpled at him, then put her hand in his. Setting one slender foot on the step, she gathered up her skirts with the same minx's trick she had employed once before to emphasize the shape of her behind and show more than was strictly proper of white-stockinged ankle and permitted Connelly to assist her into the rear seat.

Watching Connelly watch Mandy's backside with obvious appreciation, Susannah did a slow burn. Realizing that her fists were clenched, she had to make a conscious effort to relax her fingers.

"Who goes in next? Miss Emily?" Finally able to tear his eyes away from Mandy, Connelly turned and held out his hand to Emily, who had been staring at him goggle-eyed since she'd first emerged onto the porch. As he spoke to her, Em blushed almost as red as her hair, mumbled something, and then, apparently overcome with embarrassment, just touched her hand to his as she all but leaped up into the buggy. Her full skirt of lime-green cambric caught on the carriage wheel. For a second she seemed in danger of either falling flat on her face or ripping her dress. But Connelly, moving quickly, freed the skirt in time to prevent either catastrophe, and Em subsided, amidst thanks and more blushes, next to Mandy.

"Miss Sarah Jane? Will you sit in back or in front?" Connelly's smile was no warmer than was polite for Sarah Jane (certainly he did not smirk at her as he did Mandy!), but Sarah Jane's cheeks turned as pink as her dress as she looked up at him.

"I—usually sit in front." Sarah Jane's voice was soft and uncharacteristically shy. She had never been at ease around men in the way that Mandy was, but she had never been so missish as to practically whisper a reply to a simple inquiry, either. Connelly's effect on her sisters was embarrassing, and Susannah owned herself surprised at the lot of them. She would never act like such a fool over any man, be he ever so handsome. Not if it killed her to behave like a rational human being.

Sarah Jane gave Connelly her fingers, and allowed him to hand her into the front seat. Seeming almost to sigh with relief when he released her hand, she scooted over to make room for Susannah beside her.

"Miss Susannah?" Connelly turned devilish gray eyes on Susannah. Forewarned and forearmed, she lifted her chin and coolly laid her hand on his. She would not simper like Mandy, or blush like Em, or stammer like Sarah Jane. She would not make a fool of herself over him.

"Thank you." His skin was warm against her own, his fingers long and elegant and strong-looking beneath her small, capable, but certainly not beautiful hand. Susannah noted the swarthiness of his coloring compared to her own fairness and the faint roughening of black hairs just visible where his shirt ended at his wrist. Dismayed at the tenor of her thoughts, she forced her eyes away.

He handed her into the front seat, then released her fingers, just as was proper. Her skin might tingle from the contact, but no one would ever realize it from her demeanor, Susannah was determined. Taking a deep but, she hoped, unnoticed breath, she smoothed her skirts and sat. With a dismissive nod at Connelly, whom she expected to follow in the buckboard with Craddock and Ben, she reached to untie the reins.

"Slide over."

"What?" Not understanding, she looked down at him, frowning.

"Slide over. I'm driving."

"I always drive."

"In light of what happened at the Likens' place, and bearing in mind that Jed Likens may well be harboring a grudge against you because of it, your father decided that it wasn't safe for you and your sisters to wander about the countryside unprotected any longer. I volunteered to drive you about for as long as he felt it was necessary, and he agreed that it might be a good idea. So slide, if you please."

"You put the idea into Pa's head! He would never have come up with such a notion on his own!"

"You underestimate your father's concern for you, I fear. Slide."

Seated above him as she was, Susannah had the novel experience of looking down into his eyes. He was smiling, but it was clear from the set of his jaw that he was quite determined. Susannah realized that she had a choice— she could meekly slide over or she could precipitate a scene in front of her sisters that might reveal more of the strange intimacy that had sprung up between herself and Connelly than she wanted them to know. Either way, she was likely to find herself doing as he said.

Drat the man! What evil genie had been snickering over her shoulder the day she had bought him?

She slid over as close as she could get to Sarah Jane without making it obvious that she sought to put herself as far from Connelly as she could.

Connelly climbed up beside her and settled himself in the seat. Reaching for the reins, he finished untying them, then snapped them gently against Darcy's back. Watching critically as he turned horse and buggy in a direction that would point them the right way down the road, Susannah could find nothing to fault in his handling of the reins. She recalled that he had listed driving to an inch, whatever that meant, among the things he could do.

As the clean male scent of him filled her nostrils and she felt the brush of his arm against her own, Susannah gritted her teeth. The day was beautiful, the sun bright, and the gentle breeze no more than pleasantly warm as it caressed her face. It was Sunday morning, and her mind should have been occupied with godly thoughts.

But instead she could think of nothing but the man so close beside her and the very ungodly way he made her feel.

17

The church bell began to ring just as the buggy crested the rise that brought the First Baptist Church of Beaufort into view. It was a small, one-story building made of brick and tabby, whitewashed so that its walls took on a pearly glow where the sun's rays touched them through the sheltering trees. The spire was roofed with shiny new copper, and the bell that swung within had been shipped just the year before all the way from Philadelphia. Huge twisted oaks shaded the church itself, while the white and pink blossoms of weeping cherry and crabapple trees turned the tiny cemetery beside the church from a beacon of sorrow into an oasis of peaceful beauty. The trees' gentle perfume scented the air.

A semi-circular drive turned off the main road to provide access to the church. Connelly drove to the shallow steps that led up to the wide double doors, then pulled Darcy up. They were not as early as Susannah had hoped to be; several other conveyances were already hitched along the drive.

"Here we are, ladies." Connelly tied the reins to the knob and stepped down from the buggy. The absence of his lean body beside her made Susannah want to slump with relief. She had been tense for every single minute of the twenty minutes or so that he had sat beside her. Every syllable he uttered, every movement of his body, every breath he took added to the raw heat that had built until it was now practically sizzling her flesh. Never in her life had she thought to be so physically aware of a man. Her violent response to him shamed her.

Once on the ground, Connelly turned, clearly meaning to assist them down. But Emily and Sarah Jane, unaccustomed to such courtesies and, Susannah suspected, not much desiring a repeat of the awkward business at the house, descended to the ground on their own.

That left Mandy in the rear and Susannah in the front. Susannah would have descended along with Em and Sarah Jane had not her way been blocked by Connelly on one side and Sarah Jane on the other. Mandy scooted to the edge of the rear seat, one hand on the top of the front seat as she summoned Connelly with a come-hither smile. Really, where had the child learned such tricks? Susannah wondered, vexed. Not wanting to watch Connelly playing the gallant with her sister, Susannah slid along the seat toward the opposite side of the buggy, meaning to descend on her own. She was not about to compete with her little sister for their bound man's attention. Besides, she had absolutely no desire to feel his hand on hers again.

"Oh, no, you don't," Connelly said. Susannah heard him quite distinctly but had no idea what he meant until, to her consternation, he caught her around the waist and hauled her back toward him. A fleeting, embarrassed glimpse at her sister showed Mandy's eyes wide with surprise as Connelly lifted her bodily from the buggy with as little difficulty as if she had been a small child. Susannah was flushing when he set her on her feet, conscious of the tightness of his grip and the gleam in his eyes and Mandy's astonished gaze.

For what seemed like a very long while he held her so, looking down at her with that expression that was not quite a smile in his eyes. Fortunately, he had swung her around so that his back blocked Mandy's view of both their faces, because Susannah was sure she must be beet red.

"Will you please let me go?" she hissed, horribly conscious of their audience, when he made no immediate move to release her.

"Ian," he said softly. "Will you please let me go, Ian?"

Sarah Jane and Em, already walking up the steps, glanced around to see if their sisters were following. Mandy was still in the buggy, probably curious as a cat and put out as well. The sound of a new set of wheels scrunching over the drive alerted Susannah to the arrival of another vehicle. He had to let her go at once, and she could not make a scene to secure her release. What a scandal she would cause if she did!

"Will you please let me go, Ian?" The words were forced through her teeth, though a slight, polite smile was pinned to her lips for the benefit of any onlookers. Summoning that smile was as difficult as anything Susannah had ever done. The self-satisfied smile that curved his lips and lit his gray eyes as she succumbed to his blackmail made her want to hit him. But when she identified the newcomer by his booming voice, she was heartily glad that she had held rein on her temper.

"Morning, Miss Susannah, Miss Sarah Jane, Miss Emily! Is that you there in that buggy, Miss Amanda? You just wait where you are a minute, and I'll come get you down. No need to be troubling that gentleman there." Hiram Greer's greeting made Susannah stiffen. Ian's—no, Connelly's, she would not let him coerce her into thinking of him by his given name!—hands dropped away from her waist. They both turned at the same time to watch

Hiram Greer tenderly assist a tiny, wizened old woman clad from head to toe in flowing black to alight from the carriage drawn up behind their own.

"It's good to see you, Mrs. Greer," Susannah said with as much poise as she could muster. Keeping her smile firmly in place, she moved to greet Greer's mother. "I'm glad to see that you felt well enough to come to church this morning. We've missed you."

In the meantime, Greer hurried to the buggy where Mandy still sat and reached up to hand her down with an extravagant compliment, the exact nature of which escaped Susannah's ear. His next words, however, captured her full attention.

"Name's Hiram Greer," he said, and Susannah turned in time to see him hold out his hand to Ian—no, Connelly. For an amazed moment, she gaped, and then she realized that the change in their bound man's appearance was so remarkable that Greer didn't recognize him.

"Excuse me for just a minute, Mrs. Greer," she mumbled and practically ran the few paces necessary to reach the two men, who stood face to face with Greer's outstretched hand still waiting between them. Greer, clad in garments of the finest material that had been tailor-made for him, looked almost slovenly next to the other man in his pieced-together raiment. Much of the difference had to do with Greer's stocky build and florid complexion, which put him at a marked disadvantage when compared with Ian's lean height and the stark beauty of his face.

"Ian," she began nervously, for his expression as he looked at Greer was not reassuring. Realizing what she had said and mentally kicking herself for the slip, she tacked on, "Connelly. Ian Connelly, you remember Hiram Greer."

"I do." He nodded curtly. Greer, his face slowly reddening, dropped his hand.

"Why, you must remember our bound man, Mr. Greer," Mandy said carelessly, hooking her hand in the crook of Greer's elbow and tugging him toward the church steps. "You advised my sister against buying him, did you not? But I must tell you, he's become almost one of the family. Susannah quite dotes on him."

"Mandy!" But Susannah bit back the rest of her protest, and no one save the man standing beside her heard. He looked down at her, his expression hard to decipher.

"Your lovely little sister's not used to playing second fiddle to anyone, is she? She seems to have gotten her nose put out of joint because I prefer you to her." He didn't sound as if the prospect of Mandy's displeasure disturbed him overmuch. As Susannah absorbed exactly what it was that he had said, her eyes widened. Did he mean it? He smiled down at her, a teasing grin that answered her question as well as any words: of course not! Like Mandy, the blackguard would flirt with a post.

"Miss Redmon!" An imperious voice caused Susannah to glance around. Mrs. Greer had reached the foot of the steps and was gesturing impatiently. "Give me your arm! My legs aren't as steady as they could be."

"I'm coming," Susannah replied and turned to do so.

"Susannah." Harried, she glanced back to discover a faint, disturbing gleam in her bound man's eyes as they rested on her face. "I like the way my name sounds when you say it in your pretty voice. Nobody's ever called me Ian quite the way you do."

To Susannah's confusion, the gleam intensified, and the teasing nature of his grin changed into something entirely sensual. His expression conjured up images of hot, sweaty bodies and carnal love. Horrified, Susannah immediately banished such thoughts. Flushing to the roots of her hair, as much at her own wicked imagination as at his words, Susannah turned her back on the teasing devil and hurried to old Mrs. Greer's side.

The morning church service lasted till noon, the afternoon service till six. Not everyone stayed for both sessions, but the Redmon family had no choice. By the time they arrived home, it was dusk. Susannah was hoarse from singing and her fingers were sore from playing the clavichord, but she felt cleansed, as she always did after a day spent in the house of the Lord.

Ian, beside her, was silent, and she thought that so much unaccustomed praying might have tired him out. Her sisters were quiet too, each in her own way. Sarah Jane looked uplifted, Emily bored, and Mandy out of sorts. Susannah sighed inwardly as the buggy rocked to a halt, and she glanced around to get a glimpse of Mandy's pouty face. Trouble lay ahead from that quarter, Susannah feared.

Tired or not, Ian was quicker at descending than the girls. He handed out Susannah first—she had decided that it was best just to accept the courtesy and thus not afford him the opportunity for any more embarrassing displays—then Sarah Jane, Mandy, and Em. Mandy didn't even smile at him this time, but hurried on into the house. Susannah, following her sisters, braced herself for a confrontation or, alternatively, an evening spent enduring Mandy in a fit of the sulks. But Mandy, pleading a headache, took herself up to her room immediately after she entered the house, leaving the dishing up of supper and the other evening chores to her sisters. Susannah, for one, did the extra work willingly. Mandy in a temper was a complication that she would just as soon not have to deal with that evening.

It was long after supper when the knock on the door came. The girls were already abovestairs, and her father, exhausted by a long day of preaching, was asleep. Susannah was just setting aside the dough to rise for the morning's bread before going up herself. But she knew what the knock presaged, and she was already resigning herself to the inevitable when she opened the door.

This time it was Seamus O'Brien who stood there, hat in hand. He was the father of Ben's sweetheart Maria, and there was a hangdog quality about him as he stood there shuffling from foot to foot that made Susannah's heart go out to him, tired though she was.

"What can I do for you, Mr. O'Brien?" she asked quietly.

" 'Tis Mary." Mary was his wife. "Her stomach's paining her something fierce. Can you come?"

Mary O'Brien had been suffering from severe stomach cramps for more than a year. Seamus had even gone so far as to get a doctor to her, but the doctor had found nothing wrong with her and gone away. As money was tight, he had not been sent for again. Instead, Susannah would go, perhaps once a month, though it seemed to be more frequently of late, to sit with Mary and do what she could to ease her until, once again, the pains went away.

The source of the pain was a mystery, though Susannah had begun to suspect that Mary was seriously ill. But there was little she could do but offer comfort to the woman and her family. Such things as life and death were in the hands of the Lord.

"I'll get my case," Susannah said, glad she had not undressed. Seamus was waiting for her when she emerged moments later, a shawl thrown over her head. Together they hitched Darcy to the buggy and headed down the road toward his house.

When she arrived, she shooed Maria, who was the oldest daughter and a very nice girl for all she made Ben forget whether he was on his head or his heels, and the rest of the children off to bed. Seamus went on about his late evening chores, then sat in a chair before the fire, reading the Bible aloud to his wife. Susannah, meanwhile, eased Mary as best she could with herbs and hot moist towels and comforting pats, until at last the woman fell asleep. From experience, Susannah knew that that meant the worst of the pain was over for a few weeks. She was free to seek out her own bed and get what sleep she could.

Which would be, at most, perhaps four hours, Susannah estimated as she wearily refused a squawking chicken pressed on her by a volubly grateful Seamus as payment and climbed up into the buggy. Darcy, used to such midnight outings, was very patient and had occupied the time since she had left him hitched in front of the house by cropping all the grass he could reach. Now, knowing that they headed for his barn, he shook his head so that the harness rattled and set off for home at a brisk trot.

It was perhaps one o'clock in the morning. All the world seemed to sleep under the mantle of darkness. Only the singing of crickets and the occasional hoarse cry of a lonesome bullfrog marred the quiet. Susannah, wanting to hurry along home, clucked to Darcy as he slowed a bit, pricking up his ears at something along the roadside that she could not see. Probably a raccoon, or even a bit of blowing bush, though Darcy was not ordinarily skittish. Still, just being out and about in the dark seemed to spook horses as well as humans. As often as she was out alone in the middle of the night, she never quite got used to the isolation of it. She was a grown woman, and one moreover who prided herself on being as practical and level-headed as they came. Certainly she didn't believe in haunts or piskies or evil spirits that arose to flit about the world by moonlight. But still, with the moon floating like a pale ghost high overhead and the tips of the pines that lined the road swaying in homage to the wind that blew gray wisps of clouds across the sky, it was easy to imagine any number of things. For example, that she was not alone. . . .

A bullfrog erupted with its characteristic bellowing "jug o'rum!" nearly under Darcy's hooves. The horse, who ordinarily would have ignored such a familiar disturbance, danced a little. Susannah, her own nerves tightening, pulled steadyingly on the reins.

"What the devil was that sound?"

The gravelly voice, coming as it did seemingly out of nowhere, startled Susannah so much that she screamed and nearly lost her hold on the reins.

18

Darcy, upset at the commotion, nickered and broke into a canter. Fortunately Susannah recovered both her wits and her reins in time to pull him in before he got completely out of control. As the horse dropped back down to a trot and she got her breathing under control, Susannah slanted a furious glance into the back seat at Ian. She had recognized his voice almost at once, though the sheer unexpectedness of hearing it under such circumstances had thrown her off for a vital, scary instant.

"You scared the living daylights out of me! What do you think you're doing, hiding away in the back of my buggy in the middle of the night? How did you get there, anyway?"

"I wasn't hiding. I stretched out on the back seat while I was waiting for you, and I must have fallen asleep. As to how I got here, I heard you set out from the barn and followed you. On foot, I might add. 'Twas a goodly walk, and I don't appreciate having to make it. I told you this morning that I'd be driving you wherever you needed to go."

"That's ridiculous!"

"You've got no business driving around by yourself, particularly at night. I can't believe nothing's happened to you yet."

Susannah snorted. "What in the world do you suppose could happen to me around here? The worst would be if Darcy threw a shoe and I had to walk home."

"The worst would be if some piece of slime like Jed Likens decided to catch you alone and teach you a lesson. Or any man, coming upon a woman out by herself in the middle of the night, might decide to take advantage of the opportunity. You're setting yourself up to be raped, if not murdered."

"Jed Likens is all talk. He's not going to hurt me! He wouldn't dare, for one thing. Nobody around here would do something like that. Why, I've been driving around by myself for years and never had a bit of trouble."

"You've been lucky, is all. As long as I'm around, I'll drive you. Particularly at night. There's no use even arguing about it, because I mean what I say."

Hampered by having to conduct the conversation over her shoulder while she drove, it was difficult to express the true degree of her indignation at his high-handedness. Susannah pulled Darcy up, tied the reins, and slewed around to glare at him. The moonlight washed over the front seat, illuminating her as clearly as if it had been day. But the buggy's leather top blocked most of the light from reaching the back seat. Ian's face was in deep shadow, though she had no trouble making out the sheer bulk of the man or the gleam of his eyes.

"You forget yourself, Connelly." She called him that quite deliberately and with just a shade of unnecessary emphasis. "I am the mistress here. You are the servant. You do as I say, not the other way around."

There was a brief, pregnant silence. He folded both arms along the top of her seat and leaned toward her. The action was almost menacing, and it was all Susannah could do to stop herself from drawing instinctively away. She stayed where she was through sheer force of will, chin up, eyes defiant, though it meant that his face was only a few inches from hers when he spoke at last.

"I'm tired, because it's real late and I haven't been to bed yet. My feet hurt from following you for miles over a damned bad road in shoes that I haven't had a chance to break in. My knees hurt too, from kneeling in your church most of the day. I'm hungry, and I'm not feeling any too cheerful as a result of all that. So if you mean to argue with me tonight, be warned that you do it at your peril."

"I am not arguing with you," she said coldly, turning her back on him and reaching to untie the reins. "I am stating a fact. One that you would do well to remember. Now, if you will kindly sit back and close your mouth, I'll take us home."

"Susannah," he said, "I'll drive."

"No," she said, "I will. And it's *Miss* Susannah, as you know very well."

He said nothing but stepped down from the buggy. Obviously he meant to settle the discussion by physically taking possession of the reins. He looked very tall and leanly muscular, standing beside her in the road with one hand on the curved frontispiece, ready to haul himself back aboard, only this time in her seat. His black felt hat was pushed to the back of his head, and his coat had apparently been left at home. The dull gold of his waistcoat shimmered in the moonlight. So did the icy gray of his eyes in that devilishly handsome face.

He put one foot on the step and started to heave himself up. Susannah, reins in hand, snapped them smartly against the horse's back.

Unaccustomed to such treatment, Darcy shot forward. The buggy jolted,

Susannah's head snapped back, and Ian fell from the buggy to land with an audible thud on his rump in the road.

Served him right! Gloating, Susannah glanced back at him, grinned, and waved, then kept Darcy at a smart pace as she headed for home.

As soon as she reached the barn, she roused Ben from the loft to put Darcy and the buggy away. She headed for the house as fast as her feet would take her. Her one fear was that Ian would reach home before she was safely inside. He would be in a rage, she knew, and, brave as she was feeling, she still wasn't quite foolish enough to want to face him until he had had a few hours to cool down.

But of course, from where he had exited the buggy it was quite a long walk home.

Grinning at the thought of him trudging along on his supposedly tender feet, proud of herself for having gotten the better of him and no longer very sleepy at all, Susannah went up to bed.

Half an hour later, just as her lids were beginning to droop, a scraping noise and then a soft thump roused her to full consciousness. Startled, she sat bolt upright in her bed. A series of small stealthy creaks set her heart pounding. Something, or someone, was moving across the roof of the rear porch toward her window.

Her window was open, as it always was in hot weather. The simple muslin curtains billowed on the breeze. The inky sky beyond the window was bright with stars, alive with scuttling clouds—and then, so abruptly that she had to blink to make sure she wasn't imagining things, a tall, dark shadow blocked her view of the night.

The porch roof, only one story high, ran beneath her window. Someone was using it to gain access to her bedchamber.

Ian! Susannah knew who it was even before he threw one long leg over the sill and slid inside.

"What are you doing in here? Get out of my room!" she whispered fiercely, clutching the bedcoverings around her neck and glaring at him as he stalked toward her.

"Oh, no," he said, his voice vibrating with fury for all its menacing hush. "Not just yet."

He reached down, yanked the bedclothes out of her grasp, and threw them aside. Though it was dark in the room, it was not so dark as to hide her deshabille from his gaze. Pale moonlight mottled the bed, lending Susannah's prim white nightgown a translucence she was sure it had not possessed earlier. Glancing down at herself in horror as his eyes ran assessingly over her from her high, frilled neckline to the tips of her small bare toes, Susannah felt as exposed as if she had been naked. With a soft cry of mingled anger and protest, she scrambled to draw her legs beneath her. Crouching in the center of the feather mattress, her arms clamped over her breasts, she turned her face up to his. The long rope of her hair, braided for sleeping, spilled down over one shoulder. Tawny, curling tendrils formed a halo around her face. Her wide mouth was clamped into a straight, angry line. Her eyes blazed a bright green-gold.

"If you dare . . ." she began furiously.

"Oh, I dare," he said, reaching out to catch her by the elbows and haul her up and over until she was kneeling on the edge of the mattress and he was looming threateningly above her, his face just inches from her own. "Make no mistake about that, Susannah. I dare."

"Take your hands off me!" Her whisper was shrill with outrage. "And it's *Miss* Susannah!"

He laughed. The sound was soft, unpleasant. "I don't like being knocked on my ass in the dirt, *Miss* Susannah. I don't like being left in the middle of the night to walk three miles home over a pitiful excuse for a road. And I especially don't like having a prim little minister's daughter look down her nose at me every time I turn around. That I don't like at all."

"If you don't leave my room this instant, I'll scream." The depth of his fury should have frightened her. But Susannah was angry herself, and when she got angry, as her family liked to say, Susannah didn't fear the devil himself.

"Scream, then. Go ahead."

He had her there. She wouldn't scream, and he knew it. The very idea of having her family discover him in her bedroom, with all the explanations that would entail, was enough to make her cringe.

"No?" His voice was soft, taunting. "I didn't think so."

His hands tightened around her arms, and he pulled her up against him. Her breasts pressed against his chest. Her belly brushed his abdomen. Her thighs lay against his. Heat engorged her body, flushing her skin, setting her blood to boiling. The sheer shock of it saved her. She jerked back from him as convulsively as if he'd been a poisonous snake.

"Let me go! Connelly, I'm warning you!" It was a furious whisper.

She had managed to put some six inches between their bodies, though she remained all too blindingly conscious of the hard, warm length of him so near. Her head was thrown back so that she might meet his gaze head on. His hands remained tight about her arms.

"I'm getting bloody tired of you calling me Connelly in that haughty little way you have, too. You've ruled the roost around here for far too long, I'm thinking. Now the time's come to pay the piper."

"Meaning you?" Her voice was scathing. His eyes narrowed, and then one corner of his mouth moved upward in a way that Susannah misliked.

"Meaning me." So quickly that Susannah hadn't time to guess what he meant to do, his hands moved up to encircle her throat. He held her gently but implacably, his palms a high, warm collar while his thumbs tilted up her chin.

"My name's Ian, Susannah. This time I'll make damned sure that you don't forget it."

Then, even as Susannah reached up to clutch his wrists, tugging frantically in an effort to free herself before what she longed for and yet dreaded more than anything else in the world could happen, his mouth came down on hers.

19

Just as Susannah had feared, that kiss changed everything. Instead of punishing her, it was soft and warm, but insistent. His mouth moved over hers, brushing against her lips, nibbling at the corners of her mouth.

Before it could go any further, she tried to draw back.

"Ian," she began shakily, pulling her mouth free.

"That's right, Ian," he said with satisfaction and kissed her again.

At this second touch of his mouth on hers, Susannah's body caught fire. Her hands, which had been tugging halfheartedly at his, stilled and curled around his wrists. Her lids fluttered down. Her heart speeded up, sending her blood pounding in a pagan rhythm that was foreign to anything she had ever experienced. His hands moved to cradle the base of her skull beneath the heavy braid, and her head lolled back against his hands. Her neck had suddenly grown too weak with wanting to support its weight.

"Susannah. Open your mouth for me, Susannah." His whisper was hoarse, raspy. His fingertips stroked the tender skin at the nape of her neck. His mouth brushed gently over her lips.

Susannah trembled and obediently opened her mouth. Never in her life had she expected to feel the way he was making her feel—as if she were on fire, her blood boiling in her veins, her skin searing all the way down to her toes from no more than the soft touch of his mouth. Vaguely she remembered the rough, crude way he had invaded her mouth before. Even that less than lover-like kiss had set off flares of wanting in the most secret regions of her body. But when she parted her lips this time and his tongue slid inside, there was nothing rough or crude about this taking of her mouth.

His hands still cradling her head, he slanted his mouth over hers, touching her tongue with his, stroking her teeth and the roof of her mouth. She must have made a slight movement, or a sound, because suddenly the hands holding her head went rigid and his kiss grew fiercely insistent. Before Susannah could go limp with wanting or cry out with need or do any one of the dozen or so other things that her burning body seemed to want to do, he withdrew his mouth from hers. Her lids lifted, and she blinked, dizzy. His eyes seemed to glow with a reflection of her own heat as they gleamed down at her. Restlessly his thumbs stroked the soft underside of her chin.

"Oh, my goodness," she whispered, her eyes moving down from his to focus on that beautiful, sensuously curving mouth.

Her words surprised a laugh out of him. It sounded curiously shaken, and when she glanced up to meet his eyes she saw that they were not laughing at all, but ablaze.

"I love the way you talk," he said, and then, as if he could not help himself, his mouth came down on hers again. This time he did not have to tell her to open her mouth. She parted her lips for him instantly, sighing into his mouth and leaning her weight full against him. Instantly her breasts, pressed against the unyielding strength of his chest, swelled, and her nipples hardened almost painfully. Her thighs, resting against the taut muscles of his, contracted. And her secret place made contact with a curious bulge in the front of his breeches that in a matter of seconds grew both enormous and rocklike. Spinster that she was, she still knew enough about men to recognize what was happening to him. The knowledge made her quake.

"Susannah." Her name on his lips was a mere breath of sound, muttered into her mouth. He slid his hands down her back, stroking her shoulders and the length of her spine through the thin cotton nightgown. His arms wrapped around her waist, pulling her tight against him so that she could feel every muscle and sinew of his hard body pressing against her through their clothes. Susannah, knowing with the one tiny part of her mind that was still capable of rational thought that what she was about to do was hideously wrong, prelude to a sin that would haunt her forever, nonetheless lifted her arms to wrap around his neck and kissed him back.

At her sudden fierce response he stiffened, and then his kiss changed. His lips grew harder, more demanding, his tongue urgent in its forays into her mouth. With a strange growling sound that emerged from somewhere deep in his throat, he bent her backward over his arm. One hand came up to crush her breast. Her nipple pressed into his palm, pebble-hard.

Susannah whimpered, not with pain or fear but with acute wanting. She needed him, needed him as desperately as ever a starving man needed food or a thirsty one, water. Her body ached for him, trembled for him, cried out for him. The very savageness of his embrace, where before he had been gentle, told her that, surprising as it seemed, he burned for her too.

When he reached down, scrabbling for the hem of her nightgown to draw it up from the back, she made no protest but even undid the single button at her neck so that he could pull it over her head and throw it aside. Then, for just a moment as she knelt naked before him, the soft breeze from the open window caressing her skin, she was conscious of a dreadful moment of doubt. But the doubt was not about whether she should lie with him, in direct violation of every tenet of morality she had ever believed or been taught. She had already made her decision about that, maybe as long ago as when he had pulled her into bed with him that night in the parlor. The doubt was about whether he would look at her, naked, and find her wanting. If he should turn away from her now for such a reason, she would be forever shattered.

His eyes were on her, touching her everywhere. Instinctively Susannah sank back on her heels and crossed her arms in front of her body in the classic pose of exposed femininity, one arm shielding her breasts, the other at the juncture of her thighs. Her wariness shone from her eyes as they lifted to his face. He paid no heed to her concern but reached down to gently catch both her hands and pull them wide.

Susannah did not fight him. She had too much pride for that. In that instant in which she hovered between heaven and hell, she seemed to see her own reflection in his eyes. Plain square face, unruly curling hair confined in a plait as thick as his wrist, obstinate chin tilted defiantly up. Creamy pale skin, neck and shoulders acceptably attractive, with her collarbone showing through her skin and a frantic pulse beating in the shadowed hollow of her throat. Breasts that, like her hair, were the bane of her existence, too round, too full, almost the size of ripe cantaloupes and tipped with distended, darkened nipples half as long as her little finger. Below them her waist, its ridiculously small measurement only making her breasts seem larger in contrast. Then the lush swell of her hips, like her breasts emphasized by the marked indention of her waist. The soft curve of her belly, with its small dark navel, dipping down to the sable triangle of curls where her legs met. Her legs themselves, milky-skinned and smooth.

Looking up at him, at the starkly handsome, dark angel's face that legions of women before her had certainly swooned over, Susannah acknowledged herself for what she was—a plain woman, well past the first blush of youth, who was so lacking in attractiveness that she had never even had a beau. Her body was overwhelmingly ripe, so much so that, in the years before she had learned to hide it, it had elicited shocked stares whenever she had ventured out without a cloak. Her face was as unremarkable as a cabbage.

She waited, trembling, for him to turn away in disgust. Or, worse than that, to say something very, very kind as he sought to spare both himself and her feelings.

His eyes had grown very dark as they lingered on her breasts. By the time they moved over the rest of her body, then lifted to meet her eyes, they were almost as black as the night outside.

"By God, you're beautiful," he said in a harsh, grating voice that she could just barely hear. "But then, I knew you would be."

"Beautiful? Me?" Dumbfounded, she looked up at him suspiciously. His hands still held hers. He squeezed her fingers, then released them, a curious crooked smile twisting his mouth.

"Gorgeous," he said, his hands going to his neckcloth. With a few deft motions he untied it and tossed it on the floor.

"Exquisite," he added, unbuttoning the buttons she had so recently reattached to his waistcoat, then sending that garment flying as well.

"Breathtaking." He shrugged out of his shirt.

"Sublime." He hopped from foot to foot as he pulled off his shoes.

"Sublime? Oh, Ian! You're teasing me!" Not knowing whether to laugh or cry, Susannah wrapped her arms around herself and rocked back and forth. Bare now except for his breeches and the white swathe of bandages around his chest, he peeled off his stockings. His wide shoulders were thick with muscle, his broad chest shadowed with curling black hair. His abdomen was ridged and hard-looking, his waist and hips narrow. Then, as his hands moved to the buttons on his breeches, Susannah averted her eyes. The rest of his person must go unassessed.

"Teasing you?" He sat down beside her on the bed, one arm sliding around her back. In the one brief, sidelong glance she managed before embarrassment overcame her, Susannah saw that he was naked. Magnificently naked . . .

"No, Susannah, I am not teasing you," he whispered as he pressed a tiny, stirring kiss to the pulse point just below her ear. His hand was doing something behind her back. As her hair loosened, aided by his fingers threading through the thick mass, she realized that he had untied the ribbon that bound her braid. Surrounded by a tawny cape of cascading curls, she watched as he pulled back a little to run his eyes over her. She blushed, hotly, one hand moving to cling to his where it rested on her waist, but she did not try to cover herself. The glitter in his eyes told her that he wanted her. Whether he was teasing or not, that glitter was enough for her.

His hand came up to cup and weigh a breast. His thumb ran over her nipple. Susannah caught her breath as his touch shot through her body like a lightning bolt. Her nipple hardened embarrassingly under his hand.

"Beautiful," he said thickly, watching. His hand tightened on her waist, the hand that had been caressing her breast rose to tip up her chin, and he was kissing her again.

She loved the way he kissed. Intoxicated, Susannah's head fell back. Her arms encircled his neck. A ribbon bound his hair, too, at his nape. Susannah felt indescribably wanton as she tugged it free and then slid her fingers into his crisp black hair. He lowered her to the mattress, then came down beside her so that she lay flat on her back with him on his side looming over her. Susannah's eyes closed as he pressed hot kisses to her lids, her cheeks, her temples. Trembling, her mind emptied of everything except the raw need of her own body that was threatening now to rage out of control. As his hands stroked over her breasts and belly and thighs, she arched her back. His touch was almost unbearably gentle against her overheated skin. Deep inside her, in the darkest, most secret regions of her heart, she had yearned for this—a man to love her, a man to put his hands on her breasts, and kiss her mouth, and initiate her into the secrets of carnal love.

How she had hungered after carnal love—and Ian! They were now inextricably bound together in her mind. Whatever came of this night's work—and Susannah refused to think about that until the morrow—she would be unrepentant. What she and he were doing might be a sin, but to go to her grave without ever experiencing this glorious bursting passion would be an even greater one.

His fingers wandered over her belly, explored her navel, found the soft nest of dark brown curls. Susannah went perfectly still for an instant as he delved between her thighs. He touched the scalding center of her, and she cried out.

Immediately his other hand was on the back of her head, pressing her face into his shoulder.

"Shhh," he whispered. Her mouth opened against his skin and, half-mad with wanting him, she bit down on the bunched muscle of his shoulder. He went momentarily rigid.

"Damn," he said. "Ah, damn."

She didn't even need his knee sliding between her own to spread her legs wide. Reacting out of an instinct older than time, she opened to him like a flower. Both his legs were between hers, and she could feel the burning hardness of him against her soft inner thigh. He was panting, his breaths ragged in her ear, and his fingers as he slid his hand down to stroke the hot, damp flesh between her legs seemed to tremble.

Afraid she might hurt him, Susannah stopped biting his shoulder and instead pressed quavering, clinging kisses to the place where his neck and shoulder joined.

"Damn," he said again. Sounding as if he was having to force the words out, he muttered, "This might hurt. I meant to take more time. . . ."

Even as he groaned the warning into her ear, he was positioning himself above her. The hand that had been driving her crazy slid behind her to close over her rump, and he squeezed. Susannah gasped, arching up against him as he first prodded her with his shaft, then eased himself inside.

It didn't hurt. That was her first giddy thought. It didn't hurt, though it seemed as if he might be stretching her a bit.

Instead it felt wonderful, marvelous, better than anything she could have imagined, so good that she couldn't lie still beneath him but had to . . .

"Ian! Oh! Ian!" Her nails dug into his shoulders, and her pained cry was muffled against his chest as, with a single hard shove, he broke through her maidenhead and thrust himself deep inside her.

20

"It's over. The hard part's over." Ian kissed her ear.

Susannah could feel his arms trembling with the effort of holding himself still. He was wedged deep inside her, his big body hunched over hers, which had gone stiff with surprise at the sudden sharp pain of his invasion. She had known that, for a female, the loss of virginity could be excruciating. Whenever a group of women got together, at church or at social gatherings or on someone's porch, the pain of mating and childbirth were popular topics. So she had known—but not known.

Imagination was no substitute for reality.

Already the pain was fading, to be replaced by no more than a slight soreness. She grew more and more aware of her bent, spread knees and his body lying between them, of his arms shaking as they wrapped her close to his chest, of the slight abrasion of his stubbled cheek pressing into her neck and the heat and ragged pant of his breathing in her ear. He was inside her, very much inside her. She could feel the huge swollen length of him filling her.

This, then, was carnal love.

Her arms slid around his neck, and she kissed the sandpapery side of his cheek.

He gave a gasp as if he were dying. His arms tightened around her body until she thought the breath must be forced from her lungs. Pressing fierce, hot kisses into the side of her neck, he began to move his hips.

For a moment, just a moment as he pulled out and then drove deep again, Susannah lay as if frozen. Then, as he repeated the process and repeated it again, fiercely, scalding bursts of pleasure washed over her in waves. What he was doing to her was beyond anything she had ever imagined, far more earthy and intimate and shocking. It was every dark, shameful facet of the tales from the marriage bed she had heard by way of whisper and innuendo for years brought to life, and worse. Yet she gloried in it. If that meant there was something morally wrong with her, then so be it. For the moment at least, she could only cling to the hard male shoulders that bunched and strained above her, and rejoice.

He kissed her mouth hotly, slid his lips down her throat, over her shoulder bone, up the soft slope of her right breast—and then closed his mouth, very gently, around her nipple and began to suck.

Susannah moaned, arching her back as ecstasy exploded within her. At her response he shivered, tightening his grip on her. Then, in a quick series of convulsive heaves, he thrust into her again and again and again.

"Oh, God!" With that bit of blasphemy on his lips, he drove deep inside her one final time, then shuddered and went still.

Later, a long time later, he drew in a deep, shaken breath, lifted his head from its pillow on her shoulder, pressed a quick kiss to her mouth, and rolled off her. Susannah should have been relieved to be free of the hot, damp weight of him. But she was not. She felt both vulnerable and bereft, and more naked than she ever had felt in her life.

Glancing sideways, she saw that he lay sprawled on his back with his arms flung over his head, seemingly unconcerned about what he exposed. Unable to help herself, she dared a quick glance down his body, then, blushing scarlet, promptly averted her eyes. If being blatantly, unconcernedly nude in her presence did not disturb him—and it certainly didn't appear to—then his nudity shouldn't bother her, either, not after the unbelievable intimacies they had shared.

But it did. She couldn't help it, but it did.

His eyes were closed, and she thanked the Lord for that. Moving stealthily, she rolled off the edge of the bed, found her nightgown on the floor, and pulled it over her head. Her body was sticky with his sweat and her own, and what she really craved more than anything else at that moment was a bath. But that would have to wait until she was alone. More important at the moment was that she cover herself. She did not think she could face him otherwise.

With the savage pleasure of their coupling already fading into memory, she found herself growing increasingly uneasy. What did one say to a man after such an experience? More to the point, what did she, Susannah Redmon, plain spinster daughter of a minister, say to Ian Connelly, her sinfully handsome bound man, after he had just finished deflowering her with her full consent and cooperation in her own bed?

She could not call him Connelly after this or step back into the role of mistress to his servant. Not that she had ever really managed to assume that position with him, of course. He was, in his own way, as obstinate and ornery as she was herself, and he had been distinctly unservile from the first moment she had laid eyes on him.

A soft snore from the bed drew her gaze back to him. Disbelievingly, she realized that he had fallen asleep. Relieved not to have to deal with him until she had had time to compose herself and yet oddly affronted that he could just fall asleep after so momentous an event, she swept her eyes over him, conscious of a craven urge just to let him lie. She could dress and slip down to the kitchen and not have to deal with him at all. But of course she could not do that. The sky outside the window was already brightening. Soon it would be dawn, and the household would be up and about.

She could not let their bound man be found naked and snoring in her bed.

"Ian." Susannah leaned over him, prodded his shoulder. Her touch was tentative, almost shy, and it did no good whatsoever. The insensitive lout snored on. She prodded him harder, then shoved his shoulder good and proper with the flat of her hand. His snore suspended in mid-rattle. "Ian, wake up!"

Without warning his eyes opened, and he blinked as if he could not quite remember where he was. Then, discovering Susannah leaning over him, his mouth curved into a slow, sensual smile.

"You were worth waiting for. I knew you would be," he said, or at least that was what she thought he said, though the words didn't make much sense. She guessed he must still be half asleep. "Come back to bed."

He reached up and caught her hand. Susannah tugged it free.

"No, I . . ."

To her consternation, one of the roosters suddenly crowed outside her window. A second rooster followed suit. Unbelievable as it seemed, it was dawn already, and her father and sisters would be stirring.

"You have to go," she said urgently, turning away from him to snatch his clothes from the floor and then almost throwing them at him. "Hurry!"

He sat up, shaking his head and running his fingers through his hair as he ignored the garments that littered the bed around him. "Listen, Susannah, I . . ."

"Hush!" Frowning, putting a finger to her lips, Susannah moved to stand before the door. There was no lock on it, because there had never, until now, been a need for one. Though she was customarily the first one up, it was not inconceivable that one of her sisters, missing the usual sounds of Susannah dressing and going downstairs to start breakfast, might rise and investigate. At the thought of being discovered in such a fix by Sarah Jane or Mandy or Em, or, God forbid, her father, Susannah's blood ran cold.

Seeing her agitation, Ian grimaced but heaved himself off the bed and began to dress. Susannah had never watched a man clothe himself before, and for all her anxiety she was fascinated. It was quick work, as he had far fewer garments to concern himself with than did she or any other woman of her acquaintance. In a matter of minutes he was standing on one leg and then the other as he pulled on his shoes, and then he shrugged into his waistcoat. He draped his neckcloth around his neck, and his hair ribbon was tucked into a pocket.

Decent now, he came toward her, moving quietly but purposefully, till he stood before her. There was nowhere Susannah could go to escape him, though the urge to run was strong in her. It was all she could do to look at him, knowing the knowledge of the few hours just past was there in his eyes. Only in moments like these, when she stood so close to him, did she remember how very tall he was in comparison with herself. She tilted up her chin, trying to quell the sudden renegade quickening in her loins as her eyes moved over his wide chest, barely clad in the opened shirt and unbuttoned waistcoat, then slid past his broad shoulders to his face. Impossible to believe that she had lain naked with him less than half an hour before. The crisp chest hair that curled over the edge of his bandage had rubbed over her naked breasts; she had dug her fingers into those hard-muscled shoulders, and, unbelievably, bitten them. And his mouth—had she really passionately kissed that beautiful mouth?

When her gaze finally met his she was scarlet. Amusement twinkled at her from his gray eyes, though he was too wise to risk a smile.

A sound from the hall outside the door made her stiffen. She glanced around in alarm.

"I'm going," he whispered, sounding resigned. Before she realized what he meant to do, he cupped his hands around her face and bent his head to kiss her mouth. His kiss was quick, hard, and unexpectedly passionate. Susannah shivered as her hands rose to grip his wrists, and she closed her eyes. He pulled away, turned his back, and was gone. By the time Susannah opened her eyes again, he had disappeared into the rapidly lightening gray of the dawn.

Twenty minutes later she was washed, dressed, and in the kitchen. To her consternation, Sarah Jane was there before her, shaping the dough Susannah had left to rise the night before into loaves.

Susannah checked for an instant as her sister looked at her gravely, then forced herself to move on into the room as though nothing at all were amiss. If her cheeks were hot, why, she could only hope Sarah Jane wouldn't notice.

"What are you doing up?" she asked as casually as she could. Fortunately, the fire needed building. Dropping to one knee before it, she was able to turn her back to Sarah Jane as she fed the few sticks left from the previous night into its hungry orange mouth. She straightened to pour water into the kettle and set it on its crane over the fire, all the while keeping her face averted from Sarah Jane.

"I heard you come in last night. It was very late, and when you didn't get up on time this morning I thought you might be tired."

So Sarah Jane had heard her come in. What else had her sister heard? The possibilities made Susannah squirm.

"Mary O'Brien took a bad turn last night. I did what I could for her, but I fear it wasn't much. She is dying, I think." Susannah, left with no excuse to linger, turned away from the now-crackling fire and came to fetch the bread from her sister. She would act as if all were as usual if it killed her, which, considering her guilty conscience, it just might.

"Don't say so! What a tragedy it would be should those children lose their mother! The youngest is only two years old."

"I know." Sliding the bread into the oven, Susannah felt a little better. If Sarah Jane possessed any damning knowledge, she surely would have revealed it before now. " 'Tis as God wills, though."

"Yes."

A step on the porch outside made Susannah stiffen. But it was only Ben, entering with an armful of firewood.

"Dump it into the basket, please."

Ben complied, then turned to pick up the pan Susannah had filled with grain for the chickens.

"I went to get Craddock up, but he weren't in his cabin. Connelly said he hadn't seen him since supper last night."

"You saw Connelly?" That particular form of Ian's name almost stuck in her throat, but Susannah forced it out. Her heart started to pound as she considered the possibilities. Had Ben seen him jumping from the porch roof, perhaps, or even sliding from her bedroom window? "I'm surprised he was up and about."

"He's always an early riser, Miss Susannah. This mornin' he even beat me gettin' dressed."

Susannah breathed a little easier. Apparently Ben had seen nothing untoward. "Perhaps Craddock is already in the barn milking the cow."

Ben shook his head, but before he could say anything more, another step on the porch brought Susannah's head swinging around. This time her worst fear was realized. Ian walked into the kitchen. He was clad in a white, collarless shirt and black breeches, though not the same ones he had worn to exit her bedroom, Susannah thought. These were older, well-mended garments, presumably from the same source as his church clothes. He wore no coat or waistcoat, and his silver-buckled shoes had been exchanged for sturdy work boots. His hair was wet, as though he had recently stuck his head into a bucket of water, and slicked back into a ribbon at his nape. He had shaved, and the cheeks that had so recently been rough with black stubble were smooth again. If she had not known better, Susannah would have guessed from his demeanor that he had just passed a long night of untroubled sleep.

Certainly he appeared alert, and even restless. His eyes were gleaming as they immediately sought her out.

For an instant, just an instant, as her gaze met his, time seemed suspended, and Susannah forgot to breathe. He was so tall, so masculine, and so very handsome that the mere sight of him was enough to stop her breath. He was her illicit lover now. At the thought, her whole body tingled, and with the best will in the world not to do so she had to drop her eyes and turn away. To cover her confusion, she moved to the flour bin and began to dip out corn meal into a bowl for the morning's breakfast.

"Good morning, Connelly." Sarah Jane's composed greeting made Susannah conscious that she had not said so much as a word to the new arrival, where ordinarily she would have spoken to him much as Sarah Jane had. She had to compose herself and start behaving normally or she might as well hang a sign about her neck proclaiming what she had done.

"Miss Sarah Jane," Ian replied. His deep clipped voice sent a shiver down her spine. Stop it! Just stop it! Susannah told herself fiercely, and she drew in a long breath of steadying air. She could not be sure, not with her back turned, but from the prickle at the nape of her neck she thought he was watching her still. Glancing over her shoulder, she discovered that she was right. His eyes were on her, their expression disturbing.

Dear Lord, if he continued to look at her like that, the fat would be in the fire indeed!

"Susannah, have you seen my *History of Plymouth Plantation*? I seem to have mislaid the book, and I wish to use a passage from it in Sunday's sermon." Her father was frowning abstractedly as he entered the kitchen fully clad except for his coat. His preoccupation with his book was fortunate, Susannah thought, because it prevented him from observing her guilty start.

"It is in the bookcase to the left of the door as you enter the parlor, Pa." She had to work to keep her voice steady.

"Good morning, Sarah Jane. Good morning, Connelly," the Reverend Redmon said, as their presence impinged on his consciousness. Glancing back at Susannah as they murmured replies, he added, "Did I hear you go out last night?"

"Mary O'Brien was ill again." Susannah knew her answer was terse, but it was all she could do to talk at all. Would her father somehow sense the tension that wound her stomach into knots? If Ian still watched her with that expression in his eyes, would her father notice and guess what they had done? At the thought, she felt physically ill.

"You took Connelly with you, I assume?" It was no more than a casual inquiry. Susannah knew that, but still she could not help the fiery color that crept up her neck to her face.

"I went with her, Reverend," Ian interposed, and Susannah knew that he did it to protect her. He, at least, must be aware of the torment her father's presence was causing her.

"It was good of you to rouse yourself at so late an hour. I appreciate your care of my daughter more than I can say."

Shame and guilt twisted together to squeeze Susannah's heart until she thought it must wither. Her back to the men, she bent over the flour table, her fingers sinking deep into the cool meal.

"It was my pleasure, sir, believe me," Ian said. Susannah, listening, hoped that she was the only one to hear the undertones that lay hidden beneath that statement. Unable to bear being in the same room with the pair of them a moment longer, she dropped a handful of meal into the bowl and glanced at her father. He was looking at Ian, his expression one of total innocence. Of course he was unaware of the undercurrents that swirled around the room. Even if told point blank of what she had done, her father would never believe such a thing of her. Guilt stabbed Susannah anew.

"Shall I fetch your book, Pa?"

"No, no. I shall get it myself and take it upstairs with me. I fancy I have a little time before breakfast?"

"About half an hour."

"Good." The Reverend Redmon took himself off. Susannah, desperate for a moment in which to compose herself, sought some means of temporarily ridding herself of Ian as well.

"It will be a while yet until the food is ready. If—if you will take the grain from Ben and feed the chickens while he milks the cow, it would be a great help." Though she spoke to Ian, Susannah still could not bring herself to look directly at him. She threw the words over her shoulder while she made a great show of adding more meal to the already heaping amount in her bowl.

"Yes, ma'am." If there was a slight derisive edge to Ian's voice, Susannah tried not to hear it. Though she immediately bent her head to her task again, she was aware of him with every nerve in her body as he took the pan of grain from Ben and, with Ben following, headed out the door.

Left alone with Sarah Jane, Susannah's shoulders, which she hadn't until that moment realized had been tensed, slowly relaxed. That is, until she turned around with bowl in hand to find Sarah Jane regarding her speculatively.

"I do believe Connelly has an eye to you, Susannah," Sarah Jane said. "He was certainly particular in his attentions yesterday. And the way he looked at you . . . ! Why, it practically made me shiver to see!"

Susannah felt herself redden. "Don't be silly, Sarah Jane," she said briskly and moved toward the fire. She would add the corn meal to the water she had already set to boil to make corn mush for breakfast.

"You fancy him, don't you? I can quite see why. He's the handsomest man I've ever laid eyes on, even if he is a bit frightening. At least, he frightens me. I daresay it is different with you. You've always been so brave, after all. But, Susannah . . ."

"That's quite enough, Sarah Jane. You are letting your imagination run away with you." Susannah, her back to her sister, threw a pinch of corn meal into the boiling water with rather more savagery than the task called for.

"Perhaps I am. But just in case I am not, pray do not lose sight of what he is, sister. And that is a convict, and our bound servant, be he ever so handsome. He's not to be thought of as a husband for you, and there is no possibility of anything else."

"You sound like me lecturing Mandy." Susannah managed a strangled laugh.

"He doesn't look at Mandy the way he looks at you, so in my opinion that makes you the one in danger."

"I don't need your advice, Sarah Jane!" Susannah threw a hunted look over her shoulder at her sister.

"Don't you?" Sarah Jane asked quite gently. Coming to stand beside Susannah, she took the bowl from her hand. "Then why are you using this to make corn mush?"

Looking down at the bowl, Susannah was left speechless as she saw that the substance she had been adding to the kettle a pinch at a time was not corn meal at all, but ordinary flour.

21

Late that afternoon, Susannah was so tired she felt ready to drop. The day had been unusually hot, though it was beginning to cool down just a little as the broiling sun progressed in its westward migration. With Craddock gone, doubtless off on another drunk, the most onerous of the physical chores had fallen to her and Ben. Ben was at that moment mucking out the pig pen; Susannah, with Old Cobb the mule's sporadic help, was plowing the west field. Emily trailed along behind her, setting roots into the furrows so that they might, at some date that seemed impossibly far in the future, harvest a crop of sweet potatoes. Mandy was in the house preparing the evening meal, and Sarah Jane was out delivering baskets of food to needy parishioners.

"Gee up, Old Cobb!" Susannah said for what must have been the hundredth time, jiggling the reins against the mule's shiny brown back before reaching down to grab the tall handles of the triangular-shaped wooden plow as he started forward. Old Cobb was deaf as a post, and talking to him was useless. But talking to animals was a habit of hers, and, whether he heard her or not, Old Cobb understood the jiggling of his reins. Flicking his ears back and forth, he took maybe three dozen plodding steps before stopping again.

"Drat this mule!" If she had been prone to swearing, Susannah would have sworn a blue streak. Old Cobb was as cantankerous as an ailing octogenarian, and she wasn't in the mood to cater to his idiosyncrasies just then. She was wringing wet with sweat, dirty as a pig, and still had over a quarter of the field yet to plow. The reins looped around her neck chafed her skin. Blisters were forming on her palms. Her legs ached, and her back felt as if it would break in two at any moment. If rain did not threaten for the morrow, she would have called a halt and had Ben, or Craddock if he returned in a condition that permitted him to work, finish up the next day. But everything from the sheer oppressiveness of the heat to the behavior of the fuzzy brown and yellow caterpillars as they crawled across the ground foretold a storm blowing their way, and the sweet potato crop needed to be put in before it hit.

"Susannah, I am so tired."

Susannah glanced over her shoulder to discover that Em, who had caught up with her, was stretching, a hand pressed to the small of her back. Like Susannah, Em wore a deep-brimmed sunbonnet and her oldest frock. Her sleeves were turned back to well past the elbows and her skirt tucked up at the waist so that most of her muddied-to-the-knee petticoat was in plain view. She looked as miserable as Susannah felt, and Susannah had to smile at her.

"I know. I am, too. Come on, let's get this done, and then we'll go in and sit and let Mandy and Sarah Jane dish up supper."

As Em didn't usually do much when it came to putting supper on the table, this inducement didn't hold the appeal for her that it did for Susannah. But still, when Susannah gently jiggled the reins to get the ornery old mule going again, Em fell in behind, bending every few inches to push a potato root into the churned-up soil.

They had nearly reached the end of the row when Susannah, glancing up, spotted Ian. He was in the act of straddling a split rail fence about halfway up the field. Just the sight of him sent a thrill through her body, tired though she was. She had not set eyes on him since breakfast, when Pa had conscripted him to translate some book of French sermons he had unearthed and hoped to use in his preaching. Now, watching Ian stride toward her, his long legs eating up the distance between them, she was stricken with an attack of shyness that was almost painful.

But it was clear that no such affliction troubled him. If it did, he would certainly not be striding toward her so purposefully.

Willing herself not to blush—though she was already so red from the heat that it was possible no one would be able to tell if she did—Susannah pulled Old Cobb to a halt and turned to wait for Ian to catch up with her.

"What . . . ? Oh." Em, coming up behind her, looked puzzled until she followed Susannah's gaze to Ian, who was almost upon them. Susannah, leaning tiredly on the plow, realized that he was angry only when he stopped in front of her and she found enough calm good sense to permit her to look up into his face.

"What the devil do you think you're doing?" Ian demanded. The greeting was not what Susannah had expected, and for a moment she blinked in surprise. He stood with feet planted apart and fists on hips, glowering down at her. With his black felt hat shading his face and his shirt loosened at the neck and rolled up to his elbows, he looked maddeningly fresh and cool. As her eyes swept him from head to toe, Susannah felt even dirtier and sweatier than before, and she didn't much like the sensation.

"It's called plowing, I believe." If her reply was tart, it was an exact expression of how she felt. Her embarrassment receded as her temper warmed, and Susannah suddenly had no trouble at all facing him.

"It's a man's work. You have no business doing it."

"Unfortunately, at the moment I have no man to do it for me. Craddock has taken himself off again, and Ben is employed elsewhere. This is not the first time I've plowed a field, believe me."

"Give me the reins. I'll do it. You may take Miss Emily's place and plant the seeds."

"Roots," Em interjected, clearly fascinated at this exchange. Both principals to the conversation ignored her.

"You? Plow?" There was a scornful note to Susannah's laugh, and to her expression, too, as her eyes ran over him. "Don't be ridiculous."

Straightening, she grimaced at a twinge in her back and lifted the reins, ready to send Old Cobb on his way again. Ian stopped her by the simple expedient of grabbing the leather straps just above where she held them.

"Damn it, Susannah, I am not utterly useless. Give me the reins."

Neither noticed the widening of Emily's eyes at Ian's easy familiarity toward her older sister.

"You cannot plow." Susannah, stating an established fact, spoke flatly.

"Can I not?"

"We both know you cannot. As a farmer, I'm sorry to remind you, you *are* utterly useless."

"Give me the reins."

"All right. All right! If you wish to try, you may certainly do so. Only let me warn you that you may get a trifle dirty in the process."

His eyes narrowed at her tone. Then, with a swift glance at Emily, who was watching him as if he'd suddenly grown a second set of ears, he merely reached to lift the reins from Susannah's neck by way of reply.

Susannah, following his eyes to her spellbound little sister, let him put the reins around his own neck without additional comment. She stepped out from behind the plow and, with her arms folded over her bosom and her head cocked derisively, watched him position himself in her place.

"So plow," she said when he glanced at her.

"I will." He turned his eyes to the mule. "Giddyup!"

Old Cobb just stood there, swishing his tail back and forth. With another sideways glance at Susannah, who, for all her combined exhaustion and annoyance was starting to grin, he slapped the reins authoritatively against the mule's broad back.

Old Cobb, unfortunately, never did take well to authority. He gave a honking bray of extreme insult and bolted. With the reins looped around his neck, Ian never had a chance. One moment he was snapping them against the mule's back, and the next he was flying over the plow to land face first in the dirt. His fall freed the reins and sent his hat sailing. Old Cobb galloped, braying and kicking all the way, to the extreme far end of the field.

Susannah, looking from the bucking mule to Ian's long body sprawled nose down in the dirt, snickered. Catching her eye, Em did, too. By the time Susannah reached Ian's side, she was laughing so hard that tears streamed from her eyes. Emily, beside her, was in like case.

"Oh, dear," Susannah said unsteadily as Ian still hadn't moved. "Do you suppose he's hurt?"

"I—I hope not." Like Susannah, Emily was practically holding her sides. Laughter erupted from both of them in great bursts, though Susannah exercised a truly heroic effort to control her amusement as she hunkered down at the fallen hero's side.

As she touched his shoulder, Ian rolled over and sat up, his expression disgusted. As Susannah had foretold, he was now considerably dirtier than he had been just a few minutes before. He was so dirty, in fact, that she and Emily went off into fresh gales just looking at him as he tried to brush himself off.

"You knew that was going to happen." His eyes accused her.

"I did not."

"Yes, you did. You did it on purpose."

"You're being childish again." She tried to speak severely, but it was hard when giggles kept threatening to erupt.

Ian opened his mouth, then clamped it shut again with a speaking glance at Emily. Realizing that he was perfectly capable of saying whatever it was he meant to say with or without an audience, Susannah glanced up at her sister.

"You may as well go back to the house, Em. I doubt we're going to get any more planting done today."

"Do you mean it? Thank goodness! My legs feel as if they're ready to fall off! Do you want me to help you catch Old Cobb?"

"No, go on. He'll come better to me anyway. Be sure and put the roots where it's dry."

"I will." Em shot a wide grin at Ian, who still sat in the dirt with his knees drawn up before him and his arms resting on his knees. "Thank you so much!"

"You're welcome." If there was a sour undertone to that, it appeared to sail by Em without touching her. Clutching the basket of roots under one arm, Em trudged off toward the house, the very picture of exhausted relief.

Before Susannah could properly register that she was now alone with Ian, his hand shot out to close over her wrist. When she looked down at him, surprised, his smile was silky.

"So you think I'm funny, do you?"

"Just a little. Sometimes."

His eyes narrowed at her. "I'm tired of being the butt of your jokes. Maybe it's time to move on to something I find amusing."

"Such as?" The question was a mistake. Susannah knew it as soon as it left her mouth.

His smile widened, turned wicked. "You'll see."

Then, with a sudden tug on her wrist, he brought her tumbling down into his arms.

"Now let's see you laugh," he taunted as he held her, struggling, on his lap.

"People can see—the girls—let me up this instant!" Susannah cast a frantic look around. They were out in the middle of an open field that was bordered on one side by the public road and was within shouting distance of both house and barn. Anyone could come along and discover them together. "Let me up!"

"Not till you're as dirty as I am." And with that the scoundrel tumbled her in the just-plowed field, rolling over and over with her caught up in his arms until her hair tumbled from its bun and her skirt twisted about her legs and a generous coating of dirt covered her entire person.

"Ian! You've probably uprooted half the field!" she protested when at last he turned her over onto her back and let her lie there, panting, while he leaned on an elbow above her. But then, as she took a good look at herself and him, she had to laugh again. If there had ever been two filthier people in the world, she had never seen them.

"You're beautiful when you laugh." He'd been grinning, too, but the grin died as he looked down at her and his eyes turned serious.

"I'm not."

"You are."

"Not."

"Now who's being childish?" he countered. "If I say you're beautiful, you're beautiful. I'm counted something of a judge, you know."

Susannah wasn't sure she liked that. "I'll just bet you are," she said dryly.

He sensed her withdrawal and picked up her hand to press it to his mouth. "I'm thirty-one years old. I've had women. I won't deny it. But there has never been anyone in my life like you."

"How many times have you said that, I wonder?"

Ian had the grace to look slightly abashed. "All right. A few. But this time I mean it."

Susannah eyed him. The amusement left her face, and her expression suddenly bordered on grim. "You want something from me, I know. What is it, your freedom? Do you think you can romance me into tearing up the Articles of Indenture?"

He was holding her hand now, rubbing his thumb lightly over a small, swelling blister at the base of her forefinger. "Would you believe me if I told you the only thing I want from you is—you?"

For a moment, as his words sank in, Susannah's heart seemed to stop beating. Covered with dirt as he was, he was still so dazzlingly handsome that it hurt her to look at him. He had lost the ribbon that bound his hair, and the thick black locks hung loose around his face. His mouth, that perfectly carved, always sensual mouth, was twisted into a whimsical little smile. His eyes beneath the thick black slashes of his brows were as gray as the storm that threatened. As he met her gaze, there was no smile in them at all.

She could almost believe him.

Susannah snorted at her own idiocy.

"Believe it or not, I'm not that big a fool," she said crisply, and, before he could prevent it, she rolled to her feet.

Then, without ever once looking around, she walked to the end of the field where Old Cobb was contentedly pawing up the just planted tubers and chomping them down. Pretending to be headed for another target entirely, she waited until his attention was distracted and then grabbed his harness. He threw up his head and brayed his displeasure, but she had him fast. Patting his nose consolingly, Susannah began to lead him toward the barn. If he chose, Ian could bring the plow. If not, she would send Ben back for it. But until she had had a chance to sort through everything that had happened and how she felt about it, she would not put herself within Ian's reach again.

As she had told him, she was not that big a fool.

22

Despite her exhaustion, Susannah did not sleep well that night. She came in, endured Em's and Sarah Jane's exclamations over her dishevelment and Mandy's ominous silence. Clearly Em had recounted the scene in the field for her sisters' delectation, and Sarah Jane had chimed in with what she had observed in the kitchen that morning. As a result, her sisters were agog. Always they had taken Susannah's presence in their lives as a given, regarding her as so much older than themselves as to be in almost a different generation. Certainly they took it for granted that she had no interest in men. Now their view of her was threatened, and suddenly their relationship was turned topsy-turvy. Mandy oozed jealousy, while Em regarded her oldest sister with sudden awe and Sarah Jane adopted a motherly manner toward her that made Susannah feel like an errant child.

She was too tired even to eat supper. For the first time in any of their memories, Susannah went straight up to bathe and then fall into bed, leaving the other three to serve the meal and clean up. Sarah Jane and Em, alarmed at this unprecedented abdication, carried up the tin bath and the steaming kettles of water to fill it on their own initiative. Mandy, for all her pouting, brought Susannah a plate of toast. After reassuring them for what must have been the dozenth time that there was nothing wrong with her that sleep wouldn't cure, they finally left her alone, though Sarah Jane and Mandy looked worried and Em almost frightened. Susannah knew that she was dismaying them, but she was just too tired to worry about anyone else's upsets save her own. Just for this one night, she had to take care of herself. Susannah sank into the tub with a long sigh, meaning to indulge in the luxury of a good soak, which she scarcely ever found the time to enjoy. But in the end she was too tired to do more than wash quickly, soap and rinse her hair, and get out. She fell into bed with her hair still damp, only to awaken more than once. Part of her problem, she suspected, was that she was accustomed to sleeping with her window open. Tonight she had closed it and wedged it shut with a stick.

When the cock crowed the following morning, sheer force of will had her up and about as usual. She was still tired, more from emotional upheaval than from anything else, she suspected, but she refused to give in to it. Sarah Jane trailed down to the kitchen after her, clearly concerned lest Susannah be sickening with something. Susannah assumed the mantle of her old self with determination, and it wasn't long before Sarah Jane was responding to her just as she always did. Her sister made no mention of Ian, and for that Susannah was thankful. During the long, restless night she had come to an inescapable conclusion: she had to put Ian, and the brief explosion of flaming passion they had shared, firmly from her mind. Their bound man must once again become merely Connelly to her, because there was simply no other choice. At this point, what had happened between them was an aberration, one isolated incidence of surrender to the weakness to which the flesh was prey. Such a fall from grace as she had taken could be forgiven, by herself and by God—if it happened once. But even if she wished to, which she emphatically did not, she could not sustain an existence as Ian's paramour. The role of illicit lover was not for her. Such a deliberate choosing of a path rife with secrecy and sin went against every bit of moral fiber that remained to her. Besides, it was only a matter of time before they were caught together, and then the scandal would taint not only herself but her sisters and would probably kill her father. Even if they were not caught, there would, sooner or later, be consequences of the most unmistakable kind. At the thought of conceiving an illegitimate child, Susannah felt physically ill, and it was then that her decision was irrevocably made. The cost of loving Ian was simply too high.

The only way that she could even consider continuing their relationship was if she married him. But, as Sarah Jane had pointed out, to marry a bound man would create its own scandal. Though, were she truly in love with Ian and were he truly in love with her, she would be willing to weather the storm of that. But he was not in love with her, she knew it as well as she knew that the cock would crow the next morning. Should marriage be broached between them, Susannah would be forced to question his motives. Seven years was a long time for a man to be legally enslaved. It was quite possible that he would be willing to marry her in exchange for his freedom. But Susannah would not marry a man, not even Ian, who chose her for such a reason. She had too much pride and too much fear of the hurt that she must inevitably suffer. For it would be fatally easy to let herself love him, and to love Ian Connelly when he did not love her back would be, for Susannah, hell on earth.

That one glorious lesson in carnal love would have to last her the rest of her life. She only hoped that there was not already a child growing inside her that must forever bear the burden of her shame.

Surely God would not be so harsh.

But to be safe, she made Him a bargain: if He would let her not be with child, then she would end her relationship with Ian once and for all. All that remained was to tell Ian of what she had decided.

But it did not help her resolve to feel Ian's eyes on her during breakfast, even while he discussed with her father various equitable means of distributing church funds among the needy and she replenished bowls and mugs and chatted with her sisters. It did not help to find Mandy watching Ian like a cat at a mousehole or to see Em glance from herself to Ian and then at Sarah Jane more than once. It did not help to know that she had not yet found the courage to address Ian to his face as Connelly, though she had managed to greet him with composure when he entered the kitchen and pass food and drink his way.

It would take time and effort to brick over this fissure he had opened up in her heart. But brick it over she would, simply because there was no other choice. If even contemplating giving up the joy and laughter and, yes, the physical passion that her relationship with Ian had brought into her life hurt, then hurting was the price she had to pay for her sin. Take what you want, an old saying went. Take what you want, and pay for it.

The first step, the one she dreaded most, was telling Ian—no, Connelly! —what she had decided. His reaction was not likely to be pretty, but she meant to stand firm. She had fallen from the path, but she meant to go forth and sin no more, as the Bible exhorted a different sinner.

But persuading him of her resolve was likely to be one of the two hardest things she had ever done in her life. The other was giving him up.

Hiram Greer arrived unexpectedly in his buggy just as they were getting up from the table. As one who considered himself a close family friend, he entered through the back door with only a courtesy knock. As stocky and red-faced as ever, he was clad in an obviously new frock coat in a deep shade of maroon that was an unfortunate match to his complexion. He swept his hat from his grizzled head as he entered and greeted the ladies with a polite bow. The Reverend Redmon was afforded a handshake and a clap on the arm. Even Ben came in for a nod, but Ian he completely ignored. Mandy, who usually was only as nice to Greer as she had to be, positively beamed at him as he announced that he had come to steal her from them for the morning, if she was agreeable. He had to go into town, he said, and thought she might like to accompany him and do some shopping. Mandy clapped her hands in what appeared to be genuine delight as he said this, though all three of her sisters looked at her with astonishment. It was unheard of for Mandy to agree to spend fifteen minutes that she didn't have to in Greer's company.

"Why, thank you, Mr. Greer. I'd truly enjoy that—if it's all right with Pa, of course." Mandy turned a dimpling smile on her father, who looked taken aback.

"I have no objection, though 'tis Susannah you must ask," the Reverend Redmon said hastily. "She knows more about these things than I do."

As Mandy had been accustomed for most of her life to turning to Susannah for permission to do everything from wading in the creek to putting up her hair, Susannah could not help but feel that this sudden appeal to their father was directly attributable to her sister's jealousy over their bound man. Susannah suspected that it was Mandy's way of demonstrating that she no longer considered her eldest sister as her mentor, but rather as a rival for a man she wished to attract. Her acceptance of Greer's invitation was likely intended to impress Ian with how attractive other men found her. Susannah loved Mandy dearly, but she had no illusions about her character. Where men were concerned, she expected to reign supreme. If any man gave any indication of preferring another to her lovely self, then Mandy declared war. Even if that other was the sister who had stood in place of a mother to her for the last twelve years.

And to think she had bought a bound man in the hope of making her life easier!

"You may go if Sarah Jane or Em goes with you," Susannah said, though Mandy had not asked her. "There are some things you may pick up for me in town as well. It is very kind of you to invite Mandy, Mr. Greer. It will save Ben from having to make the trip."

Susannah, with Sarah Jane's help, began clearing the table as she spoke, but she did not miss Mandy's glance of dislike.

" 'Tis Miss Mandy who is kind to consent to accompany me."

"I'll just go get my bonnet," Mandy said. "Em, Sarah Jane, which one of you wants to come with me?"

"I will!" Em said at once. Susannah had to smile. She guessed that Emily feared that, if she didn't go, she might be conscripted to finish planting sweet potatoes. The threatened storm still had not struck, though the heat was even more oppressive than it had been the day before. Perhaps there would be time to finish plowing the field before the rain hit.

Sarah Jane did not object, and so Em ran upstairs with Mandy to fetch a bonnet. Susannah stopped clearing the table to write out a list of the supplies she needed from town. Greer stepped over to her father's side and put a hand on his shoulder. The Reverend Redmon, who'd clearly been preoccupied with otherworldly thoughts, turned vague hazel eyes on his visitor, as if he couldn't quite, for just a moment, place him.

"You've had no trouble out of him?" Greer asked in a confidential tone, jerking his head to indicate Ian, who had shouldered a heavy carton of books that the Reverend Redmon meant to take up to the church. As Greer spoke,

Ian was in the act of carrying the box out the door. The Reverend Redmon turned his silvery-white head to look after the bound man with a puzzled frown.

"Who? Connelly?" the Reverend Redmon asked, sounding surprised. "Why, no. In fact, he's been a considerable help to me. I consider that Susannah did a fine day's work when she brought him home to us. He's a very well-educated man."

Greer's mouth tightened, and his hand fell away from the reverend's shoulder. "He's a very violent man. I'm surprised you're willing to trust him around your daughters. There's no telling what he might be capable of."

Ian, coming back through the door, obviously heard that. His stride checked for the barest instant, and his eyes, focusing on Greer, hardened. For a moment, as his lip curled, Susannah was vividly reminded of the ferocious looking creature she'd first seen on the block. How much had changed in the short time since some twisted combination of pity and temper had compelled her to buy him! Then Susannah realized something that had eluded her: the last fortnight, for all the pain it was going to bring her, had been worth the cost. Had she not gone to the auction that day, her life would have been immeasurably poorer.

Clearly Greer did not recognize, or did not properly appreciate, the threat implicit in Ian's expression. There was going to be trouble, Susannah saw, unless she acted quickly to head it off. Glancing around for inspiration, she seized on the first chore that struck her mind.

"If you would slop the hogs for me before you go, I would appreciate it," she said to Ian in a low voice, hoping both to distract him from Greer's insults and to remove him from the other man's vicinity. With an unreadable glance at her face, Ian accepted the malodorous bucket she pressed on him and turned toward the door.

"That's fitting work for him, all right, slopping the hogs!" Greer chortled. Susannah, pushed beyond bearing, rounded on him before either Ian, who turned menacingly, or her father, who looked surprised, could say a word.

"Slopping hogs is good honest work, and no decent man or woman should be ashamed of doing it! I am surprised at you, Mr. Greer, for making sport of something that I and my sisters do every day!"

Greer looked taken aback. As he had hopes of one day wedding Mandy, he took pains to win over the approbation of Mandy's family, especially Susannah and her father. He wet his lips, and an unbecoming flush rose to mottle his cheekbones. "Miss Susannah, I assure you I did not mean . . ."

"We're ready!" Mandy popped her head through the door and beckoned to Greer, cutting short the awkward moment.

"Don't forget my supplies," Susannah said, brushing past Greer as if he were invisible and handing her list to Mandy.

Greer, following her over to the doorway, made one more attempt to right himself in her eyes. "Miss Susannah, I never meant to give you offense, and if I did so unintentionally I apologize."

"That's quite all right, Mr. Greer. I understand that you cannot help it," Susannah said coolly and showed him her back as she returned to the table and her work. Her spine was ramrod stiff, and he looked at it with a helpless expression for a moment before Mandy dragged him from the room.

"Mr. Greer is not the most sensitive of souls, perhaps," her father sighed as he put his hat on his head and headed out the back door.

"No, he is not," Susannah said, her nose in the air.

"Susannah."

Ian, bucket still in hand, turned toward her. His voice was barely above a whisper. Sarah Jane had moved into the hall to see her sisters off, so for a moment the two of them were alone. His familiarity would have to come to an end, but this was neither the time nor the place to go into the explanation she envisioned, so she contented herself with raising her eyebrows at him.

"Are you sure you weren't born a duchess and somehow got misplaced?"

"What?" The question made no sense to her. She frowned, puzzling at it, and as she puzzled at it he grinned and turned to follow her father outside.

Susannah, staring after him, felt the impact of that grin like a dagger to her heart.

23

Summer lightning was snaking through the dark clouds that sat on the horizon as Susannah hurried toward the west field. With the breakfast things cleared away, she had hoped to harness Old Cobb and, with Ben's help, finish putting in the sweet potato crop. But Old Cobb had been missing from his stall, and when she checked she had discovered that his harness and the plow were gone from the barn as well. Had Ben decided to undertake the plowing on his own? It was not like the boy to display so much initiative.

Now, topping the small rise that separated the west field from the barn, Susannah stopped in surprise as the mystery was resolved. The west field, with considerably more than three-quarters of its rich, black dirt freshly turned over, lay before her. There was no mistaking the identity of the tall, black-haired man who strode along behind Old Cobb, face taut with concentration and muscles straining as he gouged the plow deep into the small section of heat-dried earth that remained. Ian was plowing, unbelievable as it seemed. Ben came behind him, planting tubers in the newly dug rows.

Susannah pushed her bonnet brim up out of her eyes and stood, fists on hips, watching. The rows Ian made were not as straight as the ones she had put in, but they were acceptable.

He looked up then and saw her. He was nearly a quarter of a mile away, but she could feel his eyes on her. Susannah lifted a hand in salutation, then slowly turned and retraced her steps to the house. It was clear that she was not needed in the field.

Ian Connelly never ceased to surprise her. As a gift to her, plowing that field ranked way ahead of candy or flowers. Her back still ached from the day before. She would have been wrestling that plow again this morning, while Ben took over Em's job of planting. Old Cobb had taken a dislike to Ben, and if Old Cobb disliked the person working him he refused to budge so much as an inch.

In the kitchen, Sarah Jane had her head bent over some mending. The pungent scent of the okra soup bubbling over the fire lay heavy on the air.

"I thought you were going to finish putting in the sweet potato crop." Sarah Jane looked up in surprise as Susannah entered.

"Ian and Ben are doing it."

Sarah Jane's expression became quizzical. "Ian?"

Suddenly conscious of what she had said, Susannah flushed. She glanced at her sister and sighed. Keeping secrets had never been something she excelled at. Lying and dissembling did not come easily to her.

"You were right, Sarah Jane. I fancy him." The relief of confessing even such a small portion of the truth was like lancing a boil.

"Oh, Susannah! I knew you did. 'Tis as plain as the nose on your face." Sarah Jane's hands, which had been busily weaving a needle and thread through a hole in a petticoat, came to rest in her lap.

"He's not your—typical—bound man." Susannah, for want of something to do, walked over to stir the soup.

"No, he's not that."

" 'Tis foolish, I know. I'm determined to put it behind me. How ridiculous it must appear, a spinster of my years pining over a handsome face!"

Sarah Jane looked at her pensively. "Not ridiculous, Susannah. You could never be that. You know, it had never occurred to me before Connelly came on the scene that you might wish to have your own life away from us, with a husband and children of your own. Has it been a dreadful sacrifice, dear?"

Susannah looked around at that. "A sacrifice, taking care of you and Mandy and Em and Pa? Don't be silly, Sarah Jane. I love you all more than I can say." Moving over to the flour bin and sliding back the lid, she began to scoop out white flour to make biscuits for the midday meal. Sliding the lid closed again, she added, with an attempt at lightness, "Besides, as Em pointed out not so long ago, no man has ever offered to take me away from all this. Had there been such an offer, and had I wished to accept, I assure you that I would have done so."

Sarah Jane smiled but shook her head as she picked up her needle again and began to ply it. "I think that, had it not been for us, you would have had an offer. Several offers! Since Connelly appeared, you've been, I don't know, different—younger seeming, and—and pretty. Did you let yourself, Susannah, you could be quite lovely, I think."

"Me?" Susannah was glad to be able to laugh a little. "How very sweet of you to say so. But I don't aspire to be lovely, thank you very much. Any more than I aspire to sprout wings and fly."

"There are some bachelors among the congregation."

A genuine, though wry, smile curved Susannah's lips. "Indeed there are. And not one of them would I have if he was offered to me on a platter with an apple stuck in his mouth. Now don't start matchmaking, Sarah Jane. I am content as I am, I promise you."

"Are you?" Sarah Jane's eyes flicked up to Susannah's face and held. "Are you really, Susannah?"

Susannah met Sarah Jane's troubled gaze, but, before she could come up with an answer that would satisfy her without being a total lie, the unmistakable sounds of a carriage pulling up and of their younger sisters' voices and footsteps on the front porch distracted both women. Not that Susannah was sorry to have the conversation cut short. Sarah Jane knew her as well as anyone in the world, and Susannah was afraid that, if she said much more, Sarah Jane might be able to read between the lines.

The first fat drops of rain splattered on the window glass not long after Hiram Greer, after much buttering up of Susannah, took himself off. Thunder rolled, lightning flashed, and in moments a soaked-to-the-skin Ben barrelled through the back door.

"That's some downpour!" he exclaimed, spluttering and shaking his arms so that water droplets showered the floor like rain.

"Here, Ben, take this," Em said, scooping up the towel that hung from a peg by the dry sink and handing it to him with a shy smile.

"Why, thank you, Miss Em." Ben took the towel, apparently all unconscious that Em's heart was in her eyes as she looked at him. Susannah, watching, felt a sudden pang of sympathy. She knew exactly how Emily felt. Mandy, who must have been watching too, snorted. Mandy had little patience for what she considered Em's childish heartburnings.

"Where's Connelly?" Sarah Jane voiced the question that Susannah had not liked to put into words.

"He went on down to his cabin. He, ah, had an accident."

"An accident?" Susannah spoke more sharply than she intended. She could have bitten her tongue as soon as the words left her mouth, but there was no way to recall them or the tone in which they had been spoken.

"Oh, he's not much hurt. He, uh, told me not to tell y'all about it." Ben, having mopped himself up, bent to dab at the puddle he'd created on the floor. He looked up, met Susannah's eyes, and shrugged. "Guess I don't work for him, though, do I? Old Cobb kicked him."

"Kicked him!"

"You know how the danged old—uh, mule—hates thunder. Connelly was pickin' a stone out of his hoof when it thundered. Next thing I saw, Connelly was flying down the field. I don't think the kick hurt him much, though. Leastways he was able to get back up. He swore a blue streak, let me tell you. It'd been rainin' for a few minutes, and the field had already started turnin' to mud. He was covered with it, and he looked mighty funny, too. Course I didn't laugh. Connelly's not the kind of fellow you'd want to laugh at to his face."

Em giggled. Ben grinned at her. Sarah Jane smiled at Ben's telling of the story, but her eyes were thoughtful as they rested on Susannah's face.

"Maybe I should go check on him," Mandy suggested brightly.

Susannah gave her a quelling look. "No, I'll go. He might really be hurt, and I need to change his bandage anyway. Em, would you go fetch my medicine case?"

Emily nodded and went to do as she'd been bid. Mandy, eyes suddenly stormy, glared at Susannah.

"You just think you can get him for yourself! It isn't fair!" With that outburst, Mandy turned and ran from the room. Susannah, Sarah Jane, and Ben stared after her. Then Sarah Jane and Ben both moved their gazes in almost perfect unison to fasten them on Susannah.

Susannah, flushing, was saved from having to say anything by Emily's return with the medicine case.

"My goodness, whatever's wrong with Mandy?" she asked, wide-eyed. "She almost knocked me down going up the stairs."

"Mandy's just a little upset," Sarah Jane said grimly. Then, looking at Susannah, she put the mending aside and stood up. "You go on. I'll dish up lunch."

Meeting Sarah Jane's eyes, Susannah read her sister's silent support there. With that one exchange of glances, Susannah realized that, whatever she did about Ian, she could count on Sarah Jane's unconditional love.

The knowledge heartened her. Taking the medicine case from Em, she pulled a shawl from a peg by the door, draped it over her head, and walked across the porch and out into the rain.

Her shawl was soaked and her dress of tan and brown striped cambric was wet to the knees by the time she reached the little row of cabins behind the barn. Miss Isolda, her prize sow, snuffled at her hopefully as she went past the pigpen. Susannah clucked at her and her piglets, who were out of their shelter rooting happily in the rain and mud. Darcy whickered from the barn, and Clara could be seen crouching in the loft, staring down at Susannah through the small open door that hay was hauled through. Brownie was probably curled up in the stall with Maybelle the cow. The two of them were great friends. Of Old Cobb she saw and heard nothing. It occurred to her that after what had happened, Ian might have left him to fend for himself in the field.

Accordingly, the whereabouts of Old Cobb was the first thing she asked him when he opened the door in response to her soft tap.

"If I'd had my way, the bloody animal would be floating, hooves up, in the stream, but I think Ben put him in the barn."

Wordlessly Ian pulled the door wide to invite Susannah inside. She stepped past him, very aware that he was clad only in breeches and stockings, both liberally covered with mud. His bandage was still in place, though smears of mud adorned that, too. That he had been washing was obvious from the dirty water in the bowl on his washstand and the half-filled pitcher beside it. A small fire crackled in the rock fireplace set into the long wall at right angles to the door, and Susannah guessed from its meager size that he'd just lit it before he began to wash.

Reaching the center of the small room, she turned to face him, clutching her medicine case with both hands and holding it protectively in front of her. This was the perfect opportunity to tell him of her decision, and the very thought of it was making her as nervous as a cat in a room full of rocking chairs.

"Where did he kick you?" She asked the question almost at random. Better, she thought, to take care of his medical needs before she spoke her piece.

"I didn't think that boy could keep a secret." Ian closed the door, then, with no more than a glance at her, headed for the washstand, sounding resigned rather than angry. "I suppose you had another good laugh at my expense."

"*I* didn't."

The slight emphasis on the pronoun struck him immediately. He stopped sluicing his arms with water to glance at her again.

"You didn't. Then who did? Miss Mandy? Miss Sarah Jane? Miss Em? The whole household?"

"Something like that." His very disgruntlement made her smile. Imperceptibly she relaxed, her fingers easing their grip on the medicine case. Looking around, she discovered the table at her back and set the case down there.

"So where did he kick you?" she repeated patiently.

Ian touched a spot on his rib cage that was covered by the bandage. "Right here. Hurt like—hurt a considerable amount at the time, but I don't think anything's broken."

"If you'll come sit, I'll check it for you. I need to look at your back anyway."

"My back's fine."

"Then I need to take the bandage off. Will you come sit?"

"Let me change my breeches first. I've gotten more dirt on me in the last two days than I ever have before in my life."

Even as he spoke, he rubbed his arms and chest with a towel, then reached down to unfasten his breeches. Susannah, understanding that he meant to strip in front of her, felt her mouth go dry. As his navel and a narrow vee of hair-darkened skin below it were revealed, she quickly averted her eyes. But the image of him as he looked standing there, next door to naked, his black hair wet and tousled around his head, his sinfully handsome face not one whit marred by the frown that drew his brows together, his broad shoulders thick with muscle, and his bare, corded arms rippling as he undid his breeches, was already burned into her brain.

Susannah had a dreadful feeling that she had made a mistake in bearding him alone. But how else was she to say to him the things that needed to be said? She certainly didn't wish for an audience to hear that she never meant to lie with him again.

"What possessed you to try to plow the field, anyway?" She was looking steadfastly out the single window at the front of the cabin as she spoke.

"*Try* to plow—I'll have you know I did plow it, every inch of it! We'd just finished when the bloody beast picked up a stone." He sounded absurdly proud of himself, like a small boy bragging of his accomplishment. Susannah heard the slither of cloth and deduced that he was stepping out of his breeches. The picture her mind conjured up tantalized her, but she did her best to dismiss it as she watched the falling rain.

"Good for you." Her soft reply was evidently not the accolade he sought, because he grunted. Seconds later, he was behind her, moving so quickly and quietly that she wasn't even aware he was there until his arms slid around her waist, drawing her back against him.

"Ian . . ." The feel of his hard arms holding her made her eyes shut involuntarily, but immediately she forced them open again and sought to pull away.

"As to why I did it," he near-whispered in her ear, his mouth nibbling her lobe in searing punctuation, "the answer's obvious: no man worth his salt, not even such a useless fribble as you clearly consider me to be, is going to watch his woman breaking her back over work he should be doing himself."

Then he bent his head to press a kiss to the sensitive place where her shoulder joined her neck, and at the same time one hard warm hand left her waist to cover her breast.

Susannah gasped, going weak at the knees. Summoning the last reserves of determination she possessed, she tore herself out of his arms and put the width of the small room between them before whirling to face him.

Of course, when she whirled, she had not realized that he would be stark naked.

24

"You're—you're not dressed!" Her shocked gasp sounded foolish, and, as soon as the exclamation left her mouth, she *felt* foolish stating something so obvious. But it was the shock of seeing him in all his naked glory, of course, that surprised such idiocy out of her. And, naked, he was certainly glorious. His tall, leanly powerful body, with its broad shoulders and narrow hips and long, muscular legs, was made to be seen without clothes. Susannah stared because she could not help herself, then wrenched her eyes back to his face.

"No, I'm not," Ian agreed affably, starting toward her. A faint smile curved his lips, and she guessed that he was well aware of the effect his nudity had on her.

Distrustful of that smile and of his catlike approach, Susannah took a step backward, only to have her bottom come up hard against the table. She reached behind her, groping, to find her medicine case.

"I—I need to look at your back."

"To hell with my back." He reached her before she could get a good grip on her case and pulled her into his arms. Susannah's breath caught as the solid warm strength of him enveloped her, as her nostrils filled with essence of man, as her hands encountered sleek bare skin.

She pulled free.

"Sit down," she said sternly, and somewhat to her surprise he did. His nudity discomposed her, and she tried to look no further than the broad bare back that was presented for her inspection. Her hands not quite steady, she removed a small pair of scissors from her medicine case and cut away the bandage.

"Well?" he asked when she didn't say anything, trying to turn his head around so that he could view the damage.

"It's better. Much better," Susannah said, and it was the truth. The swelling and infection were gone; her salve had taken care of that. But the thin red lines that criss-crossed his back remained, and she feared that they would do so forever. Slightly raised and lighter than the rest of his skin, scars would forever brand him.

Turning back to her medicine case, she replaced the scissors and reached for the jar of salve. Perhaps, did she apply it again, it might alleviate some of the worst of the scarring.

"That's not the remedy from hell, is it?" He was watching her as she unscrewed the lid, and from the way his brows drew together over his eyes she realized that he was only half-teasing.

"Yes."

He leaped up, causing Susannah's eyes to widen and then, immediately, to be averted from certain unmentionable parts of his anatomy that moved with him.

"Oh, no you don't. No more torture." He held up both hands in front of him, much like a small child hoping to ward off a parent with medicine, and shook his head.

"But, Ian, this will help it heal."

"My back's healed enough, thank you very much. I still have lively memories of when your salve helped heal me the last time."

With a deft movement he reached out and nipped the jar from her hand. Despite her protests and grabs for her property, he returned it to its place in the medicine case and firmly closed the lid. Before Susannah realized what he meant to do, he turned and caught her in his arms, pulling her hard up against him. Taken unawares, thrown even more off balance by the tender smile that curved his mouth, she had not, for one weak moment, the will to resist. Her body tingled all along its length at being pressed so closely to him. His broad bare shoulders loomed in front of her, and the wedge of black hair on his chest tickled her nose. Susannah breathed deeply, inhaling the warm, musky scent of him. Her pulse speeded up. Her head tilted back so that she could meet his gaze.

His eyes were smiling down at her, but there was a disturbing hint of passion behind the lazy humor. The almost bruising grip of his hands on her arms told her he wanted her; so, against her skirt, did the unmistakable hardening of that part of his anatomy that she could not think about without blushing. His eyes confirmed what she already knew.

Whatever his motives, he wanted to lie with her again. Right that very minute.

He bent his head, clearly intent on kissing her. Susannah drew a deep, ragged breath—and stomped on his bare foot for the second time since she had known him.

Yelping, he released her. "Damn it to bloody hell!"

Susannah was able to put the length of the room between them before she had to turn and face him. He was glaring at her and rubbing the toes of his abused foot against the calf of the opposite leg. Of course he was still as naked as he had ever been, but Susannah, after one brief, comprehensive glance, refused to be disconcerted by his lack of modesty any longer. With steely determination, she refused to let herself look below his chin.

"And why, pray, did you do that?" He sounded aggrieved.

Susannah swallowed. All the diplomatic phrases she'd spent the last few hours thinking up went right out of her mind.

"I don't want you to touch me again," she said baldly.

"What?" The single word was incredulous. He started toward her. Holding up a hand to ward him off, Susannah took a single, nervous step backward. She would have taken more, but to her dismay her back came up against the cabin's front wall and she was left with nowhere to go.

"Please. Hear me out." To her relief he stopped walking, folded his arms over his chest, and stared at her as if waiting for her to continue.

"What—happened between us—was as much my fault as yours, and I admit that. But it shouldn't have happened, and it can't happen again. I don't know what kind of women you're used to, but I can't—I can't. . . ." Her voice trailed off at his darkening expression.

"Can't what?" he asked with awful politeness.

"Can't—oh, you know what!" Susannah threw the words at him. She would have turned her back to hide her blush, but she was afraid he would come up behind her and take her in his arms again, and that, she couldn't endure. What she was doing was hard enough without having to fight the effect his touch had on her at the same time.

"Can't make love with me? Why not, Susannah? I thought you did it very well, myself. For a beginner."

He was going to be difficult. She could tell by the mocking undertone to his voice and the almost savage glint in his eyes. Well, she had expected it. What she had to do now was say what she had come to say and get out. Whether he liked it or not was immaterial.

"I'm prepared to tear up the Articles of Indenture, and if necessary to make it official I am sure I can get Pa to agree. He only wanted to rehabilitate you anyway, and I'm sure he feels we've done that. You can have your freedom and go back to England, or wherever it is you want to go, as long as it's away from here." Her decision to give him his freedom had been made some time within the last few minutes, without her even realizing that it had been done. But as soon as the idea popped into her mind, she knew it made horrible, perfect sense. If she didn't let him go, she would never be free of him. As long as he remained where she could see him, where she could hear his voice, where she could touch him if she so much as stretched out a hand, she would be in danger of tumbling into his arms at any moment. The attraction he held for her was too frighteningly powerful. If she were to keep her pact with herself and God, Ian had to be put beyond her reach. It tore her heart out to send him away, but the alternatives, all the alternatives, were infinitely worse.

"You're telling me you want me to leave?" If his eyes had been angry before, it was nothing to what they were now.

"I'm telling you that I'm prepared to give you your freedom," she said steadily. "That's what you've been angling for, isn't it? Well, you've got it, so your campaign was successful and you can congratulate yourself. You don't even have to concern yourself with paying back the money I spent to acquire your Indenture, if that is indeed troubling you. 'Tis a large sum to lose, I own, but under the circumstances I feel it's well worth it."

"Oh, you do, do you?" His voice was silky, which Susannah had discovered meant trouble. His expression had grown increasingly ominous as he had listened to her, and it now resembled the thundercloud that at that moment sent lightning zig-zagging down toward the fields. "So you think I seduced you in order to cajole my freedom out of you, do you? Well, here's what I think: you used me for stud service, and now you're willing to pay me off to be rid of me so no one will find out about your guilty little secret. That's the truth with no bark on it, isn't it?"

Susannah flushed furiously. But before she could rebut his extremely insulting charges, he was speaking again, in a low, rumbling voice more frightening than any shout. As he spoke, he began to move slowly, almost menacingly, toward her. His gray eyes pinned her like a butterfly to the wall.

"Well, let me tell you something, *Miss* Susannah: I could have had my freedom any damned time I wanted from the moment I arrived. Do you really think a piece of paper saying you own me could keep me if I wanted to go? I stayed because I chose to, because it amused me to discover just how hot the minister's prim daughter was under her ugly skirts. And you know what? I'm not done being amused, and I'm not going."

He was almost upon her now. Susannah, aghast at his words, flayed by the fury she saw in his eyes, and growing increasingly angry herself, retained just enough reasoning ability to know what she should do: run. If he laid hands on her in such a temper, she feared to think what might be the result. In a physical fight with him, she stood not a chance in the world. And what did she really know of him after all? Every instinct she possessed shouted that he would not strike a woman, but the alternative—that he might try to subdue her with the potent sexual power he knew he held over her—was almost more frightening.

To melt in his arms after her proud speechifying and the horrible, hideous things he had replied would shame her more than anything else she had yet done.

He grabbed for her even as Susannah turned, scrabbling to open the door. The door flew back on its hinges, but too late; he caught her arm. Whirling her around, he grabbed her waist with both hands, bringing her up hard against his nakedness and leering down into her whitening face.

"Don't worry, sweetheart. If you don't want me, I doubt I'll lack for company for long." He bared his teeth at her in a taunting travesty of a grin. "Comparing sisters is always so interesting, don't you think? Though of course you wouldn't know."

The foulness of that took Susannah's breath away.

"If you touch one of my sisters . . ."

"Yes? What will you do? Gnash your teeth?"

"I'll shoot you, you disgusting swine!"

He snorted. The expression on his face was so angry that he could have been first cousin to the Devil himself. "You couldn't even shoot Jed Likens, so I doubt you'll shoot me. Anyway, I'm prepared to take my chances."

"Let me go!"

"With pleasure, *Miss* Susannah. I've learned all I wanted to know about you in any case. Underneath your church-going exterior you're as hot as any whore I've ever had—and as fickle." He released her without warning, and Susannah almost fell as she stumbled back over the threshold. The rain pounded down on her unprotected head as she caught herself and straightened to face him, her eyes spitting fury in their turn. For an instant, he stood in the aperture, the light from the fire outlining his naked body with a red glow, making him seem even taller and more breath-stoppingly muscular than she knew him to be. His gray eyes blazed with rage, and his mouth was tight with it.

Then, "I'll see you at supper," he said quite gently, and closed the door in her face.

Susannah spent nearly an hour in the barn with her animals before she considered herself composed enough to go back inside and face her sisters. She probably would have lingered longer had not Ben entered through the front door on some errand or other. Before he could discover her lurking disconsolately in the shadows, Susannah slipped out the back and circled around the pigpen again as she headed for the house. Miss Isolda and her piglets were snug, out of the rain with the others this time, and there was no inquiring snuffle to lighten the utter misery of her spirits.

Fortunately, the long-awaited invitation to the Haskinses' party had been delivered in her absence, and Mandy and Em were up in their room excitedly poring over fashion plates as they discussed what Mandy would wear. Thus, only Sarah Jane was in the kitchen to witness Susannah's return to the house.

Sarah Jane took one long look at her sister and rushed to enfold Susannah in her arms.

"What did he do to you?" she demanded fiercely. "And don't say nothing, because it's there in your face!"

Since their mother had died, no one had ever thought to mother Susannah, and it was surprisingly comforting to be able to rest her head, for just a moment, on Sarah Jane's slight bosom. But to give in to the fury and hurt that twisted her insides into knots was just plain weakness, and weak Susannah was not.

So after one brief, luxuriant moment she stiffened her spine, lifted her chin, and stepped away from Sarah Jane, who let her go but stood arms akimbo as she regarded her elder sister with a frown.

"If he's hurt you, I swear I'll skin him!" Sarah Jane said. That their bound man was the person to whom Sarah Jane referred was understood between them.

To hear such words from meek Sarah Jane and to see her looking so ready to do battle on her older sister's behalf surprised a quavering grin out of Susannah.

"I'll wager Mr. Bridgewater has no notion you can be so ferocious," Susannah said and drew a quick, cleansing breath that was almost, but not quite, as unsteady as a sob.

Sarah Jane's teeth snapped together at the soft sound, but when she spoke her voice was coaxing. "What happened, honey? Can you tell me?"

Susannah shook her head. "Nothing." Then, at the exasperation on Sarah Jane's face as she used the forbidden word, Susannah added quickly, "Nothing, really. C-Connelly and I just—quarrelled."

"Connelly?" From the tilt of Sarah Jane's head, it was clear she had picked up on the telling change in the way Susannah had referred to their bound man.

"Yes, Connelly. From now on," Susannah said, as if making a vow.

"Ah." It was a sound of understanding. Recovering her self-control by the second, Susannah smiled wryly at her sister.

"Yes, ah."

"You're doing the right thing."

"I know. But it's hard."

"Oh, Susannah." Sarah Jane draped both arms over Susannah's shoulders and touched her forehead to her older sister's for just a moment. "Life hurts, doesn't it? I'm going to miss you all dreadfully when I marry Peter."

Susannah felt tears sting the backs of her eyes. Pressing a quick kiss to Sarah Jane's cheek, she pulled away and brushed her fingers over her lashes to remove any suspicious moisture.

"If you're not careful we'll both be weeping, and then what will Mandy and Em think when they come down?"

Sarah Jane laughed shakily. "That we've both gone mad, probably. Are you really going to let Mandy go to that party?"

"I said I would, so I suppose so. Though it's probably a mistake."

"Well, I think . . ." Sarah Jane went on to give at some length her view of parties at which dancing was featured, and by the time she was done Susannah's person was nearly dry, her emotions were under firm control, and supper was bubbling over the fire.

25

As Ian had threatened, he came in to supper, bringing her medicine case, which he deposited on the kitchen floor without so much as a word spoken to Susannah. Indeed, he didn't speak to her at all during the meal or even look at her, though he was charm itself to Mandy and Em. He even tried out one of his roguish smiles on Sarah Jane, who promptly froze him with a look so frosty that afterward he left her alone. But it was Mandy who came in for the lion's share of his attention—and Susannah secretly seethed.

His behavior was no better at breakfast, or at the noon meal, or at supper. He ignored Susannah almost completely, though not blatantly enough to attract the notice of the Reverend Redmon or Ben. But Susannah was perfectly well aware of what he was doing, and all three of her sisters could hardly fail to miss his startling change of allegiance. Their reactions to the new order varied wildly.

Sarah Jane stopped just short of being openly rude to him. She fixed their bound man with a gimlet glare whenever he put himself within her range of vision. Which mark of disfavor, if he was even aware of it, Ian blandly pretended not to notice. Mandy, making the most of opportunity, contrived to sit next to him at nearly every meal and responded to his most commonplace remark with dimpling smiles and oodles of charm. Em, fascinated by the byplay between her elders, watched with bemused attention, observing first one and then another of the principal players as if she were watching horses in a race. The situation might have struck Susannah as funny had she been in any mood for laughing and had she not been so closely involved. But she was involved, like it or not, and she was not laughing. She felt like a drowning person struggling with all her might just to keep her head above water.

Having Ian as her enemy was as excruciatingly painful as anything she had ever experienced. She had not realized how much she had come to look forward to his ready smiles and teasing, to glances that made her feel attractive, to the mere brush of his hand. She had not realized how much sheer joy he had added to her previously humdrum life. Now the joy was gone, vanished like the sun with a dark cloud over it. She felt like a prisoner in her own home, sentenced to being near the thing she wanted most in the world without ever being allowed to have it.

Even if she could have, she would not have restored her relationship with Ian to what it had been. If she was suffering, then she would just have to suffer, because his paramour she would not be. But to watch him turn on Mandy those same glimmering smiles and admiring looks he had once reserved for her alone was more hideous than any torture she could ever have imagined.

A week passed, and Susannah was ready to go stark, staring mad. Craddock had not returned, and Susannah would have been concerned about him had she been capable of feeling concern for anyone save herself. Still, it was ridiculous to worry about a man who periodically went off on a three- or four-day drunk; doubtless this bender was just longer than the ones that usually took him.

A consequence of Craddock's absence was not so easily dismissed, however; Ian spent much more time than heretofore about the farm, doing many of Craddock's chores. From Ben Susannah heard some amusing tales of his misadventures, not that she felt much like laughing at them, though it seemed that he really was learning something about farming. Not that she was in a position to judge his progress. Wherever Ian was, she tried her best not to be. Mandy, on the other hand, seemed to discover a previously unsuspected interest in all things out of doors. If Ian tried his hand at milking the cow, like as not Mandy held the bucket. If Ian fed the animals, Mandy called them in. If Ian drew water from the well, Mandy was there to drink it.

Afraid of scolding Mandy for fear of drawing a charge of sour grapes (which carried the additional sting of being at least partially true), Susannah did her best to take the danger out of the situation by ordering Em to stay with Mandy at all times. Em, obedient even though she did not quite grasp the finer points of the situation her presence was supposed to prevent, faithfully trailed her sister like a shadow. Wherever Ian was, Mandy followed, and wherever Mandy went came Em.

Not unnaturally, this irked Mandy considerably. But when she protested, Sarah Jane lent her voice to Susannah's, as Susannah was not very popular with Mandy just at that moment, to proclaim the impropriety of a girl of Mandy's age being alone with their young, handsome, and very virile bound man. Susannah's case had been quite different, as Sarah Jane explained quietly to Mandy when she thought Susannah couldn't hear (though Susannah, who unbeknownst to her sisters was cleaning the sitting room, heard every word the two exchanged in the adjoining kitchen). Being a mature woman of twenty-six who had been on the shelf for many years, Susannah was not considered at risk from their bound man, Sarah Jane said. No one had thought anything untoward about their association, simply because impropriety between the two seemed so unlikely. Everyone knew that Miss Susannah Redmon's morals were above reproach. Thinking evil of Susannah was like thinking evil of the Reverend Redmon himself: in other words, simply impossible to do.

Overhearing that, Susannah felt like the biggest hypocrite alive. If anyone knew . . . But no one did, except for Ian, and, scoundrel though he was, it seemed he wasn't talking.

She supposed she should thank God for that, but she didn't even feel like praying anymore. It was all she could do to make it through each day.

On the few occasions when she had to be in Ian's company—at mealtimes and on the way to church, for example—she spoke to him as little as possible and with careful civility. He would reply, when there was no help for it, but his words were so hard and cold they could have been carved from ice. When he had to glance her way, his eyes were as unyielding as granite.

Susannah's heart ached. She bore up grimly by telling herself that even the worst pain eventually lessened. For solace she turned, as she had in times of dire trouble in the past, to her kitchen: when Susannah was emotionally upset, she cooked. Under these circumstances, the table practically groaned at every meal under the bounty with which she filled it.

Steaming pots of rice and red beans, greens flavored with bacon grease, spoonbread, spicy sausages, caramelized yams, crawfish, catfish, flounder, and crab joined such staples as baked chicken and dumplings, ham, cornbread, stewed tomatoes, black-eyed peas, mock oysters, and sweet potato pie. Every member of her family left the table groaningly replete at every meal. Everyone, that is, except Susannah herself. She could scarcely eat more than a few mouthfuls at a time. The hollows beneath her cheekbones and the new prominence of her collarbone might have pleased her had she been in any condition to notice.

The Haskinses' party was to be held on the coming Friday evening, and Mandy was to attend with Susannah as her chaperone. Susannah, for all that she and Mandy were not on the best of terms, was busy two days before sewing her sister's gown. For years she had fashioned the best of their garments, because dressmaking, like cooking, was a skill at which she excelled. This particular dress was to be fashioned of the green silk Mandy had purchased in town and made to a design that Mandy had discovered on a fashion plate and coveted—fitted through the elongated bodice, with the newly fashionable pagoda sleeves, which were tight to the elbows and then flared to end in frills of lace above the wrist. The skirt, which was full and sweeping, was made to be worn over panniers, and for all Susannah's present annoyance with Mandy she was fashioning this most important dress with painstaking care. She and Mandy might be at outs, but she still wished for her sister to be the loveliest young lady present.

Susannah had only to make a few minor adjustments to sleeves and waist, add the dark green velvet bows that she meant to use for adornment, hem, and press it, and the dress would be done. When Mandy, followed by the faithful Em, came in from gathering the eggs Susannah meant to use in a custard pie for supper, Susannah sent her up to her room to change into the new dress, then bade her return to the kitchen for the final fitting. Mandy, nothing loath to oblige her sister in this instance, did as she was told.

All four girls were in the kitchen when Ian strode in the back door. For a moment, he stopped at the sight that greeted him. As his gaze ran over the young women, his eyes narrowed. Susannah supposed the four of them made quite a tableau. Mandy, the centerpiece, stood on a small stool. Clad in the new dress, with her auburn hair tousled and excited roses in her cheeks, she was beautiful. Susannah, her mouth full of pins, knelt at Mandy's feet, carefully marking the hem. Em, frowning with concentration, held a strip of the same silk of which the gown was fashioned against Mandy's curls. Susannah felt a bow matching the dress would look best in Mandy's hair, while Mandy and Em favored a cunning lace frill. Sarah Jane stood by Mandy's side, frowning as she pinched the material tighter at the waist.

Mandy beamed at Ian and held her arms out away from her sides to invite his attention to the dress.

"Isn't it beautiful?" she asked rapturously.

"Beautiful," he replied. "But no more beautiful than its wearer."

"You are such a flatterer," Mandy said, dimpling, and shot him a glance of unbridled adoration. On the floor, Susannah nearly swallowed a mouthful of pins. Sarah Jane did her one better: she glared at the intruder. Em, aware of the tension in the room but not exactly sure of the cause, giggled.

"Did you want something, Connelly?" Sarah Jane asked brusquely, thrusting a pin through the loose material at Mandy's waist so carelessly that Mandy yelped and jumped.

"Yes, Miss Sarah Jane, I did." He moved toward the girls, looking Mandy over critically. "If you wish to be completely fashionable, I would suggest making the panniers a little wider. When I last was in London, they were wearing them so wide that ladies could rest their elbows on their skirts."

"As that was some time ago, doubtless our fashion plates are at least as up-to-date as your memory." Finished with the hem, Susannah spat the pins into her hand, then spoke without so much as looking at Ian. The tautness of her voice brought a protective frown to Sarah Jane's face, while Em and

Mandy, oblivious of everything save fashion for the moment, frowned down at the maligned skirt. "If Sarah Jane's finished, you can step down, Mandy."

Sarah Jane nodded, though her eyes were fixed on Ian. "Are you going to tell us what you wanted?"

At practically the same time, Mandy gave a little shriek. "I can't move! I'm too full of pins!"

"Allow me to assist you, ma'am," Ian said and moved forward to catch Mandy under the arms and swing her down. Mandy's hands flew to his shoulders; when he set her down she was laughing. They were standing close together, so close that the new green skirt billowed over the lower part of Ian's legs, and Mandy gazed up into his eyes with a dazzling smile. He was smiling too, lazily, as he looked down at her. For a moment they stayed as they were, his hands on her waist, her hands on his shoulders, while the other three Redmon girls stared. Mandy's fragile auburn-haired beauty was the perfect foil for Ian's tall, black-visaged handsomeness. Together they were breathtaking.

Susannah felt her stomach clench and anger heat the blood in her veins. "Mandy!" she said sharply, even as Sarah Jane said, "Connelly!"

Both looked around. Mandy smiled smugly. Ian raised his brows.

"What did you want?" Sarah Jane spoke first, her words sharp. Ian smiled at her, a mocking smile that told Susannah that he was quite well aware of the reason behind Sarah Jane's sudden coldness toward him. He dropped his hands from Mandy's waist and turned away to address himself to Susannah.

"That big sow of yours broke through the fence. She's haring off through the fields with her young ones after her." There was a certain malicious undertone to his voice that told Susannah that he relished bringing her such calamitous news and had deliberately waited as long as he could to deliver it, too.

"What! Miss Isolda?" Susannah clambered to her feet, her eyes wide with mixed annoyance and alarm. "Why didn't you tell me sooner? She's probably halfway to town by now!"

But she didn't wait for his answer, which of course could have provided a far different picture from the half truth he had told her about the sow just to vex her. Picking up her skirts, which fortunately were old (though that consideration for them never even entered her head), and quite forgetting her bonnet, she ran out the back door toward the barn to see if she could get a glimpse of the escapees.

When Susannah caught sight of the sow, she didn't know whether to laugh or cry. Stopping on the rise just past the barn, she stood for a moment, huffing and puffing from the speed of her pursuit. Fortunately, Miss Isolda and her piglets hadn't gone far. Unfortunately, they'd been stopped by the scent emanating from the pieces of sweet potatoes that had just been planted in the west field. Six little pigs and a very large sow were spread out over the field, their noses busily scooping tubers from the dirt as they gobbled down what they considered a delicacy.

"Oh, no! Sooo-ey! Pig, pig, pig!" But under the circumstances, calling them proved useless, as Susannah had feared it would. Miss Isolda looked around, fat pink snout quivering, droopy black ears twitching, and regarded her with beady black eyes that were bright with intelligence. With a grunt, she returned to her rooting.

There was nothing for it but to get a rope, catch Miss Isolda, and drag her back to her pen. Her piglets would follow her, Susannah hoped.

"I put up a board so the rest of them couldn't get out," Ian said behind her. "She's the one who broke through."

"What did you do, just stand there and watch?" Susannah asked nastily, whirling to glare at him. Without waiting for his reply, she stalked off to the barn and returned with a rope.

When she returned, Sarah Jane, Mandy, and Em had joined Ian on the rise.

"Good. I'm going to need all the help I can get," Susannah greeted them grimly. Sarah Jane, who had always been somewhat afraid of the hogs, nodded, her expression resolute but a little nervous. Em grinned. Mandy looked appalled.

"But I can't! Truly! Look, I'm wearing my new dress!"

It was true. Mandy was still wearing the green silk dress. Susannah acknowledged the fact with a grimace.

"Stay here, then." Susannah started down the rise, with Sarah Jane and Em following. Ian, the swine, stayed with Mandy, his arms folded over his chest and a kind of smile playing about his mouth that told Susannah he expected to be amused. That he was her bound man and that she could order him to help her, or even to catch the pigs himself, occurred to Susannah, only to be immediately dismissed. From the moment she had bought him, Ian Connelly had done precisely what he wished to do and nothing more. If she ordered him to help her, he would laugh in her face.

At least burning rage was a good antidote to pain.

"Sooo-ey! Pig, pig, pig!"

All three girls called the pigs, who seemed scarcely aware of the humans who were descending on them with varying degrees of resolution. At least they seemed unaware until one of the girls got close. Then the pig under pursuit would trot some distance away and commence his rooting again.

"Miss Isolda! Pig, pig, pig!" Susannah said coaxingly as she approached the huge sow, rope in hand. Miss Isolda's back reached nearly to the top of Susannah's thighs, and she must have weighed somewhere in the neighborhood of six hundred pounds. But she was a gentle creature, with a fondness for having a spot behind one floppy black ear rubbed or her back scratched. She was white with large areas of black and managed to keep herself surprisingly clean, considering that her favorite method of bathing was a lolling roll in the mud.

Susannah had already fashioned a loop in one end of the rope and needed only to drop it over the sow's neck. Which, of course, was easier said than done. In her favor was the fact that she had raised Miss Isolda from a piglet smaller than her own half-grown piglets were now. Against her worked the sow's intelligence—and greed.

The third time Miss Isolda trotted away from her dangling snare, Susannah had to stop herself from stomping her feet. It was blazing hot, the glaring sun was making her head ache, two of her sisters were stumbling around in the dirt as futilely as she was herself, and her third sister was standing up on a hill with their bound man, flirting madly while the pair of them snickered at the goings-on in the field below. The thought of Ian's amusement should she give way to temper was what kept Susannah from doing it. She would catch Miss Isolda and remain outwardly calm while doing it, or die in the attempt.

Susannah decided to use the sow's greed as a weapon. Bending, she burrowed in the hot, crumbling soil until her fingers encountered a tuber. Drawing it out, she held it in her hand as she approached the sow.

"Pig, pig, pig!"

Miss Isolda was barely interested—until she saw the tuber. Then her round little eyes brightened, and she sniffed the air. Her pink snout quivered.

"Pig, pig, pig!" Susannah repeated encouragingly, holding out the tuber in her left hand while her right readied the loop. Approaching the sow, she leaned down.

Miss Isolda lunged for the root. Susannah squeaked in sheer surprise at her speed and dropped the coveted delicacy. The sow's head went down, Susannah's hand holding the loop snapped up—and somehow or another the sow was caught.

"Hooray!" The cheer came from Em. Looking around, Susannah grinned triumphantly at her and Sarah Jane, who seemed to slump with relief.

"Come help me lead her out," Susannah called. Even as Sarah Jane and Em moved to comply, trudging over the uneven rows, Susannah glanced over her shoulder to see what Mandy and the human swine made of her success.

Mandy and Ian stood facing each other. Mandy had her hands on Ian's shoulders. Ian was holding her waist. As Susannah watched, Mandy stood on tiptoe to plant a kiss on Ian's smiling mouth. Even from that distance, Susannah could feel the heat that shimmered in the air around the too-beautiful pair.

At first she didn't believe what she'd seen. Then she did believe. Jealousy so hot and fierce that it could have melted stone exploded through her veins.

26

It took perhaps half an hour to drag and coax Miss Isolda back to her pen. Her piglets followed, just as Susannah had hoped they would. Ian had wedged a discarded door into the hole the sow had made in the fence, and with the part of her mind that was still capable of reasonable thought Susannah acknowledged Ian's presence of mind in taking quick action to keep the rest of the hogs in. With the larger portion of her brain, she went over and over the scene that had just played out on the hill. Every time she recalled Mandy going up on tiptoe to press her lips to Ian's, she wanted to kill.

Once Miss Isolda and her piglets were safely penned, Susannah sought out Mandy, who had followed the triumphant pig-chasers and now stood some little distance away observing the pigs' return to everyday life. Ian stood beside her, a half-grin quirking his mouth as he ran his eyes over Susannah's sweat-and-dirt-streaked person.

"Always so elegant," he murmured, apparently to no one in particular.

Susannah's blood boiled anew. She hated him, fiercely, savagely, hated him so much in that moment that she would have laughed had God sent a lightning bolt down from heaven to smite him dead. But she kept her rage under tight rein for fear he would guess the full extent of it—and its cause.

"Amanda," she said in a dangerously quiet voice, shifting her eyes to her smiling little sister, "go back to the house."

Mandy's eyes met hers and widened. Her smile faltered, and she opened her mouth as if she would argue, apparently thought better of it, and closed it again. With a sidelong glance at Ian, she did as she was bid, deliberate allure in every line of her lithe figure as she carefully lifted her hem clear of the grass and swayed toward the house.

Unfortunately for her efforts, Ian's eyes never moved from Susannah's face.

When Mandy was out of earshot, Susannah focused entirely on Ian. He was not smiling now, nor frowning either, but just looking down at her from his great height with an expression she could not decipher. The bright afternoon sun lent reddish glints to his black hair; it lightened his gray eyes to a shade near silver; it cast the classical beauty of his features into high relief, including the sensual curve of his mouth.

Just looking at his mouth made Susannah want to kill him. Again she grabbed her runaway temper by the tail and strove for icy dignity.

"You are a thorough-going villain," she said, her voice cold and precise. "You are a cad, a knave, and a scoundrel. A mongrel dog has more morals than you. A cat in heat has more shame. A hawk on the hunt has more pity. I saw you kiss Mandy, and I know that one reason you did it was to get back at me. But Mandy is only seventeen years old, and she is a total innocent! If you had any conscience at all, you would leave her alone. But of course you don't, do you? Then let me tell you this, Ian Connelly, and I hope you mark it well. If I ever again have the slightest reason to believe that Mandy, or Em, or Sarah Jane for that matter, is at risk from you, I will go straight to my father and tell him all that has occurred between us, so that the shame of it is out in the open. I will then sell you to Georges Renard, who is the wickedest reprobate in these parts, and all without telling you what I have done. Then, when Mr. Renard comes to haul you away in chains, I shall laugh. And make no mistake: I mean what I say with all my heart. I will not allow my innocent little sister to make the same mistake I made with you."

"Your 'innocent little sister' could give you lessons, sweetheart," Ian said and smiled at her. It was a slow, coarse smile, and it struck terror and something else, something far more primitive and base, clear down to Susannah's soul.

"Are you telling me that you—that Mandy . . ." Words failed her. Ian's smile widened, and his eyes took on a mocking glint.

"A gentleman never tells," he said. "And you of all people should know that I am, above everything else, a gentleman."

"You are a black-hearted swine!" Susannah hissed, having lost her grip on her temper.

"But then, we both know you have a weakness for swine, don't we?" he said. He reached out, chucked her under her chin, and walked past her to head, presumably, for the barn, before Susannah could recover enough to reply.

Fists clenching, Susannah glared after him. How it was possible to hate so intensely a man who'd taken her to heaven and back only a few days before was impossible to fathom. But hate him she did, so much that the taste of it was as tangible as bile in her throat. But to stalk after him and pound him with her fists, or a handy rock, or a ripped-from-the-wall-of-the-barn board was beneath her dignity. Besides, it would do no good at all. He was far bigger than she, and he would relish the chance to subdue her with his superior strength. Instead of attacking Ian, she needed to talk to Mandy. If his hint had any basis in fact, then the dilemma confronting her now was nothing compared to the trouble she faced.

If Ian Connelly had lain with her sister, then something would have to be done. An arranged marriage? Susannah couldn't even consider that possibility without feeling sick on several counts. First, Mandy was far too good for the likes of him. Second, the scandal of such a marriage would be even greater were lovely, eligible Mandy the bride than it would be with her on-the-shelf, less-than-lovely self in the role. And third, Susannah would be sick unto death every time she saw, or even pictured, the two together as husband and wife.

Much as she loved her little sister, much as she hated the blackguard who claimed to have seduced them both, she could not deny the fact that Ian Connelly, cur that he was, was the one, the only, man she had ever wanted for herself.

Mandy could not have him! But neither, a small voice of reason insisted, could she.

The first thing to do, of course, was seek out Mandy and discover from her the truth of the matter. Ian Connelly lied as naturally as he breathed.

Still, Susannah was deathly afraid. Feeling as if her feet had turned to lead, she turned and walked toward the house.

Sarah Jane and Em were on the back porch washing up. Like Susannah, they were dirty and sweaty, with their bright cotton dresses sadly crumpled and stained and their hair falling around their faces. Ordinarily it would have amused Susannah to see fastidious Sarah Jane, in particular, so disheveled, but she was not, at that moment, in the mood to laugh.

"Where's Mandy?" Susannah asked, tight-lipped.

"She went up to her room to change." It was clear from Sarah Jane's frown that she knew something was amiss. It was equally clear from her manner that she had not observed that embrace on the hill. "Is there something wrong?"

Susannah made some innocuous rejoinder and went in pursuit of Mandy. She wanted no witnesses for the conversation she meant to have with her erring sister.

Mandy was in the large front room she shared with Em, struggling to pull the green silk dress off without dislodging the pins. Her head was lost somewhere inside the bodice, and it was clear that she was not aware of Susannah's entrance.

Without a word Susannah moved to help her, grasping the waist and deftly easing the voluminous skirt up and over without catching Mandy's hair, skin, or underclothes on the pins. Talking to Ian, Susannah had been furious, but, now that she faced her well-loved little sister, the fury was all gone. Fear had drained it right out of her. Instead, she felt curiously removed from the situation, like an observer rather than a heartsick participant.

"Mandy, I am going to ask you something, and I hope you will tell me the truth. Just how far has this—thing—between you and Connelly gone?"

Mandy looked guilty. To one who knew her as well as Susannah did, the signs were unmistakable. Her lids fluttered and dropped, she swallowed almost imperceptibly, and the rose of her cheeks darkened an infinitesimal degree. Subtle signs, all, but Susannah read them and went cold.

As an obvious delaying tactic, Mandy reached for the dress of figured cambric that lay on the bed behind her and pulled it over her head. Automatically she presented her back to her sister, and just as automatically Susannah began to fasten the gown. When Mandy spoke at last, it was over her shoulder: "What do you mean, how far has it gone? How far do you imagine it's gone?"

"Have you—been intimate with him? 'Tis for your own well-being that I need to know."

"Susannah!" Mandy's shock at the suggestion was not feigned. Susannah knew her sister well enough to know that. She felt a peculiar easing of the hard knot that her insides had become, and a great sense of relief for Mandy's sake as well. Her fingers found the last hook, joined it to the corresponding eye. With the dress fastened, Mandy had no further excuse not to turn toward her sister.

"Whatever made you think such a thing?" Mandy asked. Though she might be innocent of the direst charge, Mandy was guilty of something. What it was, Susannah did not know, but the signs of an uneasy conscience did not evaporate; Mandy twitched a fold of her skirt into place and did not look at Susannah as she spoke.

Susannah regarded her, unsmiling. She had raised Mandy from a child of five and knew the slightest nuance of every response of which she was capable. The mother-love she had always felt for Mandy was still there, but so was a new realization of her little sister as a woman grown—and a rival. Mandy was lovely; Susannah knew she was not. Mandy was charming, in an engaging, innocent way that knocked men over like bowling pins. Mandy was alluring, so alluring that she could have her choice of nearly every available man in the county.

But she could not have the man Susannah wanted.

Jealousy was a sin, and sick, gnawing jealousy toward one's own sister was a greater sin. But Susannah couldn't help the way she felt. Despairing, she realized that Ian Connelly, the bounder, the villainous cur, had somehow managed to insinuate himself into her heart and would not be cast out. Like the victim of a demonic possession, she was locked in a fierce battle to regain control of her heart and soul.

The worst part of it was that the man who inspired all this tribulation wasn't in love with either her or Mandy. He had used and manipulated them both for his own obscure ends, whatever they might be.

Like herself, Mandy was being made a fool of by their bound man. But unlike herself, Mandy at least had the excuse of being only seventeen years old.

"I saw you kissing him, on the rise." Even putting it into words was difficult. Susannah had to struggle to banish the too-vivid picture from her mind. Remaining detached was the only shield from pain she had left, and she clung doggedly to it. "You know as well as I do that what you did goes far beyond the bounds of what is permissible with any man, and especially with him. We made an agreement, you and I. You were to behave yourself with Connelly, and I would let you go to the Haskinses' party. You've broken the agreement."

"Are you saying you won't let me go?" Mandy's eyes widened, and her voice grew suddenly shrill.

Susannah nodded unhappily. "I hate to deny you the treat, but playing such games with Connelly is dangerous, and . . ."

Defiance blazed in Mandy's eyes. "I will go to that party, and you can't stop me! You're only my sister, Susannah, not my mother, so you may as well stop acting like what you're not! I will go! And if you think to tell Pa about Connelly and have him stop me, you'd best think again. Because if you tell on me, then I'll tell on you, and I'll wager you've more to hide of your relationship with our bound man than I do!"

"Mandy!" Susannah was shocked. Mandy's sherry-brown eyes blazed brightly at her, then brimmed with tears.

"I mean what I say," she insisted. Snatching up the green silk gown, she ran past Susannah toward the door. "And you needn't think I need you to finish my dress, either, because I don't! I'll do it myself!"

Susannah was left with her mouth open and her hand partially raised to stop her as Mandy clattered down the stairs.

27

 "Miss Redmon! Miss Redmon!"

"Shut your mouth, you little bastard, or by God I'll shut it for you!"

"Mr. Likens! No! Think what you are doing! Susannah! Susannah, come quick!"

Susannah was halfway down the stairs when the commotion began. The last cry was Sarah Jane's, and it sounded urgent.

Grabbing her skirt up out of the way, Susannah bolted down the stairs and out the back door as if her petticoat were on fire.

The scene that met her eyes froze her for no more than an instant. Jeremy Likens had obviously been running to her for assistance. His father had come after him, had caught him just past the henhouse, and was now, with a fist in Jeremy's straw-colored hair, dragging him screaming back up the hill. Sarah Jane, with Mandy and Em behind her, was fluttering about the foot of the path where it started up the hill, yelling at Likens to let the boy go but obviously too fearful of the man to intervene physically.

At last Susannah had a target for the wrath that had been building inside her for days.

"The devil take you, Jed Likens!" she said furiously. Mindful of what had happened the last time, when she had thought to hold Likens at bay with the fowling piece, she snatched up another weapon instead—the stout broom that leaned in a corner of the back porch. Then she charged up the hill.

"Susannah, be careful!" Sarah Jane cried as Susannah rushed past her.

"I'll go get Ian!" Mandy said and ran to do so.

"Hurry, Susannah! He's hurting Jeremy!" Em screamed, and she and Sarah Jane fell in behind her. Angry as she was, Susannah barely noticed that she had reinforcements.

"Miss Redmon! Miss Redmon! Help me!" Jeremy was sobbing. His father shook the boy by the hair like a dog with a rat in its teeth.

"Shut up! Shut up!" Likens dragged the flailing boy on, lifting his feet practically clear of the ground.

"Jed Likens, you let him go!" Susannah was closing fast.

"Damn you, church woman, you stay out of this!" Likens glared ferociously at Susannah over his shoulder and shook Jeremy again.

"Let him go! At once, do you hear?"

"He's my boy! I'll do what I please with him! You just keep your old-cat nose out of it!"

"Miss Redmon, he done killed Ma this time!"

"Shut your mouth, boy! Shut your mouth, I say!"

"Let him go, Mr. Likens!"

"I'll be damned if I do!"

"I've no doubt you'll be damned anyway, Jed Likens," Susannah said grimly, coming up behind them at last. Gritting her teeth, she reversed the broom so that the soft straw pointed toward her and brought the handle, solid oak with a three-inch circumference, down hard on Jed Likens' back.

"I'm gonna kill you for that, you goody two-shoes bitch!" he screamed, releasing Jeremy and whirling. Susannah whacked him again. Sarah Jane and Em screamed.

"Run, Jeremy!" Jeremy did run—toward his father as Jed Likens sprang at Susannah. Susannah beat him furiously about the shoulders with the broom until Likens managed to grab the staff and wrest it from her hand. Sarah Jane and Em screamed again, Likens smiled an evil smile, and Jeremy leaped on his father's back as Likens swung the handle at Susannah's head.

Susannah ducked, throwing up an arm. The stout stick caught her arm just below the elbow. Susannah saw stars. She cried out at the pain of it and, stumbling, fell down.

"Stop it, Pa! Stop it!"

Likens reached around, caught Jeremy by the shirt collar, and threw him viciously to the ground. He lifted the handle high again to deliver the coup de grace to Susannah.

"Susannah!" Sarah Jane and Em screamed in unison and leaped forward to grab Likens by the arms. He knocked both of them aside. Sarah Jane fell on her backside, and Em fell forward onto her knees. Susannah was already struggling to rise. . . .

"I'll learn you to interfere with what don't concern you!" Likens snarled and swung the stick in a furious, swooshing arc at Susannah's head.

Susannah threw up an arm, ducked, and screamed. So did Sarah Jane and Em.

But the blow never fell.

"You've made a mistake, Likens. A bad mistake," a gravelly voice said, and Susannah looked up to find Ian standing between Likens and herself, one hand holding the staff, which he had caught in mid-swing. Susannah sagged, bracing both hands against the ground to keep herself from collapsing. Never in her life had she been so glad to see anyone as she was to see Ian.

"This ain't none of your concern, neither," Likens blustered. But his face had turned ashen, and his eyes darted shiftily to the side as if plotting his escape.

"Did he hurt you, Susannah?" Ian asked without ever glancing down at her.

"He hit her with the broom. I thought he was going to kill her," Sarah Jane said in a shaken voice before Susannah could reply.

"It takes a brave man to beat up women and children." There was a note to Ian's voice that Susannah had never heard before. "Very brave. Now let's see how brave you are with me."

What followed was one of the most sickening, yet rewarding, sights that Susannah had ever witnessed. Ian beat Jed Likens to a pulp before sending Ben, who had come running breathlessly up in time to get in on the tail end of the action, galloping into town to bring back the authorities.

"Now you're going to jail," Ian told the barely conscious Likens, who lay on his side, groaning.

"The constable won't never put Pa in jail," Jeremy said miserably. He shed no tears for his father but stood looking down at him rather as one might a temporarily helpless poisonous snake.

"He will this time," Ian said positively and moved to rest a hand on the boy's shoulder. "He hit Miss Redmon this time. Maybe he can get away with hitting your mother, but he can't get away with this."

"I better go check on Annabeth. She may be badly hurt," Susannah said, beginning to recover. She had gotten to her feet during the almost entirely one-sided battle and had watched with revulsion and some awe as Ian hammered his fists into Jed Likens' body with a force that was both lethal and methodical. Ordinarily she would have cried out against the violence of it, but if ever a man deserved to be beaten senseless, Jed Likens did. He had meted out such punishment to his wife and children more times than Susannah could count.

"You're hurt yourself," Ian said roughly, his eyes meeting hers across the dozen or so feet that separated them. "Someone else can go this time."

"But . . ." Susannah began to protest automatically, although her arm ached like a sore tooth.

Sarah Jane, whose arm was around Susannah's waist, supporting her, nodded.

"You're right," she said to Ian. "I'll go. Em, you can come with me. Mandy, you stay here with Susannah. She looks pale."

Ian smiled approvingly at Sarah Jane. To Susannah's fascination, Sarah Jane smiled rather shyly back. It seemed that even Sarah Jane was not proof against that roguish charm.

"Come on, Em, and you too, Jeremy," Sarah Jane said. Starting up the hill, with Em and Jeremy trailing behind, she paused and turned to glance at Ian.

"I think you probably saved Susannah's life," she said softly. "Thank you, Ian."

It was a landmark concession. Ian's eyes narrowed at Sarah Jane, as if assessing the subtle offer of friendship. He nodded once before moving to Susannah's side.

"Believe me, it was my pleasure. You're welcome, Sarah Jane."

Susannah gaped from Sarah Jane, who was smiling warmly at their bound man, to Ian himself, the devil who had succeeded in storming the last of the Redmons' four citadels. Because Mandy, of course, was his for the asking. (For all her preoccupation, Susannah had not missed hearing Mandy shout that she was going to fetch "Ian.") Em had been dazzled by him from the first and perfectly ready to regard him not only as an equal but as a totally superior being. As for herself, well, there was no point in delving into exactly how she felt about the man. Suffice it to say that ever since he had entered her life he had managed to fill it to overflowing.

Sarah Jane and Em went up the hill, with Jeremy now running ahead. Likens had subsided into total insensibility and lay sprawled on the path. Mandy stood by Susannah, gently pushing up her sister's sleeve so that she might view the injured arm. Ian joined them.

"Let me see," he ordered quietly, and Mandy stepped back. He reached out to grasp Susannah's wrist. As his long, hard fingers circled her arm, Susannah looked up, almost involuntarily, to meet his eyes. They blazed down at her for a moment, stealing her breath. Then, with something that felt very much like tenderness, he slid his hand up her forearm, turning her arm so that he might see the darkening bruise. The movement of her arm hurt so much that Susannah cried out.

"I should have killed him," Ian said through his teeth after a moment, glancing at Likens with loathing. Looking down again at Susannah, who had turned white, he cursed under his breath.

Before she realized what he meant to do, he stooped, caught her around the knees and the shoulders, and lifted her into his arms. Cradling her high against his chest, he started off down the hill.

"I can walk!" Susannah protested, scandalized at the spectacle they must make. She squirmed a little in his grasp, very conscious of Mandy trailing silently behind.

"Hush," Ian said firmly. "Just for once, will you please?"

Susannah was left with nothing to say. He carried her onto the back porch, through the kitchen, along the hall, and up the stairs. To Susannah's embarrassment, he strode right into her bedchamber and deposited her, quite gently, on her bed.

"She needs cold compresses on that bruise," Ian said to Mandy as her sister entered the room. "I've got to go back and make sure Likens doesn't move until he can be hauled off to gaol. You stay with Susannah."

He started for the door, stopped, and looked back over his shoulder.

"And Mandy," he said softly, "if you have to sit on her, make sure she bloody well stays put for at least long enough to get her arm taken care of."

28

The music was beautiful. The haunting alto of a violin was joined by the sweet notes of an indulcimor to fill the long, narrow ballroom with intoxicating sound. Susannah, who loved music, could barely keep from tapping her toes to the beat. She sat with the dowagers, of course, and didn't mind a bit even when old Mrs. Greer, who like herself was a guest, sat down beside her and bent her ear with a long list of her ailments. Indeed, the upkeep of such a conversation was undemanding, requiring only an occasional smile or nod, leaving her free to indulge herself by listening to the music and watching the spectacle unfolding before her.

More than fifty people were in the room, and the tall windows had been opened to allow circulation of whatever air might be stirring on so sultry a night. Sheer silk curtains of palest cream fluttered with the occasional breeze. The walls were hung with yellow brocade, and the domed ceiling boasted no fewer than half a dozen well-lit chandeliers. Two marble fireplaces had been set into each of the long walls, and they were filled now with masses of pink and white camellias. More camellias decked the tops of the windows and bloomed in the corners. The wooden floor had been given a high polish, so that it gleamed with reflected light. Upon its surface pranced her neighbors, clad in their finest.

Only the Greers, Hiram and his mother, and a married couple, the Lewises, were members of her father's congregation. The rest, wealthy planters and their families for the most part, belonged to St. Helena's Episcopal Church in town. Susannah might have felt a little strange if it hadn't been for her enjoyment of the music. It was not often that she found herself in such opulent surroundings or gave much thought to her attire. She was wearing her best Sunday black poplin with the white fichu around her shoulders and the silver pin at her breast, and her hair, uncovered, was styled just as she always wore it, in a thick bun at her nape. Watching the dancers, Susannah was increasingly conscious of her own sartorial deficiencies. The men wore either cadogan wigs or their own natural hair, powdered and pulled back into a tail. Their long-tailed coats were elegant, as were their clocked stockings and waistcoats of embroidered satin or brocade. But the ladies put the men to shame. Resplendent in flowered silks and striped satins and gleaming brocades, with their hair, powdered or not, artfully arranged in intricate puffs and rolls or pulled back from the face and allowed to fall to one side in thick sausage curls, even the plainest woman looked magnificent. Even old Mrs. Greer, who was in black like herself but whose gown was made of gleaming satin and topped by a lace mantilla, was in her best looks. Susannah felt like a dowd, not for the first time in her life. But tonight, for some reason, the feeling galled her. Maybe she should make herself a few new dresses, in brighter hues. . . .

But that was foolishness, of course. What she needed were serviceable clothes, not pretty ones. She was not a frivolous young girl like Mandy, after all, and she would very likely make herself ridiculous if she should try to rig herself out in the latest fashions at this stage in her life. She was mutton, not lamb, and it would serve her best to remember it.

Her eyes sought Mandy, who was standing at the opposite end of the room. Todd Haskins, on one side, plied her with lemonade, while on her other side another young man, Charles Ripley, Susannah thought his name was, offered her a nibble from a plate of cakes. Even the beautiful green silk dress that Mandy was so proud of was not quite so elegant as the creations worn by most of the other women, which had certainly come from dressmakers in Charles Town or even Richmond. But Mandy was certainly the loveliest girl present. Susannah beamed with pride as, after scanning the crowd, she was confirmed in her judgment of that.

The musicians were playing a minuet. Watching the pirouetting, posturing couples, Susannah could only marvel. The dance was graceful, stately, beautiful. Had it been possible, she would have loved to participate. Her body almost swayed at the thought. But it was not possible, of course, and even had it been she had only to consider how foolish she would look twirling about in such a fashion. Like a dowdy, near-middle-aged crow in a sky full of bright young butterflies, she thought, and almost snorted at the mere idea of making such a cake of herself.

Of course she had expressly forbidden Mandy to dance, and Mandy, who was a good girl at heart, showed no disposition to disobey. Lovely or not, it was not proper for a Baptist minister's daughter to engage in such behavior. Mandy knew and accepted that as well as Susannah did.

"Miss Redmon, how do you do? 'Tis been an age since we have seen you, I vow."

Her hostess, Lenora Haskins, Todd's mother, stopped beside Susannah's chair to smile down at her. There was perhaps a touch of condescension in that smile, because, of course, the Haskins moved in a more rarefied social stratum than the Redmons, but on the whole it was kindly.

Susannah exchanged pleasantries with Mrs. Haskins, then settled back down to nod at Mrs. Greer and listen to the music.

It was nearly an hour later when she realized that she had not seen Mandy for some time. Frowning, she scanned the ballroom, where a lively country dance was now in progress. There were gowns of butter yellow and carnation pink and magnolia-blossom white swirling about the room, but nowhere could she spy the least hint of apple green silk. The ballroom was on the ground floor, with its long windows open to the night. Mandy, tired of having to stand about on the sidelines unable to dance, must have gone out onto the gallery. The question was, just who had she gone out there with? She had been unusually quiet ever since the afternoon when Ian had fought with Jed Likens, then carried Susannah upstairs. Pouting was nothing out of the ordinary for Mandy, of course, but a quiet fit of the sulks, if that was what this mood was, was a new departure. Susannah did not know quite what to make of it or whether or not to try to cajole her sister out of it. She did know that she was suddenly concerned about her sister's whereabouts.

"Excuse me, please," Susannah said to Mrs. Greer, cutting the old woman off in mid-flow. Mrs. Greer looked taken aback, but Susannah was already making her way unobtrusively along the wall toward the open windows.

There were two couples on the gallery, as far away from each other as it was possible to be and blanketed by shadows, but Susannah saw at a glance that neither girl was Mandy.

The lawn stretched out in front of her, dark and alive with chirping crickets and croaking frogs and singing locusts. To the right were the stables. To the left were the swampy deltas where the Haskins grew their rice. Surely Mandy would not have gone either way.

"Can ah help you, ma'am?" A wizened old man, one of the Haskinses' slaves who had been passing out refreshments on silver trays inside the ballroom, materialized in front of her as she stood hesitating in one of the apertures, looking back over the guests with a frown. As if she could have somehow missed her own sister, of course.

"I'm looking for my sister," Susannah said. "Miss Amanda Redmon. She was wearing a green gown. Have you seen her?"

The old man frowned and shook his head. "No, ma'am, can't say that ah have. But ah'll ask Henry, if you'd be pleased to wait a minute."

Susannah watched as he made his way across the room to where Henry, who was the Haskinses' major domo, supervised the proceedings. As her eyes swept the crowd, she noticed three things: the festivities were growing increasingly merry, Todd Haskins was in the ballroom, dancing with an excessively attractive blonde—and Hiram Greer wasn't.

Had Mandy gone off somewhere with Hiram Greer? If so, Susannah did not know whether to be worried or relieved. Greer was well-known to them, and he would not harm Mandy, but that she should choose him for a companion was odd. Susannah was not well enough acquainted with the guest list to say for sure who else might be missing. But all the young men she had observed previously seemed to be present.

"Henry said Miss Redmon done went 'round to the rose gardens. Uh, he said she was escorted."

Susannah didn't want to ask the identity of the escort, fearing to rouse questions about Mandy's conduct if she made too much of it. The old man already looked worried, although perhaps that was his habitual expression.

"I see," she said, as noncommittally as she could. "And just where are the rose gardens, if you please? I've heard they are quite something to see."

"The easiest way to get there is to come out the back and go down past the kitchen," he said, beckoning. Susannah followed him, hoping that her progress would go unremarked. He pointed the way from the back door, and Susannah thanked him. Hurrying past the kitchen, which was a small brick building separate from the house, she was struck by the laughter and merriment that floated, along with appetizing aromas, out of the structure's open windows and doors. The slaves were having their own version of a good time, it seemed, even as they served the guests at the house. A dark-skinned woman wearing an apron and a turban appeared, bearing a steaming, obviously heavy platter of crab pastries in her hands, and sauntered along the covered passageway that led to the main house. More refreshments for the guests were on their way.

A man sat alone in the dark on the steps at the side of the kitchen. He was in the shadows, and she would not have noticed him at all had it not been for the tip of his cigar, glowing red. Sparing him hardly more than the glance it took to identify the source of the red glow, Susannah hurried past.

"Susannah." It was Ian. She would know that gravelly voice anywhere. Susannah stopped, waiting while he unfolded himself from the step and came across the lawn to join her. Despite the fact that Jed Likens had been taken to jail just as Ian had foretold, he had been released the day before with a stern warning to behave. Ian had been livid when he had heard, and adamant that Susannah go nowhere outside of shouting distance of the house by herself. Her father, angered as she had rarely seen him by the huge purple bruise on her arm, had roused himself from his usual abstraction to add his stricture to Ian's. Susannah had not disagreed, partly because she was afraid that Jed Likens might just be stupid enough and mean enough to try something and partly because taking one or the other of her sisters with her when she walked about the farm or down the road was a pleasure rather than a hardship. Fortunately, no one had summoned her to sit with a sick person at night lately. When that happened, as it inevitably would, then she would decide whether or not to allow Ian to escort her, as he clearly expected to do. The question of whether it was worse to risk a solo encounter with Jed Likens and his ilk or with Ian was never far from her mind, and she hadn't yet found an answer to it. Though her rage at Ian had been largely dissipated by his actions that afternoon four days ago, Susannah was still wary of him. She wanted him, and the feeling only grew worse with every new day that passed. She yearned for his laughter and companionship and teasing, and, yes, for the heartstopping effect he had on her senses. She missed him with every fiber of her heart and soul and body, but still she refused to give in to her yearning. If she could just remain strong, just keep out of his arms and out of his bed until the hunger for him passed, as it was bound to do sooner or later, she would be her old self again.

Like getting over an illness, getting over a man took time. Her best course of action was to avoid being alone with him, she knew, and that she had done for the last four days. Tonight, when he had driven them to the party, a silent Mandy had been along as a buffer, and Mandy would be with them again when they returned home. Though of course, since he was a bound man and a servant and quite beneath the touch of the Haskinses and their guests, he was not so much as allowed inside the house. They'd fixed him a plate of food in the kitchen, and he'd been left to cool his heels outside until his owners should decide to return home again.

Susannah was surprised to find that he had accepted these strictures, made known to them in a most subtle way by Henry when they had arrived, with no more than an ironic smile. She had almost been moved to protest on his behalf, but Mandy had already swept past them into the house and she had feared that such a protest would look too peculiar. She would not want anyone to get the idea that she fancied their bound man. Even if she did.

But here he was, standing next to her in the moonlight, while the scent of lilacs from the bush by the kitchen door wafted over them and the heart-stirring strains of a violin drifted through the air.

"Where did you get the cigar?" she asked him as he drew on it again, making the tip flare briefly before fading. He removed the cigar from his mouth and looked down at it with what she thought was a real affection.

"One of the slaves gave it to me. From Mr. Owen's desk, he said."

Mr. Owen was Owen Haskins, Todd's father and their host.

"I didn't know you had a fondness for tobacco," she said, somewhat embarrassed as it occurred to her that, even if he did, he had had no money to buy any since she had known him.

"There's a great deal you don't know about me, my girl. My liking for cigars is the least of it. What are you doing out here alone in the dark?" The tone of the question was severe, and Susannah was both unexpectedly touched by his concern and a little annoyed by his assumption that it was his right to question her.

"I'm looking for Mandy. And might I remind you that I survived for twenty-six years before I met you, and without a bodyguard."

He drew on the cigar again as if he relished the taste. "Is that how old you are? Twenty-six?"

"Yes. Though I suppose I should not admit it."

"You look younger."

Susannah glanced up at him sharply, then laughed. "You need not waste your silver tongue on me. I know I do not."

"I would have thought you just a couple of years older than Sarah Jane, and at a guess I put her at twenty-one or so. Is she older, then?"

"She's twenty, and I'm six years her senior."

"Why such a large gap between you?"

Susannah's face clouded. "My mother gave birth to three little boys who died in infancy between me and Sarah Jane. She was never the same after that, though she loved Sarah Jane and Mandy and Em, of course. Still, when the last little boy, the one after Em, died just a few hours after birth, I think she was happy enough to go with him. I think losing so many children just sapped her will to live."

"Was your mother like you?"

Susannah smiled reminiscently and shook her head. "She was more like Mandy. Very gay and beautiful. I take after my father in looks, and the Lord only knows who in disposition. Certainly not him."

"Your father is a saint."

"Yes," Susannah agreed, pleased that he had noticed.

"But, on his own, he could never have kept the church and the farm and your family afloat."

"He is not very practical."

"So you took on the responsibility for everything, including raising your sisters. It must have been very difficult for a young girl, especially at first."

"I managed. And, speaking of sisters, I really must go look for Mandy. She supposedly went to the rose garden, accompanied by an unknown gentleman."

"Ah." He fell into step beside her, and her heartbeat quickened. He didn't touch her, not by so much as a single brush of his arm, but she was aware of him with every pore. "And so you must play mama and go drag her back to the party."

"Something like that, yes." At least he did not seem concerned that Mandy was with another man. Susannah had wondered if he would be. The moon, a full frosty white ball about one quarter of the way along on its journey across the starry night sky, sent their shadows snaking out before them. Ian's looked very tall and elegant next to her own, which was—squat. The realization was lowering.

"So you gave up your own girlhood to take care of your sisters—at what age?"

"My mother died when I was fourteen."

"Forcing you to become a woman overnight."

"Someone had to try to fill my mother's place. Her passing left a huge hole in all our lives. My father was distraught, the girls were hardly more than babies, and there were meals to fix and the house to clean and the congregation to see to. There was no one to do it but me, so I just—did it."

"It must have been very difficult. But you've succeeded admirably, I must admit. The entire community obviously holds you in great respect, and your sisters are a credit to you. Though I don't think any of them realizes what a gem they have in you. Not even your father."

"If you mean my family doesn't appreciate me, you may be right," Susannah said. "They love me instead, which is better. And I love them."

She could feel his eyes on her face, though she steadfastly did not look up at him. Not that watching his shadow was a large improvement over watching him, but at least a shadow could not make her tingle with awareness. From the corner of her eye she saw his cigar glow red.

"You," he said slowly, "are a very nice woman."

That made her laugh, though the sound was a shade brittle. "Thank you so much."

"It's quite a compliment," he persisted. "Most of the women I've known are not really nice at all. Their every seeming act of kindness invariably has an ulterior motive, and they are grasping and greedy and out for what they can get."

"If what you say is true, then perhaps you need to expand your circle of acquaintances. Though I'm positive you exaggerate. Take your mother, for example; surely you would exempt her from such a condemnation." It was a delicate probe for information. Suddenly she was greedy to know more about him.

Ian laughed, but the sound was peculiarly unamused. "My mother would boggle your mind. She is as unlike you and your family as any creature could possibly be."

"Is she? In what way?"

He glanced down at her and dragged on the cigar again. For a moment he hesitated, and Susannah thought he might turn her question aside. But he did not. "My mother is not very—motherly," he said slowly. "In fact, she has said on more than one occasion that, had circumstances not forced her to, she would never have borne children. I have been a particular thorn in her side."

From his tone, Susannah immediately understood that his relationship with his mother was not a good one. She glanced swiftly up at him, to find that he was taking another deep drag on his cigar. Of course, to have a son who was a criminal might be just a little hard on a mother, but she was not going to point that out when the subject of his mother was obviously a sore one.

"Tell me about your life before you, ah, ended up with us."

"Before I became a convict, you mean?" He was smiling a little now as he glanced down at her, and Susannah was relieved to see the return of his lazy humor as she allowed the subject of his mother to drop. "What would you say if I told you that I was rich as Croesus and had half a dozen fine mansions at my disposal and that the most strenuous work I ever did was play cards all night and watch other men race my horses and sign my name to bank drafts?"

For a moment Susannah stared at him, very much taken aback. But the twinkle in his eye gave him away. "I'd say you were a very great liar, which I've known all along."

He shrugged and took another drag on the cigar, which was scarcely more than a stub by now.

"I'll tell you the truth some other day, then. Right now, we are on a mission to rescue your errant little sister, are we not?" He took a final drag and tossed the cigar away. Its still-glowing tip traced a bright arc through the darkness before it landed on the path in front of him, and he crushed it out with his toe.

Clearly the subject of his past made him uncomfortable. Imagining the surroundings he must have come from—if he could speak of his mother in such a way, his childhood must have been harsh—she felt a rush of sympathy so strong that it was all she could do not to reach out, pat his shoulder, and say, "There, there." Picturing his reaction to such an action made her smile. He would undoubtedly be horrified. Whatever else he was, Ian Connelly was a proud man.

"This way. I think." For his sake, she willingly fell in with his attempt to change the subject. From the sweet perfume that seemed heavier even than the sultry air, Susannah deduced that the rose garden must be nearby. She glanced around and saw a dark tangle of bushes surrounding a small, white-roofed pavilion. Tucking her hand in his elbow, the action instinctive rather than by design, she steered him in the right direction. When she realized what she had done and would have removed her hand, he caught it, returned it to the crook of his arm, and held it there.

29

"Susannah," Ian said, "I asked you once before, and you never answered: have you ever had a suitor?"

Her gaze flew to his face, to find that he was looking down at her with a flickering smile. But his eyes, touched to silver by the moonlight, were grave.

"I don't see that that's any of your concern," she answered in a constricted voice, glancing down at the thick grass on which they trod to avoid looking at his face. The entrance to the rose garden was right in front of them. She had perforce to draw nearer to him as they stepped onto the path that was paved with thousands of tiny, ground-up shells that sparkled in the moonlight and crunched beneath their feet. "And I wish you would stop flirting with me. I've already offered you your freedom, and I have nothing else to give."

"You're fun to flirt with, and, as I told you before, I don't want my freedom at the moment. And you still haven't answered my question."

He was clearly not going to let the matter drop. Susannah hesitated but decided that continued coyness on the subject would only make him think that the answer embarrassed her. Which it did, a little, but that she would never admit.

"Very well, then, if you must have it. No, I have never had a suitor." Her pity for him over his poor, deprived childhood had quite vanished. Hostility edged her voice.

"You have now."

"What?" Her brows knit, her head jerked around, and she stared at him. He grinned at her.

"Consider me your suitor, why don't you? Talk to me. Smile at me. Laugh with me. Flirt with me. Let me court you a little. Courting is an experience that shouldn't be missed."

"You're being quite ridiculous." He was teasing her, she knew, but still the picture he conjured up flustered her. Ian Connelly, did he put his mind to it, could charm bees right out of their hive, she thought. And he was charming her now, though she fought strenuously against falling under the spell of his handsome face and devilishly smooth tongue.

They had reached the center of the garden, where the small, round pavilion stood. Susannah would have skirted it, to exit the garden on the far side. It was becoming increasingly clear that wherever Mandy was, she was not here.

"From all I've seen, you've missed out on most of the pleasures that make life worth living. Haven't you ever done anything just a little daring?" He was drawing her inside the pavilion as he spoke. Susannah resisted.

"Yes," she replied, so tartly that her meaning was unmistakable. He laughed.

"Besides that."

"I really must find Mandy. She could be looking for me. She . . ."

"To hell with Mandy," he said, quite firmly. "Let Mandy, and the rest of them, take care of themselves for a while. Come play with me, Susannah. You need to play."

"Come into my parlor, said the spider to the fly?" Susannah misquoted tartly, still holding back.

He laughed again. "Something like that," he admitted, not a whit chagrined as he practically tugged her inside the open-sided little structure. "You learn fast, don't you, my darling?"

Susannah caught her breath, then hoped he had not heard the telltale gasp. "Yes, I do, and I'm not your darling, so you may save your blandishments for someone naive enough to be taken in by them."

"Prickly little puss, aren't you?" He turned to face her, catching both her hands and raising them, one at a time, to his lips. His lids lowered as he kissed her knuckles, and she saw that his lashes were thick and as black as ink, blacker even than his hair.

"Stop that," she said, but her voice was unsteady. There was still a foot or so of space between them, but she was tinglingly aware of every inch of his hard body. Like herself, he was clad in his Sunday-go-to-meeting clothes, and he looked more the gentleman than any of the so-called ones inside the ballroom. The peaked roof of the pavilion kept the moon from shining on them directly, but its muted glow reflected off the lawn and the garden and allowed her to see his face. He was smiling down at her, the merest curve of his lips, and she thought the expression in his eyes looked almost tender. Her heart lurched, and she knew all her hard-won resolutions where he was concerned were on the verge of flying out the window.

"Do you hear that? Listen." Ian cocked his head as the sweet strains of music whispered past their ears. ". . . Da – da – da – da – dum . . ."

"Alas, my love, you do me wrong to cast me off so discourteously. . . ."
Susannah, entranced by his deep voice intoning the familiar notes, could not
resist adding words to the music: ". . . who but my Lady Greensleeves?"

Her voice soft and true, she sang the haunting melody until he picked it
up and joined in. Only then, with his eyes not quite smiling as they searched
her face, did she realize how apropos the words were. She broke off, biting
her lip in chagrin.

He shook his head at her. His black hair, drawn back from his forehead
and secured at his nape with a ribbon, was struck by a stray moonbeam that
made it shine like a starling's wing.

"You sing like an angel," he said. "I could listen to you forever. Go on.
Please."

Thus encouraged, she took a breath, then picked up the tune again and
sang it through. He bent his head close to hers, humming along, and Susannah
was entranced. Before she quite knew how it had happened, he had drawn
her against his chest, grasping one of her hands while with the other he
guided her in a graceful pirouette. Then he drew her close once more, took a
few mincing steps forward which she mimicked dreamily, and twirled her
again before bowing, to which courtly gesture she responded with an instinctive curtsey. It was only then, as the song came to an end and the spell was
broken, that Susannah realized what they were doing and jerked free of him.

"We were dancing," she said in an awful tone, as if accusing him of the
vilest of acts. He grinned at her.

"And very elegantly, too." As he saw the expression on her face, he
added, "Why is it so wrong to dance? I knew as soon as I saw how much you
love music that you could be a wonderful dancer. You sing, and play, and lose
yourself in it. Even from the very back of your church I can see that. Dancing
is just another way of appreciating beautiful music."

It sounded so logical that Susannah found herself nearly persuaded. She
frowned direly. "That tongue of yours could coax the devil out of his horns,
Ian Connelly!"

He laughed and caught her hands again when she would have turned and
left him. "I would it were true. If so, then I would persuade you to forget
about your notions of what is proper and what is not, just for a little while. If
you'd let me, I'd teach you how much a part of the music you can be. Hear
that tune?"

Almost unwillingly, Susannah tipped her ear toward the source of the
lilting melody. It had a soft, dreamy quality that made her eyes half close.

"It's a waltz." Ian began to hum. His voice had a deep, raspy tone to it
that stirred something deep inside her. When he began to sway in time with
the cadence of the violin, she allowed him to pull her closer. Before she knew
quite how it happened, she was clasped against his chest. One of his arms was

wrapped around her waist, while the other held her hand in a tight, warm grasp.

"One-two-three, one-two-three, one-two-three four," he counted, as Susannah falteringly tried to match her steps to his. It was difficult, because being so close to his body distracted her. His chest was hard as a board against her swelling breasts; his thighs were as powerful as steel springs against her weakening legs. She could smell the musky scent of him, feel the heat of his body, see the black stubble that had grown since his morning's shave to darken his chin. More than she had ever wanted anything on earth she wanted to touch that stubble, to feel its roughness beneath her fingers. . . .

The thought disturbed her so much that she stumbled, and trod on his toe. She was mortified, but he only laughed and refused to let her stop. Instead his arm tightened, and he picked up the pace until he was whirling her around the inside of the pavilion at such a clip that she was soon breathless.

When the music stopped she was leaning against his chest, her hair falling down her back, laughing. He was laughing, too, his eyes alight with it, his face almost boyish as he chuckled. It was then, as she looked into his face and laughed and quite forgot how devilishly handsome he was in her sheer joy at being with him, that she realized, purely and simply, that she loved him.

Not that she was in love with him, though she was that, too. But that she loved him, for the man he was, quite apart from his heartbreaker's face.

At the realization, her heart threatened to shatter into a million tiny pieces. She was going to be hurt, badly hurt, perhaps mortally hurt, by this love that had come upon her unsought and unbidden, and she knew it. But there was nothing she could do, now, to escape her fate. Like a person caught in quicksand, she had been sucked deeper and deeper until she had no hope of pulling free.

All her fine resolutions vanished in the face of this new knowledge. How could she distance herself from a man who meant more to her than the very air she breathed?

Something of what she was feeling must have shown in her face, because he stopped laughing and looked down at her intently.

"What's wrong?"

"Let me go," she said and tried to pull free. She had to put some distance between them, had to separate herself from him for a little while, just enough time to think this shattering new truth through. She had barely enough wit left to know that if he discovered how she felt he would have her at his mercy.

But he wouldn't let her go. He caught both her hands and held them trapped against his chest.

"Alas, my love, you do me wrong . . ." he began softly, even as his eyes possessed her.

"Stop it!" The song cut her to the heart, and she tried again to pull away from him. But his arms slid around her waist and his hands locked behind her back and he refused to release her. Her hands were free, pressed flat against his chest. She supposed she could have slapped him to secure her release, but at the thought of striking him she felt sick. What she really wanted to do was slide her arms around his neck. . . .

Her hands clenched. He looked down at those tell-tale fists pressed against his chest, and for a moment he went very still. His arms tightened until she was molded against him, with scarce enough room between them to run a thread between their two bodies. His eyes flickered up from her hands to meet hers. The gray depths were suddenly as dark as the darkest pit, and unsmiling.

"Kiss me, Susannah."

It was a seductive murmur, hot and deep and full of temptation. His head bent over hers, bringing his mouth tantalizingly close. There was heaven and hell combined in his face. Muddled by his nearness, she could not decide if he was demon—or savior.

"I—can't." Her voice was anguished.

"Yes, you can. You've been safe all your life, Susannah. Take a chance. Take a chance on me."

"Ian . . ."

"Kiss me."

"I can't do this. I . . ."

"Kiss me."

". . . know it's wrong and . . ."

"Kiss me."

His eyes blazed at her suddenly. The heat was so palpable that she felt her mouth go dry. She longed, yearned, to go up on tiptoe and slide her arms around his neck and press her lips to his. . . .

No longer able to resist, she did.

At first he kept his lips closed, while she pressed her mouth to his in feverish entreaty. Now that she had bitten of the apple, she felt like a woman possessed. She wanted him. She needed him. She craved him. Her hands shook as they ran over the broad shoulders in the rough linsey-woolsey coat. Her knees shook too as she pressed her thighs against his. Her heart pounded, her lips quivered, and a steamy hot liquid boiled to life deep inside her to pulse through her veins.

"Oh, Ian. Ian." It was a broken little cry.

"God, I love the way you talk," he muttered against her mouth. Then, as if her voice whispering his name had exploded the iron control he'd been exerting over himself, his arms tightened around her until she could hardly breathe, and he bent her back over one arm and kissed her with a torrid hunger that turned her brain to mush and her body to jelly and her morals to air.

Susannah locked her arms around his neck and clung, kissing him just as feverishly as he kissed her. When he lowered her to the wooden floor, she went willingly. When he pulled at her skirts, she moaned and arched her back. When he unbuttoned his breeches and positioned himself between her legs, she lifted her bottom off the hard cold floor to meet him.

He grasped her bare hips beneath the frothy tangle of white petticoats and black skirts, plunging deep. She cried out at the fierce pleasure of it as, shuddering, he filled her to bursting. Her nails tore at his coat. Her teeth locked on his shoulder. He caught her thighs, lifting them high even as he took her again and again and again.

It was fast, this taking. Fast and hard and hot and glorious. Eyes closed, lips parted to gasp in air, Susannah writhed and bucked and strained toward the ecstasy that she knew awaited her. She wanted it. She needed it. She didn't think she could live without it.

When it came, it was as searing as an explosion of ball lightning. Flames swept her, hot licking flames that made her quiver and twitch and cry out. She was whirled away on the firestorm, barely aware of him echoing her cry as he held himself quaking inside her. Her arms were still clasped tight around his neck when he collapsed.

Little things, like the lush scent of roses and the thick, humid heat and the buzz of a mosquito, roused her in what could not have been more than a few minutes, though it seemed an eternity had passed. Her eyes blinked open, to find that she was staring up at the beamed, pointed roof of the Haskinses' outdoor pavilion. When she looked to the left, she could see the starry night sky through the structure's open sides. If she listened, she could hear the lilting strains of a violin.

Reality hit like a shock of cold water. She was lying sprawled on a hard, cold wooden floor that was bruising her bare bottom, the skirts of her best Sunday dress were pushed up around her waist, leaving her naked from her navel down; her legs were spread wide, and her bound man, half naked like herself, was lying in what felt like the sleep of the dead between them, the male part of him still inside her.

Anyone could come along.

"Ian!" She pushed at his shoulder. Awake after all, he turned his head, planting a kiss in the general vicinity of her left ear.

"Ian, get off me! Let me up!" She pushed at his shoulder again, urgently this time.

"You are clearly not a woman who likes to savor the afterglow," he grumbled but obligingly rolled off her. Susannah scrambled to her feet, not surprised to find that her knees were shaky as she yanked her skirts into place and straightened her fichu. Ian lay on his back, his hands folded beneath his head, watching her. His breeches were unbuttoned and his person was indecent to the point of putting Susannah to the blush, but he didn't seem one whit bothered by it.

Modesty, as she had already learned, was not his strong suit.

"Get up! Anyone could come along!" she whispered fiercely. Her hair hung in a hopeless tangle down her back, and her dress was crumpled. The skin of her face felt chafed where his bristly cheeks had rubbed hers. A scent clung to her, a musky aroma that she remembered from her first experience with him.

Only now she knew what it was: the smell of carnal love.

30

"Stop, Susannah. You're only making it worse. Let me," Ian said in a resigned voice as he watched Susannah's frantic efforts to restore her hair to some semblance of order. Without brush or comb, it was almost impossible to tame the curly mass. She had coiled it twice, thrusting her pins deep into the center of the bulky knot, only to have the pins spring out again and her hair tumble down her back.

"Hurry, then!" At the thought of being discovered, Susannah felt sick at her stomach. Mandy might be looking for her by this time. Or anyone might decide to visit the rose garden. The scandal would be all over Beaufort by dawn tomorrow.

"There's no need to panic." Ian cupped her face in his hands and tilted it up to his. She felt the warmth of his palms on her face, the rough tips of his fingers brushing her cheekbones, and had to fight the urge to close her eyes. Shameful or not, she could not regret what they had done. She loved him.

"If someone should come . . ."

"If someone should walk in here, right now, all they would see is a woman whose hair has fallen down. I'm fully clad, you're fully clad, and there's no scarlet letter blazing on your bosom. Your guilty secret is quite safe."

Put that way, it sounded even worse than she had thought. Was that what he was, her guilty secret? Susannah moaned.

"Now what?" Sounding mildly exasperated, Ian dropped a quick, hard kiss on her mouth and turned her around. Susannah forced herself to stand still as he ran his fingers like a comb through the wild mane of her hair.

"What we did was a sin, and I knew it was a sin . . ."

"Susannah . . ."

But she rushed on, disregarding the interruption. ". . . and—and still I did it anyway!"

His fingers stopped moving, and for a moment he went very still behind her. His hands left her hair to close over her shoulders. Gently he turned her about.

"Sin, like beauty, is very much in the eye of the beholder," he said. Looking up into his face, her eyes flickering over the stark masculine beauty of it, Susannah shook her head.

"Sin is—sin," she said in a strangled voice.

Ian's eyes darkened. "Making love to you is the closest I've come to heaven in a very long time. I don't want to hear any more talk of sin."

"Whether we talk of it or not doesn't change the truth."

"You're a very stubborn woman, did you know that? And a very beautiful one."

"Oh, Ian!" Her laugh trembled on the verge of tears. "I'm not! Be honest for once, and admit that I'm nothing at all above the ordinary. In fact, I'm rather plain."

"You're beautiful, and I'm always honest. You just don't know the truth when you hear it."

"You lie as easily as you breathe." Her accusation was both humorous and despairing.

"I breathe a sight more easily, believe me. Do you know your hair makes me think of a wild palomino filly I once saw galloping free on a mountain in Spain? That horse was a deep, burnished gold, and your hair is just that color."

"My hair is plain brown." It was a struggle to keep a grip on reality while he beguiled her, but Susannah tried her best. It would not do to let herself believe the preposterous things he said.

"And your eyes remind me of a sunlit pool hidden deep in a forest glade."

"They're hazel."

"Your mouth is as soft and generous as your nature, and the color of squashed raspberries."

"Squashed raspberries?" That sounded so very unromantic in comparison with his other poetic images that she couldn't help repeating it in a quizzical tone.

His mouth lifted up at one corner, and humor twinkled to life in his eyes. He looked so very dear, smiling down at her in that familiar teasing way, that she had to smile back at him almost mistily.

"Crushed rose petals, then. Something very lush and pink."

"I see."

"And your figure puts Venus to shame. How can you say you're not beautiful?"

"Who," Susannah asked, frowning, after the briefest pause, "is this Venus?"

For a moment he stared down at her, incredulous. He started to laugh and hugged her close against him. Susannah rested her forehead against his shaking chest, slightly miffed at being the source of his amusement.

"Venus, my darling," he said in her ear, "is one of the most famous classical figures in the world. But I can understand why your father, when he was educating you, might have kept you from all knowledge of it."

"Why? What's wrong with it?" Suspiciously she lifted her head to look up at him.

"Nothing is wrong with her. She's very beautiful. She's also very, uh, voluptuous, and almost completely nude. To the ancient Romans, she was the goddess of beauty and love."

"Oh." At the implications, Susannah felt her cheeks pinken.

"So when I tell you you're beautiful, you're to believe me. Is that clear?"

"But . . ."

"Say yes, Ian," he ordered.

Susannah surrendered. "Yes, Ian," she murmured obediently. As a reward he kissed her.

When he lifted his head, her arms were looped around his neck and her eyes were dreamy.

"And you taste good, too." He was pressing soft kisses all over her face. Susannah closed her eyes and leaned closer against him. "And you smell good —so fresh and clean, and always with the faintest hint of lemon. Why lemon?"

At that she opened her eyes. "I rinse my hair with it." She sluiced the juice over her head nearly every time she washed it, in a secret, silly hope it might lend a vestige of color to the thick mass of her hair. Though her hair could not be as nondescript as she had supposed if he could describe it as palomino gold—but of course his was the kind of tongue that had ended up ousting Adam and Eve from Eden.

"Miss Susannah actually has a hidden vanity! I don't believe it! There's hope for you yet."

He kissed her mouth again, more lingeringly, and her eyes fluttered shut. Susannah felt her reason slipping away again. She wanted nothing more from life than to be allowed to stay where she was forever, in his arms.

"Susannah! Susannah, are you there?"

Susannah jumped away from Ian like a scalded cat.

"Mandy!" she whispered frantically, her hands flying to her hair.

"Susannah!" The crunch of shells told Susannah that Mandy was entering the rose garden. Susannah hugged the shadowy center of the pavilion, glad that it was raised some few feet from the ground, not daring to look around lest Mandy should perceive her movement and catch her in such a state. Fortunately, trellis work rose halfway up the structure on three sides, providing some cover.

"Hold still. I'll do it." He stepped behind her, caught her hair in both hands and twisted it deftly into a long rope. Then he coiled the rope in a neat figure eight on the back of her head and secured it with precisely four pins. It usually took her at least three times that number.

"How did you do that?"

"Practice." He handed her the rest of the pins.

"I'll just bet!" She stowed them in her pocket.

"Mandy . . . Miss Mandy, please let me explain! I love you. . . ." The voice belonged to Hiram Greer, and it was clear from the sounds of his footsteps that he was following Mandy.

"Go away! Don't you dare say such things to me! Susannah!"

"What on earth . . . ?" Susannah glanced quickly down at herself. "Am I presentable? I must go to Mandy."

"Miss Mandy, I meant no disrespect. Please believe that. . . ."

"If you don't quit following me I shall scream! Susannah!" Mandy was getting shrill.

"You look fine. Every bit the minister's prim daughter again." Something in Ian's voice made Susannah frown. Her eyes lifted to his.

"Ian . . ."

"Susannah!" It was a wail. "Oh! How dare you! Take your hands off me!"

Then came brief sounds of a scuffle, a sharp rip that could only be tearing cloth, and a slap. Susannah and Ian exchanged brief, startled glances.

"Mandy!" Susannah cried, breaking away and moving out into the bright moonlight. "Mandy, I'm right here!"

Standing at the top of the shallow steps that led from the pavilion, she could see Mandy about twenty feet away on the sparkling path. She was struggling in Hiram Greer's arms.

"Mandy! Mr. Greer, unhand her at once!"

"Susannah! Oh, thank goodness!" Mandy glanced around, then tore herself out of Greer's surprise-slackened grasp.

"Miss Susannah! Uh . . ." Greer stuttered to a halt as Susannah hurried toward her sister. "It's not what it looks like. Uh . . ."

"They told me you'd gone to the rose garden, and when I came out to find you he insisted on coming with me, again. He's been following me about all night, though I didn't want him to, and—and he said I was a tease, and he —grabbed me!" Mandy broke off with a sob and ran to Susannah, who was approaching along the path toward her. To Susannah's dismay, real tears poured down Mandy's cheeks. Susannah saw that the bodice of Mandy's gown was torn, revealing the white lawn of her chemise.

"Mr. Greer," she said in an awful voice, wrapping her sobbing sister in her arms and speaking past her bent head. "What have you done?"

Greer looked shamefaced. To his credit, he did not try to run away but rather walked sheepishly toward the entwined pair. "She was being too free with some of those boys. I tried to tell her, but she walked away from me. I couldn't just let her go outside by herself, could I? Anything could have happened to her."

"Keep him away from me!" Mandy sobbed.

"I meant no disrespect," he said, and Susannah realized that his voice was faintly slurred. As he drew closer, it was clear from the general look of him and the smell of alcoholic spirits that hung about him that he'd imbibed rather freely. Suddenly Susannah realized why the party had grown so boisterous just before she had left it: the Haskinses had been serving strong drink to their guests. "I guess I—got carried away."

"I guess you did!" Susannah said coldly, while Mandy turned around to glare at Greer.

"He—he kissed me and—and pawed me and—and ripped my beautiful dress. Oh, Susannah, can we please go home?"

"Indeed we can. Mr. Greer . . ."

"I'll take care of this, Susannah." A quiet voice said behind her. Only then did Susannah realize that Ian had walked up behind her and now stood at her back.

"Oh, Ian, what must you think of me!" Mandy burst into fresh tears and hid her face in Susannah's shoulder.

"As I told you before, Mandy, when you kissed me, I think you're very young and very unaware of the dangers that men pose to innocent girls." Ian spoke quietly. Susannah was sure that his words did not carry even as far as Hiram Greer. "I still think that."

"I'm so ashamed," Mandy whispered.

"You've no reason to be ashamed, baby." Susannah—stunned at the revelation of the truth behind that kiss she had so reviled Ian for and overcome with her own guilt at her activities of the night—patted Mandy's back. If anyone had done something to be ashamed of, it was she, not Mandy. As Ian had said, Mandy was guilty of nothing worse than being very young and innocent.

"He didn't—hurt you?" Ian's question was very gentle.

"Not—really. But . . ." Mandy sobbed again.

"You're very lucky," Ian said to Greer in a louder voice. "Because if you'd done more than just rip her dress, I'd have killed you. You're a grown man, and you know as well as I do that, for all her flirting, she's no more than a naive little girl."

Susannah, occupied with comforting her weeping sister, barely noticed when Ian stepped around her and Mandy, who still clung to her. What occurred after that happened so quickly that by the time she guessed what Ian was about, it was all over: with a sickening *thwack!* his fist connected with

Greer's jaw. The other man reeled backward, to collapse on a hapless rose bush, crushing it.

"I hope you broke his jaw," Mandy said passionately, glancing around at the sound, but Ian shook his head and flexed his fingers at the same time.

"I didn't," he said regretfully. "I didn't hit him hard enough. He'll have a bruise, but that's about all."

The ride home was accomplished in comparative silence, though Mandy occasionally burst out with fierce animadversions on the character of men in general and Hiram Greer in particular. When they reached the house, Ian lifted both girls down. Mandy, her hand clutching her torn gown together at the neck, started up the steps toward the door as soon as her feet touched the ground.

"I'm sorry for what I thought about you and Mandy. I should have known better," Susannah murmured as Ian's hands lingered on her waist. Her eyes met his and clung; her fingers curled around his hard biceps. For a moment, there in the shadow of the buggy, he pulled her close.

"Yes, you should have," he whispered, dropping a lightning kiss on her mouth. "I told you that I wasn't interested in your sisters. Maybe, just once, you should try believing me."

"I . . ." Susannah began, when Mandy interrupted, calling to her from the porch.

"Susannah, are you coming? I think I'm going to be sick!"

"I have to go." She pulled free, though he caught her hands and held them in both of his.

"One of these days I'm going to get you alone, without your damned family anywhere around, and you won't have any excuse to be rid of me." His smile as he kept her hands a moment longer was wry, but it was still a smile, and the look in his eyes did strange things to her heart.

"Ian, I . . ." She almost did it. She almost confessed that she loved him there and then. But Mandy stomped her foot impatiently on the porch.

"Susannah!"

"I'm coming," she answered absently. Then, to Ian, she whispered almost shyly, "Tomorrow. We'll talk tomorrow."

"Yes," he said. "We'll talk."

His eyes never left her as she rounded the buggy. Susannah could feel them, warmly possessive, on her back. As she reached the porch and Mandy and slid a comforting arm around her sister's waist, there was the jingle of tack and the rumble of wheels, and the buggy moved off.

31

For the first time in his life, Ian thought he might be in love. The notion made him grimace with mingled humor and disgust. He was lying on the damned uncomfortable bed in the tiny cabin which was now, unbelievably, his home, his arms folded under his head, quite unable to sleep. Matchmaking mamas had been throwing their daughters at his head for years. He'd kept nearly a score of actresses and opera dancers under his protection, at separate times of course, in the decade since he'd come of age. His last mistress, Serena, had been as beautiful a woman as a man could hope to find anywhere, with glossy black hair, flashing dark eyes, skin the color of honey, and a figure that nearly rivalled Susannah's for ripeness. Serena had suited him perfectly, and he'd grown quite fond of her during the six months of their association. But never had she stirred anything in him that so much as approached what he felt for Miss Susannah Redmon.

It amused him to think of her that way, calling to mind as it did the image of her as he had first seen her. Prim, plain, and bossy of nature, a dowdy colonial spinster with an air of command, she'd been something quite beyond his ken. She was still something quite beyond his ken, though he had good reason to know that the prim spinster was only a facade that hid a vibrant, loving woman whose soul was as beautiful as Serena's face. And he had lived long enough, and hard enough, to realize that a soul, unlike a face, was beautiful forever. If one meant to keep her, her soul was the part of a woman that mattered.

Not that Susannah wasn't physically beautiful, too. She was, when he had her naked and hungry, with her skin flushed and her mouth soft and her eyes dreamy with passion, while her glorious hair cascaded down around her face and body like a curly lion's mane. Her body, with its full, ripe breasts and hips and tiny waist, was enough to stop his breath. Strip her of her dull clothes and proper exterior, and she was a different being entirely. Taught properly—and he had every intention of being very thorough with her lessons—she would be the best bed partner he'd ever had. Even now she was wild and hot and, once he got her past her curious notions of morality and sin, as eager for their lovemaking as he.

He could almost picture himself being faithful to a woman like that. Quite probably, if he had her in his bed every night, he'd lack the energy, if not the will, to stray.

Was he thinking of marriage? That he should even entertain the idea surprised him. But what other course was open to him with a woman like Susannah? However different she was from the ladies he was used to, she was, indubitably, a lady. In some ways, the ones that really mattered, she was a far greater lady than those who ruled the *ton*.

He could not use her as his mistress. Some unsuspected delicacy of mind shrank from even thinking of her in such a context, though he had bedded her twice, and damned hotly, too. But if he slept with her, she had to fall into one of two categories: mistress or wife.

Miss Susannah Redmon would never be happy as his mistress. Now that she'd given herself to him, not once but twice, she would be thinking in terms of persuading him to take her to wife. He knew how her mind worked as well as he knew his own.

She had said they'd talk on the morrow. Did she mean to propose? Managing as she was, that seemed quite likely. He wondered how she'd go about it. Picturing various scenarios made him grin.

Ian chuckled aloud as he wondered what she would reply when he told her he was really a marquis.

The entertainment value of that thought was his undoing. He never heard the door open, never saw the man who crept across the floor until suddenly, without the slightest warning, a huge dark shadow loomed over his bed.

His first, instantaneous thought was that Likens, the bastard, thought to exact some sort of revenge on him instead of Susannah, which suited him very well. His second was that Greer, the fool, still muddle-headed from drink, had followed them home and hoped to pay him back for that clout on the jaw.

The one foe he didn't consider, while his mind ranged with lightning quickness over various possibilities even as his body tensed for violent response, was precisely the one that, instants later, his attacker was revealed to be.

"This time you die, Derne," the specter growled, and a knife flashed as it hurtled down toward his chest.

Impossible as it seemed, his enemies had found him again.

32

Susannah was singing as she shaped dough into loaves not long after dawn the next morning. The tune had run through her dreams all night long, and even now she couldn't seem to get it out of her head. She could almost see Ian's face bending close to hers, just as it had when she had sung for him the night before. She almost could see the tender light in his gray eyes and the teasing smile that curved his beautiful mouth.

"Alas, my love, you do me wrong to cast me off so discourteously. . . ."

Not even particularly caring whether or not she was alone, she pirouetted once or twice on her way to pop the bread into the bake oven. As Ian had said, sin, like beauty, was in the eye of the beholder. Maybe dancing wasn't such a very great sin. And maybe he truly found her beautiful.

She was going to marry him. Susannah smiled giddily at the thought. She was going to take a chance on him, just as he had urged her to. She was going to do something daring, and dangerous, and probably foolish. She was going to grab life with both hands, while she had the chance. She was going to ask Ian to make her his wife.

There would be a scandal, of course, and the neighbors would buzz, and a few of the adamant sticklers among the congregation would look down their noses at her for a while, but Susannah had discovered, somewhere during the course of the long night, that she simply didn't care.

She wanted Ian, and she meant to have him. Take what you want, said God. Take what you want, and pay for it. Only this time, she wanted to be Ian's wife, and she was willing to pay the full price.

Anything.

What beautiful children they'd have, she thought dreamily as she added water to the kettle and hung it over the fire. Sturdy, black-haired little boys, girls with his perfectly carved features and gray eyes—or maybe they'd look like her. She would love them regardless, of course. But she hoped they would all look like Ian. How peculiar it would be, to find herself the mother of such a gorgeous brood!

Maybe a child had already started to grow within her. This time the thought excited her rather than filling her with dread. How wonderful it would be to have a child of her own—and Ian's—to love!

Pa would not object when she told him that she loved Ian and meant to marry him. She didn't even think he'd be too sorrowful, though she couldn't be absolutely positive about that. Ian was a bound man and a convict, after all. But Pa had never tried to keep her from doing anything she was determined to do, and he wouldn't—couldn't—stop her now. She hoped he wouldn't try. He liked Ian, after all, and she knew his primary concern was her happiness.

Ian was what made her happy.

Happy. Susannah realized that she'd forgotten what it felt like to be happy. Not since before her mother had died, when she'd lain in bed in the mornings and awakened to the smell of breakfast cooking and the sounds of her mother singing as she moved about the kitchen, had life seemed so full of possibilities. For a long time now her world had been leeched of joy. She'd done what she had to do, gotten through each day, picked up the standard that her mother had dropped. She had given unstintingly to those she loved. But she had not been happy.

She'd been resigned, rather. Sometimes content. Certainly ready to settle for the half-loaf that she had thought was to be her lot. To raise her sisters in lieu of children of her own. To keep her father's house rather than establish her own home. To watch as, one by one, her sisters found love, married, and had children. To be left, in the end, on the shelf and alone.

But Ian had changed all that. He had exploded into her life like a cannonball, and nothing had been the same since. She had not been the same since. She much preferred the foolish, reckless, and even sinful woman she was with Ian to the dried-out spinster she'd been before.

Maybe she would even let him teach her to dance.

At the thought, Susannah giggled. She was still giggling like a girl when Ben walked into the kitchen. Biting her tongue to stop her laughter, looking across at him almost guiltily, Susannah saw that he had not brought in the sticks for the fire. Instead, his hands were empty, and his fingers clenched and unclenched nervously.

"Somethin's amiss," he said without preamble, before she could question him. His thin young face wore an expression that Susannah had never before seen on it.

"What is amiss?" she asked, leaving off pouring molasses into a crock for the table to stare at him. A cold fear began to fill her heart, though she couldn't say exactly why. It was just a feeling, a bad feeling. . . .

"Connelly ain't nowhere around, and his cabin looks like a hurricane's been through it. I think he's gone, or been took, or somethin'."

"What?"

Susannah stared at him for the space of a heartbeat while a peculiar iciness spread throughout her body. She put down the molasses bucket almost too carefully and walked to the back door. Once there, she lifted her skirts clear of her feet and ran.

Ian's cabin was indeed a shambles. The door hung on its hinges, the bed was turned on its side, and the mattress had been flung across the room and ripped so that its cornhusk stuffing covered everything. The rest of the furnishings looked as though they had been flung about by a madman, or by someone in a furious rage. The pitcher and bowl from the washstand lay shattered on the floor. Even the mirror that hung above the washstand was broken.

Ian was not here. Nor was he in the barn, or the fields, or anywhere else that Susannah, in that first frantic rush, thought to look. By the time she returned, still almost running, to the cabin, the entire household was gathered there, talking among themselves.

"Something's happened to Ian!" she said, mounting panic sharpening her voice as they clustered around her.

"Now, Susannah, you don't know that," Sarah Jane said.

"Maybe Mr. Greer did something to him." Mandy sounded scared.

"Or Jed Likens," Em said.

"Craddock ain't never come back," Ben looked nervously around. "It's been a long time, too. Maybe whatever got him got Connelly."

"Ben! You hush your mouth!" Sarah Jane sounded almost fierce.

"We have to search for Ian." Susannah was striving to remain calm. She had to remain calm, for Ian's sake, and think. It was clear to her that a terrible struggle had taken place in that cabin. Maybe a fight to the death—though with whom? And who had won? If Ian had been the winner, where was he? She wrapped her arms around herself, shivering despite the already stifling heat.

"You don't know that anything bad's happened to him, daughter. Maybe a bear got in here, or a bunch of raccoons." The Reverend Redmon turned back from studying the inside of the cabin, took one look at Susannah's white face, and put an arm around her shoulders. His expression told her that he didn't put much stock in his own suggestions. There was something else there, too. She could see it in his eyes, feel it in his touch—he had just realized how she felt about Ian. But there was no condemnation in the gentle hazel gaze, and his touch was warmly comforting.

"Yes, I do. I can feel it," Susannah said. It was the truth. Deep inside her she could feel it beginning already, the sharp ache of loss. She remembered it from when her mother died. Only now it was a thousand times worse.

She pulled away from her father and walked inside the cabin. The chaos made her shiver, and yet she could not leave. There was something here, something that she was missing. . . . Picking her way through the mess, she touched things: an overturned chair, the upended bed, a pile of cornhusk stuffing from the mattress, the mattress itself. It was then, as she looked at the mattress, that she realized what had troubled her. The mattress had not burst. It had been slit open cleanly, as with a knife. A large, dark brown stain formed an irregular circle near the slit.

Scarcely daring to breathe, Susannah knelt and touched that stain. It was still damp.

"Blood," she said, horror rising in her throat and threatening to choke off all other utterance as she looked at the substance on her fingers. "Dear God, it's blood!"

"Susannah. Daughter, come away." From behind her, her father reached down and practically lifted her to her feet.

"It's blood, Pa! Ian's blood!" She knew it instinctively, with a deep, certain knowledge that she could not explain. Still staring at her stained fingers in shock, she was led unresisting toward the door.

"Be strong, child. God sends us no burdens that we cannot bear. If something has indeed befallen Con—uh, Ian, then you must strive to remember that it is His will."

"A pox on God's will!" Her passionate outcry caused her father's arm to drop from around her shoulder.

"Susannah Redmon, I am ashamed of you!" he said sharply, his gentle eyes suddenly stern as he condemned her for her blasphemy. Never in her life had her father spoken to her so or looked at her like that. But Susannah was too distraught to care. She could do no more than stare at her stained fingers and, despite her passionate disavowal, try to pray, as prayer was the only remedy she knew, the source of help in time of trouble that she had turned to all her life. Please, God, let Ian be all right. I'll give him up this time, I promise. I'll never lie with him again. I'll never dance again. I'll never question the teachings of the church again. Just let him be all right. Please. Please. Please. The cry ran feverishly through her brain.

Looking down into her whitening face, her father's expression softened. His arm came back around her shoulders as he urged her out into the light.

"There, I know you didn't mean it," he squeezed her shoulder. "You're a good, God-loving girl. Sometimes the heart just rebels at the pain and suffering that are a mere mortal's lot in life."

"I just found him," she said brokenly. "I can't lose him now. I just can't, Pa!"

"There, there," the Reverend Redmon said. He sounded almost helpless in the face of his eldest daughter's misery. Always before it had been Susannah who had been strong, and he did not seem to know what to do in the face of her distress. Then, as he stared at her bent head, his spine stiffened, and he seemed to grow an inch or so taller.

He beckoned to Ben, who stood with Sarah Jane and Mandy and Em a little distance away.

"Go to town for the constable, and tell him to bring some men for a search," the Reverend Redmon said to Ben with quiet authority. It was the first time in years that Susannah had heard that tone from him, and she glanced up at him in surprise. Suddenly it was as if she were seeing him the way he used to be, before her mother's passing had torn the heart from him. She had forgotten how strong he had been then, strong despite the gentleness that had always been so intrinsic a part of his nature. When she was a little girl, she had thought that her pa was omnipotent. He was the most powerful, bravest, smartest man in the world, and she had adored him. For a moment, just a moment, that was the man she saw again.

"In the meantime, daughter, let us go into the house. We'll do no good by standing about here."

Susannah rested her head against her father's shoulder as they went.

33

Two months passed. Two months that were closer to hell on earth than anything Susannah had ever experienced. Two months of unrelenting misery, of an ache so deep that she could not cry, of grief so debilitating that it seemed as if she would suffocate under the weight of it. It took every ounce of strength and courage and stubbornness she possessed just to get through the hours from one gray dawn to the next. And with Ian no longer in it, that was the color of her world: an unremitting gray.

She very much feared he was dead, although every now and then a tiny flicker of hope would insist he was not. But if he was not dead, then where was he? That he had simply run off, as the constable suggested, she could not, would not, believe. He would not just leave her without a word. Not after what had passed between them. She was as certain of that as she was of anything in her life.

Officially he was listed as an absconded bound servant. Handbills were printed up with his description and distributed as far away as Richmond. He was subject to arrest on sight. But not a single sighting of him was made.

A body was found by searchers in a nearby swamp, and for a little while Susannah's sense of dread heightened to sheer terror. The corpse had been partially dismembered by hungry alligators, making identification difficult. At the thought of Ian, her beautiful Ian, suffering such a fate, Susannah threw up. But eventually the dead man was discovered to be the missing Craddock. It was widely supposed that, while in a drunken state, Craddock had stumbled into the swamp and either drowned or been killed by the alligators that mauled him. Though she knew she should have felt proper sorrow at their farmhand's tragic end, Susannah was conscious only of a profound relief. Through the funeral service and burial she could summon scarcely a single prayer for the repose of Craddock's soul. What kept running through her mind, over and over again, was, Thank God. Thank God. Thank God it isn't Ian.

A week or so later another corpse was found. This man had been buried in a shallow grave scooped out beneath the carpet of fallen needles that blanketed the piney woods. Searchers were drawn to the site by the strong odor of his body as it returned to the dust from which it was made. From the first it was clear that the dead man was a stranger, so Susannah felt only the mildest curiosity about the mystery that had the rest of Beaufort abuzz. Who was he, where had he come from, and how had he come to be buried there in the woods? The questions went back and forth, though Susannah was unconcerned with the answers. All she could think was, at least it isn't Ian.

Hiram Greer still called at the house, under the pretext of bringing news about the search for their missing bound man. Mandy refused to accept his renewed apologies and stayed clear of him. But as no one else knew of his transgression and Susannah was too frightened of missing the smallest bit of information to forbid him the house, he stopped by every few days. Indeed, she couldn't even summon the energy to hold a grudge against him for his behavior that night in the rose garden. She simply preferred to forget about it, because remembering also brought with it sharp, searing memories of Ian.

At least she was not with child. Her monthly courses came and went just as before. She knew that its arrival was a blessing from God, but still she mourned the dream children she would never have just as she mourned Ian.

She was so upset that she couldn't even cook. Never before had she been unable to take solace in her kitchen, and the circumstance would have alarmed her had she been able to summon an emotion other than grief. But she could not. Despair filled her to the exclusion of all else. Besides that, she felt nothing.

Sarah Jane's wedding approached, and Susannah had to rouse herself to make preparations for that. At least, if she wept as she stitched her sister's wedding gown, it was assumed that her tears were at the prospect of the parting that grew ever nearer. Only Susannah knew the truth: the tears were for herself, for the wedding to Ian that she would never have. For their dream children, who would never be born. For the bright, shining future that had been dangled before her, then snatched so hideously away.

Susannah acknowledged her own selfishness, but such was her malaise that she could not even summon a feeling of shame.

Her family watched as she grew pale and listless, and worried. It was Sarah Jane who suggested that they travel to Charles Town, which was a distance of some forty miles away, to escape the August heat for a fortnight. Such seasonal migrations were common on the part of the planters and their families—indeed, the Haskinses and Mrs. Greer and several other local aristocrats had already removed themselves for the remainder of the summer to the town homes they maintained there—but the Redmons, being of plain farm stock, had never even considered doing such before. The festivities and social activities that marked the summer months in Charles Town were anathema to the Reverend Redmon. Though he approved of Sarah Jane's idea—a change of scene might be just the thing to restore Susannah's spirits—he declined to make the trip with the perfectly legitimate excuse that, if he went, there would be no one to preach of a Sunday. Ordinarily Susannah, too, would have scoffed at the idea of such a journey—after all, who would do her work while she was gone?—but such was her pain that she let her father and Sarah Jane make the arrangements without protest. Only when it occurred to her that in Charles Town she would not be able to instantly hear any information that might turn up about Ian did she think to object, and by then it was too late, because they were already aboard the ship that spent the summer months plying the coast.

Even at sea, it was suffocatingly hot. Susannah and her sisters spent most of the voyage on deck, seated under a canopy rigged for the ladies' comfort. The constant motion rendered both Susannah and Sarah Jane vaguely nauseous, and for a while they contented themselves with closing their eyes and enjoying the warm breeze on their faces. Mandy and Em were so excited they could scarcely sit still, and they kept jumping up to exclaim over the silver flash of a jumping fish or the sighting of a distant sail. The company was congenial, and the atmosphere on the deck was rather like that of a church social. As the hours slid by and her nausea receded, Sarah Jane even managed to partake of some lemonade and cakes and enter into her younger sisters' banter. Susannah, on the other hand, only grew sicker and wished the journey might soon end.

It occurred to her that, without Ian, nothing gave her pleasure anymore.

It was almost dark when the *Bluebell,* for that was the ship's name, sailed briskly into Charles Town Harbor. They had missed the tide, the captain explained, and there was a strong west wind blowing. Thus he meant to anchor the *Bluebell* in the bay overnight and dock in the morning. Meanwhile, the passengers could go ashore by longboat.

There were eleven passengers all together, and so the longboat was crowded. Susannah, who made it down the swaying rope ladder more by sheer force of will than anything else, was afraid that she was going to be actively sick as the small boat pitched up and down over the bobbing waves. Some combination of heat and motion had rendered her stomach most unreliable. She closed her eyes, gritted her teeth, and prayed to reach shore without disgracing herself.

When at last the boat tied up at the landing, the sun had sunk clear beneath the horizon, leaving behind streamers of bright pink and orange and gold to unfurl across the deepening purple of the sky. A grinning sailor practi-

cally lifted Susannah onto the dock. Sarah Jane, Mandy, and Em, who'd dis-
embarked just ahead of her, hovered over their sister with solicitous murmurs.

"Happen she's just got a touch of the mal de mer," the sailor said as he
moved away to help unload the baggage. "Give her a bit to get her land legs
beneath her, and she'll be right as a trivet."

Susannah gritted her teeth and opened her eyes. "He's right," she said
faintly to her sisters. "Just let me stand here for a minute. I know the dock
isn't moving, but it feels like it is. I'm a poor sailor, I fear."

"Let me go see about a carriage," Sarah Jane said, looking around. "I
understand they can be hired right in front of the dock."

"You can't go alone." Susannah spied her own trunk being lifted from the
longboat and tottered over to sit down on it with a sigh of relief. If only she
could lie down. Her head was swimming, her stomach churned, and, when
she glanced toward town, the horizon with its jagged row of buildings and two
tall steeples seemed to tilt on its side. If she turned her head out to sea, her
case was even worse: beyond the tall bare poles and furled sails of ships at
dock and anchored in the bay was the rolling ocean. With a shudder she
turned her gaze to her immediate surroundings.

All about her was a bustle of activity. Arriving and departing passengers
hugged and wept over their loved ones. Sailors exchanged ribald quips and an
occasional curse. The chatter was punctuated by loud booms and clattering
rattles as barrels were unloaded from a nearby ship. Coarse rope nets loaded
down with bales of cotton were hoisted into the air by creaky winches.

"I'll take Em with me, then, and Mandy can stay here with you," Sarah
Jane said, looking worriedly at Susannah's pale face.

Mandy looked disappointed, but she didn't argue. Of course she was as
eager to get a glimpse of Charles Town as Em, and Susannah felt she herself
would be better for a few moments in which she could simply rest. With
Mandy, or even Em, to keep an eye on, closing her eyes would be sheer folly.

"All three of you go. I'll be fine right where I am. If I just sit still a
minute, maybe my stomach will discover we're back on land."

Sarah Jane looked from Susannah to Em to Mandy, then nodded with
reluctant agreement. "We'll be right back."

Susannah waved them off. Then she slumped and closed her eyes. If only
she could lie down. . . .

Just what made her open them again she didn't know—a tingle, a prickle
of awareness, a magnetic current that shivered down her spine? But open her
eyes she did, to focus rather hazily on the motley stream of humanity that
passed some few feet beyond her perch at the edge of the dock.

A woman in a bright scarlet dress and fantastic feathered hat stood chat-
ting with a soldier whose uniform was as vivid a red as her gown. Two boys
chased one another, apparently battling over the ball that the first one held. A

family of seven, the woman obviously expecting again, walked slowly toward the lowered gangplank of a ship. A tall man in a swirling blue cloak with a three-cornered black hat pulled low over his eyes overtook the family and seemed headed toward the same gangplank.

Susannah's eyes widened, her mouth dropped open, and she rose from her makeshift seat as if a string run from her feet through her body and out her head had jerked her upright.

"Ian," she said hoarsely. Then, louder, "Ian!"

It couldn't be, of course. But the walk, the way the man carried himself, struck a terrible chord of familiarity. It couldn't be, and yet . . .

"Ian!" It was a cry now, and several passersby turned to look. Nearing the end of the gangplank, the man glanced back over his shoulder. The hat shaded his eyes, and the upstanding collar of the cloak made it impossible to see the lower third of his face. But still, the very way he moved his head caused her stomach to clench.

"Ian!" She started after him, moving as if she were in a daze. How could it be—but her heart screamed that it was. The lady in scarlet and her soldier companion stared openly as she passed them. Susannah barely even knew they were there.

The man seemed to hesitate, then continued on his way. If anything, he quickened his pace. Susannah began to run.

"Ian!" More people turned to look. The mother of the family Susannah had just observed clutched her youngest closer to her skirts as Susannah rushed past. Susannah never even saw them. She ran as if she were chasing the ghost he must be, ran as if he would vanish in a puff of smoke if she didn't reach him within seconds. She ran until her heart threatened to burst in her chest and her blood pounded in her temples, and she could scarcely draw breath. And yet she was aware of no physical discomfort at all.

"Ian!" She reached him, caught at his cloak. Her fingers closed over the smooth cool wool and tugged. If it were not he, if she had chased and pulled at the cloak of a stranger, she would be thought insane. Maybe she was insane. Maybe the grief had cost her her reason. But she knew—she knew . . .

With her hand clutching his cloak, there was nothing he could do but turn. He did, and for a moment, a wonderful, terrible moment, Susannah found herself staring up into eyes as gray as a storm rolling in from the sea. A muscle twitched at the corner of his beautiful mouth. The straight elegant nose, the high cheekbones, the square, almost cleft chin—all were unchanged. His cheeks and chin were shadowed with a faint black stubble. One of her hands rose of its own volition to touch that sandpaper cheek.

"Ian," she whispered, sure of him now. Her grip tightened on the fold of his cloak that she held as if she feared to release it in case he should disappear.

For an instant, no more than an instant, she simply stared up into his face. Then a returning wave of weakness caught her unaware. She swayed, surprised to find his face blurring into fuzzy twin images.

For the first and only time in her life, she fainted dead away.

34

When Susannah opened her eyes, it was dark. Not the dark of midnight, but the gray, gloomy dark of enclosed spaces. And she was in an enclosed space, she discovered with a frown. She was lying flat on her back on a thin mattress raised some few feet off the floor, staring up at a three-foot-wide wooden shelf not too far above her head. On her left was a smooth, wood-paneled wall. On her right—and she turned on her side to get a better view—was a tiny, box-like room. A black iron stove and a small table and chairs were the only furnishings. An oddly situated round window was the sole source of light. Curiously, the entire chamber seemed to sway.

She was looking away from the wall into which the door was set and thus heard rather than saw the striking of flint on steel. By the time she turned her head around, he was cupping his hand around the wick of an oil lamp.

Ian.

The wick slowly caught and flared. He put the globe back on the base and turned to face her.

Ian.

He sat in a chair propped against the door, clad in black breeches, a white shirt with an elegantly tied neckcloth, a pair of shiny black boots, and a waistcoat of dull silver satin that she had never seen before.

"Ian." This time she said his name aloud, disbelievingly, as she struggled into a sitting position. Her head ached, her stomach churned, but she could not take her eyes from his face. Was she asleep and dreaming, perhaps? Was he a phantom who would vanish when she awoke?

"Hello, Susannah."

Hello, Susannah? *Hello, Susannah?* No phantom, surely, would greet the love he returned from the afterworld to comfort in so prosaic a fashion. Susannah's eyes narrowed as they swept over him. No phantom, surely, would sit with booted legs crossed negligently at the ankle, his hands folded on his stomach, his eyes hooded as he watched her. No phantom, certainly, had the stubble of a day's growth of beard darkening his cheeks!

He was as real and solid as she was herself. *Hello, Susannah?* Was that all he had to say after more than two months of agonized separation? Was that all he had to say after she had grieved herself sick over him, mourning him with a painful intensity that put the sorrow she had felt for her blessed mother to shame?

"Hello, Susannah?" She echoed his greeting aloud, her tone disbelieving. Her eyes were wide with incredulity.

"I daresay you've been wondering where I disappeared to." He sounded faintly uneasy and even shifted from his negligent position to lean forward, his hands clasped between his spread knees.

"You daresay I've been wondering. . . ." Still stunned when she began, Susannah snapped her teeth together in the middle of that second sentence as the reality of the situation came home to her like a clap of thunder. He was not dead. He had never been dead! From the look of him, he had never even been hurt and had simply taken himself off when it had suited him to do so, the swine! And why not, pray? He'd even told her, once, that he meant to do so when it suited him. After all, he had gotten what he'd wanted, hadn't he? He'd tamed the minister's prim daughter, to use words he had employed himself. He had bedded her, not once but twice, and found her plenty hot, too. On that never-to-be-forgotten occasion when she had offered him his freedom, he had told her that he stayed because pursuing her amused him. But then he had caught his quarry, and, with the hunt over, he had apparently ceased being amused. So he'd moved on to greener pastures, without a thought for the woman he left behind.

"Yes, you might say I've been wondering where you had disappeared to," she managed in a tight voice before rage swamped her. Hot blood flooded her veins. Fire blazed from her eyes. She shot to her feet, her fists clenching and unclenching at her sides as her gaze swept the room for a weapon. He was not dead, yet; but, as God was her witness, he would be when she got through with him!

"Now, Susannah, if you'll just be calm I can explain. . . ."

That placating offer was a classic case of too little, too late. With a wordless cry of rage Susannah spied a poker leaning against the stove, grabbed it with a single lunge, then turned to annihilate the black-souled scoundrel who had stolen her heart and trampled it carelessly into the ground.

"You rascally knave! I thought you dead!" She rushed toward him, the poker lifted high overhead and held with both hands. When a pair of strides brought her within range, she brought it crashing down toward the glossy black crown that had haunted her days and nights for more than two months. She'd make a ghost of him yet!

"Wait a minute!" He threw up a hand and flung himself to the side. The poker caught his upper arm, drawing a pained yelp from him even as the chair tipped beneath his weight and pitched him to the floor. He yelped again as he landed hard, but he had no time to recover before she was upon him. She got in a few more good licks before, cursing, he grabbed the shaft of the poker and wrenched it from her hand. With a wordless cry of rage at being thus disarmed, Susannah whirled and sought a new weapon.

"Damn it, Susannah!" He surged to his feet with the quick grace of a cat, casting the poker aside.

"You lily-livered cad!" She found another oil lamp on the table—fortunately unlit—and hurled it at him even as he spoke. Jumping to one side, he just managed to get out of the way, and the lamp shattered against the wall.

"That's just about enough!" He was roaring now, and even as she discovered a pair of wick-scissors and flung them at him he lunged forward, caught her around the waist, and bore her, kicking and shrieking, to the floor. The hard wood moved beneath her back. The ceiling slanted over her head. A round metal cylinder freed by the shattering of the lamp rolled across the floor past her feet. But Susannah was barely aware of these things. She was kicking and scratching and biting at the silver-tongued cur who was scrabbling to pin her to the floor.

"Ouch!" he said, as her teeth sank into his shoulder. Grabbing her wrists, he pinned them beside her head and jerked his shoulder out of range. Shifting one hard thigh, he managed to pin her kicking legs to the floor. Holding her thus, poised a little bit above her so that she could not bite him, her hands and legs secured so that they could inflict no damage to his person, he had her fast. Susannah glared up at him, so furious she could have chewed nails—or his too-handsome nose!

"Get off me, you repellent oaf!"

"If you'll just listen. . . ." There was that placating tone again. What tale did he think to spin her this time, pray? Did he really imagine that she was such a fool that he could sweet-talk her out of her anger? Yes, he probably did, because she had given him every indication in the past that she was such a fool. But that was in the past!

"I'll never listen to another word you say! I cried over you, you stinking polecat! I couldn't sleep, or eat, or do anything but grieve! I worried my father! I worried my sisters! I quit taking care of the congregation! And all because of you, you varmint! You insect! You worm!"

"Now, Susannah . . ."

"Don't you 'Now, Susannah' me! You got what you wanted from me, and you left! That's the truth, so don't try to dress it up with pretty phrases! You're a no-good cur, and a . . ."

He shut her up by the simple expedient of transferring her wrists to one hand and clamping the other over her mouth. Furious, she made muffled sounds of outrage and tried to pull her face free, but it was useless.

"I realize you think that you have cause to be angry with me, but when you hear me out you'll see that I had no choice but to leave as I did. I was coming back, I swear I was. I just had some—business—to attend to first." He spoke rapidly, his gray eyes earnest as a saint's as he looked down into her face. As if she would fall for his tricks again! Susannah glared up at him, her body rigid under his, her expression furious beneath his silencing hand.

He frowned, as if searching for words that might sway her. Not likely, Susannah thought, and fixed him with a gimlet stare.

"You may have difficulty believing this—hell, I know you're going to have difficulty believing this, because you never have believed a word I've said—but I did not commit the crime with which I was charged. I did not, in fact, commit any crime at all. The information laid against me in England was false, my true identity concealed, and the court bribed to find me guilty. I was supposed to be murdered in Newgate, I think. But fortunately bribery works both ways. I traded my signet ring to a guard, and he put me in with a gang of convicts to be transported. Else I doubt I'd be alive today."

Susannah's gaze must have expressed her skepticism, because his frown deepened and his eyes took on an almost pleading look that might, at some previous time in their association, have moved her, though now it emphatically did not.

"Being on a convict ship was hell, but I was determined to survive. If I could stay alive, I thought, then I could return to England and exact vengeance on those who had so betrayed me and reclaim all that was mine. The piece of paper that said I was little better than a slave for seven years meant nothing to me; I had no intention of honoring it for longer than I had to. When you bought me at auction, I thought it would be easy. I would rest and regain my strength and then leave. But I didn't plan on falling in love with you, or on my enemies in England discovering that I had escaped their net and coming after me. The night I left, I was attacked by one of my enemies' minions who'd been sent to kill me. During the course of our battle, some things he said led me to the conclusion that he had come to your farm with instructions to rid the world of me once before, only to murder poor Craddock by mistake. If you recall, on the night Craddock disappeared I was not in my cabin."

Though he didn't say it, Susannah could not help but remember precisely where he had been the night Craddock disappeared—in her bed. If he thought the memory would aid his cause, then he was about as wrong as it was possible for a human being to be. As for his falling in love with her—hah! He must think she was a want-wit, to believe that after what he had done! Disappearing without a word was not something she would do to someone she loved! Something in her expression must have displayed how infelicitous she found his words, because after studying her face he continued almost wearily.

"Be that as it may, he came back for a second try at me, and I killed him instead. But I knew I had to leave, because if one came after me and failed, there would be more. Once it was known that I had survived the fate that they had planned for me, they would not stop until they succeeded and I was dead. They couldn't; there is too much at stake for them now. I had to leave you, Susannah. If I had not, I would have put you and your family in almost as much danger as I was in myself."

He searched her face again, as if looking for a sign. She snorted against his hand, and to her surprise he removed it.

"You must know that your explanation, while very affecting, is about as clear as mud. Who is after you, pray, and why?"

She raised her eyebrows at him as she asked the question. He hesitated, as if searching for words. Then he sighed.

"As I told you before, Susannah, though you chose not to believe me then either, I am—or was—a very rich man. I am the Marquis of Derne, to be exact, eldest son and heir to the Duke of Warrender. Only my mother prefers that my younger brother inherit in my stead, and she and my brother conspired together to rid the world of me. Having gone so far, they cannot now turn back. They will see me dead at any cost, unless I can put a crimp in their plans, which I hope my return will do."

For a moment, just a moment, Susannah weighed his words. That he was a marquis, a nobleman, she could almost believe. That would explain much about him, from his looks, to his arrogance, to the effortless elegance that seemed as much a part of him as breathing. And he had told her, as they had walked toward the rose garden on the night of the Haskins' party, that his mother was not very motherly and that he was a thorn in her flesh. . . .

But then she caught herself and flushed a little at her own gullibility. He was on the verge of talking her around again! What she must fix in her mind, and keep fixed there, was the fact that, had she not by the merest coincidence happened to be on Charles Town's dock as he passed, she would never have seen him again!

"That is the purest drivel I have ever heard in my life! The Marquis of Derne indeed! Surely you do not think I am such a fool as to believe you?"

"But it is the truth, I swear. I . . ."

"Tell me," she interrupted ominously, as the floor tilted beneath her as it had been doing during the whole of their exchange, "am I correct in assuming we are aboard some sort of ship?"

At that he looked slightly apologetic. "You fainted, and the ship was ready to sail. I could not just leave you lying there on the dock. Besides, as soon as you recovered your senses I knew you would prate of seeing me to all and sundry, and I would just as soon not have the authorities waiting at quayside when we dock in England, ready to haul me off to gaol as a runaway indentured servant. I saw your broadsheets, you know."

The accusing look that accompanied this last passed right over Susannah's head.

"Are you telling me that we are on a ship bound for England?" she gasped.

"Yes."

That bald statement made her close her eyes. "Dear God!"

"You'll like England, I promise you. It's cool there, with none of your hellish heat. And . . ."

"If you do not get off me this very instant, you are going to be extremely sorry," she interrupted in an ominous tone, her eyes opening in her whitening face. "Because I am not a good sailor, I warn you, and I am about to be extremely sick!"

35

As the weather drove him from the deck for the sixth time in as
many days, Ian thought ruefully that being confined to a cabin with
Susannah was rather like being swung in a sack with a vixen. A very
sick vixen. When she had said she was not a good sailor, she had dramatically
understated the case. She had been violently ill for the entire three weeks the
Corinth had been at sea.

He cautiously opened the door to their cabin and stepped inside. A
lantern swayed from the ceiling to which it was affixed, its yellow glow permitting him to see at a glance just how much danger he was in. The vixen was
propped up in her bunk being handed a bowl that appeared to contain rice
gruel by Mistress Hawkins, whom for the price of a few shillings he had hired
to care for Susannah. Mistress Hawkins, who was thin and rather bent and
well past middle age, turned to stare suspiciously at Ian as he entered. Despite her title, which would seem to indicate the married state, she was travel-
ing with another female and seemed to have a profound distrust of men.

" 'Tis glad I am you've come, me lord. I mun be gettin' on back to my
cabin. Birdie—that's Mistress Tyler, my travelin' companion, to you—just
sent me word that she's feelin' the motion herself and needs me to do for her."

"Will you be able to come tomorrow?" If he sounded anxious, Ian
couldn't help it. The prospect of caring for Susannah, who was as sick and
weak as she was furious with him, was daunting. It was quite possible that she
would refuse to let him do anything at all for her.

"Depends on how Birdie does."

"Please try." She nodded, plumped the pillow behind Susannah's back
with a vigor that nearly caused Susannah to spill her gruel, turned and crossed
the room to where Ian stood just inside the doorway with the same air of
unease as a cat on tacks. Wordlessly she held out a bony hand. Ian looked at it,
then searched in his pocket and withdrew a coin from the small store that he

had earned during the two months that he had been gone from the farm. It would have been ample for his needs had he not had to pay extra for his "wife's" passage once it was discovered that she was on board. The trifling amount that remained had to last them until they reached England and he could make contact with his bankers.

"Good evenin' to ye, then, me lord. Me lady." Mistress Hawkins inclined her head, stepped around Ian, and left the cabin. When the door shut behind her, Ian tensed. If fireworks were on the agenda for the night, they would begin now.

"I cannot believe that you told her you are a marquis and that we are married." Susannah sounded peevish. Ian was relieved. After having endured her throwing things every time he stuck his head in the door for the first week after they sailed, screaming at him for the next week, and giving him the silent treatment for the third, he found it a pleasure to hear her speak to him in something approaching a reasonable tone.

"I am a marquis. And would you rather I had said you were my mistress?" Ian said that last before he thought. As soon as the unfortunate word left his mouth, he winced in anticipation.

"I am not your mistress!" Ill and pale as she was, Susannah was still capable of flashing him a glare that made him want to cringe. He supposed that he reacted as he did because he had grown so accustomed, in that first week, to a missile following hard on the heels of such a look.

"I did not mean to imply that you are," he said in the same soothing tone that he had used for the entirety of the voyage. "What I am trying to say is that, had I not told her you were my wife, she would have assumed you were my mistress."

"You should have secured me a separate cabin!"

"Darling, I hadn't enough money for a separate cabin. Not that there are any. The ship is packed to overflowing."

"Don't call me darling!"

"It was a slip of the tongue." Ian fought an impulse to raise his eyes heavenward. Susannah in a snit would try the patience of a saint, and God knew that he was no saint. But he felt that, after putting her through the hell she had apparently suffered after he'd left, he deserved anything and everything she could dish out. Funny, he had never considered that she might grieve for him. No one had ever cared for him enough to mourn his loss before. She'd cried over him, she'd said. He couldn't imagine his strong, feisty Susannah weeping.

It was a humbling experience to realize that he had the ability to cause her so much pain. He had thought that he would get his affairs in order and then return to take up where they had left off. He'd pictured their reunion as characterized by delightful surprise on her part. He had never in his wildest dreams anticipated spitting fury or that she would grieve herself sick in the meanwhile.

"How are you feeling?" Stupid question, he knew, but there were precious few topics that she wouldn't seize on as a pretext for giving him a tongue-lashing. He slid out of his coat and draped it over the back of a chair as he waited for her to answer.

"Sick." That one-word response emboldened him to approach. He rested an arm against the upper bunk that was his by default and gazed down at her.

"You're looking better." That was not precisely true. She was clad in her long-sleeved lawn chemise because, as he'd carried her aboard in her Sunday-best black and nothing else, she had no nightdress, and the low, scooped neck showed off her creamy neck and shoulders. A coverlet tucked beneath her armpits hid the rest of her from his view, but he had no trouble remembering what he could not see. Her hair hung in a loose braid down her back. Tiny tendrils, loosened by the tossing and turning she did in bed, framed her face in a tawny halo. Illness had thinned her face. The hollows under her cheekbones and the new, finer-drawn line of her jaw gave her an unexpectedly fragile air. Her hazel eyes, with their long, thick sweep of lashes, appeared larger and lovelier than ever with blue smudges beneath them.

To some she might appear far more attractive now than before, but to him she looked ill. He would rather by far have the determinedly plain woman he had left behind than this much more fragile version, as long as she was restored to health.

"No thanks to you. Have you thought how anxious my family must be about me? As soon as we reach land, I must turn around and go back to them. As far as they know, I have disappeared off the face of the earth!"

He had not the money to send her straight back to the Colonies, not without visiting his bankers, but there was no need to tell her that yet. Sufficient unto the day was the evil thereof, he found himself thinking. The biblical quotation narrowed his eyes. Obviously he'd spent entirely too much time around a certain Bible-thumping Baptist if he was starting to fall prey to such thoughts!

"Shall I help you with that gruel?" He was convinced that, rather than permit him to feed her in the earliest days of the journey, she would have starved. Indeed, she had refused to allow him to help her at all, even batting him away when he had tried to hold her head as she emptied her stomach with such violence that she could barely move afterward. She had not allowed him to help her undress, to wipe her face with a cool cloth, or to loosen her hair. In short, she had made it abundantly clear that she wanted nothing to do with him. Truly alarmed about her state and the lack of care she was getting, he'd confided in the captain, not everything, but merely that his wife was badly stricken with mal de mer. The captain, pleased to be of assistance to a member of the nobility, had recommended Mistress Hawkins. Mistress Hawkins was not all that Ian might have hoped for, but she was better than no one.

"I can feed myself, thank you."

Susannah's temper had mellowed somewhat, but not enough to where he had expected a positive answer. He turned away, loosening his neckcloth. As the ship heeled, Susannah cried out. Ian turned back so sharply that he hit his head on the top bunk.

"What's the matter?" He rubbed his forehead. It was just a slight bump, but still it hurt.

"The gruel. It spilled when the ship rolled. Now it's everywhere."

A glance told Ian that she had not exaggerated. The watery stuff had sloshed all over Susannah and the bunk. Her hands dripped with it; the bedclothes were saturated.

"Here, give me that." He took the now empty bowl and set it in a little rack in a case bolted to the wall. Fitted with glass doors, the case was designed to hold such gear as dishes so that they would not be flung about during rough seas.

"Now what am I to do?" Susannah looked down at herself with dismay.

Obviously she could not stay in her bunk the way it was. The answer was obvious, yet it stuck in Ian's throat. He knew how the suggestion would be received even before he made it.

"For tonight you'll have to sleep in the top bunk with me."

For a moment she just looked at him, incredulous. Then, "Hah!" she said.

Ian's lips compressed. "I have no intention of forcing myself on you, if that's what's worrying you. But your bunk is wet."

"I would rather sleep in a wet bunk than sleep with you!" she said, folding her arms over her chest and eyeing him militantly.

Ian's patience snapped at last. "You're being bloody ridiculous, Susannah," he said through his teeth. Bending, he scooped her up in his arms, straightened, and deposited her on the top bunk so fast that she had time to do no more than squeak. Her eyes flashed as she snapped her bare legs beneath her and rolled into a semi-kneeling position. Ian stepped back fast.

She didn't even take a swing at him.

"Very well, then," she said, as if making a great concession. "I will sleep up here. You may sleep on the floor."

Ian had no intention of sleeping on the floor, but he also had no intention of saying so until he had to.

"Take off your chemise, then get under the covers. It's cold in here, and you don't want to take a chill." He was already bending to strip her bunk.

"Yes, you would like it if I did that, wouldn't you? I hope I'm not so big a fool!"

Ian found that, having lost his patience once, it was harder not to lose it a second time. He threw the bedclothes on the floor, then straightened to look at her.

"Susannah," he said in a carefully even tone. "If you don't take off that chemise, I'll do it for you."

"You will not! You wouldn't dare!"

"Why wouldn't I?" His patience was thoroughly lost now, and for the first time since he had discovered how he had wronged her he felt his temper begin to heat. "There's nothing to prevent me. I'm bigger than you, and stronger than you, and I've had quite enough of your foolishness. Now take off that damned wet chemise!"

He stood with fists on hips, scowling up at her. She glared back just as fiercely. A steep dip on the part of the ship made her face change. She paled, swallowing. Watching her, compunction smote him, and his brief flare of anger died.

"Susannah," he said quietly, "please take off the chemise. You may sleep in one of my shirts."

For a moment the issue hung in the balance. Then Susannah nodded almost imperceptibly. "Very well. Though you must turn your back."

Ian said nothing, careful not to jeopardize this small victory. Crossing to the battered valise that held the few necessities that he had been forced to purchase before committing himself to a lengthy ocean voyage, he extracted one of his three shirts. Tossing it to her, he turned his back.

Which was patently ridiculous, of course. Even without seeing it, he could have sketched her body down to the tiniest detail. He knew it intimately, from the full swell of her breasts to the tender curve of her toes. He had committed to memory the litheness of her waist, the slight convexity of her belly, the roundness of her behind. His recollection of her was so precise that he could have named the exact shade of the triangle of curls between her legs.

Indulging in such detailed reminiscences was a mistake. Ian realized that even as he began to harden. If Susannah should see . . .

"All right. You can turn around."

He did, to find her sitting with knees tucked beneath her in his bunk, rolling up the too-long sleeves of his shirt. Her glance at him was absurdly defensive, and he could see why. Clad in such outlandishly large, very masculine garb, she looked adorable. Although, of course, she couldn't know that.

She threw his pillow at him. It hurtled straight for his stomach. He caught it, surprised. Had she now added mind reading to her bag of disconcerting tricks?

"You'll need it for the floor," she said and, lifting the coverlets, wriggled down into his bunk.

Ian smiled grimly but said nothing. He set the pillow aside, then gathered up the wet bedclothes. Working methodically, he spread them out over the chairs so that they might dry before morning. He blew out the lantern and shed his own clothes.

From the sound of Susannah's soft breathing, it was just barely possible that she might be asleep. Tucking his pillow beneath his arm, he set one foot on the bottom bunk and quietly levered himself up beside her.

"You are such a liar that you have to lie about everything, don't you?" Her furious hiss made the hair on the back of his neck stand up in warning. Miss Susannah Redmon, as he had discovered to his cost, was a termagant to be reckoned with when she was angry. "You said you would sleep on the floor."

And then she shoved him backward with all her might.

36

 Ian grabbed the end of the bunk as her hands shoved at his shoulders and just narrowly missed tumbling to the floor. The fright quite did away with the last vestiges of his stretched-to-the-limit patience. Being called a liar in the scathing tone that was her principal means of addressing him lately was the icing on the cake.

"Damn it, Susannah, I am not a liar!" he roared and heaved himself up and into his bunk before she could take another stab at murdering him. "Every word I have told you is the truth! You just refuse to believe me!"

"Liar, liar!" she chanted even as she threw herself toward the foot of the bunk. Thinking her just bull-headed enough to throw herself off to punish him, he grabbed one bare ankle as it flashed past and held it fast.

"How dare you touch me! Take your hand off me! Do you hear? Right now!" She had turned so that she was sitting on her backside, leaning back with her hands extended behind her propping her up, kicking for all she was worth. To keep the foot he had, Ian had to dodge and duck from the other one.

"Unfortunately for you, I don't take orders from you anymore, *Miss* Susannah," he said through his teeth, his temper going the way of his patience. "And I am bloody well tired of this tantrum you've been throwing for three damned weeks!"

"Tantrum . . . !" But whatever she had been going to add to that was superseded by a squawk as he jerked her leg out straight and at the same time hurtled atop her, his arms successfully pinning hers to her sides as he fell back with her into the bunk.

"Knave! Oaf! Cur! Get off me! Oh!"

She squirmed and ranted as he quelled her struggles by wrapping his legs around her as well as his arms, but fortunately his size made the difference, and soon he had her fast. Had she been as large as he, Ian did not like to consider what the outcome of their battle might have been; she was a hellcat when she was roused, and if he had time and leisure to think about it he knew he would be vastly amused comparing the spitting cat in his arms to the prim and righteous Miss Susannah Redmon he had first encountered.

"Ow!" He'd forgotten about the vixen's teeth. She sank them into his upper arm, and for a moment, just one moment, Ian had to battle an urge to strangle her and be done with the pesky wench.

He compromised by pinning both her wrists behind her back with one hand and catching her jaw with the other. Menacingly he leaned over her, hoping to frighten her into giving up the battle before one or the other of them got hurt.

"If you bite me, or kick me, or scratch me, or do anything else to cause me bodily injury, one more time, I'm going to . . ." His voice trailed off, because in truth he would do nothing that would harm one hair on her virago's head, and he knew it. He only hoped that she did not and would consider his lack of specifics ominous. He should have known better.

"Pooh!" she said inelegantly and then spat full in his face.

Sometimes, in the course of human relations, one partner to an exchange makes an error of a such magnitude that it forever after changes the course of their association. Having Susannah spit in his face marked such a turning point for Ian.

"That's torn it," he said, releasing her jaw to wipe his face. An almost glacial calm came over him, although he could feel fury battling to get out. "You've run your course, my darling, and if you give me one more iota of trouble I am going to take my hand to your backside and paddle you until you can't sit!"

"Don't you dare threaten me!" Clearly the woman didn't know how thin was the ice on which she skated.

"Susannah," he said, very low, thrusting his face almost into hers so that she could get a sense, in spite of the darkness, as to just how very close he was to carrying out his threat. "I am not threatening you. I have apologized a hundred times for leaving you without a word and explained a hundred times why it was absolutely imperative that I do so. I have been patience itself while you have treated me to the full range of your hellion's temper. I have told you nothing but the absolute truth, and you accuse me of lying. I have had enough. I am going to let you go, and we are going to lie together in the one dry bed we have between us and go to sleep. Is that clear?"

Silence.

Ian waited, but got no reply other than the faster than normal cadence of her breathing. After a moment, deciding to chance it, he let go of her hands and waited. Nothing. Not the smallest movement or sound, other than her breathing. He untwined his legs from around hers. Still nothing. She lay unmoving, unspeaking, the wind taken from her sails as she recognized a will stronger than hers and an anger more powerful. Ian dared to take a deep breath. He had only needed to put his foot down, obviously. Susannah was a termagant, but like all termagants she could be brought, when push came to shove, to recognize her master.

"That's better," he said and sat up, preparatory to moving to the correct end of the bed for sleeping.

Sitting up proved to be a mistake.

"Oh, is it?" she hissed, coming up off that mattress like a she-wolf and shoving him for all she was worth. Ian felt the rush of her movement, felt the soft little hands thrusting against his shoulders with an unexpectedness that compensated for her lack of physical strength, felt himself losing his balance and toppling backward, felt the cold hardness of the plank floor as he slammed into it shoulder first. Then for a moment, just a moment, all he felt was pain.

He lay there, stunned. Despite his threats, and warnings, and apologies, the beldam had actually dared push him off the bunk! The knowledge shocked him almost as much as his fall.

In the bunk, Susannah listened intently. She was still furiously angry— that he had actually threatened to spank her was the last straw—but, as the thud of his landing died away and not so much as a curse replaced it, she began to get anxious as well.

Her intention had not been to really hurt him, just to teach him that she would not be tamed, to use his infamous word, so easily. The bunk was only about five feet off the ground. Surely he could not have been rendered unconscious by so short a fall? Lying down, she peered over the edge of the mattress. It was too dark to permit her to see more of him than a shadow lying on the floor below.

The rasp of his breathing told her that she had not killed him, but other than that there was nothing. No sounds of movement, not even a groan. Hideous thought: had he perhaps struck his head?

"Ian?" Just to call him by his name gave him a victory of sorts. She had resisted even that during the time he had had her a prisoner aboard this ship. For that was what she considered herself—a prisoner. He had stolen her away from her family, from her life, for his own selfish ends, just as he did everything. Though she had to admit he had been amazingly conciliating in the face of her constant hostility. He had held her head and bathed her face most competently the first few times she had been sick, though she had made it clear that she wanted none of him. He had brought her broth, and weak tea, and tried to coax her to eat and drink. When she had flung both at him, he had silently cleaned up the mess. And brought her more, though he watched her warily as she ate. Finally, when she absolutely refused to let him tend to any of her personal needs, he had found Mistress Hawkins to tend her in his place. After that, he had absented himself from the cabin as much as possible, and when he had to enter he had crept around like a mouse. Had she been the least in charity with him, she would have had to smile to see such a tall, powerfully built man trying to make himself as inconspicuous as possible in the tiny space afforded by their cabin. It had been impossible, of course, and she had been as aware of him as if he had stomped and shouted whenever he came in. But she was not in charity with him. She was on guard against him, her heart sternly armored in case he should try to wheedle his way into it again. From the first she'd known that letting herself love him meant setting herself up for heartbreak. Well, he'd already broken her heart once, and she'd be hung by her heels in a smokehouse before she'd give him the chance again.

But she hadn't meant to hurt him. Just to demonstrate that she wouldn't be bullied.

"Ian?" she said again in a small voice. The ship pitched, but she had grown so accustomed to that that she scarcely noticed. Timbers creaked, the lantern must have swayed because it squeaked as the swivel hook which attached it to the ceiling turned—but there was no other sound.

None. Not even the rasp of his breathing.

"Ian!" She knew he wasn't dead, of course, knew it as well as she knew her own name. But still—black-hearted rogue that he was—she could not just leave him lying on the floor in the dark, possibly injured, without at least checking on him.

"Ian!" She tried one last time. Nothing.

Cautiously Susannah swung her legs over the bunk and dropped to the floor. She landed almost atop him, one foot between his sprawled legs, but still he didn't move. Growing increasingly concerned, she stepped over him and crouched beside his chest.

"Ian?" Putting a hand to his face, she encountered warm, sleek skin and the roughness of a day's growth of beard.

"That's going to cost you, vixen." The rough growl came out of the darkness even as he caught her wrist and pulled her down against his chest.

"You liar!" she wailed, knowing that she'd been well and truly had. The scoundrel had been playing possum!

"If you call me that one more time, so help me God I'll throttle you." Ian's arms came around her, and he rolled with her so that they both lay on their sides facing each other. Susannah had known, of course, that he was naked—it was impossible to live with a man in such close quarters and not realize that he slept naked—but she had not experienced the fact so vividly before. With his shirt tangled around her hips, she was nearly as bare as he. She could feel the heat of his skin, the roughness of the hairs on his legs, the steely strength of his muscles, pressing against her own soft smooth flesh. It was the first time she had been so near him in months. Had she not known the scalawag for what he was, her senses would have reeled.

But she would not respond to the lure of the flesh. She was done with sinning—and being a fool.

Against her thigh she could feel the unmistakable evidence that her nearness was affecting him in much the same way that his would have affected her, had she allowed it to. The burning heat of the swelling thing made her grit her teeth in determined rejection.

"You've had your joke. Now let me up," she said as evenly as she could under the circumstances. It had occurred to her that this was not the time to escalate their battle. Not when he was naked, and she was nearly so, and they were both so—hot.

"I believe I warned you what I would do if you did not lie quietly in my bunk with me and go to sleep?" One hand moved down to pat her backside suggestively. The tail of his shirt covered her at least that far, Susannah was thankful to discover. But still she felt the touch of his hand like a brand through the thin linen.

"If you dare . . ." she began furiously, holding herself rigid in an effort to combat the weakness that his nearness engendered.

"Susannah." His voice sounded almost weary. "Don't dare me. I find that I am averse to paddling you, after all. But you could push me to it, if you really tried."

His hand still rested against her bottom. She would have tried to dislodge it, but she had the feeling that any movement at such a moment might be a fatal mistake.

"Let me up," she managed through stiff lips.

He said nothing for a moment. Then, "Say please."

"How childish!"

"I thought we'd already established that I am childish. Now say please, Ian, let me up."

Susannah gritted her teeth. But her situation was really very dire, because she wanted nothing so much as to stay where she was. While with her head she hadn't forgiven him and her heart was still very much on guard, her foolish, fickle body seemed not to have gotten the message. His hand on her bottom awakened all kinds of shameful longings inside her. Like the wish that he would push the shirt out of the way . . .

"Please, Ian, let me up," she muttered in hostile surrender. But it was worth it, to escape him before she could make a complete fool of herself again.

"No," he said, and, though it was too dark to be sure, she thought he smiled mockingly.

It took a moment for his perfidy to sink in.

"No!" she gasped. "Why, you skunk! You pole-cat! You . . ."

He laughed. "I may be all of those things, Susannah. But I am also the man you have to please if you wish to get out of this predicament you've placed yourself in with a whole skin. It's going to cost you more than a grudging please. It's going to cost you—a kiss."

"I'd sooner kiss a . . ." She had been going to say pig, but then, remembering how he'd gibed her about her fondness for swine before, she shut her mouth with a click on the last word.

"That's just too bad, my darling. Unless you want to lie here all night, you're going to have to kiss me."

37

"I hate you!"

"That's too bad, too. Come on, Susannah. Kiss me. Or I'll have to think of some way to persuade you." He patted her bottom suggestively. It was all Susannah could do not to squirm.

"You are the most despicable . . ." Screwing up her courage—and her mouth—she pecked his mouth with hers.

"There!"

He laughed. "You call that a kiss? I barely felt it. I've taught you better, and I want to reap the results of my lessons. Now, are you going to kiss me or . . ." His fingers spread over her left buttock, and he squeezed. Susannah, galvanized, jerked away.

"All right!" she said, glaring at him although of course he couldn't see. Anything, anything, to get away from him before she succumbed to the heated languor that was rising through her body. If he did not remove his hand from her backside soon, she would be reaching down and pulling the shirt out of the way. She wanted his hands on her flesh with so much intensity that she was losing the will to fight. Kissing him might prove a mistake—though she thought she could hang on to her slipping self-control through the course of one kiss—but staying in his arms was certainly dangerous.

"A proper kiss, tongue and all," he cautioned her. Susannah took a firm grip on both her temper and her self-control and set herself to giving the swine what he wanted.

But when she pressed her lips to his he didn't open his mouth.

"That's not fair," she pulled back to say furiously. "How can I kiss you if you won't cooperate?"

"You have to persuade me to cooperate." From his voice, she knew he was smirking. "Wrap your arms around my neck. Press your breasts up against my chest. Wriggle around a little. Stroke my mouth with your tongue. Do it right, and I'll let you go."

"That's blackmail!"

"Blackmail has its uses," he observed and squeezed her fanny again. Susannah gasped and jerked free.

Seething, trying to ignore the inward trembling that competed with anger for equal space inside her, she freed her arms from his grasp—he obligingly let her—and slid them around his neck.

"Hug me tighter," he whispered. "And wriggle."

Scarlet-faced, thankful that it was too dark for him to see, Susannah tightened her grip to the point where she was plastered so close against him that her breasts felt as if they were being squashed flat. Then she—wriggled, to use his distasteful phrase.

"Ah." It was a curiously hoarse sound. "Now use your tongue."

Hesitantly, Susannah pressed her lips to his, put out the tip of her tongue, and slid it over his closed mouth.

"That's good. That's very good," he whispered. "Now slide your tongue inside my mouth. And wriggle again. I like the way you wriggle."

Susannah wriggled. His lips parted obligingly, and her tongue slid inside his mouth.

She had forgotten how he tasted. Hot, faintly musky, with the merest hint of tobacco—where had he been smoking cigars?—and wet, very wet. She moved her tongue around inside his mouth for what must have been a full minute before he responded, sucking on her tongue and stroking it with his.

"That's enough. I've kissed you," she said, withdrawing hastily. "Now let me go." But her arms still hugged his neck, and her breasts were pressed flat against his chest. After a moment—it took so long because her senses were clouding fast—she realized that he was holding her as tightly as she was holding him.

"You kissed me," he agreed, on a deep husky note that sent shivers down her spine. "What would you say if I offered to return the favor?"

No, her mind shouted. Stop, shrieked her heart. But her body, her traitorous body, on fire from her kissing and wriggling and his hand on her behind, quaked yes.

Paralyzed by the battle that raged within her, she moved restlessly. That move proved her undoing. It shifted the tails of the shirt she wore, pulling it out from under his hand, so that now his hand rested on her soft, curved flesh.

"Ahh." She could not help the small sound. The mere resting of his hand against her bare bottom awoke trumpets of passion in her blood. Unable to help it, she moved again. His hand slid down to the top of her thigh and then closed upward over her cheek.

"If you're planning to call a halt to this, you'd better do it fast," he said, sounding as if he was having trouble getting the words out. "Because you've got me hotter than a firecracker."

"No," she whispered.

"You want me to stop?" From the sound of it, even asking the question pained him.

"No." Susannah quivered and ached and burned with wanting him. Her arms tightened about his neck. Her thighs pressed his, and she—wriggled.

"No." It was a groan of satisfaction. His hand on her bottom pulled her up close against him, and his mouth slanted over hers. His tongue repaid her for the torture she had caused him, and his fingers delved into the cleft between her cheeks, stroking and exploring, and squeezing her behind. When he lifted his head to kiss her throat, Susannah was gasping and clinging to him like Spanish moss to an oak.

"I want you naked." He was unbuttoning her shirt, trailing kisses in the wake of his hands. When the last button slipped its mooring, he parted the front, and his mouth slid from halfway down her belly to the valley between her breasts and then, trailing fire, over a soft peak. As his lips closed over her nipple, Susannah cried out and arched her back.

"Easy," he whispered, tugging the shirt down her shoulders. "This is going to take a long time."

Feeling as if she were going to die if it took much longer, Susannah helped him take off her shirt. Then, and it was shameless, and she knew it was shameless but she didn't care, she slid her hands up the back of his head and pressed her breasts closer into his face. He suckled her harder, his mouth sliding from one taut nipple to the other, while his hands stroked and teased her bottom until she was gasping and writhing against him in mindless need.

"That's it," he said as her thighs parted restlessly in response to his butterfly forays. "Now lift your leg up around my waist."

Susannah did, under the guidance of his hands. They were lying on their sides, she with one leg around his body, he with his head bent to her breasts and one hand spread over her buttocks, pressing her close. He reached up, caught one of the hands that were entwined in his hair, and pulled it down between their bodies.

"You put me in," he said.

For a moment Susannah had no idea what he meant. Then, as he reached his destination and folded her fingers around his throbbing shaft, she knew. He was burning hot, and velvety soft over a turgid strength, and her first impulse was to recoil. But he brought her fingers back to him, and this time she took hold of him without having to be urged.

"If you want me, put me in."

If she wanted him. Susannah was on fire with wanting him. She was mindless with it, soulless with it, a quivering, flaming body with a will all its own. She grasped him, and guided him, and then he was inside her, filling her, thrusting urgently while she writhed and clung.

"I love you, love you, love you," she cried in the final glorious moment, when rapture burst like flaming rockets inside her. It was only later, what seemed a long time later but could not, in reality, have been more than minutes, that she realized what she had said.

Lying cradled against him, her head pillowed on a strong arm stretched out to provide what comfort it could, Susannah went cold. And her coldness had nothing to do with the drafts blowing about the floor.

He had said nothing, as he found his own release, or after, nothing, as she lay beside him on the floor. Perhaps he had been so wrapped up in the driving ecstasy that had possessed them both that he had not heard, or understood, what she had said.

Another moment passed, and then he pressed a quick, hard kiss to her mouth before sitting up. Seconds later he was on his feet, leaving her scrambling about on the floor for the discarded shirt. She knew, without knowing quite how she knew, what he meant to do.

The snap of a spark being struck confirmed her guess. The lantern wick caught and flared to life. As a warm golden glow stretched over the small cabin, Ian replaced the globe and turned to look at her, fists on hips, eyes narrowed. If his nakedness disturbed him so much as a whisker—and she did not think it did—then it was not apparent from his stance. Susannah, still on the floor although seated now with her legs tucked up beneath her, pulled the edges of the shirt together, lifted her chin, and met that searching gaze.

"Well, now," he said. "That's very interesting. Did you mean it?"

"I don't know what you're talking about." Though she did, of course. His mouth smiling at her told her that he knew it as well as she did.

"You said you love me. Did you mean it?" He was watching her like a bird might a particularly juicy worm. Susannah had to fight not to lower her eyes.

"Perhaps. At the time." Did he look faintly disappointed?

"Only at the time?"

He was not going to let the matter go, it was clear. Susannah would have stood up and turned away, but his shirt, while a perfectly adequate cover for her person from her thighs up, left a great deal of bare leg available for his inspection. It was silly to worry about letting him see her legs, of course, when he stood before her naked as a babe and she had made shattering love with him not five minutes before, but still she couldn't help it. So she faced the matter head on.

"Does it really matter?" she asked. His lips pursed.

"Yes, it does. To me. It's a simple enough question: do you love me?"

Looking up at him, trying to think of an answer that was not quite a lie and yet almost longing to say it at last, Susannah felt her throat go dry. She was setting herself up for heartbreak again, she knew, and the pain would be worse this time than before.

"Oh, if you must have it, then yes," she said, and with the best will in the world she could not keep her eyes from dropping to the floor. She sensed rather than saw him move, and suddenly he was crouching before her, his hand lifting her chin.

"Yes, what?" He was smiling, yet not quite smiling, as he met her eyes. His hair had come loose from its confining ribbon some time during the wild night and hung loose to frame his face. His mouth curved sensuously at her, and his eyes were warm and yet oddly intent.

Just looking at him made her heart swell.

"Yes, I love you, Ian," she whispered, because she couldn't keep it secret anymore.

He smiled then, a real smile, and pinched her chin.

"Now that is interesting," he said almost casually. "Because, you see, I love you, too."

As her eyes widened and her lips parted, he suddenly wasn't in the least casual as he took her in his arms.

38

No wedding trip was ever any more blissful than the remaining three weeks of that voyage. Having thrown her cap over the wind-mill, Susannah gave herself to Ian body and soul. She loved him, with a fierce abiding passion that she knew would last her her whole life long. If she did not quite trust him or his protestations of love for her, well, that was something to worry about later. For now, for however long it lasted, he be-longed to her, and that was enough. She didn't even miss her family or remind Ian that he had promised to send her home again the moment they docked. Instead she penned them a letter detailing some if not all that had happened and promised to return to them as soon as she could. In her happiness with Ian, she was able, if not to put them from her mind, at least to shove them to the back.

England, when they landed, was not what she had expected. For one thing, it was, as Ian had promised, cool. To one who was used to living in a land of steamy, near-tropical heat, it was downright cold. Gray fog drifted over the capital like a blanket the day they arrived in London, shrouding her view of most of that city's narrow thoroughfares. To compound the difficulty, what seemed to be thousands of chimney pots spewed thick, sooty plumes of smoke into the already lowering sky. Small black flakes of soot floated like snow through the air. What she did see was not impressive—tightly packed brick-fronted buildings, row upon row of them, with scarcely a blade of grass or a tree anywhere; crowds of people hurrying hither and yon, breaking into shrill altercations at what seemed the least cause; vendors hawking their wares in strident voices that Susannah could scarcely understand. Carriages of all sizes and descriptions filled the streets, travelling in both directions at shocking speeds with scant regard for safety. In one street, Ian called it Piccadilly, a black phaeton with a coat of arms picked out in gold leaf on the door came so close that its wheels almost brushed that of their hired carriage, so close that

Susannah jumped back, away from the window to which her nose had been pressed.

"What's the matter?" inquired Ian lazily. An indulgent smile played around his mouth as he watched her wide-eyed wonder at her first glimpse of London. Susannah saw that smile and knew that she was the source of his amusement, but beyond sticking her tongue out at him saucily she made no objection. She was enjoying herself far too thoroughly to take umbrage at him.

"That carriage—it nearly hit us!"

He glanced around her, out the window, then settled back into his former position—long legs stretched out in front of him, booted feet crossed at the ankles, head resting back against the worn velvet squab, arms raised and hands locked behind his head. He looked so handsome in that posture that Susannah almost leaned forward to drop a kiss on his mouth. But she knew if she did she faced the very real prospect of being pulled into his arms and treated to a session of heated lovemaking right there in the carriage. Ian's appetite for carnal love was very keen and aroused by the least little touch or smile, as she had learned with a great deal of interest. She had no wish to arrive at their destination—a hotel, Ian said, until he could get a few matters of business squared away—with her hair and clothing in disorder, so she contented herself with smiling at him.

"That was just Cambert. He likes to think he can drive to an inch, but in reality he is the most cow-handed clunch imaginable. You were quite right to fear that he would hit us, because he has such accidents frequently."

"Cambert?" Ian sounded as if the careless driver was well-known to him. But the carriage had obviously been horrendously expensive, and the bracket-faced driver had been clad in clothes that looked as if they had cost the earth. Certainly Susannah had never seen even the finest of the Beaufort gentlemen turned out in such style. For a man who had counted shillings and pence every step of the way on their journey to claim acquaintance with such an obviously wealthy London gentleman seemed far-fetched. And yet—fool though she probably was—the silver-tongued devil almost had her convinced that he really was a marquis. Certainly she wanted to believe that—and everything else he said.

"John Bolton, Earl of Cambert. He is a little older than I am, but I have been acquainted with him any time these dozen years."

Her eyes must have revealed her lingering doubt, because he sat up suddenly and grinned at her.

"You still don't believe me, do you?" Letting down his window, he yelled something at the driver. Moments later the carriage swung over into another lane of traffic and turned left.

"What are you doing?" Something about his air of smug satisfaction alarmed her.

"Taking you to see my man of business. I was going to be a gentleman and drop you off at the hotel first so that you could rest while I dealt with the hard, cold realities of life, like procuring funds so that we could eat, but I've changed my mind. Prepare to dine on crow, my darling."

Susannah frowned. "It is not that I don't believe you, precisely, but . . ."

"Oh, yes, it is. Precisely. I can't tell you how your lack of faith has wounded me, either. I'll have you know that I have never told a lie in my life."

"Pooh!"

Ian cast his eyes heavenward. "See? She doesn't believe me!" he said plaintively, as if to a higher power. Susannah had to laugh.

"Well, if you are really a marquis . . ."

"I am."

". . . and rich as Croesus . . ."

"I am that, too. Or, rather, I was. The situation is complicated here, but I am hoping that my mother, who has a great dislike of scandal and an even greater regard for her own skin, has left my money intact. She was after the title, after all, for my brother. I rather suspect that, until she has conclusive proof of my death, she will move rather slowly against my possessions and—other things."

"That is the thing I find hardest of all to believe—that your own mother, and brother, could wish you dead, and even connive at your death."

The humor vanished from his face, to be replaced by something implacably bleak and hard. "I told you, my mother is as different from you as night is from day. She has never cared for me. Nor has my brother. She has quite poisoned Edward against me."

"What of your father?"

If anything, Ian's face grew more shuttered. "My father suffered a hunting accident when I was nine. More properly, half his skull was blown away by a misfired shotgun. But he survives. At least, his body survives. He has not been in his right mind for these twenty-two years."

"How dreadful!" Susannah's heart wept for him and, with a rustle of skirts—her best black poplin, now rather the worse for wear—she moved to sit beside him and slide her arms around his neck.

"Never mind, my dear," she whispered, kissing the side of his jaw. "There is truth to the saying that those who have a trying childhood progress to a particularly satisfying old age."

"I hope so," Ian said, a touch of humor returning to his voice. One hand came up to cup the back of her head, and his lips found her mouth.

The carriage rocked to a halt.

"Damn!" Ian muttered. "Though it's just as well, I suspect. You would not like to call on Mr. Dumboldt looking as if you'd just arisen from a toss in the hay—or, in this case, the carriage."

"No," Susannah said, brushing her hand across the back of her mouth to wipe away the last traces of his kiss and lifting a hand to her hair. "I should not. Ian, perhaps you had best take me to the hotel after all."

He grinned at her, perfectly restored to himself now. "Not a chance, my darling. I want to get this straight between us once and for all."

The driver opened the door, and Ian stepped out, then turned to hand Susannah down. The building they stopped in front of was the typical tall, narrow brick row house, with a neatly lettered sign affixed to the facade that read "M. Dumboldt and sons, Esquires" in sober black letters on a gray ground.

"But how do you know he is in?" Susannah faltered.

"Dumboldt is always in," Ian said imperturbably, and, ushering Susannah ahead of him, he walked up the steps and inside without even bothering to knock. Two men were in the cluttered office off the hallway as they entered. The younger one, fully dressed except for his hat, was seated at a large desk, arguing spiritedly with the older, shirt-sleeved gentleman. From the identical profiles, it would be hard to judge the pair as anything save father and son.

"Good morning, Dumboldt. Good morning, Tony," Ian said affably as he shepherded Susannah into the room. Both men jumped as if they'd been shot, their eyes riveted to Ian and bulging. The younger one, Tony, Susannah assumed, leaped up from his desk. The older man had to be Mr. Dumboldt.

"Derne!" Dumboldt gasped.

"By God!" Tony cried.

"I have some business to conduct with you, Dumboldt. If it is perfectly convenient, perhaps we could retire to your private office." Ian was polite, but it was clear to the meanest intelligence—and Susannah's wasn't stupid—that, despite his shabby attire and the slight limpness of his neckcloth, Ian was a man the others sought to please.

"We thought—that is, we were told—uh, it had been suggested to us that you might be—uh . . . ." Dumboldt broke off as his face reddened.

"We were told that you were dead," his son said bluntly.

Ian shook his head. "Obviously, I am not. Though not from want of trying, I might add. I shall tell you the whole story, if we may be private, and ask you to make a note of it too, in case the person responsible should try again to rid the world of me. But first, I should like to make you known to my wife. Susannah, Mr. Dumboldt and Mr. Tony Dumboldt."

"H-how do you do?" Susannah's slight verbal stumble occurred because she could not like being introduced as his wife, when she was in truth no such thing. But as Ian had said, the alternative was worse, so, whether she liked it or not, she supposed she must accede to the lie.

"My lady." Both men bowed deeply. Susannah's eyes widened as she glanced at Ian over their bent heads. He grinned at her triumphantly.

"Ah—just so that we may have things perfectly clear, Dumboldt, who am I?"

"What, my lord?"

"What is my name, man, my name!" Ian sounded impatient, so Dumboldt made haste to oblige him, though he clearly considered the question peculiar in the extreme.

"Why, Ian Charles Michael George Henry Connelly, my lord."

"And my title?" His gray eyes held Susannah's. She already knew what she would hear before Dumboldt said a word.

"Marquis of Derne, Baron of Speare, Lord of . . ."

"That's enough, Dumboldt, thank you very much." He quizzed Susannah with his eyes, then turned to Dumboldt again. "Now, if we may be private . . ."

"Certainly, my lord. Certainly." The older man ushered them into his office, his manner almost obsequious. Susannah, rather dazed, listened as Ian gave a concise account of what had befallen him—leaving out such choice bits as the beatings he had endured—and whom he held responsible. It seemed that everything was true that he had been telling her over the past six weeks, from the trumped-up charge—as he was not allowed to speak at the trial, his true identity was never brought out—to the murderer who had followed him to the Carolinas.

Now it seemed that Ian Charles Michael George Henry Connelly, Marquis of Derne, lately the bound servant of Miss Susannah Redmon of Beaufort in the Carolinas, was back to exact revenge.

As they were leaving, with Dumboldt vigorously assuring them that he would take steps to see that Lord Derne did not suffer a repeat of this dastardly business, Ian turned at the door to ask, almost offhandedly, "And how is my father faring? Have you heard?"

"As to that, my lord, except for news of your supposed death I have had little contact with your family. But if anything untoward were to have befallen His Grace the Duke, I am sure I would have been informed."

"Yes." Ian set the rather shabby tricorne on his head and drew Susannah's hand through his elbow. "I suppose they did not dare do anything to him until they were certain I was dead."

"No, my lord. That is my supposition as well." Dumboldt sounded sad. "Tony has a cab waiting, I believe."

"Thank you, Dumboldt."

"It has been my pleasure, my lord, as always."

When they were once again in a carriage headed toward a hotel, Ian fixed Susannah with a wicked grin.

"Well?"

Susannah had the grace to flush. "I was mistaken in you. You have my sincerest apologies."

He laughed. "Not near good enough, my girl. Come here and start trying to make amends. I warn you that it may take some considerable time, as my feelings were considerably lacerated. Weeks, maybe. Months. Years." He opened his arms to her. Susannah, after fixing him with an admonishing look, grimaced her acceptance of the terms he exacted and moved into his arms.

There were worse punishments than kissing Ian, after all.

39

The hotel where they were established, the Crillon, was the most luxurious establishment Susannah had ever been inside in her life. The floors were of marble, the ceilings of gilt, and the walls painted with murals of woody glens and limpid blue pools and cherubs. The chamber she shared with Ian was magnificent. From the huge, intricately carved canopy bed, to the mahogany wardrobe and mirrored dressing table, to the cheval glass that was long enough to permit her to see her entire reflection, to the thick Persian carpet on the floor, everything was of the finest. Finer than anything Susannah had ever seen.

Her awe must have shown in her face, because Ian laughed and kissed her. Later, after demonstrating the thorough superiority of that particular mattress over any others they had shared, he ordered an enormous luncheon sent up and appeared to derive a vast amount of enjoyment from watching her sample the strange dishes. Susannah found most of them rather flavorless, but to please Ian she exclaimed as though it were a feast worthy of a king.

The next order of business was obtaining wardrobes for them both, he decreed. Susannah found nothing to protest in this. She was growing heartily sick of her black dress.

When Ian, driving a smart carriage he had hired from the hotel, showed her into an exclusive little establishment called Madame de Vangrisse's, Susannah almost had second thoughts. The outside was discreet enough, with a single shop window that displayed a truly lovely golden dress of lustrous satin. But once Ian opened the door, Susannah could scarcely contain a gasp. Bolts of rich fabric were tossed carelessly over plump sofas and divans in a large, plushly carpeted room. More fabric in vibrant hues spilled from niches set into one wall. Tall mirrors were everywhere, and before them postured some of the most elegantly beautiful women Susannah had ever seen. Equally elegant gentlemen lounged in chairs and on the sofas that were not covered with fabric, watching the ladies parading new gowns.

"I can't go in there!" Had Ian not been right behind her, Susannah would have backed right out the door. Such exquisite decadence was not for the likes of her! But with a wicked grin and a hand in the small of her back, Ian urged her onward.

"Of course you can. Don't be ridiculous! I've been wanting to see you in some proper gowns ever since I first laid eyes on you. Don't think I didn't notice that, while you were making Mandy and Sarah Jane and Em things, you rarely fashioned yourself new clothes."

"That's because I didn't need any."

That this conversation was conducted in whispers didn't detract from its urgency, at least on Susannah's part. She felt increasingly uncomfortable as a few of the ladies turned to glance at the new arrivals, ran their eyes over her, then dismissed her with an obviously contemptuous shrug. Ian came in for rather a longer look, but, as his attention was all for Susannah and his clothes proclaimed him the country bumpkin, he was soon ignored, too.

"You need some now. Don't let them intimidate you. You're worth more than the whole lot of them thrown together. Helen Dutton, over there"—he nodded toward a tall, serenely beautiful blonde—"may be the Countess of Blakely, but she is also one of the most notorious lightskirts in London. They call her children the Baddington miscellany, because all of them were sired by different fathers. She has seven."

He went on, murmuring naughty stories in her ear about the beautiful women, until Susannah had to laugh at the sheer preposterousness of pairing such lovely faces with such bawdy tales. She suspected that he made most of it up to set her at ease, but when she turned to tax him with it she found a shopgirl regarding them with a most supercilious pair of raised brows.

"May I be of assistance, ma'am? sir?" The girl asked frigidly. It was obvious that Susannah's attire, which had been dowdy in Beaufort and was a thousand times more so in this fashionable capital, found no favor in her eyes.

Susannah drew herself up, not liking to be addressed in such a manner.

"As you can see, I require a gown," she said firmly. The girl's manner altered slightly at this pronouncement, which was delivered in Susannah's best imperial manner despite the fact that the girl was some inches taller than she.

"You may tell Madame that Derne is here," Ian told the girl, a grin lurking around his mouth.

"Yes, sir," she said, obsequious now despite their shabby garb, and hurried off. Moments later a tiny woman with hair of an improbable shade of red approached. For an instant she peered suspiciously at Ian, and then, with a cry, she threw herself into his arms.

"It's good to see you, Bridget." Grinning, Ian returned the woman's hug with interest.

"*Mon cher* Derne!" Susannah's back grew rigid as she watched obviously rouged lips plant a kiss on Ian's mouth. "It is so good to see you again! Where have you been keeping yourself? Away from London, yes? And you have brought me a new customer?" She withdrew from Ian's arms to run her eyes over Susannah, who was regarding her in much the same way she had looked at the snippy shop girl. "A relative, perhaps?"

The implication that Susannah was not the sort of female who would be with Ian if she were not a cousin of some sort was plain, at least to Susannah, but it appeared to sail right over Ian's head.

"Susannah is my marchioness," he said, giving her chin an affectionate pinch. "She's from the Colonies, and she needs to be brought up to snuff, as you can see. I want her to have a complete wardrobe, everything new from the skin out. And we need it within a week. With one or two dresses to take with us today."

"One or two today, and the rest within a week! *Alors*, my friend, you ask much! It will be expensive, as I am sure you realize—but it can be done." Bridget turned bright black eyes on Susannah, running them assessingly over her figure. "Bah, I can tell nothing through that—that gown! We will have it off you, my lady, and then we shall see."

Bridget started off, beckoning Susannah to follow. Susannah cast a nervous look back at Ian, who grinned at her.

"Go on," he said. "She won't eat you. And I'll be right here. I'm not about to let you pick out your gowns by yourself. We'll be back to sackcloth and ashes again if I do, I know."

"Madame la Marquise, *s'il vous plaît*, we must hasten!" Bridget called over her shoulder at Susannah. Instantly the head of nearly every lady in the shop swivelled, and a dozen pairs of eyes fixed on her. A low buzz of conversation followed her as she crossed the room. Susannah held her head high, though she could not help the color that rose to her cheeks at the whispered comments.

"Did you hear who she is? Derne's marchioness!"

"Nonsense! A marquis would not marry a mouse!"

"She is that, isn't she? Well, Derne has looks enough for the both of them. Oh, look, he's here with her! I must just go and say hello. I haven't seen him this age. I wonder if he's been out of the country?"

The chatter continued, but by then Susannah had reached the sanctuary of the dressing room. Her cheeks burned, and her head was high. A mouse, indeed!

"If you will stand still, my lady, I will help you with your dress."

Susannah was scarcely aware of being undressed down to the skin.

Bridget's eyes widened as she took in the curves and hollows of Susannah's body without the concealing dress.

"*Sacrebleu,* it is a crime against nature to hide such a shape in this rag of a dress!" Bridget gave Susannah's old dress, which was flung over her arm, a disgusted look and consigned it to an assistant to be taken away. Susannah had the feeling that she would never see her best Sunday black again, and she was suddenly, fiercely glad. If she could not be beautiful, at least she need not be a dowd! It occurred to her to wonder why all of a sudden she was concerned with her appearance when it had never bothered her before. But then, without even having to think about it, the answer popped into her head—Ian. She wanted to look attractive for Ian.

"You have a beautiful figure, my lady. I make you my compliments on it."

A beautiful figure? Susannah looked in the mirror, blushed at the naked reflection that she saw there, and hastily averted her eyes. But still the comment stayed with her and provided some balm for the wounding appellation of mouse.

"And a hairdresser, hmmm?" Bridget asked as she brought stacks of fine silk underwear for Susannah's inspection. "Lisette, send Clothilde to me, at once! And bring me the gold dress from the window!"

Silk underwear! Susannah thought as she consented to have a delicately embroidered chemise put over her head. How Mandy would love that! At the thought, Susannah felt a sudden pang for her sister. All her sisters. And Pa. Much as she loved Ian, she was starting to miss her family.

Susannah was laced into a whalebone bodice of brocaded satin that pushed her breasts up to the point of indecency and made her small waist seem even tinier, had silk stockings rolled onto her legs and secured with ribbon garters, and struggled into petticoats and panniers and gold satin slippers with silk flowers and heels three inches high (they were a trifle large, but Bridget stuffed the toes with cotton and assured her they would do). She was growing more than a trifle weary of high fashion. Only the thought of being called a mouse kept her from calling a halt.

The gold dress was thrown over her head, pinned at the waist where it was too large, and removed. Measurements were taken. Clothilde arrived and proceeded to unpin Susannah's hair.

"*Ils sont beaux!*" said Clothilde, who turned out to be Bridget's sister, as she assessed the curly mane. Nevertheless, she attacked it ruthlessly with a pair of scissors, rubbed it with scented pomade, then pinned it back up. Then the gold dress was thrown a second time over Susannah's head and fastened up the back.

By that time, it seemed that she had been in the shop for hours. But Bridget assured her that only three-quarters of one had passed.

The thought of Ian cooling his heels in the front room for three-quarters of an hour was enough to send her speeding out to join him. Bridget stopped her.

"Do you not want to look in the glass?" she asked, sounding scandalized. Thus reminded, Susannah realized that she did, very much, want to look in the glass. When she did, her mouth fell open.

The young woman who looked back at her was a vision in gold. The lustrous satin gleamed under the bright lights. Cascades of blond lace fell over her hands and trimmed her skirt in wide flounces. Above the square, low-cut neckline the top half of her breasts swelled lushly and were the first detail of her altered appearance to catch her eye. Susannah would have found such a display embarrassing if every other lady in the shop had not worn her gown so. Still, it was all she could do not to cover up the vast expanse of creamy flesh with her hands.

"You do not think it is too low?" she inquired of Bridget, who was hovering anxiously.

"*Non*, madame, it is *le dernier cri!*" Bridget assured her. "Look, the hair! Is it not exquisite?"

Thus adjured, Susannah looked and was amazed. Clothilde had piled her hair high on her head in a jumble of loose curls, making her appear taller and slimming her face at the same time. Her square jaw looked almost oval, while the gold of the gown brought out gold flecks in her eyes. Her hair gleamed gold too, with the help of Clothilde's mysterious pomade.

"And the waist, it is so small! Derne will be in raptures! Though of course he already knows what that crow's gown concealed!" A knowing titter accompanied this.

At the thought of Ian seeing her thus, Susannah felt a rush of shyness. She was not ready to go before him clad so. To her own eyes she was very fine, and of course Bridget and Clothilde would tell her what it was in their best interests to say, but how would she look to him? Above all things, she would hate to appear ridiculous in his eyes. The phrase "mutton got up as lamb" arose to haunt her.

"Come, my lady, we must amaze Lord Derne," Bridget tugged her out toward the front room where Ian waited. She stumbled once, unaccustomed to heels of such dizzying height, but caught herself as she set eyes on Ian, lifting her chin and straightening her spine. However ridiculous she might appear, she would face him with dignity.

He watched her, rather idly, as she approached him, his eyes flicking over her in a cynical way that made Susannah long to lift her hands to cover her exposed bosom. Bright flags of color rose to fly in her cheeks at his expression. How dare he look at her like that! Then she saw that he had not yet realized who it was he ogled so.

"*Voilà*, my lord!" Bridget said, and Ian's eyes lifted to Susannah's face.

She watched them widen, watched them run swiftly, almost disbelievingly, over her again as he rose to his feet.

"My God," he said in a curious, shocked tone as his gaze touched on her piled hair, her dainty slippers, the cascades of blond lace that covered her hands. "My God, Susannah, you're a little beauty! Whoever would have guessed it?"

40

"Ian! Derne, is that you?" The sweetly feminine voice in no way prepared Susannah for the dazzler who rushed past her to cast herself on Ian's bosom. Ian, taken by surprise, had no time to do more than say "Serena!" before the woman was in his arms. A perfectly manicured hand threaded through his black hair to pull his head down for her kiss. Her other arm was flung around his neck.

To his credit, Ian was looking rather desperately at Susannah out of one eye even as Serena was kissing him like the lost love of her life. Which, perhaps, he was.

"Ah, madame, you must not mind. She is just a little—history, yes? From before the marriage," Bridget murmured consolingly even as Ian put his hands on Serena's waist and bodily moved her away from him.

"But where have you been, my love?" Serena asked plaintively, her slender hands grasping his coat sleeves. Her eyes running over him, she added, "And why are you dressed like a—a provincial? 'Tis not like you, Derne, you who are always top of the trees!"

"I journeyed to the Colonies, for reasons which I won't go into here. I was sorry to leave you without a word, believe me. But I've brought someone back with me whom you should meet."

"Derne is unbelievable. He is so bold as to introduce his mistress to his wife!" murmured Bridget in an aside to Clothilde, who had just joined her. Susannah heard, and her gaze sharpened. Though she had not needed Bridget to tell her that Ian and this woman had once been considerably more than friends. The way she touched him, the timbre of her voice calling him love, the fondness in his eyes when he gazed down at her said that without words. It did not occur to Susannah until later that she was not, in fact, Ian's wife. As she watched the shameless creature clinging to her man, she felt like a wronged spouse.

Ian turned the woman to face her. Susannah took one look at the exquisite, lily-white face beneath piled hair that was black as midnight, at the huge dark eyes and rosebud mouth, at the tall, lush figure displayed to perfection in a dark green gown that was even more low-cut than the gold one she herself wore, and knew that in any contest of beauty the other woman would win hands down. Even Mandy could not compete with this.

"Susannah, this is Serena, Lady Crewe. Serena, this is Susannah—my wife."

Susannah did not miss the slight hesitation in his voice before he called her his wife. She guessed, had he not already perpetrated the deception upon Bridget and Clothilde, he would have been more truthful. After all, he would not want to make Lady Crewe think that he was no longer available to warm her bed!

"Your—wife!" Serena's mouth popped open, and her eyes widened as they moved swiftly over Susannah, who spent an instant giving thanks that at least she was not still clad in her Sunday black. While she could not begin to compete with the other woman's breathtaking looks, at least she need not feel completely inferior. Susannah lifted her chin, cast Ian a darkling look, and held out her hand.

"How do you do, Lady Crewe?" she asked quietly.

Serena, too, glanced at Ian. "Such a charming accent," she purred, just touching Susannah's hand with the tips of her fingers before letting her hand drop. "A Colonial, did you say?"

"I am from the Carolinas," Susannah replied, disdaining to let Ian speak for her. The woman detested her already, that much was plain. But of course, Serena considered that Susannah had stolen her man.

"Charming," Serena murmured again and turned back to Ian. " 'Tis always good to renew old acquaintances, is it not?"

"Sometimes," he said and smiled at her. To Susannah's fury, Serena placed a hand on his arm, went up on tiptoe, and whispered something in his ear. He smiled again, shook his head, and whispered something back.

"Ah, Madame la Marquise, will you take the blue dress with you as well? The alterations are made. And I can have the rest within a few days."

Bridget's attempt to distract Susannah's attention was kindly meant, Susannah realized as she nodded her assent. But she didn't miss the kiss Serena bestowed on Ian's cheek in parting, or the pat of his hand on her behind. Bright color flamed in Susannah's cheeks, and the glance she sent his way as they left the shop was sizzling.

"If your tongue isn't burning from all the lies you've told, it should be," she said to him with a snide smile as he stowed her parcels in the carriage. Disdaining his hand, she scrambled into the carriage on her own, nearly coming a cropper as her heel caught on the threshold. But she recovered without disgracing herself and was seated with back ramrod straight and head held high when he swung inside.

"And just what lie in particular are you referring to now?" he asked almost too politely as he clucked to the horse and set the carriage in motion. Deftly he drove into the teeming traffic, but Susannah never even noticed how he squeezed between a milk cart and a barouche with scarcely an inch to spare.

"The one about me being your marchioness. Clearly Lady Crewe was upset to meet your wife." Susannah placed a faint emphasis on the last word.

"Serena is an old friend."

"Oh, yes. I can just hear you describing me in that fashion one day."

"There is no comparison between you and Serena. All right, so Serena was my mistress. I told you I'd had women. Serena was one of them. She's in the past."

"She doesn't look like she wants to be in the past."

"Susannah," he said. "You're a very jealous woman. Fortunate for you that I like it."

"What?" She blinked at him, caught by surprise at his response. He grinned, moved his hands, and the carriage turned right in a motion as smooth as silk.

"You look beautiful sitting there spitting at me like a she-cat. All I have to do is look at you, and I lust. I'm going to take you back to the hotel and take off that delectable dress and make love to you until you don't have the energy to be mad at me anymore."

The image he conjured up made her blood heat, but she was determined that he would never know it. Sticking her nose in the air, she said, "I don't feel like making love to you at the moment."

"Susannah." He said her name very softly. "Now who's lying?"

As they pulled up in front of the hotel at that moment, Susannah had no chance to reply. When they reached their room, she eyed him warily even as she kicked off the high-heeled slippers that were starting to hurt her feet.

"Shoes pinch?" he asked sympathetically. She said nothing but gave him a narrow-eyed look. He sighed.

"Witch," he said. "Come here."

"No." She unwrapped the blue dress that was nearly as lovely as the gold one she had on and stowed it in the wardrobe. In stockinged feet and shirtsleeves now, he came to stand behind her.

"Nice," he said approvingly as she took out the silk underwear and folded it away.

She closed the wardrobe door just as his arms came around her waist from behind.

"You're beautiful," he whispered. "I want you." His mouth slid down the side of her neck. The hot, stirring contact made her pulses jump, but she jerked her neck away. To her surprise, as she turned her head, she found that she could see their reflections in the cheval glass that stood beside the wardrobe. The image of the two of them together was so arresting that she couldn't tear her eyes away.

She looked very small against him despite the pile of gold-touched curls on her head. She also looked quite lovely, and arrestingly feminine. He stood dauntingly tall and well-muscled behind her, and the soft white linen of his shirt clung to his broad shoulders that dwarfed her own. His glossy black head was bent to her neck as he kissed it again, and watching his mouth move over her white flesh even as she felt the wet slide of his lips was arousing in a way she had never before experienced. His strong arms were wrapped around her waist, and her golden skirt concealed his legs. Her stillness as he ran his mouth over her neck must have attracted his notice, because he glanced up then, followed the direction of her gaze, and then his reflection smiled knowingly into her eyes.

He turned her to face the mirror more fully. Then, still standing behind her, he began to unfasten her dress. Susannah could only watch, mesmerized, as he stripped her garments from her item by item, until finally she was naked. She felt like the worst kind of voyeur as she stared at herself in the glass. She was naked and quivering as he pulled her back against him, while he was still clad in his breeches and shirt. The contrast made her quake.

"No, don't look away," he said when she would have done just that. "Watch."

Unable to help herself, she did as he bade her. Her mouth went dry as she gazed at her own body as though it belonged to someone else, gazed at the full white globes of her breasts tipped by nipples the color of brown sugar and engorged with wanting, gazed at her tapering ribcage and flaring hips and shadowy navel and the sable nest of hair between her thighs. Her legs were very pale against the stark black of his breeches, and her abdomen was very pale, too, against the swarthiness of his wandering hand. He held her with one arm about her waist, pressing her back against his body, watching her watch herself in the mirror as he caressed her. His eyes smoldered, their hot depths searing her as she met them in the glass. Susannah stared into the hard, handsome face, then dropped her eyes to her own image as his hand slid up to fondle her breasts.

He stroked her gently, his long fingers tender as they touched her, his eyes aflame now as he watched her lips part as if she had difficulty drawing in air. She glanced from his face to his hand on her swelling breasts, and suddenly a wild hot ache spiraled to life inside her and she moaned. The sound that emerged from between her lips also seemed to come from the wanton in the glass, and watching even as she experienced such pleasure was the most erotic sensation in the world. The hand that had been grasping her waist slid down between her legs, and she discovered something even more erotic than that. He played with her, and she let him, and watched while he did it, and when finally he pulled her down to the floor and unbuttoned his breeches and guided her atop him, she watched that too. She watched as her hair tumbled down and her body trembled and flushed and hoarse little cries emerged from between her parted lips. She watched as he drove into her, giving her a shivering ecstasy that caused her to arch her back and dig her nails into his chest as though she would hang on for dear life. She watched the wanton in the mirror and knew her for herself. This naked, shivering, ungodly woman was the guilty secret the minister's prim daughter had kept hidden inside herself for so long.

41

Over the next two weeks Ian showed her London. He took her to Astley's Amphitheatre, and to a street fair, and to view the wild beasts at the Exchange. She saw mummers and minstrels, a roaring lion, and a bawdy farce that made her laugh even as she blushed. He took her driving down Bond Street, where she was much amused by the sight of fashionable beaux on the strut, as he termed it, and to the museum where she was able to view what he described as a very good copy of Venus, which put her to the blush, and to Winchester Cathedral, the majesty of which awed her. The world he showed her was so removed from the world in which she had grown up that she could scarcely believe they were on the same planet. As she thought that, she was once again aware of a pang in the region of her heart and a desire, quickly stifled, to go home.

He told her about the ball. He spoke of it in a very casual way at first, which made her suspicious. He was very casual only about things that mattered a great deal to him. With a little effort, she managed to pry out of him the information she needed to make sense of his manner—on the upcoming Wednesday, his mother, the Duchess of Warrender, would be holding a grand ball to kick off the season at her town house in Berkeley Square, to which she had just removed. Ian meant to attend. Susannah had no intention of letting him go alone.

Her wardrobe had arrived the previous Tuesday, but none of her dresses suited her so well as the gold and so Susannah decided to wear that. She felt some qualms about being introduced to Ian's mother as his wife when she was not, but considering the alternative she again did not object. Besides, under the circumstances it was doubtful that any formal introduction would occur. Did one introduce one's wife to the mother who had tried to murder one?

Ian acted as lady's maid for her—he wanted to hire one, but to that Susannah objected strenuously; she had done for herself all her life and had no intention of changing that now—and very creditably, too. At least all her hooks were fastened and her hair felt secure in its new curly style on the top of her head. Just that afternoon, he had presented her with a fan with creamy ivory sticks and a charming meadow scene painted on white silk. It dangled from a ribbon at her wrist.

Ian, of course, was so handsome she could hardly take her eyes off him. He'd been fitted for a new wardrobe, and his ball dress was especially magnificent. He wore a long-tailed coat of midnight blue, a white silk waistcoat with an extravagant design of birds and flowers embroidered on it, and a pair of black breeches so tight that he joked that he feared to sit. His white silk stockings were clocked with gold, and his shoes had red heels. He'd been wearing nearly identical shoes and stockings when he'd been sent to Newgate, he informed her, and he had managed to retain them for exactly one day. They'd been stripped from him while he slept, and he'd been lucky to replace them with the shoes of a prisoner who had died. Susannah, both fascinated and appalled as she remembered his awful brogues, had begged to hear more of his experiences in the notorious prison, but he was in the process of tying his neckcloth (a weighty matter for a gentleman, she'd discovered) and thus could not converse without the danger of ruining its delicate folds.

The street leading to Berkeley Square was thronged with carriages. All of fashionable society seemed to be going. By the time the carriage had been driven away by a coachman Ian had hired for just that purpose and they were making their way through the crush of people ascending the stairs, it was nearing midnight. Susannah, having learned that London kept very different hours from Beaufort, was not much disturbed when the watch called the hour.

She was, however, disturbed about the prospect of the ball itself. Never had she attended such a grand affair—it made the Haskinses' party look paltry in comparison—and she had not the slightest idea of how to go on.

"Stick close to me," Ian advised when she whispered her concern to him. Susannah, who could have hardly done anything else with her hand tucked firmly in the crook of his arm, thanked him for the advice.

Ian was greeted on all sides with much exclamation, and he patiently explained again and again that he had been in the Colonies (he didn't explain exactly how he had come to make such a visit) and had brought back a bride. By the time they reached the door, where a portly butler, who looked far more like Susannah's idea of what a marquis should be than Ian did, sonorously announced the new arrivals, Susannah felt as if she'd been introduced to half of London.

When it was their turn to be announced, the butler took one look at Ian, and then a second. His eyes popped.

"Mr. Ian!" he said. "I mean, my lord! We were given to understand that you were . . ."

He broke off and coughed delicately into his white glove. Ian grinned with wry understanding.

"Dead," he finished. "Yes, I know. How are you, Reems?"

"Very good, my lord. It's very good to see you, if I may say so, my lord. The staff will be in alt when I tell them that you're, ah . . ."

"Resurrected?" Ian suggested with a gleam. "You'd best announce us, Reems. We're holding up the line. Ah—this is my wife."

Reems goggled at Susannah, who smiled weakly. Really, the lie was getting harder and harder to bear. Something was going to have to be done, soon. . . .

But before she could decide exactly what, Reems intoned, "The Marquis and Marchioness of Derne!"

A ripple of astonishment seemed to run along the receiving line that snaked out in front of them until Susannah, following Ian's gaze, saw a tall, blond-haired woman at the head of the line turn to face them. She looked only at Ian, and as their eyes met she seemed to sway slightly and pale. But then she appeared to take herself in hand. Head high, she waited as Ian, Susannah in tow, made his leisurely way toward her. Had it not been for the tension in the arm beneath her hand, Susannah would have thought him perfectly at ease.

They reached her at last. Susannah saw that the lady was older than she had first supposed, and not so lovely. Her hair was not blond but powdered white, and she wore a light maquillage that did not conceal the deep lines that bracketed her mouth. Or perhaps it had, until she had set eyes on Ian.

"Mother." Ian inclined his head, but his smile was not a pleasant one.

"Derne." Any woman who could call her own son by his title instead of his name was not one that Susannah wanted to know. She bristled in instinctive defense of Ian as his mother glanced her way.

"You've married?" Her voice was husky, and there was a tiny nerve at the corner of her mouth that seemed to have gone mad. It twitched rhythmically, like a pulse. That was the only sign she gave that she was less composed than she seemed.

"While I was enjoying my delightful sojourn in the Colonies. As a matter of fact, Susannah very likely saved my life." He smiled again, but this time it was no more than a baring of his teeth.

"We must all owe her a debt, then." She looked again at Susannah. "As Derne does not introduce me, I suppose I must do it myself. I am Mary, Duchess of Warrender."

"I know very well who you are, ma'am," Susannah said, and she did not smile.

"Ah." The Duchess swayed again but did no more.

"I suggest we repair to the library to talk, Mother. After all, we have not seen each other in—how long?"

"A long time," she said tonelessly and allowed Ian to draw her hand onto his arm.

"Is Edward here? 'Twould be best if he heard this, too."

"We will leave Edward out of this, if you please." For the first time her voice was sharp.

Ian shook his head. "There is no way to leave Edward out of it, I fear. But come, we will talk in private. There are too many ears to listen here."

Indeed, Susannah was aware that they were being stared at on all sides. As Ian started off through the crowd, polite smiles pinned to his face and his mother's, she got a glimpse of Helen Dutton, Countess of Blakely, the notorious lightskirt (or so said Ian) of Madame de Vangrisse's establishment. The lady was with a rather elderly, very fat man who kept a firm grip on her arm and talked very fast at her with an angry look on his face. If that was her husband, Susannah suddenly understood the reason for "the Baddington miscellany." She would not like to be married to a man like that. A few other faces looked vaguely familiar, but Susannah was able to put names to none of them until she saw Serena, Lady Crewe, staring angrily after them just as Ian opened a door in the hall and stood back, allowing first Susannah and then his mother to precede him.

"Does she have to hear this?" The Duchess nodded jerkily toward Susannah as Ian closed the doors behind them.

Ian nodded. "Susannah deserves to be in on the denouement. Were it not for her, your plan just might have succeeded."

The duchess flashed Susannah a look of hatred, then crossed the room to stand nervously before a large, leather-topped desk before turning to face them again. She was framed by shelf after shelf of leather-bound books set into the wall, and her face was lit by a fire that blazed in the hearth to the right of the desk.

"What is preventing me from putting a period to your existence right now, and to your wife's, too?" There was a note of almost gloating triumph in the duchess's voice as she raised her hand to reveal a silver pistol. Ian stared at it for a moment and then with a jerk of his head motioned to Susannah to get behind him. Of course she did no such thing. Instead she stared at the weapon with horror and dawning fear. Was the woman really mad enough to shoot them both, with several hundred witnesses gathered in the house? She prayed not, but sidled a step closer to Ian. Perhaps she could throw herself between him and the bullet or at the very least push him out of the way.

"Before you pull the trigger, you should know what I, or rather Mr. Dumboldt, whom I commissioned to look into this, has discovered. We know the truth about Edward, Mother. The whole tale is written down, with names of witnesses and dates. Should anything happen to me, it will be an open scandal throughout England. And, of course, Edward will not inherit."

"I don't know what you are talking about." Her voice was hoarser than before, and Susannah thought her hand trembled. Susannah edged closer to Ian. She could not stand it if he were to be killed before her eyes.

"I am talking about the date of Edward's birth, Mother. He is three months older than you have always claimed. At the time of his conception, my father had been away on the Continent for six months. Therefore Edward cannot be my father's issue."

"That is not true!"

"Dumboldt has found witnesses who swear it is, including the midwife who delivered him. He has also discovered evidence of the identity of Edward's real father. All this is in writing, Mother, and will be revealed if I die or disappear. The scandal will ruin Edward's life, to say nothing of yours."

The duchess's face contorted violently. Her mouth shook. Her hand shook. Susannah took another sidling step toward Ian, to be rewarded by a sidelong glare before his attention focused on his mother again.

"I've always hated you, Derne. You were the most repellent little boy. Your father doted on you, and you were in flaming need of a birch applied to the seat of your breeches, which remedy he would not countenance. If I had had my way, you would have been sent to a foundling home."

"Which brings us to another point—my father," Ian said, his voice far too casual for the subject matter. Susannah's gaze left the wobbling gun to fly to his face. "You arranged for that hunting accident that befell him, didn't you? He had found out about the circumstances surrounding Edward's birth and was threatening to divorce you."

"That's not true!" Her mouth shook again.

"Isn't it? If I could prove that to the satisfaction of a court of law, I'd have you locked away for the rest of your life, mother or no."

She laughed then, a high, hysterical sound. The pistol wavered again. "That's the ultimate jest, isn't it, and with all your investigations you haven't discovered it and never will! Well, I'll make you a present of the information. I am not your mother, for which I devoutly thank God! Your mother was a nobody from the country whom your father dallied with and wed only because she was expecting you. When she died at your birth, he was relieved, because she'd been totally unsuitable to be the Duchess of Warrender. Then he wed me, a Speare, whose bloodline goes directly back to William the Conqueror. I was, and am, suitable to be a duchess! I was so suitable he wanted everyone to believe that his heir was my son. Well, you are not, and never will be. You're the son of a slut, conceived under a hedgerow somewhere in Sussex! You're unworthy of the name you bear!"

For a moment the silence in that room was so thick it was tangible. Then, with a dive so fast and low that Susannah didn't even see it coming, Ian was across the room and grappling with the duchess for the pistol. He wrested it from her hand, then stood looking at her without pity as she dropped to her knees and covered her face with her hands.

"Thank you for telling me, Your Grace," he said with icy courtesy, pocketing the pistol. "You've set me free."

Then, taking Susannah's arm, he half-led, half-pulled her from the room without a second glance at the silent, kneeling woman he left behind.

Toward morning, when he got Susannah home, his lovemaking was especially passionate. Afterward, she held him wrapped in her arms until he fell asleep.

42

When Susannah awoke the next morning, it was nearer to noon than to dawn. Ian slept beside her, his breathing harsh and heavy. They were both naked, their clothes strewn around the room, and sunlight spilling through a chink in the curtains streamed across the bed. A sunny day in London! Susannah marveled. It was the first she'd seen since she arrived.

She knew, though she didn't know how she knew, that last night a chapter in her life and Ian's had come to a close. He was free of the nightmare that had hurtled him from his rightful world into hers. He could live his life out as he was meant to live it—as a rich, pampered English aristocrat. So where did that leave her?

For all their pretending, she was his mistress, not his wife. As she faced the truth of that, Susannah felt like Eve seeing her nakedness for the first time —she was flooded with shame. She had not been raised to be a man's mistress. It went against everything she had ever been taught.

How her father would grieve if he could see the depths to which she had fallen! Picturing his face, and Sarah Jane's, and Mandy's, and Em's, if they could see her as she was at that moment, Susannah felt sick. She was no better than a harlot, a common whore. She had sinned, and gloried in the sinning! Most of the members of her father's congregation would likely consider her doomed to eternal hellfire.

Susannah shivered and looked down at Ian, to discover his gray eyes open and narrowed on her face.

"What's amiss?" he asked without preamble. Susannah hesitated a moment and then decided to say what was on her mind.

"I cannot continue on in this way any longer," she said, not looking at him. "I must go home."

"What?" He sat up then and brushed the hair back from his eyes. "Don't be ridiculous. You can't go home. You have to marry me."

As proposals went, that one was decidedly lacking.

"Are you asking me?" she inquired with a flicker of hope.

"Hell, no. What is there to ask? You've been with me now for almost three months. Neither one of us has a choice anymore. We have to get married, or you'll spend the rest of your life branded as a whore."

That hurt. It hurt so much that Susannah walled it up inside and refused to think about it.

"It's very good of you to worry about my reputation." If there was an edge to her voice, he missed it completely.

"It is, isn't it?" He stretched, yawned, and rolled out of bed. "Now that you've awakened me, I might as well get dressed. I need to see Dumboldt about some matters. You may amuse yourself shopping or however you like." He paused, as if struck by an idea. "Since we both agree to the necessity, I might see about getting a Special License while I'm out. I have a friend whose uncle is a bishop, and he might be able to oblige me. If I can get the license today, we can be wed tomorrow, if that suits you."

"So soon?"

"If it were done when 'tis done, then 'twere well it were done quickly," he quoted, and grinned at her before he padded into the anteroom to shave. "Take a maid from the hotel with you when you go out. It's not done for a marchioness to go about alone in London, remember."

Susannah watched him dress, as she had every morning for nearly three months, and brooded. When, fully clad, he leaned over to drop a kiss on the top of her head and a wad of banknotes in her lap, she knew she had her decision made.

So, when he would have turned and left her, she reached up to wrap her arms around his neck and kiss him an almost desperate good-bye.

"I can stay," he said on a surprised note and put one knee on the bed as if he would come into it with her.

For an instant longer Susannah clung. She forced a laugh and released him. "Go do your business," she told him and smiled.

"You're looking very tempting."

She had the sheet tucked under her armpits, but he was as familiar with her body by now as she was and his eyes ran over the shapely form beneath the thin linen knowingly.

"Later," she said, waving him off, though the word stuck in her throat.

"All right, later," he agreed, "but only because I need to see Dumboldt. When I come back you just might succeed in luring me back to bed."

"What an exciting prospect," Susannah managed dryly, smiling though she wanted to cry. But her insouciance had the desired effect. With a wave and a grin, he was gone.

Once the door shut behind him, she did cry. Then she sat up, mopped her eyes, dressed, and packed her clothes. Fine feathers do not make fine birds, and she was no more a marchioness than he was a farmer. She was going home, back to Beaufort where she belonged, and he would be relieved of the burden of having to wed a bride who would never fit into his world. He had never meant to bring her to England with him; indeed, he had left her behind when he had left the farm. If she had not stumbled across him on that Charles Town dock, she would in all likelihood never have seen him again. Because she still didn't believe his protestations that he would have come back for her.

What they had shared had been as close to heaven as she was likely to get in this life. But now it was finished, and it was time for her to go home.

43

A little over two months later, Susannah had once more settled into the routine of her life in Beaufort. She and her sisters had had a tearful reunion, and that first night home, tormented by guilt, she had confessed some part of what she had done to her father. She'd half-expected him to order her from his doorstep like a biblical father of old, but instead he'd put an arm around her shoulders and hugged her close.

"Daughter, the love of a woman for a man is a godly thing in itself. As long as what you did was done in love, there's not so much shame in that."

Then she'd wept on his shoulder.

Sarah Jane (who'd broken her betrothal when Peter Bridgewater had insisted on going ahead with the wedding whether or not Susannah was present) and Mandy and Em treated her like an honored guest for about the first forty-eight hours, and then they rapidly slid back into their old ways of depending on her to run the household and the farm and see to the needs of the congregation. Within a week, it was as though she had never left.

A fortnight after her return, Susannah was kneeling in the garden weeding when Em, who was helping her, looked up, shading her face with her hand as she peered down the road. Susannah didn't pay much attention, concentrating as she was on clearing the dandelions out from among her carrots. When Em got to her feet and stared openly down the road, Susannah only glanced up at her with some annoyance. Really, Em was getting almost as bad about doing chores as Mandy.

"Susannah," Em sounded slightly uneasy. "If you were getting ready to have a really important visitor and you were down in mud getting all dirty, would you want to know about it in advance so you could run in the house and at least wash your hands?"

"What are you talking about, Em?" That made so little sense that Susannah stopped work to look up at her.

Em opened her mouth to say something, then shrugged fatalistically. "See for yourself," she said and nodded toward the road, where a man on a large roan horse was just pulling up in their front yard. Brownie stood up on the front porch and barked half-heartedly. Clara, on the railing, didn't even bother to stretch.

"Oh, good grief," Susannah said, getting to her feet. She was in no mood for guests at the moment. She had to get the weeding done, and then put supper on, and . . . Her eyes widened as she took a good look at the man swinging down from the horse.

She stood frozen stiff as a statue as he tied the horse to a bush and came walking toward her, scattering clucking chickens before him as he came. Beside her, Em was wide-eyed as she looked from her sister to their visitor and back.

He was the first one to speak. "Hello, Susannah," he said dryly. Then, with a nod at the younger girl, "Hello, Em."

"Your—your—marquis-ship," Em, who'd been filled in on some if not all the details of Susannah's adventure, stuttered.

"Ian," he said. "You can just call me Ian."

His eyes moved to Susannah. He stopped walking and stood with his booted feet planted apart and his arms crossed over his chest, surveying her almost grimly. Susannah, looking back, felt her heart unfreeze and start to pound in her chest. Her eyes ran over him almost greedily. Not to anyone, and barely to herself, had she admitted her hope that he might come after her. Now he stood before her, clad in an elegant blue coat and black breeches, his black hair gleaming in the sun, his perfectly carved features almost grim, his sensuous mouth unsmiling. A faint dark stubble shadowed his cheeks and chin. He was as sinfully handsome as she remembered him, and clearly put out with her.

"What are you doing here?" she managed. His gaze started at the top of her head and traveled, with slow censure, to her feet, then worked its way back up again. Susannah was suddenly conscious that she had bundled her hair up in its customary style and that the gown she wore was one that she had made herself and been accustomed to wear for gardening when he had been their bound man, and before. It was sack-like in its proportions, and dirty to boot. Clearly it found no favor in his eyes.

"What do you think I'm doing here, Miss Susannah Redmon?" he asked in a tone that managed to convey that he was keeping a tight rein on his temper. His gaze shifted to Em.

"Would you mind if I talk to your sister alone?"

Em, eyes widening, glanced at Susannah, who nodded.

"It's all right," she said. But her eyes barely left Ian. Em almost ran into the house.

"You've led me a pretty dance," he said furiously when they were alone. "And why, pray tell? I was prepared to marry you, God damn it! I told you so!"

"I don't want someone who's 'prepared' to marry me." Susannah felt her own temper begin to heat. "And I'll thank you not to use profanity here."

"You're enough to drive a man to profanity," he said through his teeth. "What do you mean, you don't want someone who's prepared to marry you? That is the most asinine thing I've ever heard in my life!"

"Then I must be asinine, because that's how I feel."

For a minute she thought he was going to step forward and shake her. But he controlled himself after a single hasty step and settled for a glare.

"Do you have any idea how I felt when I got back to the hotel, special license in my pocket I might add, and found you gone, lock, stock, and luggage? All you left for me was a two-word note: Be happy. You didn't even have the common courtesy to tell me you were going!"

"I thought you'd try to stop me." Susannah's heart was pounding now, and she was beginning to feel a sharp gladness sing through her veins. He was as mad as fire, but he had come.

"You're damned right I would have tried to stop you. Hell, I would have stopped you! I would have tied you to my wrist, if I'd had to, to keep you with me until we were safely wed."

"That's why I didn't tell you!"

He made a furious sound under his breath and reached her in one quick stride. His hands closed over her upper arms and he again looked on the verge of giving her a good shaking.

"I'm going to have to ask you to unhand my daughter, sir." The voice was her father's, and, looking over Ian's shoulder, Susannah was surprised to see him standing just a little way away, fragile-looking in his black preacher's suit with his white hair ruffled by the faint breeze, a frown in his gentle eyes as he surveyed the pair of them. Beyond him stood Sarah Jane and Mandy and Em in a cluster, staring.

"Hello, Reverend." Ian nodded without releasing Susannah. "I'm trying to persuade her to marry me, sir."

There was a moment of profound silence.

"Susannah, you finally got an offer!" Em squealed, only to be shushed by Sarah Jane and Mandy, who both looked appalled at their younger sister's gaucherie.

"Why?" Susannah shot at Ian, disregarding Em's comment completely. "Because you have to?"

"Now, that's interesting, daughter," the Reverend Redmon said, taking a step closer as his frown cleared. "You didn't mention he wanted to marry you."

"No, not because I damned well have to!" Ian shot back, ignoring the background comments as completely as Susannah did. "I didn't have to come all the way after you from England, did I? I'm even prepared to live here, if you want to. If this damned hellishly hot country is what it takes to make you happy, then we'll buy a place."

"I have to admit I didn't care for the thought of you taking her back to England with you," her father observed thoughtfully.

"What about you?" Susannah asked Ian slowly. "Won't you want to live in England? After all, you're a marquis."

"Well, don't say it like it's a deadly affliction. I can't help it, you know, any more than you can help having curly hair. I guess I can be a marquis as well here as I can there. Better, if I have you with me. We can travel to England every once in a while."

"Are you saying that you truly want to marry me?" Susannah was still cautious, although she was starting to smile.

"It surely looks that way to me, daughter," the Reverend Redmon said.

"Of course he does, Susannah!" Mandy sounded disgusted. "Why else would he come all the way across the ocean after you?"

"Yes, Susannah, I truly want to marry you. I love you, damn it. Now what do you say?" There was a red tinge to his cheekbones, as if the idea of having an audience to such private talk was beginning to embarrass him. His arms were still crossed over his chest, and he looked positively belligerent.

"Say yes, Susannah! Say yes!" the girls squealed in chorus.

"Yes," Susannah whispered, then practically flew into his arms, dirt and all. They opened to receive her, and he kissed her with a heat that brought admiring applause from the three female members of his audience when he released her—at least until their father glanced around at them, when they stopped abruptly.

"Welcome to the family, son," the Reverend Redmon said and held out his hand to Ian. Keeping one arm around Susannah, who was beaming and clinging to his side, Ian shook it warmly.

"Thank you, sir. I'll take good care of her."

"If I didn't think so, I wouldn't let you marry her." Her father's voice was gruff, but there was a twinkle in his eye as he leaned down to give Susannah a kiss on the cheek. "She has a tendency to want to rule the roost, you know."

"I know." Ian glanced down at the top of Susannah's head. "But I think I can keep her in line."

She pinched his side admonishingly. He jumped and clapped a hand to the threatened part.

"Susannah, you know that blue dress you brought home with you? Do you suppose I could wear it to your wedding?" Mandy asked on a wheedling note.

"I suppose."

"And maybe to the church social next week?" Mandy's voice was hopeful.

"Maybe."

"And will you alter it just a little? Nothing that you can't take back out, of course."

"Mandy, dear, you may have the dress with my blessing if you want it. That blue color is better on you than me, anyway."

"Susannah, you're an angel!" Mandy clapped her hands with glee.

"No, dear, I'm not," Susannah said, accepting congratulatory kisses from Mandy and Sarah Jane and Em in turn. "Believe me, I'm nobody's angel."

"Oh, yes you are," Ian said softly, catching her hand and raising it to his lips. Susannah lifted her eyes to his, and all the love she felt for him blazed at him from their hazel depths. Ian pressed a kiss to her palm, then laid her hand against his bristly cheek. "Yes, you are—you're mine."